Broken Compass

Clara Hawke

Published by Clara Hawke, 2024.

This is a work of fiction. Similarities to real people, places, or events are entirely coincidental.

BROKEN COMPASS

First edition. October 8, 2024.

Copyright © 2024 Clara Hawke.

ISBN: 979-8227615909

Written by Clara Hawke.

Chapter 1: Hidden Spirits

The Broken Compass is a sanctuary of warmth, with flickering candlelight casting soft shadows across the room, inviting laughter and hushed conversations. I run my fingers over the smooth surface of the bar, feeling the history embedded in the wood, each scratch and dent a story waiting to be told. The walls, adorned with faded photographs of explorers and maps dotted with red Xs, speak of journeys taken and dreams fulfilled, a stark contrast to the rut I find myself in. It's as if the spirits of those adventurers linger here, their laughter mingling with the aroma of aged whiskey and the sweet scent of spiced cider.

"Another round for the lonely hearts club, Sam?" calls out my friend Mia, perched on a barstool, her hair an explosion of curls that catches the light. She's a tempest of energy, a stark reminder of all the life I used to embrace before the world shrank into the confines of heartbreak. The way she winks at me makes it impossible not to smile, even as I deftly pour another round of craft beers for the regulars clustered at the end of the bar.

"Only if it comes with a side of wisdom," I retort, my voice laced with the sarcasm that has become my shield against the nagging loneliness. The patrons laugh, their good-natured ribbing filling the air like confetti, lifting the weight pressing on my chest. Mia rolls her eyes, but her grin is infectious. She knows my heart is still stitched together with fragile threads, each one vibrating with the memory of Lucas, the man whose laughter once filled my nights with joy and whose departure left a chasm in my soul.

"Sam, you've got to stop wallowing in the past," she says, her tone firm yet playful. "There are good men out there—like this one." She gestures toward the rugged stranger nursing his drink at the far end of the bar. He looks like he's walked straight out of one of those old Western films, his hat pulled low and his flannel shirt a vibrant plaid against the muted colors of the tavern. The whiskey tumbler in his hand seems to fit perfectly, cradled like a secret, and I find myself intrigued despite the reservations etched into my heart.

"I'm not interested in a dusty old cowboy, Mia," I counter, but even as the words leave my lips, I can't help stealing a glance at the man. There's something about him—perhaps it's the way his brow furrows as he contemplates the amber liquid, or the way the flickering light dances across his chiseled jawline—that sparks a flutter of curiosity within me.

"Who says he's dusty?" Mia smirks, swirling her own drink, her eyes gleaming with mischief. "He could be a breath of fresh air or a whirlwind ready to sweep you off your feet. You'll never know unless you try."

I shake my head, but a tiny spark of excitement ignites within me. Maybe I've been too cautious, too wrapped up in the tendrils of my past. But then I remind myself that I've always been the cautious one, the steady hand at the bar while others dive headfirst into life's chaos. It's a role I've grown accustomed to, but maybe, just maybe, it's time to shake things up.

As if sensing my contemplation, the man lifts his gaze, locking eyes with mine across the expanse of polished oak. A slow smile spreads across his face, and I feel the warmth of it wrap around me like a cozy blanket against the evening chill. I quickly look away, a flush creeping up my cheeks, betraying the very nonchalance I had hoped to maintain.

"Okay, I'm going to talk to him," Mia announces, sliding off her stool with the grace of a dancer. "You stay here and pour drinks like the pros we are." She winks and struts away, her confidence leaving a trail of light behind her. I watch as she approaches the stranger, my heart racing with a mix of excitement and dread.

Their conversation unfolds in hushed tones, but I can see the flicker of chemistry between them—her laughter spilling like champagne, his chuckle deep and rich, resonating across the bar. I turn back to my work, pouring another whiskey for a couple celebrating an anniversary, their fingers intertwined and laughter spilling like confetti. With every clink of the glass, my heart sinks a little deeper.

But then I catch sight of Mia leaning closer, her eyes sparkling like she's just discovered a hidden treasure, and I can't help but feel a twinge of jealousy. What is she saying that draws out such warmth from him? I shake my head, trying to dispel the thoughts, reminding myself that the world is full of fleeting connections and unfulfilled hopes.

The bar becomes a blur of faces, drinks, and laughter as the evening progresses. I serve cocktails and listen to snippets of lives intertwining, weaving tales of love lost and found. Yet my mind wanders back to that stranger, the magnetic pull of his presence igniting a flicker of hope within me. As I polish a glass, I glance in their direction again, only to find him watching me now, his gaze piercing yet warm.

"Sam, meet Jack," Mia chirps, pulling me out of my reverie. The rugged man stands beside her, his height imposing but his demeanor disarmingly friendly. He extends a hand, and I take it, feeling the strength in his grip—a reassuring warmth that sends a jolt of energy through me.

"Nice to meet you," he says, his voice a deep rumble, like distant thunder before a storm. "Mia here has been singing your praises."

"Oh, really?" I can't hide the hint of disbelief in my tone, raising an eyebrow. "I hope it was all good."

"Only the best," he replies with a charming grin, a flash of mischief in his eyes. "She claims you're the best bartender in Silver Springs. I had to see for myself."

"Well, I don't know about 'the best,' but I do have a knack for mixing drinks," I retort, the wryness slipping effortlessly from my lips. There's something refreshing about him, a vibe that crackles with unspoken possibilities. I can't help but feel the walls around my heart begin to soften ever so slightly.

As the conversation flows, I find myself captivated by his stories of hiking through the misty trails of the nearby mountains and the thrill of getting lost in the vast wilderness. The way he describes the world around him makes it seem so alive, as if every leaf and whispering wind is part of a larger narrative. He talks about a hidden lake, shimmering under the sun, where he once lost track of time, and I can't help but picture the scene—a canvas of nature painted in vibrant hues, a world so unlike the confined space of the bar.

The night stretches on, a tapestry woven with laughter, shared glances, and a growing sense of connection. With each passing moment, the ache of my past seems to ebb, replaced by the warmth of possibility. Jack is not just a rugged stranger; he's a breath of fresh air, a reminder that life can be spontaneous and beautiful even amidst the ordinary.

And as the stars twinkle outside, I feel something shifting within me, like a door creaking open after being locked for too long. Maybe it's time to let the light in.

The music swells in the background, a soft melody weaving through the chatter and laughter, while Jack leans against the bar, exuding an easy confidence that draws me in. His casual stance, arms crossed, seems to suggest he's as comfortable here as he is on those mountain trails he described. There's something about him that feels disarming—like a well-worn book that promises adventure but is still familiar enough to be comforting.

"You must get a lot of characters in here," he says, his voice deep and rumbling, echoing the sincerity in his gaze. "I'm betting you've seen some wild stories unfold."

I chuckle, nodding, my curiosity piqued by the way he engages with me as if we're already entwined in some inside joke. "You have no idea. Last week, I had a guy trying to convince me that his cat could predict the weather. He even brought the cat along to prove it."

Jack leans closer, his eyes sparkling with amusement. "And what was the cat's forecast?"

"A sunny day with a high chance of catnip," I reply, grinning as I recall the scene—the cat sprawled across the bar, utterly unimpressed by the enthusiastic forecast.

"Sounds like a wise little creature," he says, his laughter rich and infectious. I can feel my heart ease as the warmth of our banter washes over me, smoothing away the rough edges of the past.

Mia reappears, her energy pulsating through the room as she interrupts us, her cheeks flushed from the excitement of our little circle. "I was just telling Jack how you make the best spiced cider in town. It's practically a public service."

"Oh, come on," I protest playfully, waving her off. "You know that's just the cider doing the heavy lifting."

Jack raises an eyebrow, intrigued. "Is that a challenge? I think I need to sample this legendary drink myself."

I smirk, brushing a stray lock of hair behind my ear. "I'm not one to back down from a challenge. Just don't say I didn't warn you when you're downing the last drops."

"Game on," he replies, his gaze steady and full of mischief. The way he looks at me sends a ripple of excitement coursing through my veins.

With a flick of my wrist, I begin to prepare the spiced cider, layering cinnamon sticks, cloves, and fresh apple slices into a steaming pot. The scent unfurls, filling the bar with a warm embrace, and I can't help but steal glances at Jack as he leans against the bar, eyes trained on my every move. It feels as though the entire world has faded into a blur, leaving just the two of us in our own little bubble.

"What do you do when you're not charming bartenders?" I ask, my curiosity bubbling over like the cider in the pot.

"I'm a wildlife photographer," he replies, the pride evident in his voice. "Chasing light and shadows in the great outdoors is what I live for. There's nothing like capturing a moment that makes you feel alive."

I can almost picture him, hiking through dense forests and standing at the edge of a roaring waterfall, camera in hand, waiting for that perfect shot. "Sounds incredible. Do you have a favorite subject?"

"Honestly? It's all about the moments—whether it's the sunrise over a mountain range or the stillness of a deer in the morning mist. But people are a different story; they're more unpredictable, more layered. Sometimes I think capturing their essence is the hardest part," he muses, his expression contemplative, revealing a glimpse of the depth beneath his rugged exterior.

"Ah, so you're a philosopher with a camera," I tease, pouring the cider into a glass and handing it to him. "Here's your ticket to enlightenment. Just remember, the deeper the thought, the more likely you'll spill."

He laughs, taking a sip and letting out a satisfied hum. "You've officially converted me. This is divine."

"Glad to hear it," I say, my heart fluttering at the compliment. "Maybe I should charge for this."

Mia raises her glass, "To Sam, the greatest bartender and cider sorceress of Silver Springs!" The other patrons join in with their cheers, and I feel a wave of warmth spread through me. It's moments like these that remind me why I love this place and the people who fill it with laughter and stories.

But as the evening continues, I notice a change in the atmosphere. A group of rowdy patrons enters, their boisterous laughter cutting through the cozy ambiance like a knife. They're loud, the kind of people who seem to thrive on chaos. One of them—a burly man with a bearded grin—makes a beeline for the bar, his eyes narrowing as he spots Jack.

"Look who's here, playing with the locals!" he calls out, his voice booming, the laughter trailing behind him like an unwelcome storm cloud.

Jack's posture stiffens slightly, and I can see the shadow that passes over his face. "Hey, Todd," he replies, the warmth in his voice dimming just a notch.

"Didn't think you'd come back after last time," Todd continues, slapping Jack on the back with enough force to jostle him. "Thought you'd learned your lesson about sticking around the town folks."

I can feel the tension thickening in the air, an invisible line drawn between Jack and the newcomer. Mia's playful demeanor shifts, her brow furrowing as she senses the change.

"Everything okay?" I ask, my voice steady, though I can feel a knot forming in my stomach.

"Yeah, all good," Jack replies too quickly, forcing a smile that doesn't quite reach his eyes.

"Come on, let's grab a round for everyone!" Todd hollers, waving over his friends, who approach with an air of entitlement, their boisterous laughter ringing hollow.

The moment shifts; the cozy sanctuary of The Broken Compass is suddenly overshadowed by the unwelcome energy radiating from the newcomers. I stand behind the bar, caught between the tension of two worlds, one filled with warmth and laughter, and the other sharp and unyielding.

As Todd and his crew take over the space, Jack's smile falters, and I can see a storm brewing beneath his calm exterior. I glance at Mia, her eyes wide with concern, and I know I need to act.

"Can I get you something?" I call out to Todd, trying to regain control of the bar. "We have some excellent local brews."

"Yeah, whatever," he grumbles, waving a dismissive hand. "Just get us something strong. We're here to have a good time, not sip on fairy juice."

Jack shoots me a grateful glance, the tension in his shoulders easing ever so slightly. I pour a round of shots, the sharp scent of alcohol mingling with the cider's sweetness, and set them before Todd and his friends.

"Cheers to good times!" Todd bellows, raising his glass in a mock toast, but I can see the way Jack's eyes darken at the display.

As the laughter resumes, punctuated by the clatter of glasses and the smell of sweat and whiskey, I can't shake the feeling that the night has just taken a sharp turn. Jack's presence, once a beacon of warmth, now feels like a flickering candle, struggling to stay lit amid the chaos.

"What was that all about?" I ask quietly, leaning closer to him as Todd and his crew turn their backs, their raucous laughter filling the room.

"Just a little history," he replies, his voice low, as if afraid of being overheard. "Nothing I can't handle."

But I can see the strain in his eyes, the weight of unspoken words. The shadows that linger there hint at something deeper, a narrative fraught with tension that has yet to unravel. And as the laughter grows louder, I can't help but feel that we're both on the precipice of something unexpected, a collision of past and present that could either shatter or forge a new beginning.

The energy in The Broken Compass shifts, a tangible tension wrapping around us as Todd and his rowdy friends settle in, filling the space with their brash laughter and boisterous banter. It's like throwing a boulder into a serene pond; ripples of unease spread out, unsettling the comfortable rhythm of the night. Jack's demeanor tightens, the easy charm he wore slipping into something more guarded as he leans closer to me.

"Are you okay?" I ask quietly, concern slipping into my voice, even as I keep my eyes on the loud newcomers.

"Yeah, just... old ghosts," he replies, though the weight of his words lingers in the air like the faint scent of smoke from the fireplace. The glimmer in his eyes dims, and I feel a strange mix of determination and frustration stirring inside me. I want to help him confront whatever it is that's troubling him, but I also don't want to push too hard.

As I pour a couple of beers for Todd's group, they start regaling each other with exaggerated stories of past exploits, their laughter crashing against the walls like a tidal wave. "You remember that time we almost got arrested for skinny-dipping at the lake?" Todd bellows, slapping a friend on the back, causing a ripple of chuckles to erupt.

I roll my eyes, but I can't help but feel a flicker of amusement, the absurdity of their antics cutting through the tension, if only for a moment. Just then, one of the friends, a lanky guy with an obnoxiously loud shirt, leans over the bar, pointing directly at Jack. "What about you, cowboy? You got any good stories? Or are you just here for the free drinks?"

The question hangs in the air, charged with the expectation that Jack will rise to the bait. I can see the tension tighten around him like a noose, and my heart races at the thought of how he might respond.

"Actually, I was just about to tell a story about the last time I went hiking," Jack says, his voice smooth but laced with an underlying strain. "We stumbled upon a bear that decided we were more interesting than the berries."

The group goes silent for a heartbeat, intrigued. Jack carries on, weaving a tale of narrowly escaping a close encounter with the bear. I can't help but admire his ability to redirect the attention, a skill I know well as a bartender. But as he continues, I notice Todd's jaw clenching, a flicker of disdain crossing his face.

"Sounds like you were just lucky," Todd sneers, his voice dripping with sarcasm. "You must be real good at running away."

Jack straightens, the easy charm slipping back into his demeanor, but there's a darkness in his gaze now that makes me uneasy. "Luck's all part of the adventure, isn't it?" he replies, a challenge simmering beneath the surface.

Todd chuckles, but it's a mocking sound, and I can see the camaraderie of his friends waver, sensing the tension. "You don't need to get all defensive, cowboy. It's just a joke," Todd replies, though the veiled threat lingers like smoke in the air.

Mia leans in closer to me, her eyes wide. "What's going on there?" she whispers, her excitement dampened by concern.

"I don't know, but it feels like we're teetering on the edge of something," I reply, trying to keep my voice steady. The energy in the bar has shifted, and I can feel it. It's not just Todd's taunting; it's something deeper, a history that seems to stretch back into the shadows.

"Let's not let them ruin our night," Mia suggests, her hand gripping the edge of the bar, a determined glint in her eyes. "You're the best bartender in town; show them what you've got!"

Before I can respond, I decide to channel Mia's enthusiasm into action. I clear my throat and call out to the room. "Who's ready for a round of shots on the house?"

The offer seems to catch Todd off guard, and his expression shifts from scornful to surprised. "What's the occasion?" he barks, folding his arms over his chest.

"Just a little celebration for surviving another day in Silver Springs!" I quip, flashing a bright smile. The crowd cheers, caught up in the spontaneous excitement, and I quickly prepare a selection of shots, stacking them neatly in front of me.

Jack watches, a flicker of admiration in his eyes as I navigate the chaos, but I can still sense the tension between him and Todd. I serve the shots with flair, bantering with the patrons, coaxing laughter back into the atmosphere like a magician pulling rabbits from a hat.

"Here's to good friends and great adventures!" I declare, raising my glass, hoping to drown out the negativity with laughter. The bar echoes with cheers, and even Todd begrudgingly joins in, though his smile is a mere facade.

As the drinks go down, the energy begins to shift back towards the positive, laughter bubbling over the sound of clinking glasses. Jack, buoyed by the camaraderie, loosens up a little more, sharing more of his stories—adventures in the mountains, the thrill of capturing the perfect photograph.

Yet, just as the warmth settles back into the room, the atmosphere thickens again, like a storm cloud rolling in. Todd leans over to Jack, a dangerous glint in his eye. "You know, not all of us appreciate the company of outsiders," he says, low enough that only we can hear. "Some of us think you should know your place."

Jack stiffens, and for a moment, I can't breathe. I watch as the air thickens, charged with an energy that feels almost electric.

"Why don't you back off, Todd?" I interject, my voice sharp and assertive. "This is our space, and everyone is welcome here."

Jack shoots me a grateful look, his tension easing just a notch as he shifts slightly, but the threat in Todd's eyes remains unwavering.

"Just remember, it's a small town. You never know when you might need a friend," Todd retorts, leaning back, a smirk tugging at his lips as if he holds all the cards.

The laughter around us feels fragile, the buoyancy of the night teetering on the edge of collapse. I can sense Jack's discomfort, the way his hands curl into fists on the bar, his calm facade cracking ever so slightly.

"What are you trying to say?" he asks, his voice low but edged with determination. "Because if you have a problem with me, you can say it to my face."

The bar goes silent, the buzz of laughter snuffed out like a candle in a storm. I feel the heat rising, the weight of tension settling heavily over us, as if the walls themselves are holding their breath, waiting for the inevitable storm to break.

"Easy there, cowboy," Todd replies, feigning a casual demeanor that fails to mask the threat simmering beneath. "I wouldn't want you to get hurt. This town has a way of dealing with outsiders."

The implication hangs in the air like a loaded gun, and I can feel the hairs on the back of my neck stand up. There's a history here, a darkness that threatens to spill into the open.

Suddenly, a loud crash reverberates through the bar, a drunken patron staggering into a table, sending glasses shattering to the floor. Gasps ripple through the crowd, and in that moment of chaos, I see Jack's eyes flash with something more than concern—a spark of fear mingled with defiance.

"Maybe it's time to go," he says quietly, the tension in his voice matching the fraught atmosphere.

Before I can respond, Todd laughs mockingly, "You think you can just run away? You're in our territory now."

I step closer to Jack, my heart pounding as I gauge the situation, feeling the stakes rise with every word exchanged. "This is our place, Todd," I retort, the fight igniting within me. "We're not afraid of you."

But just as the air thickens with a mix of bravery and defiance, the front door bursts open, a gust of cold air sweeping through the bar. A figure stumbles in, drenched and shivering, eyes wild and frantic.

"Help! You've got to help me!" they cry, panic evident in their voice.

The room falls into an icy silence, and I exchange a glance with Jack, the weight of uncertainty hanging heavily between us.

As the tension reaches its boiling point, I can feel the world shift beneath our feet, the night unraveling in a way I never saw coming. What happens next will change everything.

Chapter 2: A Chance Encounter

The bell above the door jingles, breaking my reverie as a woman steps inside. She's a whirlwind of vibrant energy, with chestnut curls cascading down her shoulders and a smile that seems to light up the dim bar. Mabel, I learn, is her name, and she immediately draws the attention of every patron in the room, like a sun breaking through an overcast sky. I lean against the counter, my cocktail shaker resting between my palms, feeling a sudden jolt of interest I haven't felt in ages.

As she approaches the bar, her laughter bubbles up, light and infectious, slicing through the muted conversations and clinking glasses. It's a sound that beckons to the very core of me, stirring something long dormant, like a whisper from a friend long forgotten. I pour her a whiskey sour, the bright yellow liquid swirling in the glass like a tiny sunset trapped in crystal.

"What's your name, handsome?" she asks, leaning on the bar with a casual confidence that makes me instinctively straighten.

"Jake," I reply, trying to match her energy, though I can feel the weight of my usual reserve pressing down on me. "And you're Mabel. I heard the universe sent you to liven up my night."

"Flattery, Jake? Is that your secret to keeping customers?" she teases, her green eyes sparkling with mischief.

I chuckle, feeling the corners of my mouth curl upward as I slide the drink towards her. "I'd be lying if I said it's not part of my charm. But I promise, my cocktails are worth it too."

Mabel takes a sip, her expression shifting from playful to contemplative. "Wow, that's surprisingly delicious. I was expecting something more... pedestrian. Like me."

I furrow my brow. "What's wrong with being pedestrian?"

Her laughter bubbles up again, spilling over like the drink in her glass. "Oh, come on! You're talking to a woman who, until last week, spent her days buried in a soul-sucking office job, pondering life decisions over endless spreadsheets. I think I deserve a little pedestrian in my life."

As I mix another drink—a concoction of muddled mint, fresh lime, and rum—she continues, the words tumbling out in an animated stream. "But I quit! Just like that. Packed up my desk, said my goodbyes, and I'm off to chase my dream of becoming a writer." She lifts her glass, a triumphant grin lighting her features. "No more spreadsheets, no more beige cubicles! Just me, a laptop, and the world."

The boldness in her voice ignites a flicker of admiration within me. "That's pretty brave. I mean, stepping away from a steady paycheck for a dream? Not many people can say they've done that."

"Bravery, or insanity?" she retorts with a wink. "But you know, Jake, it's not just about chasing the dream. It's the fear of regret that drives me. I don't want to be that person who looks back on their life and says, 'What if?'"

Her words hang in the air between us, a shared vulnerability that makes me realize how much I need to hear them. In her, I see a glimpse of the adventurous spirit I once had, before the world turned its back on me, wrapping me in layers of disappointment and stagnation.

"So, what's your story?" she asks, leaning forward, genuinely curious.

I hesitate, my usual walls threatening to rise. Sharing my life with a stranger feels risky, like opening a wound I've kept carefully bandaged. But there's something about her earnestness, her desire to connect that pulls me in. "I used to have big dreams too, you know," I finally admit, my voice low, almost a whisper. "I wanted to be a musician. Played guitar and wrote songs like it was my lifeblood. But then life happened—responsibilities, choices that felt right at the time but ended up being... well, not."

"Ah, the universe's little detours," Mabel nods, her expression understanding. "Tell me you haven't given up on music completely?"

"Not entirely," I confess, feeling a flicker of hope light up my chest. "I still play sometimes, but it's more of a pastime than a passion now. Work keeps me busy, and my nights are mostly filled with pouring drinks and listening to other people's stories."

"Like mine?" she teases, her smile bright enough to rival the neon lights outside.

"Exactly. But your story—your leap of faith—it's inspiring. It makes me wonder what I'm missing out on."

Mabel leans back, a thoughtful look crossing her features. "Maybe you just need a little push. What if I wrote a character based on you? A bartender with unfulfilled dreams, who meets a spunky writer determined to help him reclaim his lost passions?"

I laugh, the sound feeling foreign and exhilarating. "That sounds dangerously close to a rom-com plot. What if your character ends up falling for the bartender?"

Her grin widens, eyes sparkling with mischief. "Now you're talking! But here's the twist: the bartender helps the writer realize her dreams while she helps him find his voice again."

I can't help but feel a rush of warmth at the thought. "And what if they both realize that chasing dreams is far more enjoyable together?"

"Exactly! A partnership of dreams! They might just find themselves in the process," she says, her voice laced with excitement. "How perfect would that be?"

The conversation flows effortlessly, the weight of my solitude beginning to lift like morning fog giving way to sunlight. With every sip she takes, every story she shares, I feel a sense of lightness growing inside me, coaxing out the remnants of the person I used to be—the hopeful musician, the dreamer, the man unafraid to chase the impossible.

Mabel leans against the bar, her vibrant presence infusing the air with an electric energy that makes my usual evening routine feel almost ancient. She swirls her cocktail, the bright yellow hue catching the dim bar lights like liquid sunshine. "You know, Jake, I've always believed that a good drink can spark creativity. And if that fails, at least it can help with the existential dread."

I can't help but chuckle, my heart warming at her candidness. "I should bottle that philosophy and sell it. 'Elixirs for the Soul'—it has a nice ring to it."

"Just imagine the marketing!" she replies, her eyes dancing with enthusiasm. "We could host workshops. 'Drink Your Way to Enlightenment!' I can see it now, a crowd of hopefuls with glasses in hand, ready to solve the world's problems one sip at a time."

Her laughter is a melody I could listen to all night, and I feel a curious lightness blooming within me. It's like I've stepped into a movie where everything feels possible, and for the first time in ages, the weight of my routine begins to feel a bit less oppressive.

"So tell me, what's your story?" she asks, her gaze steady and encouraging, as if she's coaxing out a secret I've kept locked away.

I hesitate, the familiar tug of insecurity pulling at my thoughts. "It's not nearly as exciting as yours," I admit, wiping down the bar, avoiding her piercing green eyes. "I spend my nights serving drinks to people who are often more interesting than I am."

"Come on, every bartender has a story," she prods gently. "You're like a therapist with a better view of the action."

I laugh, then lean in slightly, lowering my voice as if sharing a conspiracy. "Okay, if I'm being honest, I once played in a band. We had our moments—drunken parties, a few gigs where we almost made it big, and then... life got in the way. Responsibilities, bills, you know how it goes."

"What happened to the band?"

I pause, the memory bittersweet. "We were good, but life pulled us in different directions. I ended up here, mixing drinks instead of melodies. Sometimes I wonder what could've been, but…"

Mabel raises an eyebrow. "But what? It's never too late, you know."

I shake my head, a playful smirk tugging at my lips. "Look, if I start strumming a guitar again, I might start writing 'desperate ballads' and 'heartfelt odes to missed opportunities.'"

"Maybe those are the best kinds!" she counters, her voice vibrant. "We all need a little heartbreak in our lives to make the happy endings feel worth it."

Her passion is infectious, and I feel the edges of my hesitance start to soften. "Alright, Miss Writer. If you're so sure about chasing dreams, what's your first story going to be about?"

"Ah, that's the million-dollar question," she says, twirling a lock of hair around her finger. "I've got a million ideas racing in my head, but they're like kittens—adorable but impossible to wrangle. I think I want to write something about love, but not the fairy tale kind. More like the messy, complicated kind."

"Do you have any personal experience with that messiness?" I ask, half-teasing.

Mabel feigns shock, placing a hand over her heart dramatically. "How dare you assume such a thing? I'm a pristine example of what happens when you let life get too predictable."

Her eyes sparkle with mischief, and I can't help but smile. "Predictability can be comforting. Like a well-worn pair of shoes."

"Or a safe but boring salad," she quips, her grin widening. "What's the point of a salad when you could have nachos?"

I nod in mock seriousness. "Now you're talking sense. A life without nachos is no life at all."

Just as our laughter fills the air, the bar door swings open again, and in walks a man clad in a leather jacket, his expression as stormy as the clouds gathering outside. His presence seems to suck the energy from the room, and I can feel the atmosphere shift as he strides up to the bar.

"Hey, Jake," he grunts, his voice gravelly. "Get me a whiskey—neat."

"Coming right up," I reply, glancing back at Mabel. Her expression has changed, a flicker of recognition passing over her features. I pour the drink, the amber liquid swirling in the glass, wondering what kind of storm brews beneath that leather exterior.

"Do you know him?" I ask, my curiosity piqued.

"Unfortunately, yes. That's Rick, my ex." Mabel's tone shifts, laced with a mix of humor and resignation. "He's the perfect example of why nachos are far superior to salads. Sometimes, you just get a little too... predictable."

Rick shifts his weight, leaning against the bar with a brooding intensity that seems to fill the space between us. "Still mixing drinks, huh?" he sneers, his gaze flicking to Mabel. "And how's the writing career going? Still chasing dreams, or are you just drowning in mediocrity?"

The insult hangs in the air, heavy and unwelcome. Mabel stiffens beside me, but then I see the fire in her eyes spark back to life. "At least I'm chasing something, Rick. What are you doing—clinging to the past while pretending you're not drowning in regret?"

Rick opens his mouth to retort, but before he can find his words, Mabel leans over the bar, her voice dropping to a conspiratorial whisper. "You know what's funny? I was just telling Jake here how I'm going to write a book, and maybe it'll feature a bartender who helps a lost soul find their way."

"Wow, that's groundbreaking," Rick scoffs, but there's an edge of uncertainty creeping into his voice.

"Maybe I'll make the lost soul a little too predictable," Mabel adds with a sly smile, turning back to me as if the storm brewing behind us no longer exists. "What do you think, Jake? Can a character like me save a character like him?"

The tension crackles in the air, but there's an unmistakable camaraderie blossoming between us, each barb thrown by Rick only bringing Mabel and me closer together. As I pour another drink, I realize I'm no longer just a bartender, but a participant in this unfolding drama—caught in a web of dreams and confrontations, where Mabel's fiery spirit reignites a flicker of hope within me.

Mabel leans closer, her voice conspiratorial as she continues to engage Rick with an easy confidence that only adds to her allure. "You know, Rick, it's amazing how people can surprise you. Like, for instance, Jake here could write a bestseller about the very moment you walked in." She turns her head slightly, shooting me a playful wink that warms my chest. "A story of redemption. It's got layers!"

Rick's expression darkens, his brows furrowing as if she'd just thrown a glass of cold water in his face. "Redemption, huh? Maybe you should take a closer look at your own life before you start giving others advice. Last I checked, you were still wearing that 'crazy writer' badge."

I can see the tension tightening around Mabel's mouth, but she's not about to back down. "And yet here I am, still standing, while you—" she gestures toward him with her glass, "you're still sulking at the bottom of the bottle."

A silence stretches between them, thick and heavy like the humidity that clings to summer evenings. The bar, which had been so vibrant moments before, now feels charged, as if everyone is waiting for the inevitable explosion.

"Enough of this," Rick snaps, his irritation palpable. "You're not as clever as you think, Mabel. All this chatter about dreams and stories? It's just a smokescreen for the fact that you're scared. Scared to put yourself out there and actually be vulnerable."

For a moment, I can see Mabel waver, the bravado dimming like a flickering candle, but then she lifts her chin defiantly. "You're wrong, Rick. Vulnerability isn't weakness; it's courage. Something you wouldn't know anything about."

"Courage?" he scoffs, taking a deep swig of his whiskey, the amber liquid reflecting the strained light above the bar. "If you were truly brave, you'd face your fears head-on instead of hiding behind a bar and a half-baked cocktail recipe."

"Good thing I have a better idea of who I am than you ever did," she retorts sharply, the confidence flooding back into her tone. "At least I'm willing to take risks, even if they lead to failure. That's more than I can say for you."

Rick slams his glass down on the bar, shattering the moment. "Keep playing the victim, Mabel. You'll only end up back where you started. Alone."

Mabel's face flushes with a mix of anger and hurt, but before she can respond, I step in, unable to bear the tension any longer. "Alright, Rick, how about we just enjoy our drinks and keep the melodrama for the stage?"

Rick narrows his eyes at me, assessing, before finally rolling his shoulders back as if shaking off the weight of the moment. "Whatever. Just don't get too cozy with her, bartender. This isn't some fairy tale."

"Fairy tales are overrated," Mabel shoots back, her voice steady, but I can see the storm brewing behind her eyes. "Sometimes, reality's far more interesting."

As Rick turns away, I lean closer to Mabel, who is now swirling her drink again, a contemplative expression settling on her features. "You alright?" I ask softly, genuinely concerned.

She exhales, her shoulders dropping slightly. "I will be. It's just... annoying, you know? To have someone who claims to know you throw all that judgment around."

"I get it. Judgments can sting," I reply, placing a fresh drink in front her. "But you're here, fighting your fight, and that takes guts. Seriously."

"Thanks, Jake." She lifts her glass in a mock toast. "Here's to fighting the good fight, even when the past tries to drag you back down."

Before we can clink glasses, the bar door swings open again, and the atmosphere shifts yet again, the air thickening with another wave of unexpected energy. A tall figure walks in, silhouetted against the streetlights, and as he steps into the bar's warm glow, I instantly recognize him. It's Leo, my older brother, his presence as magnetic as ever.

"Jake! You won't believe the day I had!" he announces, striding over, his voice booming with a mix of excitement and exhaustion. He ruffles his messy hair, his smile infectious, but when he spots Mabel, his expression changes to curiosity. "Who's this? Your new muse?"

Mabel's eyes widen slightly, and she shifts in her seat. "Just a friendly drink, I promise," she says, her tone light but her eyes dancing with intrigue.

"Great to meet you!" Leo extends his hand, flashing a charming smile. "I'm Leo, the older, cooler brother. What brings you to our humble establishment?"

"I'm Mabel," she replies, her demeanor shifting from defensive to approachable as she shakes his hand. "Just trying to dodge my past and find some inspiration."

"I can relate to that," he says, his voice warm, though I sense a flicker of something beneath it—a protective instinct. "Jake's the king of escaping his past too."

"Sure, if escaping involves making cocktails and avoiding life," I interject, shooting him a look that says I'm perfectly fine, thank you very much.

Leo laughs, his attention now fully on Mabel. "Well, Mabel, consider this your official invitation to join our little family. We might be a bit of a mess, but at least it's a colorful one."

She laughs, and for a moment, it feels as though the air has shifted again, a bright thread woven into the fabric of our evening.

But just as the tension seems to melt away, the atmosphere shifts once more when the door bursts open again. This time, it's a familiar face—an ex-patron of the bar who had caused trouble in the past, and now his eyes sweep the room, lingering on Mabel with a predatory intensity.

Mabel shifts uncomfortably, her earlier bravado faltering. "Is that...?"

"Yeah, that's Doug," I reply, my stomach sinking. "He's not the kind of guy you want to be around."

Leo narrows his eyes at Doug's approach, a protective instinct flaring to life. "Jake, maybe it's time to cut off his tab."

But before I can react, Doug's voice cuts through the air, smooth and sinister. "Well, well, if it isn't the famous Mabel. Thought I'd find you here. Seems like you've traded in your dignity for a cocktail and some company. How charming."

Mabel stiffens, her earlier spark dimming under the weight of his words. "You need to leave, Doug," she says, her voice low and steady.

"Oh, I'm not going anywhere just yet," he replies, a smirk spreading across his face. "I have unfinished business."

The room feels electric with tension, the energy crackling around us. I can see Mabel's determination waning, the shadows of her past creeping back in, and the weight of the moment becomes almost unbearable.

"Let's go, Mabel," I say, stepping closer, ready to shield her from whatever Doug has in store. "You don't have to engage with him."

But as she looks between us, a fire ignites in her gaze, and she stands tall, defiance radiating from her. "No. This is my story, and I'm not backing down."

The weight of her words hangs heavily in the air, and I can feel the stakes rising, a cliff's edge hovering just out of reach. The tension mounts, leaving us all suspended, and as Doug's smirk widens, I realize this is only the beginning of a confrontation that could change everything.

Chapter 3: Unspoken Connections

Mabel arrived at The Broken Compass with a purposeful stride, her silhouette framed by the soft, golden light spilling from the bar's old-fashioned windows. It was one of those crisp autumn evenings when the world felt dipped in amber, and the promise of warm drinks and heartier conversations beckoned. I was nursing my third cup of Earl Grey, the fragrant steam curling into the air, a comfort against the burgeoning chill that had seeped into my bones.

As she approached, I couldn't help but admire how the low hum of laughter and clinking glasses danced around her like a welcome mat. Mabel had an undeniable charm; it radiated from her like heat from an oven, enveloping everyone in her orbit. Her curly auburn hair caught the light, creating a halo effect that only seemed to amplify her infectious smile. "Mind if I join you?" she asked, her voice a blend of excitement and warmth, as if she had just discovered a long-lost friend in the crowded café.

"Please do," I replied, gesturing to the empty seat across from me. "I was just contemplating the existential weight of the scone I had earlier."

She laughed, a sound that was melodic and bright. "Ah, yes, the scone dilemma. A classic. Should it be savored slowly or devoured in one glorious bite?"

"I think I went for option B," I admitted, smirking as I leaned back in my chair, reveling in the moment. "Regrettable decisions, but I'm all about living in the now."

Mabel leaned forward, her eyes sparkling with mischief. "A bold philosophy. I can get behind that. Life is too short to deny oneself pastries, especially when they have the audacity to be so delicious."

Our laughter mingled, creating a bubble of ease that seemed to push away the weight of the world outside. With each shared smile, I felt the protective armor I had wrapped around my heart begin to soften, the layers peeling back to reveal something raw and unguarded. Mabel had a way of disarming me, coaxing out stories I hadn't dared to tell anyone.

"Do you ever miss it?" she asked suddenly, her tone shifting as she toyed with the edge of her cup.

"Miss what?" I answered, a playful frown creasing my forehead.

"Your old life," she clarified, her gaze steady and probing, like a gentle tide inching toward the shore, persistent yet unobtrusive. "The people, the predictability of it all."

I hesitated, feeling the familiar pang of nostalgia rise like bile in my throat. The memories of my previous life had a habit of creeping up on me when I least expected it, a reminder of everything I had left behind. "Sometimes. But more for what could have been than what was," I finally said, my voice barely above a whisper. "I used to think I had it all figured out, but the truth is, I was just playing the part."

Mabel's expression softened, her vulnerability shining through the confidence that usually wrapped around her like a cozy blanket. "I get that. I left Boston chasing dreams, but sometimes the chase feels a lot like running away from something rather than toward anything."

"Where did you think you were running to?"

She sighed, her eyes drifting toward the window where the last vestiges of sunset flickered against the darkening sky. "To a life less ordinary, I suppose. But now, I wonder if I just traded one set of fears for another."

Our conversation flowed like a river, twisting and turning through the labyrinth of our lives, revealing hidden depths and sharp rocks that had shaped us. With every word shared, I felt the weight of my guarded heart ease, allowing me to glimpse the possibility of a connection I hadn't anticipated. Mabel was so different from me—her bravery, her adventurous spirit, and her unwavering optimism both frightened and intrigued me.

As the evening wore on, the café buzzed around us, but we existed in our own bubble, a world of shared thoughts and unspoken dreams. I learned about her childhood spent in the vibrant streets of Boston, where life felt like a series of snapshots filled with colorful characters and endless possibilities. The thought of her in that bustling city brought an unexpected warmth to my heart; she painted it vividly, from the eclectic coffee shops that served the best croissants to the old bookshops that smelled like nostalgia and whispered secrets.

"I always thought I'd end up working in one of those coffee shops," she confessed, her laughter tinged with a hint of disbelief. "But here I am, pouring my heart into a new life. It's a lot like learning to walk again—wobbly and uncertain, yet thrilling."

"Is it scary?" I asked, the question slipping from my lips before I could think it through.

"Terrifying," she admitted, a shadow passing over her bright eyes. "But it's also exhilarating. Every day is a new chance to trip and fall or dance like no one is watching."

I smiled at that, a flicker of understanding igniting between us. In that moment, I wanted to pull her closer, share all the fears that had kept me anchored to my past, and unleash the desires that flickered just beneath the surface. Yet, the nagging doubt lingered in the back of my mind, a stubborn little voice that warned me of the risks of becoming too entangled in someone else's journey.

But Mabel was relentless. "You know," she said, her voice lowering conspiratorially, "I think the only way to truly live is to embrace the messiness. The unspoken connections, the what-ifs, they're what make life worth it."

I wanted to believe her, to dive into the chaos of life with her. But as I gazed into her eyes, full of hope and dreams, I couldn't help but wonder—was I ready to dismantle the walls I had so carefully constructed? Would I be able to risk everything for a chance at something beautiful?

The question hung in the air, tantalizing and terrifying, as I took another sip of my tea, the warmth spreading through me, urging me to step beyond my fears and embrace whatever was blooming between us.

The weeks slipped by like pages turning in a well-loved book, each moment with Mabel a new chapter filled with laughter and revelation. The Broken Compass had transformed into our sanctuary, a cozy haven where we forged an unspoken pact of authenticity. It was where the aroma of fresh coffee mingled with the sweet scent of pastries, and the baristas had begun to recognize our orders before we even approached the counter.

One particularly crisp Saturday morning, the café bustled with a blend of regulars and newcomers, their voices a pleasant hum beneath the smooth jazz playing in the background. Mabel and I settled into our usual corner, the old wooden table scratched and worn from years of vibrant conversations and shared dreams. She had an armful of books—well-thumbed paperbacks, their spines cracked and pages dog-eared—gathered like treasures. "I figured we could discuss our latest literary obsessions," she said, her eyes sparkling with mischief. "You know, the ones that fuel our existential crises."

I chuckled, taking a sip of my steaming latte. "And you thought today would be the day I laid bare my soul to the judgment of literary critics?"

"Absolutely! Who needs critics when we have each other?" she teased, flipping open a book with a flourish, the pages fluttering like wings. "Besides, you might be surprised at the hidden depths I've uncovered in my readings."

I leaned in, intrigued. "Oh? Do tell."

As she launched into a passionate summary of a novel about a woman who reinvented herself after a heartbreak, I found myself captivated not just by the story but by the way Mabel's words danced in the air. Her expressive gestures painted pictures of the characters, their struggles and triumphs, weaving her own experiences into the fabric of their lives. It was during these moments that I realized how much she had become a mirror reflecting the untold stories within me.

"What about you?" she asked, her voice suddenly serious, as if she could sense the shift in my thoughts. "What's been keeping you up at night?"

I hesitated, the familiar weight of vulnerability pressing against my chest. "I guess I'm just... figuring things out," I said slowly, choosing my words carefully. "Trying to reconcile who I was with who I want to be."

Mabel tilted her head, her gaze unwavering, and I felt the urge to elaborate. "I've always been the sensible one, the planner, the girl who had her life neatly mapped out. But now? It's like I've been handed a blank canvas and a palette of chaotic colors, and I'm terrified of making a mess."

"Messiness can be beautiful," she countered, a soft smile tugging at her lips. "Sometimes it's in the chaos that we find our true selves."

As her words sank in, the barriers I had so carefully erected began to tremble. Mabel had a way of illuminating the darker corners of my heart, coaxing out the shadows I preferred to keep hidden. I longed to share more with her, to reveal the scars that still throbbed beneath the surface.

Just then, the door swung open, and a gust of chilly wind swept through the café, rattling the cups on the tables. A figure stepped inside, shaking off a flurry of leaves clinging to their coat. I glanced over, expecting nothing more than a passerby seeking warmth, but my breath caught in my throat as recognition washed over me. It was Ethan.

Ethan, with his disarming smile and easy charm, was a ghost from my past that I had hoped to leave buried. The last time we had crossed paths, it had been a chance encounter at a mutual friend's party, a reminder of all the feelings I thought I had tucked away.

"Mabel," I said, my voice low and unsteady, "that's... that's Ethan."

Her brow furrowed as she turned to look. "The ex?"

"Yeah," I replied, my heart racing as if it were trying to escape my chest. "This should be fun."

Ethan spotted me, his face lighting up with recognition. He strode toward our table, an uninvited storm cloud looming over my carefully constructed calm. "Well, if it isn't the lovely and talented—"

"Mabel," she introduced herself with a firm handshake, her confidence cutting through the tension that hung like fog in the air.

Ethan's gaze flicked between us, curiosity sparking in his eyes. "Nice to meet you. I didn't know you two were... friends?"

Mabel glanced at me, her expression curious yet unwavering. "We're getting to know each other. We were just discussing how beautiful messiness can be."

"Oh, is that what we're calling it these days?" Ethan quipped, his tone light yet laced with an undercurrent I couldn't quite place. "Because I distinctly remember a time when you categorized chaos as a catastrophe."

"People change, Ethan," I replied, my tone sharper than I intended. "I've come to embrace the chaos in my life."

He opened his mouth to retort, but Mabel interjected with a disarming smile. "And what brings you to The Broken Compass today? Seeking existential wisdom or just a good scone?"

"Bit of both, actually," he replied, his grin softening as he turned his attention to her. "And to see if I could bump into some interesting company."

I wanted to roll my eyes, but Mabel's presence grounded me. Instead of diving into old wounds and messy history, I found myself intrigued by her ability to remain unfazed by his charm. It was refreshing, almost enchanting, and it sparked something within me—an ember of defiance against the shadows of my past.

"Well, you've found it," she said, crossing her arms in a way that said she was not to be trifled with. "But be warned: Mabel is not easily charmed."

Ethan's laughter filled the air, a sound that used to wrap around me like a warm blanket. "Challenge accepted, Mabel. But I'm not here to charm anyone. Just catching up with old friends. Right, Alice?"

I nodded, feeling the remnants of tension unwind. "Right. Just friends catching up."

As Ethan settled into the seat next to Mabel, I felt a mixture of unease and curiosity. Conversations flowed like a river, unpredictable and occasionally turbulent. Mabel engaged him effortlessly, her questions sharp and witty, and I found myself caught in the ebb and flow, trying to navigate the shifting tides of my emotions.

The world around us faded as the dialogue danced, and despite my unease, a part of me relished the unexpected twist of fate. Mabel and I exchanged glances, our silent communication vibrant and electric. Perhaps this was a turning point—a reminder that the past, though haunting, didn't have to define my future. The unspoken connections we forged in that café felt like a bridge over the tumultuous waters of our lives, and for the first time in a long time, I sensed the possibility of hope on the horizon.

The atmosphere in The Broken Compass crackled with an electric tension, each word spoken hanging in the air like a fragile ornament on a tree, just waiting for the wrong breeze to send it tumbling. As Ethan settled in beside Mabel, the ease of our earlier banter transformed into something more complex. Mabel's laughter echoed against the walls, bright and airy, as she volleyed jokes back and forth with Ethan, but I could feel an invisible thread binding me to my past, stretching taut and threatening to snap.

"Tell me, what's the wildest thing you've ever done?" Ethan asked, leaning back in his chair with a devil-may-care grin that had once made my heart race.

Mabel tapped her chin thoughtfully, pretending to weigh the options. "I once tried to cook a three-course meal for a date and almost set my kitchen on fire," she confessed, her eyes glimmering with mischief. "I still have the smoke detector to remind me of that lovely evening."

I couldn't help but chuckle, the absurdity of her story momentarily dispelling the heaviness in my chest. "That's impressive," I added, eager to steer the conversation. "Setting the bar high for first impressions, are we?"

Ethan interjected with a teasing smirk, "What about you, Alice? What's your wild card?"

I felt the weight of their gaze, like two spotlights illuminating a stage where I had forgotten my lines. "Oh, you know, the usual," I said, trying to sound nonchalant. "A few years back, I tried skydiving. Didn't quite realize the 'free fall' part was so literal."

Mabel leaned forward, her eyes wide with intrigue. "You jumped out of a plane? That's incredible! I can barely handle the adrenaline of a roller coaster."

"It's a long story," I replied, taking a sip of my drink to mask the flutter of nerves that had stirred at the mention of my daring adventure. "Let's just say the parachute did open—eventually."

Ethan laughed, but there was a flicker of something else in his eyes, an unspoken challenge that made my stomach twist. "Maybe you should try something wilder, Alice. Life is short, after all. The more chaotic, the better."

Mabel shot him a look that could only be described as protective, a flicker of concern. "Let's not encourage reckless decisions, Ethan."

"Hey, I'm all about calculated chaos," he retorted, waving a hand dismissively. "Besides, a little recklessness can be a catalyst for change. Isn't that what you're all about, Mabel?"

The banter continued, the playful sparring masking an undercurrent of tension that hummed between us. I watched Mabel and Ethan slip into their rhythm, his easy charm complementing her spirited wit, and a pang of uncertainty lodged itself in my chest.

Just when I thought the conversation was settling into a comfortable groove, the door swung open once again, and in walked a familiar face—Olivia, my former boss and the last person I wanted to see. Her presence felt like a sudden gust of wind that threatened to topple everything I'd been carefully constructing.

"Alice!" she called out, her voice a blend of warmth and authority. "I was hoping I'd find you here."

"Great," I muttered under my breath, fighting the urge to hide behind my coffee cup.

"Olivia, what a surprise!" I forced a smile, hoping it didn't betray my unease.

As she approached, her heels clicking on the wooden floor, I felt the tension in the air thicken. "I've been meaning to talk to you about the new project we're launching," she said, her eyes sharp as she took in the scene. Her gaze flickered from Ethan to Mabel and back to me, assessing and calculating. "And I see you've made new friends."

"Just catching up," I said, attempting to deflect the conversation.

Mabel, ever the brave one, chimed in with a bright smile, "It's a lovely little spot, isn't it? We were just discussing our most reckless moments."

"Reckless moments?" Olivia arched an eyebrow, clearly intrigued. "I always say life begins at the edge of your comfort zone."

Ethan leaned forward, his grin widening. "We could all use a little recklessness, don't you think?"

Mabel shot me a quick glance, her expression both amused and wary. I could see her picking up on the subtle shift in my demeanor.

"Why don't you join us, Olivia?" Mabel suggested, her tone friendly yet firm. "We were just about to brainstorm wild life choices."

"Thank you, but I have some things to discuss with Alice," Olivia replied, her eyes locked onto mine, a silent demand that sent a shiver down my spine.

My heart raced as the weight of her gaze bore down on me. I could feel the conversation shifting, a tide pulling us back toward familiar shores that I had fought so hard to leave behind.

"I'd love to hear more about this project, Olivia," I said, trying to keep my voice steady. "How about we grab a table in the back?"

"Perfect," she said, her smile tight, and I could sense the challenge lurking just beneath the surface.

As we moved away from the table, I caught Mabel's concerned look lingering in my peripheral vision. Ethan's laughter faded into the background, replaced by the knot of apprehension tightening in my stomach.

Once we settled into a quieter corner, Olivia wasted no time. "Alice, I need you back on board," she said, her voice clipped and urgent. "The project's scope has shifted, and we could really use your expertise."

I hesitated, the words tumbling around in my mind like marbles. "I've moved on, Olivia. I'm focusing on other things now."

"Things that seem a bit... chaotic?" she countered, her eyes narrowing slightly. "You're still searching for direction, I can tell. Don't you think it's time to come back to what you're good at?"

My pulse quickened at her words, a mixture of irritation and longing bubbling beneath the surface. "I'm not interested in going back to what was comfortable. I'm trying to explore new paths."

"Paths that could lead to dead ends," she shot back, her voice low and insistent. "You're better than this. You have a real talent, and I won't let you waste it."

The air between us crackled with unspoken tension as I grappled with her words. Did she see me as nothing more than a cog in her machine? Did she even understand the turmoil I was facing?

Just then, the door swung open again, and a chill swept through the café, making me shiver. In walked someone I hadn't expected to see—Rachel, an old acquaintance, her expression unreadable. She scanned the room until her eyes landed on me, and a smile broke across her face, as if she had just found a long-lost friend.

"Hey, Alice! Fancy seeing you here!"

I felt a rush of relief wash over me, a welcome distraction from Olivia's penetrating gaze. "Rachel! What a surprise!"

As she approached, her energy filled the space like a warm breeze, and I could see the tension between Olivia and me dissipate, at least for a moment.

Rachel's laughter rang out, contagious and bright. "I heard you'd left the corporate world behind. What are you doing these days?"

"Exploring," I replied, glancing back at Olivia, whose expression had shifted from annoyance to calculation.

"Well, exploring sounds much more exciting than endless meetings," Rachel said, her eyes dancing with mischief. "Life's too short for that nonsense."

"Yes, exactly!" I exclaimed, grateful for the reprieve.

But as the conversation flowed, I couldn't shake the feeling that my past was rising like a tide, threatening to pull me back under.

"Listen, I really need to talk to you, Alice," Olivia interrupted, cutting through the laughter like a knife.

My stomach twisted, caught between the urge to escape and the knowledge that running wouldn't solve anything. The moment hung heavy in the air, charged with potential and dread, as I realized that some conversations were inevitable.

Rachel's smile faded slightly as she sensed the shift, her eyes darting between us. "Everything okay?"

I swallowed hard, caught between the two worlds that had begun to clash around me. "Yeah, everything's fine," I lied, knowing the truth lurked just beneath the surface.

As Olivia leaned closer, her voice dropping to a conspiratorial whisper, I braced myself for the inevitable confrontation. But just as she opened her mouth to speak, the café door swung wide once more, and the world outside rushed in, carrying with it a sudden gust of uncertainty that sent a shiver down my spine.

I turned instinctively, curiosity piquing as I watched a tall figure step inside, shrouded in shadows. My breath caught as recognition flashed through me, and my heart raced with a mix of excitement and trepidation.

There, standing at the threshold, was someone I never expected to see again. A figure from my past, stepping back into my life at the most inopportune moment, their gaze locking onto mine with an intensity that sent shockwaves through the room.

And just like that, the calm surface of my carefully crafted existence began to ripple, the world tilting precariously as I braced for the impact of whatever was about to unfold.

Chapter 4: A Turn of Events

Rain pattered insistently against the window, each drop a tiny drumbeat urging me to face the tempest brewing within me. The dim light of my living room flickered as I paced, my mind swirling with thoughts like the storm outside. Mabel had just arrived, her hair damp and tousled, a picture of chaotic beauty as she burst through the door, shaking off the remnants of the storm. It was one of those evenings that felt heavy with secrets, the air thick with an energy that promised change.

"I can't believe this is happening!" she exclaimed, her voice bright like the flash of lightning outside. She was radiant, a spark of life amidst the gloom, and the way her eyes shone made my heart thump a little harder.

I stopped pacing, taking in the enthusiasm that radiated from her, yet beneath that brightness, I caught a glimpse of the uncertainty she tried to mask. "What is happening?" I asked, half-teasing, half-serious. I loved to prod her, watching as the layers of her thoughts peeled away, revealing her true feelings.

"I've been selected for the writer's retreat in the mountains! You know, the one everyone dreams of attending." Her voice climbed higher with every word, and I couldn't help but feel a twinge of envy. Mabel had a talent that flowed effortlessly from her pen, words spilling like rain after a drought. I admired her ability to capture moments, weave tales that felt like they breathed, and here she was, stepping into a world I only dared to dream about.

"That's incredible! You deserve it!" I clapped my hands together, trying to infuse my words with enough sincerity to outweigh the twinge of disappointment lodged deep in my chest. "When do you leave?"

"Next week." She smiled, but the corners of her lips quivered slightly. "I'm excited, but..." She hesitated, biting her lower lip, a gesture I had grown to adore. "It's right around the anniversary of, well, you know."

The mention of that date twisted something inside me, a reminder of heartbreak that lingered like the humidity in the air. A year had passed since my world cracked open, and I had spent countless days staring at the same four walls, grappling with memories that danced just beyond my reach. "Yeah, I know." I took a step closer, letting the warmth of her presence seep into my bones. "How do you feel about it?"

"I'm excited for the opportunity, but…" She trailed off, her gaze drifting to the rain-slicked window, where the shadows of trees swayed like specters in the storm. "I don't want to feel sad while I'm there, you know? I want to focus on my writing."

I understood that yearning, the need to create something beautiful amidst the chaos, yet the thought of her leaving made my stomach twist. It was as if the universe had orchestrated this moment—her opportunity against the backdrop of my vulnerability. "You could always stay here," I blurted out, the words tumbling from my mouth before I could wrestle them back.

She blinked, her expression a cocktail of surprise and intrigue, the storm outside fading momentarily as we locked eyes. "Stay here?"

"Yeah," I continued, buoyed by a mix of boldness and desperation. "Just for a few days. I mean, why would you want to be alone during a time that feels so heavy?" The words hung in the air, thick and electric, like the charged atmosphere before a storm breaks.

Mabel's brow furrowed, and I could see the wheels turning behind those bright eyes. "But what about the retreat? It's such an opportunity…"

I took a step forward, closing the distance between us. "Opportunities can wait. You don't have to chase everything alone. Besides," I added, leaning in a little, "the mountains will still be there when you're ready. And what if I have a few writing exercises up my sleeve? You could focus on your work without the weight of that day looming over you."

Her hesitation melted slightly as she searched my face, seeking something—reassurance, perhaps, or maybe a spark of possibility. "You'd really want me to stay? Just like that?"

"Absolutely." My heart raced, a wild drumbeat echoing the urgency of my plea. "It would be fun! Just us, no distractions. We can make it a little adventure." The idea of having her here, close enough to feel her warmth, was intoxicating.

Mabel let out a soft laugh, her eyes dancing with a mixture of mischief and disbelief. "Adventure, huh? You make it sound like a treasure hunt, only the treasure is a pile of half-finished manuscripts and existential crises."

"Exactly! Who wouldn't want to dig through that?" I grinned, the tension easing as I reached for her hand, intertwining our fingers. The storm outside raged on, but inside, the atmosphere shifted to something lighter, a tentative hope blossoming between us.

"Alright, let's do it," she said, her voice steady now. "But only if you promise to keep the snacks stocked. I can't create on an empty stomach."

"Deal," I replied, my pulse quickening at the prospect of sharing these days with her. We shared a knowing look, a moment of unspoken agreement that carried weight far beyond the mundane.

As we settled onto the couch, her presence was a comforting balm against the storm outside. The rain drummed a steady rhythm, a backdrop to our laughter and playful banter. The world outside seemed to fade away, leaving just the two of us, a cocoon of warmth and shared dreams.

And as the evening wore on, I couldn't shake the feeling that this twist of fate was more than just a chance encounter; it was the beginning of something profound, a chapter unwritten, waiting for us to discover what lay ahead.

As the rain drummed steadily against the windows, the atmosphere inside transformed into a sanctuary. The world outside was drenched in shadows and moisture, but here, in this small living room, warmth enveloped us like a soft blanket. Mabel nestled deeper into the couch, her laughter weaving through the air, punctuated by the occasional clap of thunder, which seemed to echo her joy.

"Okay, so what's the plan?" she asked, propping her chin on her palm, her curiosity piqued. "Are we going to brainstorm a novel about two quirky best friends stranded during a storm? Or perhaps a romance between a writer and her best friend who also happens to be a former heartthrob?"

"Only if the heartthrob is me," I shot back, grinning as I threw a pillow her way. "Otherwise, I don't want to hear it. I can only write so much while nursing my ego."

She laughed, catching the pillow mid-air, and tossed it back at me with surprising force. "Fine! You're the heartthrob, and I'm the quirky best friend with a penchant for disastrous life choices and bad coffee. It's practically a bestseller already."

The playful banter flowed easily, and for a moment, the shadows of the past felt like a distant storm cloud, far removed from the laughter we shared. But even amid the levity, a twinge of anxiety clung to my thoughts like humidity in the air. This was no ordinary evening; it was a threshold, a juncture where the past met the present, where my heart and head tangled in a wild dance of emotions.

"Tell me about the retreat," I prompted, leaning back to take in her animated expression. "What's the vibe? Will there be mountains? Wildflowers? Maybe a handsome stranger to distract you from your work?"

Her face lit up as she spoke, her passion igniting a fire in the room. "Oh, absolutely! The brochure said it's this gorgeous old lodge nestled right by a lake, surrounded by towering pines and wildflowers in full bloom. They even have workshops led by published authors! I'm not just going to sit in a cabin and stare at a wall, you know."

I couldn't help but smile at her enthusiasm, yet the thought of her immersing herself in that world while I wallowed in my own solitude felt like a punch to the gut. "And what about all those 'handsome strangers'? Are they there to offer literary advice or just to distract you?"

"Probably both," she teased, her eyes twinkling. "But I've got to keep my focus on writing, right? That's the whole point."

"Sure, until one of them shows up with a rugged smile and a tragic backstory," I countered, pretending to sulk. "Then it's all over for your manuscript."

"Stop!" she laughed, covering her mouth as she shook her head. "I can't have you scaring me away from potential romances with your melodramatic narratives. What if I want a rugged stranger to sweep me off my feet?"

"Then I suppose I should be prepared to be utterly heartbroken," I replied, my voice feigning a dramatic quiver. "Tragic, really. My best friend off gallivanting in the mountains while I'm stuck here drinking overpriced wine and binge-watching bad reality TV."

"Oh, come on! You know you'll survive." Mabel rolled her eyes, but there was a softness in her gaze that made my heart skip. "Besides, you're way more than just my binge-watching partner. You're my biggest cheerleader."

The sincerity in her words wrapped around me like a warm embrace, but just as quickly, doubt crept in. Would she see me as just a cheerleader? What about the other feelings swirling beneath the surface, bubbling and threatening to spill over? I swallowed hard, grappling with my own insecurities.

"I suppose," I said, forcing a casualness into my tone, "you'll come back with all sorts of new ideas and experiences that will make me feel even more inadequate."

She leaned closer, the playful mood shifting as she placed a hand on my knee, grounding me with her warmth. "You're not inadequate. If anything, you've been a constant source of inspiration for me. This friendship we have—it's rare, and I don't take it lightly."

The sincerity in her gaze made my heart race, and I caught myself holding my breath, waiting for the punchline that never came. Instead, we sat in silence, the room echoing with unspoken words, the thunder rumbling outside as if the universe itself held its breath.

Mabel broke the tension with a lighthearted remark, pulling me back from the brink. "And if you're really feeling inadequate, I can always introduce you to my rugged stranger when I get back. I'm sure he'd be thrilled to meet the heartthrob of the storm."

"Ah, yes. I'll get him to write a glowing review about my dance skills at the next karaoke night," I quipped, my laughter mingling with the sound of rain, but inside, a part of me resisted the idea of her returning with stories that would include someone else.

The evening stretched on, our conversation meandering like the river we could hear in the distance. As the storm raged outside, I found myself caught in a whirlpool of emotions—excitement at her presence, fear of losing her to new adventures, and an inexplicable longing to redefine our friendship into something more profound.

Just as the thought settled uncomfortably in my mind, Mabel glanced outside, her brow furrowing slightly. "You know, I didn't expect the weather to turn like this. It feels like the storm is here to stay."

"It certainly feels that way," I replied, my heart pounding at the possibilities unfolding around us. "But storms can bring clarity, right? Maybe it's a sign for us to discover something new."

"Or a sign for me to admit that I'm terrified of leaving." She looked back at me, and I caught the glimmer of vulnerability in her eyes. "What if I go up there, and I can't write? What if I let everyone down?"

"Then you'll have the most dramatic story to tell," I said, squeezing her hand gently, anchoring her to the moment. "But you won't let anyone down. You're too talented for that. You've got a fire inside you that just won't quit."

The room hummed with energy, both of us grappling with fears and aspirations, the boundaries of our friendship shifting in ways that felt both exhilarating and terrifying. In that intimate moment, amidst the raging storm, I couldn't help but wonder if perhaps this was the pivotal moment we both needed—one that might lead us to the truths lurking just beneath the surface, waiting for the right storm to break them free.

The rain continued to tap a syncopated rhythm against the window, a persistent reminder of the tempest both outside and within. Mabel and I sat in the living room, the air thick with unspoken sentiments, each heartbeat amplifying the gravity of our conversation. I stole glances at her, hoping to decipher the thoughts that danced behind her expressive eyes, knowing all too well how easy it was to let fear and uncertainty shadow the brighter possibilities.

"I can't shake the feeling that this storm is a sign," Mabel mused, gazing out at the sheets of rain blurring the world beyond the glass. "Like maybe the universe is saying something important."

"Right? It's like a cosmic warning," I said, allowing my fingers to lightly brush against hers, igniting a spark that sent a thrill through me. "Or it's just Mother Nature reminding us who's really in charge. She's a dramatic one, that lady."

A soft chuckle escaped her lips, and I basked in the warmth of her laughter. It had been so long since I'd felt this light, the clouds of past disappointments giving way to the warmth of her company. "But what could it mean?" she asked, turning her focus back to me, her eyes glinting with curiosity.

I hesitated, wrestling with the words that fluttered around in my mind like startled birds. "Maybe it means we need to embrace change. After all, change can be a good thing, right? Even if it feels terrifying?"

Mabel leaned back against the couch, her expression thoughtful. "You make it sound so simple. Just embrace it and everything will magically fall into place?"

"If only it were that easy," I replied, a smirk creeping onto my face. "But hey, we've already survived one awkward karaoke night together. What's a little existential crisis compared to that?"

"Fair point. Though I'll have you know I'm still traumatized by that performance," she said, her mock seriousness making me laugh. "I didn't think we could butcher 'Don't Stop Believin' that badly. It was like a high-pitched cat fight in a karaoke bar."

"Ah, but we owned it! I'm still pretty sure the audience was more entertained by our sheer enthusiasm than our vocal skills." I leaned forward, daring to draw nearer, my heart racing with a mixture of excitement and dread. "But seriously, if you don't go to the retreat, what does that mean for you? You've been dreaming about this opportunity."

Her brow furrowed, the weight of her decision clearly pressing on her. "I know, but it's also the first anniversary of, well, everything. How can I celebrate this amazing chance while also remembering that day?"

"Celebration doesn't erase the past," I said softly, my voice steady despite the turmoil inside me. "It honors it. You can embrace the new while still carrying the memories of what shaped you."

Mabel met my gaze, her eyes searching mine as if weighing my words against her feelings. "And what if the new becomes overwhelming? What if I lose myself in all of it?"

The vulnerability in her question hung in the air, heavy and ripe with implications. I wanted to reach out, to reassure her that she wouldn't lose herself, that I would be there—yet a part of me hesitated, aware of the tightrope I was walking between friendship and something deeper.

"Then we figure it out together," I said, my voice dropping to a whisper. "I won't let you drift away. Not when you've just started to explore who you are."

A flicker of hope crossed her face, and I felt a surge of warmth spread through me, igniting a fire of determination. "How about this: If you decide to stay, we create our own retreat here. A writer's sanctuary of sorts. Just us, the rain, and an endless supply of coffee and snacks."

Her laughter broke the tension, and she smirked. "As long as you promise to keep the coffee strong and the snacks plentiful, I might just consider it."

"Deal," I replied, feeling a thrill rush through me at the prospect of this new adventure—together.

We settled into a comfortable silence, the rain outside continuing its relentless symphony. The shadows shifted as lightning danced across the sky, illuminating her features, framing her face in ethereal light. I took a deep breath, the moment stretching, the air heavy with possibilities.

Just then, Mabel's phone buzzed on the coffee table, the sharp sound cutting through the ambiance like a knife. She reached for it, glancing at the screen. "It's my mom," she said, her tone shifting. "She's been calling me all evening. I should probably answer."

"Of course. It's not like she has any idea you're in the middle of an existential crisis or anything," I replied, a playful smirk tugging at my lips, but deep down, I felt the tension creeping back in.

As she answered, her expression transformed, shifting from lighthearted to serious, her brow furrowing deeply. "Hey, Mom. Is everything okay?"

The conversation spiraled into a whirlwind of concern, her mother's voice urgent yet muffled, the distance between them seeming to stretch further than the physical space of the room. Mabel's eyes widened as she listened, her lips parting slightly in shock. "What? No, that can't be—"

Panic gripped me as I leaned closer, trying to catch her words. "Mabel?"

"Okay, okay, I'll be there as soon as I can," she said, her tone tight, and when she hung up, the air between us crackled with an unexpected tension. "I have to go. My grandmother... she fell. She's in the hospital."

My heart sank, and the storm outside raged louder, mirroring the chaos erupting within me. "Oh, Mabel, I'm so sorry. Do you want me to come with you?"

"No," she said quickly, a look of determination crossing her face, but I could see the vulnerability lurking beneath. "I need to handle this. But I can't leave things like this. I need to know—"

"Know what?" I pressed, the urgency in my voice rising as I stepped closer. The connection we had was slipping through my fingers, and I felt a desperate need to anchor her here, to not let the moment dissolve into uncertainty.

"Will you wait for me?" she asked, her eyes searching mine, the weight of her question hanging between us like the storm clouds outside.

"Always," I whispered, even as the words hung heavy, echoing the fragility of our situation. And then, just like that, she was gone, leaving me standing in the storm, the door swinging shut behind her, leaving me alone in the cacophony of rain and thunder, my heart pounding with uncertainty and longing.

I had wanted so much more than just friendship. But now, in the aftermath of her sudden departure, I was left grappling with the reality of what could slip away—a connection forged in stormy nights and unspoken dreams, now teetering on the brink of something neither of us could quite name.

Chapter 5: Fractured Dreams

The moon hung low in the sky, a pearl against the velvet backdrop of night, casting silvery beams through the window, illuminating the clutter of our cozy living room. Mabel sat across from me, her laughter ringing like chimes in a gentle breeze, as she recounted another of her wonderfully absurd childhood stories. Her brown hair fell in soft waves, framing her face, and with every word she spoke, I felt the warmth of our connection wrapping around us like a knitted blanket—secure, comforting, yet somehow stifling.

"...and there I was, eight years old, convinced I could convince the neighbor's cat to take a bath by singing it a lullaby. Can you believe it? I must've been a real piece of work!" She chuckled, a mix of disbelief and fondness coloring her tone.

"Not just a piece of work; you were a master of disaster," I quipped, grinning as I imagined the spectacle. "I bet Mr. Whiskers didn't know what hit him."

Mabel leaned back against the couch, her eyes dancing with mirth. "Oh, he definitely looked at me like I was a lunatic. I mean, I can't blame him. Singing to a cat? What was I thinking?"

The evening air was thick with the fragrance of chamomile tea and the lingering scent of the lavender candles flickering on the mantelpiece, creating an atmosphere that felt almost enchanted. Yet beneath the surface of our shared laughter lay an undercurrent I could no longer ignore. As the days slipped by like grains of sand, I found myself increasingly entangled in a web of vulnerability, one that was slowly tightening around my throat.

Each night spent with Mabel chipped away at the armor I had fortified over the years. She was passionate, driven, with dreams that sparkled like the stars above. I admired her tenacity, but with admiration came a creeping dread that clawed at my insides. Her aspirations felt like a mirror reflecting the jagged edges of my own failed ambitions. I had tucked those dreams away in a box labeled "Too Fractured to Fix," but as she painted her future with such vivid strokes, I couldn't help but feel the weight of my own regret.

That particular night, after the laughter had dimmed and our conversations turned to the deeper shades of life, I felt exposed—raw. Mabel had shared a piece of herself, a hope to start her own business, and I had found myself at a crossroads, teetering on the edge of envy and self-loathing. "Why not?" I had asked, but the words had come out harsher than I intended. A silent storm brewed in my chest, a tempest threatening to break through the fragile calm we had created.

"Why not what?" she'd asked, her brow furrowing slightly.

"Your dreams," I snapped, almost biting the words off at the end. "Do you really think it's that easy? You think just because you want it badly enough, the universe will oblige?"

A shadow passed over her face, and I immediately regretted my tone. Mabel, with her unyielding optimism, seemed like a lighthouse to my shipwrecked soul, yet I was too caught in the undertow of my insecurities to acknowledge the light she shone.

"I didn't say it would be easy," she replied, her voice steady but tinged with hurt. "But I believe it's possible. Isn't that worth something?"

That was when I retreated, unable to face the truth of her words, unwilling to confront the reality that I had allowed my own dreams to wither while I kept my focus on surviving. I retreated into the solitude of my room, burying myself in a fortress of blankets, hoping to ward off the creeping darkness that threatened to suffocate me.

The next day, the sun rose with an innocent brightness, but I felt shadowed, as if the weight of my self-inflicted isolation had cast a pall over the world. My mind replayed the night's conversation like a broken record, each iteration echoing the pain of pushing away the very person who dared to shine a light into my darkness.

"Did you feed the cat?" I asked, knowing it was trivial, but unable to summon the energy to tackle the real issue.

Mabel's expression shifted from concern to confusion, her brow knitting as she processed the sudden shift in my mood. "Uh, yeah, I did. You okay?"

"Fine," I snapped, perhaps too sharply. "It's just cat food. You really should keep your focus on more important things."

Her lips tightened, and for a moment, I saw the hurt flash across her face, a crack in the otherwise radiant facade. "What do you mean by that? It's important to me!"

The tension thickened, wrapping around us like a fog. I could feel the emotional wall I was building, brick by brick, and the realization sent a chill through me. I had been here before, caught in a cycle of isolation and regret, each failed connection carving deeper scars into my heart.

"I mean..." My voice faltered, lost in the tangled thoughts that twisted like vines in my mind. "I just don't want you to waste your time on things that don't matter."

"What doesn't matter to you might matter to me," she replied, her tone now laced with the steel of confrontation.

And there it was, the raw honesty that had drawn me to her in the first place, now crashing against the walls I had erected. The fear of losing her gripped me with an iron fist, and I knew I was pushing her away just as I had done in the past, just as I had always done whenever someone dared to get too close.

"Maybe we should just take a break," I blurted, my heart pounding with the weight of the words, the dread of losing something precious threatening to consume me.

Her eyes widened in disbelief, a mixture of shock and sorrow cascading over her features. "A break? Seriously?"

In that moment, I felt as if I were teetering on the precipice of a chasm, knowing that with a single misstep, I could plummet into the abyss of my fears, fracturing the fragile dreams we had begun to weave together. But as I stared into her eyes, those pools of warmth and understanding, I also knew that the alternative was to stand firm, to fight against the tide of my insecurities.

The silence that hung in the air after my words felt like an echo of a distant thunderstorm, ominous and heavy, pressing against my chest. Mabel stood frozen, her expression caught somewhere between disbelief and hurt, the kind that had the power to unravel the most tightly knit bonds. I regretted my impulsive proclamation, but the fear of intimacy clawed at my insides, whispering insidious thoughts that tangled my resolve.

"I mean it, Mabel," I said, trying to soften the edges of my harshness, but the words came out more like a plea than a promise. "Maybe some distance is what we need. Just to… recalibrate."

"Recalibrate?" she echoed, her voice strained, as if she were piecing together a puzzle with missing parts. "Is that what you call pushing someone away?"

I could feel the heat rising in my cheeks, a flush of embarrassment mixing with my simmering anxiety. "That's not how I meant it!" I shot back, my defenses rising instinctively, even as guilt gnawed at my conscience. "I just—"

"Just what?" Her tone sharpened, and for the first time, I saw a flicker of frustration break through her usually sunny demeanor. "Are you afraid of what we're building here? Because if you are, maybe we need to have a real conversation about it instead of playing emotional dodgeball."

Her words were like ice water splashed across my face, shocking me into a moment of clarity. I couldn't keep pretending that everything was fine, that I wasn't a quivering mess beneath my carefully curated façade. "I don't want to lose you," I finally admitted, the truth spilling from my lips like an unguarded secret. "But I feel like I'm always one misstep away from ruining everything."

Mabel crossed her arms, the warmth in her eyes dimming as she processed my admission. "And you think shutting me out is the answer?"

"I don't know," I said, frustration bubbling in my chest. "Maybe I'm just trying to protect myself from making a fool of myself again."

"Protect yourself?" She shook her head, disappointment mingling with incredulity. "You're not a fool, and you're not going to make a fool of yourself. You're... you're amazing. Just let yourself be that."

"I don't feel amazing," I muttered, looking away. "I feel like a haunted house, full of cracks and creaks. I'm terrified that when you get too close, you'll see right through me and run."

Her sigh was heavy, the weight of it pressing against my heart. "Then let me help you with that. Let me in."

"Letting you in means facing things I buried a long time ago," I admitted, my voice barely a whisper. "And I don't know if I'm ready to dig all that up."

"Then we'll dig it up together," she said softly, her tone shifting, a gentle invitation rather than a demand. "It doesn't have to be all at once. We can take our time. I'm here for the ride, remember?"

I opened my mouth to respond, but the words caught in my throat. I was paralyzed by the fear of what might come tumbling out if I allowed the floodgates to open.

"I just—" My voice faltered again, and I could feel the walls closing in around me. "I don't want to burden you with my baggage. You've got your own dreams to chase. I don't want to hold you back."

"Burden?" she repeated incredulously. "You think your life is a burden? If that were true, I wouldn't have accepted your invitation in the first place. I want to know you, every single facet. It's not a chore; it's a privilege."

The sincerity in her words brushed against my heart, warming the icy edges that had taken up residence. But a dark thought crept in: what if she learned about my past? What if the shadows lurking in the corners of my mind overshadowed the bright connection we were building?

"I just... I don't want to ruin what we have," I murmured, staring at the patterned rug beneath my feet, as if it held the answers to my fears.

Mabel stepped closer, closing the physical distance between us. "You can't ruin anything if you're honest with me," she said, her voice soft yet firm. "The only way this falls apart is if we stop talking. So let's keep talking."

I nodded, the lump in my throat slowly easing, though I still felt like I was perched on a tightrope, swaying in the winds of uncertainty. "Okay. I'll try."

"Good," she said, a small smile breaking through the tension. "Now, how about we start with something simple? What was the most embarrassing moment of your life? Surely, it wasn't trying to sing to a cat."

The sudden lightness of her suggestion pulled me back from the edge. I couldn't help but chuckle, the sound spilling out like a release valve. "Alright, but don't laugh too hard."

"I make no promises," she shot back with a wink.

As I recounted the time I tripped onstage during a school play, the laughter between us returned, a balm for the frayed edges of our earlier confrontation. Mabel leaned in, eyes wide, her encouragement making me feel less like an actor in a tragedy and more like the lead in a quirky romantic comedy.

"Honestly," she laughed, "if you had told me that you were a stage-diving cat serenader, I might've lost my mind."

"Just wait until I tell you about my ill-fated dance recital," I replied, feeling the tension of the night slowly evaporate.

We shared more stories, the laughter flowing freely, creating a tapestry of connection that seemed to stitch up the gaping holes of fear and doubt. But even amidst the joy, a lingering weight rested in my chest, a reminder of the fragility of our growing bond.

Later, as we settled into the comfortable silence that sometimes followed our laughter, I couldn't shake the sense that beneath the surface of our playful banter lay unresolved emotions, waiting for their moment to surface. Mabel's dreams loomed large in my mind, a beacon of light and possibility, while my own fears whispered of potential failure, urging me to retreat.

"Promise me one thing," she said suddenly, her voice breaking the quiet like the crack of a thunderclap. "When you feel the urge to push me away, you'll fight against it instead."

I looked into her eyes, deep and earnest, and felt the truth of her request settle over me like a cloak. "I promise," I said, though I felt the words tremble on my tongue, as if they were a fragile glass waiting to shatter.

And as we sat there, the air thick with unspoken challenges and a flickering candle casting playful shadows, I couldn't help but think that our journey had just begun, both exhilarating and terrifying in its vast unknown.

The warmth between us lingered, a fragile thread woven from laughter and unguarded moments, yet the tension hovered just below the surface like a restless ghost. The evening air was thick with possibility, a tension that made my heart race in anticipation and dread. After our moment of vulnerability, I felt the weight of our unspoken fears pressing down on us, but for now, we danced around the edges of deeper truths, circling one another like moths drawn to a flickering flame.

"I need to get back to work," Mabel finally said, breaking the spell that had wrapped around us like a cozy blanket. "I'm up to my ears in sketches and plans for the new business. Want to see what I've got?"

Her enthusiasm was infectious, and for a heartbeat, I was tempted to dive headfirst into her world of dreams and ambitions. But I hesitated, grappling with my own uncertainties. "Sure, I'd love to," I replied, trying to sound enthusiastic, but the words felt heavy on my tongue.

Mabel retrieved her sketchbook from the coffee table, flipping through pages filled with swirling ideas and vibrant drawings. Each stroke of her pencil seemed to bring her vision to life, and as she described her plans, her eyes sparkled with an energy that lit up the dim room. I couldn't help but admire the passion that radiated from her, but alongside my admiration came the gnawing fear of inadequacy, a whisper that slithered into my thoughts, taunting me with reminders of my own unrealized aspirations.

"See this?" She pointed to a rough sketch of a boutique café, the outline of the building set against a backdrop of trees. "This is where I want to open my shop. Something cozy where people can gather, read, drink coffee, and feel at home. I want to create a community space."

I nodded, the vision beautiful and vivid, yet I couldn't shake the gnawing sensation in my gut. "It sounds amazing," I said, forcing a smile that felt a touch too tight. "You really have thought this through."

"Thanks! I'm excited, but it's also terrifying. I mean, what if it fails?" She looked at me, searching for reassurance, her vulnerability peeking through her confident exterior.

"That's the risk of following your dreams," I replied, my voice steadier than I felt. "You never know what will happen, but you can't let fear dictate your path."

She smiled, but I could see the flicker of doubt lurking behind her eyes, a reflection of the very fears I wrestled with daily. "Exactly. And I'd rather try and fail than always wonder 'what if.'"

Her words echoed in my mind, a mantra I had convinced myself was true. But the truth was, I felt stuck in the mire of my own regrets, too fearful to leap into the unknown. I swallowed hard, grappling with the knowledge that while she was daring to chase her dreams, I was still standing on the sidelines, paralyzed by my insecurities.

We spent the next few hours lost in a blend of sketches and stories, her laughter mixing with the gentle clinking of tea cups. Yet, as the sun dipped below the horizon, casting a golden hue across the room, I felt the walls I had carefully constructed start to wobble.

"Mabel," I began, summoning my courage. "I think we need to talk about the elephant in the room."

She looked up, her brow furrowing slightly. "The elephant?"

"You know, the one that's been sitting between us since the whole 'let's not push each other away' thing."

Her eyes narrowed, but there was an undertone of curiosity mixed with concern. "What about it?"

"I've been thinking..." I paused, my heart racing as I searched for the right words. "I don't want to be the reason you hold back on your dreams. I mean, what if this whole... us thing becomes a weight on your shoulders?"

The silence that followed was palpable, thick enough to slice with a knife. "I can handle my own weight, thank you very much," she replied, her tone sharp. "But you don't get to decide what's a burden for me. This is my journey, not yours."

"Right, but I care about you!" I exclaimed, frustration bubbling beneath my skin. "And I don't want you to look back one day and regret your choices because you felt tied down."

"Caring about me means supporting my choices, not second-guessing them!" Mabel shot back, her voice rising. "I thought we were on the same page about this!"

"We are, but—"

"No buts!" she interrupted, crossing her arms defiantly. "You need to trust me. I want you in my life, but if you keep pushing me away, it'll hurt us both."

The air crackled between us, a palpable tension that felt like a prelude to a storm. I wanted to argue, to pull her back into my web of doubts and fears, but I could see the frustration etched across her features. She was standing firm, and I was left grappling with the realization that I was the one causing the distance between us.

I opened my mouth to respond, but before I could find the words, the doorbell rang, slicing through the tension like a sharp blade. Both of us turned, surprise flashing in our eyes. "Who could that be?" I wondered aloud, a sense of foreboding creeping in.

Mabel sighed, the moment of anger dissipating as she pushed herself up from the couch. "I'll check. Maybe it's a delivery."

As she moved toward the door, my heart raced. Something about the unexpected visit felt ominous, as if the universe had decided to intervene at just the wrong moment. Mabel opened the door, and I caught a glimpse of her expression transforming from curiosity to shock.

"Hello, Mabel," a voice said, smooth and dripping with familiarity.

I shot up from my seat, the realization crashing over me like a tidal wave. It was Claire, the woman from my past whose shadow still loomed over my present. The air turned electric, charged with an intensity I hadn't anticipated.

"Mabel, I—" I started, but the words stuck in my throat, the sudden appearance of my ex-lover bringing back a flood of emotions I thought I had buried.

"What are you doing here?" Mabel asked, her voice edged with confusion and surprise, mirroring my own tumultuous feelings.

Claire stepped inside, her presence filling the room with an unsettling mixture of nostalgia and dread. "I came to talk," she said, her eyes flickering between us, assessing, judging.

The air was thick with unresolved tension, and I could feel the ground shifting beneath my feet. Mabel's gaze darted to me, confusion blending with something deeper—maybe suspicion, maybe hurt.

And in that moment, as I watched the two women in my life lock eyes, I realized that the fragile connection I had begun to build with Mabel was hanging by a thread, swaying precariously in the wind. I felt the walls of my carefully constructed world beginning to crumble, the echoes of my past threatening to collide violently with the dreams of my present. The choice was clear, but the consequences loomed large, and I was caught in the crossfire, unsure of which direction to take.

Chapter 6: Breaking Down Walls

I could feel the tension in the air, thick and suffocating, as Mabel stood before me, her hands fisted at her sides. The golden light from the late afternoon sun streamed through the kitchen window, casting a warm glow on the wooden table between us, but her expression was anything but warm. It was a mixture of hurt and determination, a glimmer of vulnerability that made my heart ache. "We need to talk," she said, her voice steady yet laced with an undertone of desperation.

I swallowed hard, the words hanging in the air like uninvited guests. This wasn't how I imagined our evening. I had hoped for laughter and shared stories over dinner, not an emotional standoff that felt like a ticking time bomb. But her eyes—their usual spark dulled by an unspoken weight—dared me to retreat into silence, which I knew was not an option. I nodded, my stomach knotting, and gestured for her to sit.

The chair creaked beneath her as she lowered herself into it, the tension between us palpable. I poured us each a glass of iced tea, the refreshing clink of ice against glass a stark contrast to the unease bubbling in the pit of my stomach. As I handed her a glass, our fingers brushed, and I felt a jolt of electricity—an ache for the connection we shared, tainted now by unvoiced fears.

Mabel took a sip, her gaze locked onto mine. "You've been pulling away," she said, her voice quiet but firm. "I see it. And I know you think it's easier to hide behind those walls, but it's not. It's hurting you—and it's hurting us."

I clenched my jaw, the heat rising to my cheeks. "I'm not pulling away," I protested, though the words felt hollow as they left my lips. It was a lie dressed in a flimsy cloak of denial, and she saw right through it.

"You are," she countered, leaning forward slightly. "And I get it; trust is hard. But if we're going to make this work, you have to let me in." Her voice softened, and there was a tremor in it that made my heart flip. "I want to know what's really going on with you. The real you."

The vulnerability in her eyes chipped away at my defenses, and for the first time in a long while, I felt the urge to be honest. I took a deep breath, feeling the weight of my emotional walls pressing down on me, but I knew if I didn't start dismantling them now, they would crush us both. "It's... complicated," I admitted, my voice barely above a whisper. "I guess I've always been afraid of getting hurt. I mean, who hasn't? But for me, it's like every time I start to feel something real, I sabotage it. I can't help but think of all the times it's gone wrong."

"Like with your family?" Mabel asked, her tone gentle but probing.

My heart clenched at the mention of my family. "Yeah," I said, almost choking on the word. "Growing up, I was always the one trying to hold everything together. But when the cracks started to show, I felt so powerless. It's hard to trust someone when you've seen how quickly things can fall apart."

"I know how that feels," she said, her voice steady, her eyes reflecting a shared understanding. "I've failed so many times. In school, in relationships. I used to think I was the problem, that there was something fundamentally broken in me. And then I realized that I was just scared. Scared of not being enough."

As she spoke, I felt an unexpected sense of kinship forming between us, like strands of a rope intertwining, binding us together in a shared struggle. It was both terrifying and exhilarating, like standing on the edge of a precipice with the wind at our backs. "I guess it's easier to hide," I said, my voice more assured now. "To put up these walls and pretend everything's fine. But that only keeps us from feeling anything real."

Her eyes glimmered with understanding, and for the first time, I could see the weight of her past failures reflected in her gaze. "Exactly," she replied, her voice dropping to a whisper. "I don't want to hide anymore. I want to know you. The real you."

The connection solidified like a tightly woven tapestry, threads of honesty and shared fear binding us together. I leaned forward, my heart pounding in my chest as I prepared to bare my soul. "What if we both let go of the fear?" I asked, testing the waters of this new territory we were forging together. "What if we embraced the messiness of our emotions instead?"

"Then we might just discover something beautiful," she said, her lips curving into a tentative smile that felt like sunlight breaking through the clouds.

But just as I began to believe that maybe, just maybe, we could build something worth fighting for, the world outside our bubble intervened. The sound of my phone buzzing on the counter shattered our moment, and I instinctively reached for it, an icy tendril of dread snaking its way down my spine as I glanced at the screen. My heart sank. The name there sent an electric jolt of anxiety through me.

"Who is it?" Mabel asked, a hint of concern etching itself into her features.

"It's my brother," I murmured, my throat tightening. I hadn't heard from him in months. A pit of uncertainty formed in my stomach, threatening to undo all the progress we'd just made.

Before I could respond, Mabel's eyes flicked to the phone, then back to mine, searching for reassurance I didn't know how to give. "You should answer," she said softly, though her expression was a mix of curiosity and unease.

With a reluctant sigh, I accepted the incoming call, my heart hammering against my ribs. "Hey, what's up?" I managed to say, hoping my voice didn't betray the swirling emotions inside.

"Can we talk?" His voice was a low rumble, serious and urgent.

"Yeah, sure. Is everything okay?"

A pause, then, "Not really. I need to see you. It's important."

As I nodded numbly, Mabel's gaze bore into me, the shift in our moment stark and disorienting. The air felt heavy with unspoken words and unresolved feelings, and I wondered if our breakthrough had just been dismantled by the very thing I had tried to escape—family drama that always seemed to rear its ugly head just when I thought I was getting my footing.

I glanced back at Mabel, her eyes filled with a mix of support and worry, and for a moment, I feared I would lose her too, just as I had lost so much before. But deep down, I knew that whatever storm awaited me, we could face it together.

As I ended the call with my brother, a familiar mix of apprehension and frustration churned in my stomach. I looked back at Mabel, whose brow was furrowed in concern. The moment we had just shared felt like a fragile glass sculpture, beautiful and delicate, and I feared that one wrong move would shatter it.

"Is everything okay?" she asked, her voice gentle but probing, like a soft hand on my back encouraging me to step forward.

"I don't know yet," I replied, feeling the tension coil around us once more. "But it's not the kind of conversation I can have over the phone." I ran a hand through my hair, the strands sticking up rebelliously. "He wants to meet."

Mabel's expression shifted, the warmth in her eyes clouded by a hint of worry. "Do you want me to come with you?"

Her offer hung in the air, a lifeline tossed amidst the storm brewing inside me. It was tempting to accept, to lean on her support like a crutch, but I hesitated. "No, I think it's best if I handle this alone. Family stuff... it's complicated."

She nodded slowly, though I could see the disappointment flickering just beneath the surface. "I understand. Just... remember that you don't have to do it all by yourself."

I managed a small smile, grateful for her understanding, but a gnawing sense of dread settled in my chest. As I watched her, the sunlight catching in her hair, I couldn't help but think how unfair it felt to drag her into the dark shadows of my past. I wanted to shield her from it, protect the fragile thing we were building.

"Let's not let this ruin our evening," I said, trying to inject some lightness back into the air. "How about I whip us up a little dinner? You can tell me about your day, and I can pretend to be a Michelin-star chef."

Her laughter rang out like a bell, brightening the dimming room. "Just as long as you promise to keep the fire extinguisher nearby."

I rolled my eyes, feigning exasperation as I turned to the fridge, grateful for the momentary distraction. "You wound me. My scrambled eggs could win awards."

As I rummaged through the refrigerator, I could feel her eyes on me, her curiosity simmering just beneath the surface. "Okay, Chef, what's on the menu?"

I paused, glancing over my shoulder. "How about a culinary masterpiece featuring... leftovers? The avant-garde dish of our time."

She smirked, shaking her head. "I should've known you'd be a culinary artist in disguise. Just make sure to add a dash of love."

"Right, because I always keep that in the pantry," I quipped back, throwing her a mock-serious look. "What's next, a sprinkle of self-esteem?"

"Exactly!" she shot back with a laugh, her smile infectious. "Can't cook without it."

We exchanged playful banter as I pulled together a makeshift dinner, the scents of sautéed vegetables and spices slowly filling the kitchen. Mabel moved around me, pouring wine and setting the table, her presence a soothing balm to the chaos brewing in my mind. Each clink of glass and rustle of fabric reminded me that despite the looming weight of my family drama, I had this—her.

As we settled down to eat, the conversation flowed like the wine, easily and naturally. Mabel regaled me with stories of her latest work projects and the quirky antics of her coworkers, and I found myself genuinely laughing, the tension of the phone call fading with each shared story. But beneath the laughter lay an undercurrent of unease, like a shadow just out of sight.

"So," she began, her tone shifting, "what's going on with your brother? You've never mentioned him before."

The question hung between us like a delicate spider web, and I felt the weight of my secrets press against my chest. I took a sip of wine, gathering my thoughts. "We had a falling out a while back. Things were... messy. I guess I thought if I didn't talk about him, it would be easier to forget."

Mabel's expression softened, understanding mingling with concern. "You don't have to share if you don't want to."

"No, it's okay," I replied, the words tumbling out before I could stop them. "I think it's important you know. It's just... complicated. My brother always had this way of making me feel like I was never enough. He's a high achiever, and I've always been the 'creative one'—the one who floats through life without any real direction."

"You're not just the creative one," she interjected, her eyes bright with conviction. "You're passionate, driven. You've built this amazing connection with your students, and that's a gift."

I smiled at her encouragement, but the shadow of my brother's disapproval loomed large in my mind. "Maybe. But sometimes I feel like that passion is just a distraction. I'm terrified of what he might say when we talk."

"Then don't let his words dictate your worth," she urged, her tone firm yet gentle. "You're not defined by his expectations. You're you, and that's more than enough."

Her unwavering support felt like a lifeline, and for the first time in a long time, I believed it. I took a deep breath, a mixture of gratitude and fear swirling within me. "Thank you," I said softly. "I really needed to hear that."

As we finished dinner, the sunlight faded into the evening glow, casting long shadows across the table. But as the night wore on, I couldn't shake the feeling that my brother's call was a storm brewing on the horizon. Mabel seemed to sense my shift in mood; her laughter faded, replaced by a quiet concern.

"Are you okay?" she asked, reaching across the table to squeeze my hand.

"Yeah, just... thinking about tomorrow."

"Whatever it is, you've got this," she said, her voice steady. "And if you need me, I'm just a text away."

Her confidence reassured me, even as the unease settled back into my bones. I knew I had to face the reality of my family, but for now, I allowed myself to relish this moment—her warmth, the glow of the candles flickering softly, and the promise of what we could build together if I could only break down the walls I had built around my heart.

But as the night deepened, a flicker of doubt threaded through my thoughts, leaving me to wonder if the very act of letting someone in would end up being the most terrifying leap of faith I had ever taken.

The moon hung low in the night sky, casting a silvery glow over the landscape, turning my backyard into a scene plucked straight from a dream. I leaned against the kitchen counter, sipping the remnants of my wine, watching Mabel as she wandered outside. She moved with a grace that drew my eyes, her silhouette framed by the ethereal light. I couldn't help but smile at the way she tilted her head back to gaze at the stars, as if seeking answers among them.

"Do you think they're looking back?" she called over her shoulder, breaking the silence.

"Only if they're interested in the latest episode of my melodramatic life," I replied, my tone teasing yet filled with an undertone of sincerity. "But I'm pretty sure they're just twinkling to make us feel insignificant."

"Ah, the existential dread strikes again," she said, turning to face me with a mock-serious expression. "I think it's a pretty good look on you, though. Very mysterious."

"Just what I've always wanted—mysterious and deeply troubled," I said with a playful eye roll, though a twinge of truth resonated in my words. The night felt heavy with unsaid things, and I could sense the impending conversation looming over us like the dark clouds of an approaching storm.

After a moment of comfortable silence, I joined her outside, leaning against the porch railing, the cool night air brushing against my skin. "What about you? Do you think the stars are judging us?"

Mabel laughed, a light and melodic sound that seemed to pierce through the heaviness of the evening. "If they are, they're probably cheering for us. I mean, who doesn't love a good underdog story?"

I nudged her playfully with my shoulder, appreciating her ability to lighten the mood. "I've never considered myself an underdog. More like the overenthusiastic sidekick who occasionally trips over his own feet."

"Every good hero needs a sidekick," she countered, her eyes sparkling. "And if you're tripping over your feet, at least you're doing it with style."

Just as I was about to reply, my phone buzzed again on the counter, interrupting the easy flow of our banter. I groaned inwardly; it was probably my brother again, relentless in his need to insert himself into my life. Mabel raised an eyebrow, concern flickering across her features. "You should probably check that. It could be important."

Reluctantly, I turned back to grab my phone. The screen lit up with a message from my brother, and my stomach plummeted as I read it: Can we meet sooner? Something's happened.

"What is it?" Mabel asked, glancing over my shoulder, her tone shifting from playful to serious in an instant.

I hesitated, the knot in my stomach tightening. "Just a message from my brother," I said, trying to keep my voice steady. "He wants to meet sooner."

"Do you think it's about…?" she started, then trailed off, her eyes searching mine for answers I wasn't sure I had.

"Probably," I said, my mind racing with possibilities. The weight of the message settled heavily over us, the easygoing atmosphere evaporating like morning dew under the sun.

Mabel stepped closer, her presence grounding me in the chaos swirling inside my head. "You don't have to do this alone, you know."

"I know," I replied, though my voice sounded distant even to my own ears. I looked at her, her expression a mix of support and concern, and I felt a flicker of warmth seep through the cold dread. "It's just… family stuff. It has a way of unraveling everything."

"Then don't let it," she insisted, her eyes fierce and bright. "You're stronger than that. You can handle this."

I wanted to believe her, but doubt gnawed at the edges of my resolve. "What if I can't?" I asked, my voice barely above a whisper.

"Then you'll have me beside you, fighting through it," she promised, her hand reaching out to grasp mine, her touch warm and steadying.

The connection between us felt electric, a bridge over the chasm of uncertainty threatening to swallow me whole. But just as I began to find solace in her words, a distant rumble of thunder echoed through the night, a reminder that storms were not merely metaphors.

"I should probably respond," I said, pulling my hand away reluctantly, the warmth of her touch lingering like a sweet ache. "I can't leave him hanging."

"Take your time," Mabel replied, her tone softening as she stepped back, giving me space. "Just remember, whatever happens, you're not alone."

I nodded, grateful yet anxious, and typed a quick response, agreeing to meet him at a nearby café. The message sent, I turned to Mabel, who was watching me closely, her eyes filled with an understanding that settled uneasily in my chest.

"Are you okay?" she asked, her voice barely above a whisper.

"I will be," I assured her, though the conviction in my tone felt flimsy at best.

As we stood there, a breeze swept through the yard, rustling the leaves overhead, and I caught a glimpse of my own fear reflected in her eyes. "Do you think I'm making a mistake by meeting him?" I asked suddenly, vulnerability seeping into my voice.

"No," she said firmly, stepping closer again. "You're facing it head-on. That takes strength."

Her confidence bolstered me, but as I looked back at the phone, anxiety pulsed through my veins. It was the unknown that terrified me most—what news awaited me and how it might shatter the delicate balance we had started to forge.

As I took a deep breath, trying to calm the storm within, Mabel tilted her head slightly, the moonlight illuminating her features. "Just remember, whatever happens, I'm here. We'll face it together."

The sincerity in her words sent a flicker of warmth through me, but just as I opened my mouth to respond, my phone buzzed once more. I glanced down, my heart sinking at the sight of another message from my brother.

You need to know something... it's about Mom.

The words hit me like a freight train, the world around me spinning. I could barely process the implications as I felt Mabel's hand on my arm, her touch grounding me, yet everything felt unmoored. I looked at her, my heart racing, my mind a whirlwind of possibilities and fears.

"Is everything okay?" she asked, her voice edged with worry.

I swallowed hard, the words lodged in my throat. "I... I don't know."

Just then, the wind picked up, a fierce gust rattling the branches overhead, as if nature itself were warning me of the storm brewing just out of sight. With my heart pounding, I stared at the screen, dread pooling in my stomach as I realized that the evening had just turned into something much more complicated than I had ever anticipated.

Chapter 7: Unforeseen Challenges

The air in my cozy apartment was thick with the scent of lavender and fresh coffee, a fragrant cocoon that had wrapped itself around Mabel and me during our quiet Sunday morning. The sunlight streamed through the sheer curtains, casting a warm glow on her tousled hair as she leaned back against the plush cushions of the couch. I couldn't help but admire how the sunlight danced on her skin, highlighting the freckles that sprinkled her nose like playful confetti. She had a way of making the mundane feel extraordinary, and in that moment, with her laughter echoing softly in the corners of my heart, I felt I could carve out a new life, one filled with hope and warmth.

Our conversation flowed like the gentle tide, rhythmic and soothing, with Mabel sharing stories of her recent adventures in the art world—each tale more colorful than the last. I could almost see the vibrant hues splashing across the canvas of her life as she animatedly recounted her latest exhibition. Her passion was infectious, and I found myself caught up in the dream of her world, a place where creativity reigned and anything was possible.

Just as I reached out to tuck a strand of hair behind her ear, my phone buzzed insistently on the coffee table. The sound shattered the serene atmosphere, and I felt an inexplicable sense of dread coil in my stomach. I glanced at the screen, my heart sinking when I saw my sister's name flickering like a warning light. It had been years since we had spoken, years filled with unresolved tension and unspoken words. I hesitated, my fingers hovering above the screen, unsure whether to answer or let it fade into the abyss of missed calls.

Mabel noticed my shift in demeanor, her expression a mixture of concern and curiosity. "Is everything okay?" she asked, her voice a gentle anchor in my swirling thoughts. I forced a smile, but it felt brittle, ready to shatter under the weight of my emotions. "It's just... my sister. She's in town."

"Ah, the infamous sister," Mabel replied, her tone playful yet laced with empathy. "Do you want to talk to her?"

The question hung in the air, heavy with implications. Part of me wanted to dive headfirst into that tumultuous relationship, to confront the ghosts of our past. But the other part, the one that had painstakingly built this sanctuary with Mabel, recoiled at the thought of disrupting the fragile peace we had created. "I don't know," I finally admitted, the admission tasting bitter on my tongue.

"Maybe it's a sign," she suggested, her gaze steady and reassuring. "You can't avoid your past forever, you know." There was truth in her words, a reality I had tried to sidestep for too long. Yet, I also felt the sharp pang of fear that maybe I wasn't ready for this particular confrontation. The phone buzzed again, this time with a sense of urgency that sent a shiver down my spine.

Mabel squeezed my hand, grounding me in that moment, and I took a deep breath. "Okay, I'll answer it," I said, my voice steadier than I felt. With a shaky finger, I accepted the call, and her voice crackled through the speaker, a mix of familiarity and estrangement that filled my heart with a storm of emotions.

"Hey, it's me," my sister said, her tone bright yet hesitant, like she was testing the waters of a pond she hadn't dipped her toes in for years. The weight of her words bore down on me, and I could hear the echo of our shared history in the spaces between her sentences.

"Hi," I replied, my voice barely above a whisper. "What's going on?"

"I'm in town," she said, and I could almost picture her fidgeting, as she always did when she was nervous. "I thought maybe we could meet up. You know, catch up?"

The invitation hung in the air, a tether between the past and a future I had only just begun to embrace. My heart raced with conflicting emotions: resentment bubbling to the surface alongside a deep-seated longing for connection. It was as if she were a character from a book I had once loved, whose plot twists had left me feeling betrayed but still yearning for the next chapter.

"I don't know if that's a good idea," I managed, glancing at Mabel, who watched me with concern etched across her features. "It's been a while."

"I know, and I'm sorry for everything," my sister replied, her voice softening. "But I want to make things right. Can we at least talk?"

I could feel the tempest brewing inside me, a swirling mass of confusion and nostalgia. "What about Mabel?" I asked, my voice trembling slightly as I caught Mabel's eye. The very thought of our delicate world fracturing under the weight of my sister's return felt like a betrayal of everything I had fought for.

"I'd love to meet her too," my sister offered, her words a soothing balm. "I think it's important for us all to be together."

The invitation felt like a double-edged sword, slicing through the comfort I had found in my newfound relationship while also extending a lifeline back to a family I had long since cast aside. I glanced at Mabel, whose expression shifted from concern to an encouraging smile, her eyes alight with warmth.

"Alright," I finally said, the word slipping from my lips like a secret I had been holding onto for far too long. "Let's meet."

As I hung up, the reality of the situation crashed over me like a wave. I felt a mix of dread and exhilaration—a heady cocktail that threatened to drown me if I didn't find a way to navigate these uncharted waters. Mabel's hand found mine again, her touch both grounding and invigorating.

"You're brave," she said softly, and I wondered if she could sense the storm raging within me. I couldn't predict how this would unfold, but the tightening knot in my chest warned me that the past rarely stayed buried for long, and this reunion could either be a bridge to healing or a tempest that threatened to sweep away everything I held dear.

Mabel and I decided on a small café downtown for the reunion, a place with an eclectic charm that seemed to mirror the confusion swirling inside me. The café, aptly named "The Cozy Corner," had become my sanctuary, its mismatched furniture and local art creating a welcoming atmosphere that felt like a warm hug on a chilly day. It was a haven where the scent of freshly baked pastries mingled with the rich aroma of espresso, a delightful distraction that I hoped would soothe the tempest of emotions brewing within me.

As we entered, the sun filtering through the large windows cast a golden hue on the wooden floors, and the soft murmur of conversations wrapped around us like a cozy blanket. Mabel ordered us each a cappuccino, her bright smile lighting up the space as she turned to me. "So, what's the game plan? You need a strategy for this," she teased, raising an eyebrow as she placed a playful hand on my shoulder.

"Game plan? More like a disaster recovery plan," I replied, trying to lighten the mood, but the weight of the impending confrontation clung to me like a stubborn shadow. "Maybe I should start with a dramatic entrance. You know, flip my hair and say something profound."

Mabel chuckled, her laughter a sweet sound that eased some of the tension in my chest. "Or you could just be yourself. That's more than enough."

I nodded, grateful for her unwavering support, yet the truth was that the prospect of facing my sister made my stomach twist into knots. I had spent years building walls around my heart, fortified by resentment and disappointment. Now, those walls felt both protective and suffocating, and I had no idea how to navigate the cracks that were beginning to show.

The bell above the café door jingled, cutting through my thoughts, and I turned to see my sister walk in. She looked different yet achingly familiar. The same wild curls framed her face, though now they danced around her shoulders like autumn leaves caught in a gentle breeze. She wore a bright yellow dress that seemed to embody a new, vibrant energy, but as our eyes locked, the warmth of her smile faltered, replaced by uncertainty.

"Hey," she said, her voice tentative yet hopeful.

"Hey," I echoed, my heart racing as she approached. I felt a wild urge to turn and run, but instead, I stood my ground, grappling with the flood of memories that threatened to engulf me.

"Wow, you look great," she said, her eyes scanning me as if trying to uncover the person I had become in her absence. "I love your hair."

"Thanks," I replied, realizing too late that I hadn't prepared for this moment, the casual niceties that felt like a rickety bridge spanning an abyss of unresolved feelings. "You look... different too."

"Different good or different bad?" she asked, a hint of humor glinting in her eyes.

"Definitely different good," I assured her, but the words felt like a flimsy safety net. I could sense Mabel's presence beside me, a solid reassurance that I desperately needed.

"Do you mind if I join?" Mabel asked, her voice steady as she extended a hand to my sister. "I'm Mabel."

"Nice to meet you!" my sister replied, her smile widening as she took Mabel's hand. "I've heard a lot about you."

"Mostly good, I hope," Mabel quipped, her eyes sparkling with mischief. "Because if not, we might have to have a chat."

My sister laughed, the sound easing the tension in the air. "Don't worry, it's all good. I'm not here to cause trouble—at least not on purpose."

We settled into a cozy corner booth, and for a moment, the awkwardness dissipated like steam from a hot cup of coffee. We exchanged pleasantries, and I noticed how effortlessly Mabel navigated the conversation, her warmth enveloping us both. It reminded me why I had been drawn to her in the first place—her ability to light up even the darkest corners of a room.

But as my sister began to recount her journey of self-discovery, the narrative took a turn that made my heart sink. "I went through a lot after we stopped talking," she admitted, her voice tinged with vulnerability. "I made some bad choices. I needed to find myself again."

I studied her, searching for signs of the girl I used to know, the one who had once been my closest confidante. "What do you mean by bad choices?" I asked, my voice cautious.

She hesitated, her fingers nervously twisting the edge of her napkin. "I got into some relationships that weren't great. I didn't know how to take care of myself, and I hurt a lot of people along the way, including you."

The admission hung in the air, heavy and suffocating. The memories of the past threatened to claw their way back into my consciousness, the sting of betrayal and disappointment bubbling just beneath the surface. "It wasn't just you, you know," I said, the words escaping before I could stop them. "I felt abandoned."

"I know," she replied, her eyes glistening with unshed tears. "And I'm sorry. I wish I could change it."

There it was—the apology I had longed for, the missing piece of our fractured history. Yet, even as she spoke, a part of me bristled at the familiarity of the sentiment. Was it genuine, or just another attempt to rewrite our story? I was grateful for her honesty, yet unsure if I could trust it. The scars from our past were still fresh, and vulnerability felt like a gamble I wasn't ready to take.

Mabel's hand found mine under the table, a silent reminder that I wasn't alone in this. "What do you want now?" I asked, my voice firmer than I felt. "What do you hope to gain from this?"

"I want to rebuild," my sister said, her gaze unwavering. "I want to understand you, to be part of your life again if you'll let me."

Her words stirred something deep within me—a flicker of hope mixed with an overwhelming sense of dread. I wanted to believe that reconciliation was possible, that we could bridge the gap that years of silence had created. But the lingering pain was a constant reminder that not all wounds healed easily.

Just as I opened my mouth to respond, a loud crash from the kitchen sent our heads whipping around. The barista emerged, looking flustered, a tray of mugs teetering dangerously in his hands. "Sorry about that! Just your typical Tuesday morning mayhem!" he announced with a sheepish grin, clearly trying to inject some levity into the chaos.

We all chuckled, the momentary distraction allowing the tension to dissipate just a fraction. I felt Mabel squeeze my hand, and I took a deep breath, steeling myself for the conversation that was far from over. As I glanced at my sister, the weight of what lay ahead settled heavily on my shoulders. It was time to sift through the ashes of our past and see if anything could be salvaged, if we could ignite the flicker of connection that had once burned so brightly between us.

The atmosphere at The Cozy Corner shifted subtly as my sister and I navigated the rocky terrain of our conversation. I could almost feel the air thickening, charged with unspoken words and suppressed emotions, like a storm brewing on the horizon. Mabel's presence was a balm, yet I could sense her tension as she leaned in, her eyes darting between us, reading the currents that ran deeper than any surface conversation could convey.

"So," Mabel said, breaking the heavy silence that hung like a curtain between us. "Tell me something you love about the city."

My sister's face brightened, a flicker of enthusiasm breaking through her earlier somberness. "I love the arts scene here. The galleries, the street art—it's all so vibrant. It's like the city is alive."

"Oh, I completely agree!" Mabel chimed in, her passion for the arts palpable. "There's something about the way creativity transforms a space, don't you think? It breathes life into the mundane."

I watched the two of them, the way their voices flowed into a comfortable rhythm, and felt a pang of longing for the sisterly bond we had once shared. "What have you seen?" I asked, trying to redirect the conversation, needing to pull her back into the present, back into the room where we sat, coffee steaming between us like an unspoken truce.

"There's a pop-up exhibit at the old warehouse on Fifth," she replied, her eyes lighting up with excitement. "It features local artists, and there's this one piece—a giant mural that captures the essence of the city. It's like stepping into a dream."

Mabel smiled, and for a moment, the atmosphere felt lighter. "That sounds amazing. We should go together. I'd love to see it through your eyes."

"Yeah, I'd like that," my sister said, her voice softening as she looked at Mabel. I could see the tension in her shoulders easing slightly, as if Mabel's effortless charm was melting the ice that had formed over years of distance. Yet, an unsettling feeling began to creep back in—a whisper in my mind that warned me we were still on shaky ground.

"I know this is all new and probably overwhelming," my sister said, her gaze shifting back to me. "But I want to know you again, to understand who you've become. And if you'll let me, I'd like to share who I am now too."

"Do you think it'll be that easy?" I shot back, the words escaping my lips before I could filter them. "You waltz back into my life after all this time, expecting a warm welcome and no questions asked?"

"I'm not expecting anything, I swear," she replied, a hint of desperation creeping into her tone. "I just want a chance to explain myself, to show you I'm different now. I know I messed up. I get that."

As she spoke, I noticed the way her hands trembled, the uncertainty etched on her face. It struck me then, in that café brimming with warmth, that beneath her bravado lay the same girl who had once been my best friend, the one who had gotten lost in a world of her own making. The past felt like a living thing between us, alive with potential but also fraught with danger.

Mabel, ever the diplomat, interjected with a bright smile. "Why don't we lighten the mood? We could order a slice of that amazing chocolate cake I saw on the way in. Nothing resolves tension like cake, right?"

The idea coaxed a smile from my sister, and I found myself chuckling despite the heaviness in my heart. "You might be onto something," I said, grateful for Mabel's instinct to defuse the situation. "Cake is always a solid plan."

Mabel signaled the waiter, and as we placed our order, I felt the tension ease just a fraction, replaced by the comforting buzz of life around us. Yet, as the minutes ticked by, I found myself wrestling with conflicting desires. I wanted to open up, to let my sister back in, but the wounds ran deep, and trust was not something I was willing to hand over lightly.

The waiter arrived with the cake, a decadent slice adorned with rich, dark chocolate ganache. It looked indulgent enough to lure a saint into temptation. We each took a forkful, and as the flavors exploded in my mouth, I was reminded of the simple joys that life had to offer, the moments that could lift even the heaviest of hearts.

"Okay," I said, setting my fork down and mustering the courage I needed. "Let's try this again. If you really want to reconnect, tell me why you're back now after all this time. What changed?"

My sister swallowed hard, the moment stretching out like a tightrope we were both teetering on. "I had to hit rock bottom," she admitted finally, her voice barely above a whisper. "I lost my job, and that was the last straw. I realized I had to face my demons and start over. I didn't want to live with regrets anymore."

Her honesty struck a chord within me, one that resonated with the struggles I'd faced in my own life. "But you're asking me to just forget," I countered, my heart racing as I laid my emotions bare. "Forget the hurt, forget the silence. It's not that simple."

"I know it's not," she replied, her eyes pleading. "But I've spent so long feeling like I'd lost my way. And if I can't make amends with my sister, then what's the point?"

Mabel's eyes sparkled with unshed tears, and I could feel the pull of empathy tugging at my heart. But it wasn't just about understanding her pain; it was also about my own. I had carved out a new life, built on the ashes of the past, and I wasn't sure if I was ready to let anyone back in, especially someone who had once hurt me so deeply.

The café buzzed around us, laughter and chatter weaving a tapestry of life that felt achingly out of reach. I shifted in my seat, glancing at the door, wondering if I should bolt or stay put. "Let me ask you something," I said, searching her face for the truth. "Are you really here to rebuild, or is this just another fleeting moment in a long line of missteps?"

"I want to rebuild, I promise," she insisted, her voice trembling slightly. "But I understand if you don't believe me yet. Just give me a chance."

The words hung in the air like a fragile promise, and I felt my heart begin to thaw, though it was still encased in a protective shell.

Before I could respond, the door swung open, and a rush of cold air enveloped us, accompanied by the sound of hurried footsteps. A figure rushed inside, shaking off droplets from the rain that had begun to fall outside. My breath caught in my throat as I recognized the familiar silhouette—James, the ex who had walked out of my life just as I had begun to open my heart to him.

He scanned the café, his eyes landing on me, and time seemed to stand still. The warmth of the room was replaced by an icy rush of confusion and dread. What was he doing here? My heart raced, caught in the throes of an unexpected confrontation that could shatter the fragile truce I was just beginning to navigate with my sister.

"Is this seat taken?" he asked, his voice smooth yet laced with something deeper, a question that held the weight of everything left unsaid between us. I felt my stomach drop, the tension in the air snapping like a taut string.

"James..." I breathed, my voice barely a whisper, caught between the past I was trying to reconcile and the present that felt like it was spiraling out of control. As the weight of the moment crashed down around us, I realized that I was standing at the precipice of chaos, teetering on the edge of a truth I had yet to confront.

Chapter 8: An Unbreakable Bond

The kitchen was alive with the scent of simmering garlic and herbs, a welcoming warmth that wrapped around me like a favorite blanket. Mabel stood by the stove, stirring a bubbling pot of marinara sauce while her curls danced rebelliously in the steam. The clattering of utensils blended with the soft hum of an old jazz record playing in the background. It was a snapshot of a perfect evening, yet I couldn't shake the feeling that the shadows lurking in the corners of my mind were ready to pounce.

"Are you going to stand there and let the pasta burn, or are you going to help me?" Mabel teased, glancing over her shoulder, her smile bright enough to light up the dim corners of the room.

"Do I look like I know how to cook?" I quipped, crossing my arms dramatically. "My idea of fine dining is instant ramen."

She laughed, a sound like the tinkling of wind chimes in a gentle breeze. "Well, that's a culinary art in its own right. But since we're trying to impress Mom, let's aim for something a little more sophisticated tonight."

"Right. Because a woman who once made me eat kale chips for dinner would be so impressed by my pasta skills," I grumbled, stepping closer to the counter, the warm air teasing my skin. I found a wooden spoon and joined her, stirring with a determined focus that belied my lack of skill.

The conversation flowed easily, a gentle current pulling us along as we chopped, stirred, and occasionally laughed at our culinary misadventures. Mabel's patience was legendary; it was as if she possessed a secret stash of tranquil zen. Meanwhile, I was more like a fizzing soda, full of chaotic energy that threatened to spill over at any moment. Yet in these simple moments, with the aroma of tomatoes and basil enveloping us, I felt a sense of peace.

The weight of the day's earlier conversations hung in the air, unspoken yet palpable. My sister had come home unexpectedly, and I had felt that familiar tightening in my chest—the instinctive urge to retreat, to shield myself from the inevitable onslaught of memories and old wounds. Our relationship was a tapestry of shared childhood experiences interwoven with threads of tension, misunderstandings, and resentments that seemed impossible to unravel. But Mabel, with her unwavering support, had been my anchor.

As we sat down to eat, the table was a feast of colors: the vibrant red of the marinara, the golden hue of garlic bread, and the bright green of a simple side salad. I watched Mabel take a bite, her eyes widening in delight, and for a moment, I felt lighter, the burdens of the past momentarily forgotten.

"This is amazing!" she exclaimed, her mouth full of pasta. "Who knew you had it in you?"

"Don't get used to it. I'm more of a takeout kind of girl," I said, feigning nonchalance as I took a sip of my wine. The rich, fruity notes swirled in my mouth, grounding me in the present. I could feel the tension begin to ease, the knot in my stomach loosening with every bite.

But just as I began to relax, the thought of my sister gnawed at me. The chasm between us felt vast and daunting. I had carried the weight of my childhood scars for so long, buried beneath layers of laughter and casual conversations. But Mabel had this way of unearthing my truths, coaxing them out gently until I felt ready to share.

"What's on your mind?" she asked, her voice softening as she pushed her plate aside. "You've been quiet since dinner started."

"I guess I was just thinking about... you know, everything," I replied, my gaze dropping to the half-eaten plate of food before me. "About her."

Mabel's expression shifted from playful to serious in an instant. "Do you want to talk about it?"

I hesitated, fear prickling at the edges of my resolve. But Mabel's eyes—always so understanding—held a silent promise of safety. With a deep breath, I plunged into the depths of my past, recounting the moments that had fractured my relationship with our sister. The echoes of harsh words, the sharp edges of betrayal, and the burden of expectations that had woven a barrier between us.

Mabel listened, her presence a comforting balm to my raw confessions. "I never knew it had gotten that bad," she murmured when I finished. "You've carried this alone for so long."

"It was easier that way," I admitted, guilt creeping in. "I didn't want to burden you. You were always so busy with your own life."

"I would have made time," she insisted, leaning forward, her sincerity palpable. "You don't have to go through this alone. You never did."

Her words wrapped around me like a hug, soothing the frayed edges of my anxiety. I realized in that moment that vulnerability was a strength, not a weakness. Sharing my scars with her felt like shedding a layer of armor I had worn for far too long.

Yet just as the evening began to settle into a comforting silence, my phone buzzed on the table. A message from a number I didn't recognize lit up the screen, and my heart sank. The casual atmosphere shattered like glass. The message held a name I had tried to forget, a reminder that the past was not as distant as I had hoped. My fingers trembled as I reached for the phone, the weight of my secret ready to resurface and disrupt the fragile peace we had just built.

The message on my phone flickered ominously, casting a blue glow on my already troubled thoughts. I hesitated, my heart thumping as if trying to escape my chest. It felt like an unwelcome ghost from a past I thought I had laid to rest, but the digital screen held the truth captive, waiting to be revealed. I should have ignored it, allowed the chaos of my evening to drown out the potential storm brewing just beneath the surface. Instead, I picked it up, my fingers shaking slightly as I swiped to open the message.

"Hey, it's Sam. Can we talk? I need to explain."

The name hit me like a bolt of lightning, electric and sharp, igniting a flurry of memories I had worked so hard to bury. My pulse raced, thoughts tumbling over one another like laundry in a dryer, each spinning round and round. Mabel, ever intuitive, noticed the change in my demeanor.

"What's wrong?" Her voice sliced through the haze, her eyes narrowing as she searched my face for answers.

I hesitated, torn between the urge to confide in her and the fear that I would only invite more chaos into our already tangled family dynamic. "It's just a message from someone I used to know," I finally managed, my voice lacking conviction.

"Someone? Or that someone?" She raised an eyebrow, the corners of her mouth twitching into a knowing smile that melted away the gravity of the moment. "You know, the 'oh my God, I can't believe you're back in my life' kind of someone?"

"The very same," I replied, unable to suppress a nervous laugh. "Can you read my mind, or do I just wear my emotions like a billboard?"

"You absolutely do. It's a gift." Mabel leaned back in her chair, arms crossed over her chest, the playful glint in her eye suggesting she was both amused and curious. "So what are you going to do about it?"

I sighed, sinking back into my seat as I fought against the whirlpool of emotions that threatened to pull me under. "I don't know. Part of me wants to ignore it and pretend like everything is fine." My fingers drummed on the table, a rapid-fire rhythm echoing my internal conflict. "But the other part... the part that feels like it's been holding its breath for years, wants to know what this is about."

"Then you owe it to yourself to find out." Mabel's voice was firm, yet soft, like a gentle nudge when you needed it most. "You can't let ghosts dictate your life. Maybe this is your chance to put it all to rest."

A chance? The idea struck me as both liberating and terrifying. I had avoided Sam for so long, carefully constructing a fortress around myself to keep the hurt at bay. Yet here I was, facing a possibility that could either bring closure or reignite old wounds. I glanced at the message again, the screen glowing with a light that felt like a siren call.

"Fine," I said, surprising even myself with my sudden resolve. "I'll reply. But if this goes sideways, I'm blaming you."

"Deal." Mabel chuckled, and her laughter was a welcome balm to my frayed nerves. "Just remember, you're in control. You get to set the tone."

Taking a deep breath, I typed a hesitant response. "What do you need to explain?" I hit send, my heart racing as if I had just bungee jumped into an abyss. I didn't have to wait long for a reply.

"Can we meet? There's a lot to unpack, and I think it's better in person."

"Great. Just what I needed." I rolled my eyes, the familiar sarcasm creeping back in as I glanced at Mabel. "A face-to-face meeting with someone who has a penchant for drama. Perfect."

"Hey, it might surprise you. Or it might make for a very entertaining story. Either way, you'll be fine." She winked, and I couldn't help but smile, a flicker of warmth spreading through me. Mabel had this uncanny ability to transform anxiety into a manageable burden, even if just for a moment.

The evening wore on, filled with lighthearted banter and laughter that danced through the air, momentarily pushing aside the unease that lingered. We finished dinner, cleaned up, and settled into the soft embrace of the couch, the comforting glow of the lamp casting a cozy light around us.

But even as we sank into the warmth of our shared moments, a weight pressed on my chest, heavier than I could articulate. "Mabel," I began, my voice faltering. "What if I open this door and find out that nothing has changed? That I'm still the same scared girl hiding behind walls I built long ago?"

"Then you rebuild," she said, her tone unwavering. "You have the tools now—strength, resilience, and the knowledge that you don't have to face anything alone. Remember, you have me, and we can take it one step at a time."

Her words settled around me, a protective shield against the storm that loomed ahead. I nestled deeper into the couch, letting her presence wash over me. Mabel had a way of making everything feel manageable, even when the weight of my past threatened to crush me.

As we shared stories of our childhood, memories tumbling from my lips like marbles rolling down a hill, I felt a strange sense of lightness. The laughter flowed easily, bridging the gap that had often felt insurmountable between us. Yet, with each shared memory, the shadow of Sam's message lingered in the background, waiting, patient as ever, like a predator in the night.

The night wore on, and just when I thought I had distracted myself enough, my phone buzzed again. My stomach twisted, anticipation mingling with dread. This time, it was a notification from Sam. "How about tomorrow at 3 PM? The café on Maple?"

I glanced at Mabel, who raised an eyebrow, a blend of curiosity and concern etched across her face. "Well, there you go. Now you have a time and place. You can't chicken out now."

"I guess not," I muttered, feeling the knot tighten in my stomach. "Why does this feel like I'm walking into a minefield?"

"Because it is," she said, her expression turning serious. "But you're not walking in alone. Remember, I'll be just a phone call away."

Taking a deep breath, I nodded, absorbing the weight of her words. "You're right. Just one step at a time."

Morning light filtered through the kitchen window, spilling warmth onto the wooden table where I sat, cradling a cup of coffee like it was a lifeline. The rich aroma of the brew mingled with the sweet scent of freshly baked pastries that Mabel had whipped up. It was a comforting start to the day, yet I felt a sense of impending tension coiling in my stomach, an uninvited guest that refused to leave.

Mabel bustled around the kitchen, humming an old tune that danced through the air, the kind of song that could lift spirits and chase shadows. "You know, if you keep staring into that cup, it might just give you answers," she teased, her voice light, but her eyes held a flicker of understanding.

"More like it'll drown me in caffeine-induced anxiety," I shot back, attempting a grin that felt like a fragile mask over my nerves. "I'm just... thinking."

"About Sam?" she asked, her tone shifting to something more serious. I nodded, the name hanging in the air like an unwelcomed specter. "Look, you've faced down worse demons. What's the worst that could happen?"

"A lot," I murmured, recalling the whirlwind of emotions tied to our history. The thrill of memories clashed with the sharp edges of past hurts. "He could just as easily make me feel like that scared little girl again."

"Or he could surprise you," Mabel suggested, pouring herself a cup of coffee. "People change, you know. Maybe he's not the same person he was back then."

I didn't respond, swirling my coffee absentmindedly, watching the steam dance upward. It felt strange to think that anything could change about Sam, especially after years of silence. What did he want now? My thoughts spiraled, and I fought the urge to grab my phone and cancel our meeting.

Mabel set her cup down and crossed her arms, a familiar challenge lighting up her eyes. "If you don't go, you'll never know. And that uncertainty will eat you alive. Trust me, I've been there."

"Okay, okay, you've made your point," I relented, letting out a breath I hadn't realized I was holding. "But I could still use a good distraction before I dive into the ocean of regret."

Mabel smirked, her playful spirit lifting the weight in the room. "How about a spontaneous adventure? We could hit the flea market downtown. I heard they have the cutest vintage finds this weekend."

"Now you're speaking my language," I said, suddenly feeling lighter. "Vintage finds are way better than existential crises."

We bundled up, the crisp air outside bracing against my skin as we made our way to the market. The streets were alive with color and sound, vibrant stalls overflowing with everything from hand-painted pottery to quirky clothes that looked like they belonged in a bygone era. As we strolled past the booths, laughter and chatter surrounded us, wrapping around me like a cozy scarf.

"This one looks promising!" Mabel exclaimed, pulling me toward a stall filled with mismatched antiques. A vintage typewriter caught my eye, its keys glinting in the sunlight, each one beckoning me closer.

"Now that's a piece of history," I remarked, reaching out to touch it, my fingers grazing the cool metal. "Can you imagine all the stories it could tell?"

"Only if you ask it nicely," Mabel replied with a grin, her eyes twinkling. "Or maybe we could start typing our own stories on it."

I laughed, picturing us sitting at a table, surrounded by coffee cups and chaos, letting our imaginations run wild. It was a momentary escape, a breath of fresh air that helped push away the anxiety gnawing at the edges of my mind.

After a few more stalls and impulse purchases, we settled on a bench, sipping hot cider and watching the world pass by. Mabel nudged me with her elbow, her expression suddenly serious. "Okay, you know I'm your sister and all, so I have to ask—are you really going to meet Sam?"

"Yes, I'm going," I said, forcing conviction into my tone. "But it feels like I'm gearing up for battle or something. I have this overwhelming urge to throw myself into a pit of alligators instead."

"That sounds about right," she said, her expression softening with empathy. "But remember, you're not that scared girl anymore. You're strong, and you have me in your corner."

Her words anchored me, but they didn't erase the storm of uncertainty brewing within. "What if he's still the same person who hurt me? What if I've built up this whole fantasy of closure in my mind, and it all comes crashing down?"

"Then you'll rebuild, again. One day at a time." Mabel's voice was steady, like a lighthouse guiding me through turbulent waters.

The warmth of her support filled me with courage, but the moment felt fleeting, as if the world was drawing a breath before plunging into chaos. I took a sip of cider, letting the warmth seep through me, but that familiar tension began to return, a dull thrum in the background of my thoughts.

After an hour of wandering through the market, we returned home, the afternoon slipping into evening like a shy child, unsure of its place. As we entered the house, a sudden weight settled on my chest. The looming confrontation was no longer a distant thought but an impending reality.

"I think I need a moment," I murmured, slipping away from Mabel, who nodded knowingly. The living room felt like a refuge as I sank into the couch, cradling my phone like a lifeline. I stared at it, the silence around me amplifying the noise in my head.

Just as I gathered my thoughts, a new message arrived, causing my heart to skip. "I'm waiting at the café."

The urgency in his words struck me, a reminder that the time had come to face the ghosts I had tried to forget. I took a deep breath, trying to calm the storm inside, but just as I was about to reply, my phone buzzed again.

"Can we talk about what happened?"

I stared at the screen, dread pooling in my stomach. Each word felt heavy with the weight of our shared history. And just as I was about to type back, my phone rang, the familiar ringtone cutting through the silence like a knife.

The caller ID flashed Sam's name, and my breath caught in my throat. This was it. I had two choices: to answer and confront the past head-on, or to let it slip away into the void, another ghost lost to time.

With shaking hands, I swiped to answer, the world around me fading into a distant murmur. "Hello?" My voice came out steadier than I felt.

"Hey," he said, his tone carrying an unexpected softness. "I know this is sudden, but I need to explain everything... and I think it's important."

The tension hung in the air, palpable and electric, as I fought to steady my breath. This was the moment that could change everything. "Okay," I said, my voice barely above a whisper, and then the line went dead.

Chapter 9: Secrets Revealed

The dim glow of the living room lamp cast a warm halo around the cozy space, an inviting refuge from the cool autumn air outside. I wrapped my fingers around the steaming mug of chamomile tea, inhaling its soothing scent as I settled into the worn, overstuffed couch that had cradled countless evenings of laughter and comfort. Mabel sat opposite me, her dark hair spilling over the back of the chair, framing her face like an artist's delicate brushstroke. She was wrapped in a soft, oversized sweater that swallowed her whole but highlighted the graceful way she leaned forward, eager to share in the intimate ambiance of our impromptu evening together.

We had spent the earlier part of the night swapping stories—her tales of a chaotic day at the bakery and my snippets of mundane office gossip. The easy laughter between us flowed like the tea, warming me from the inside out. Yet, even amidst the lighthearted chatter, I felt a heaviness settling in my chest, a storm brewing just beyond the horizon. Little did I know how true that would be.

It was my sister, Claire, who first broke the spell. She had arrived unannounced, her hair pulled back in a haphazard bun, eyes bright yet clouded with a troubling intensity. The moment she stepped through the door, the air thickened with anticipation, as if the walls themselves held their breath. "We need to talk," she said, the words dropping like stones into the still waters of our evening.

"What's wrong?" I asked, a knot forming in my stomach. Claire never came over to chat casually; there was always an urgency to her visits, as if she carried the weight of the world on her shoulders.

She glanced at Mabel, who remained silent but alert, sensing the tension that crackled like static electricity between us. Claire's gaze returned to me, her expression a mixture of fear and resolve. "It's about Mom. There's something you don't know."

The words hit me like a sudden gust of wind, disorienting and cold. I couldn't quite catch my breath. "What do you mean? I know everything about Mom. We've talked about it a hundred times."

She took a deep breath, her fingers tapping nervously against her thigh. "No, you don't. There's a reason we never talked about her family. There's a reason she left home. It's all tied up in this secret that—"

"Claire, what are you saying?" I interrupted, my heart racing. "You're scaring me."

She leaned closer, her voice dropping to a whisper, a secret shared between sisters. "I found her old journal. She wrote about it, about why she left—about us. It's not what you think."

The room felt smaller, the walls creeping in with the weight of her words. The familiar patterns of our childhood flashed through my mind, warm summer days spent in laughter, family dinners marked by love. But now, it all felt like a fragile facade, threatening to shatter. "What do you mean? What could be so terrible?"

Her eyes were wide, glistening with unshed tears. "Mom wasn't just running away from her family; she was hiding something—something about our father. She never told us who he was."

My world tilted on its axis. I felt the ground beneath me shift, as if the very foundation of my reality was crumbling. "What are you saying? She never mentioned him; she never even hinted at...at any of this."

"I know. But she was scared. There are names in that journal, names we've never heard. They're not just hers; they're ours too. Our entire lives have been built on this...this lie."

Anger flared within me, burning hot and fierce. "A lie? You think she did this to hurt us? To keep us in the dark?"

"I think she did it to protect us," Claire replied, her voice trembling. "But now...now I don't know. I just can't sit on this anymore. You deserve to know the truth."

I glanced at Mabel, her expression a blend of empathy and concern. The warmth of her presence steadied me, grounding me as I wrestled with the chaos erupting in my mind. "Mabel, I... I don't know what to do with this," I stammered, my voice shaky.

"Talk to her," Mabel urged gently, her eyes soft yet firm. "Confront her. You need to hear it from her."

I shook my head, feeling the weight of the revelation settle like a stone in my stomach. "I can't just confront her. She's my mother. How could she keep this from us? It's betrayal!"

"Maybe it's not as simple as that," Claire interjected. "You have to think about the time she grew up in, the reasons she had. Maybe it was too painful. Maybe she thought it was best for us."

I looked at Claire, her face etched with worry and resolve. The bonds of sisterhood felt strained, stretched tight against the weight of these new revelations. "Why didn't you tell me sooner?"

"I didn't know how," she admitted. "I thought I could keep it to myself, protect you from the fallout. But it's not fair to you. You deserve the truth, no matter how painful."

Mabel's hand found mine, her touch grounding me as my heart raced with confusion and anger. "We'll face this together," she whispered, her voice steady. "Whatever happens, you're not alone."

The depth of her support wrapped around me like a protective cloak, igniting a flicker of hope amid the swirling turmoil. But the path ahead felt treacherous, lined with jagged rocks of betrayal and uncertainty. I felt torn between the loyalty I owed my family and the newfound love I found in Mabel's unwavering support.

As I looked at Claire, the sister I had shared countless memories with, I realized the time had come to face the truth, no matter how painful it might be. The weight of our past pressed down heavily, but

I wasn't about to let it crush me. The journey ahead was uncharted territory, and with Mabel by my side, I felt a flicker of courage rising within me. It was time to unravel the secrets that had been buried for too long.

The air in the room felt charged, an electric buzz hovering just above the surface as I stared at Claire, each breath thickening with an unsaid truth. Mabel, sensing the intensity, tightened her grip on my hand, her warmth anchoring me amidst the swirling storm of emotions. "Okay, let's just take a breath here," she suggested, her voice calm yet encouraging. "What did the journal say exactly? We need to know what we're dealing with."

Claire swallowed hard, her face pinched in concentration. "There are names—our grandparents, uncles, people Mom cut ties with. It's like she's been living with a shadow over her life, and now it's ours too." Her voice faltered, the weight of her words hanging between us like a fragile chandelier, ready to shatter at any moment.

"Shadows can't just be ignored," I murmured, the realization dawning that we were all tangled in this web of secrets. "So what do we do? We go after our family like we're on some twisted scavenger hunt?"

"It's more like digging for buried treasure," Claire countered, her tone wry, despite the gravity of the moment. "Except this treasure is just a bunch of family drama and emotional baggage."

Mabel chuckled softly, the sound breaking through the heaviness. "Well, who doesn't love a little family drama? Just remember, the last time we dug for treasure, we ended up in that moldy basement. Not exactly a hallmark moment."

The absurdity of her words snapped something in me. Laughter bubbled up, the tension loosening ever so slightly. "True, and we did find some truly awful relics of the past. Like that horrible knit sweater Mom made for me in high school," I added, a grin spreading across my face. "It still haunts my closet."

"Ha! I still think it's a fashion statement," Mabel shot back, her eyes sparkling with mischief.

"But it's not just a sweater," I said, sobering as I glanced back at Claire. "It's more than that. What if this turns into something we can't handle?"

Claire's gaze turned serious. "We can handle it. We've faced worse. Remember when I thought I lost my wedding ring? You rallied the troops, convinced the cat had stolen it, and we ended up tearing the house apart. Spoiler alert: it was in my pocket the whole time."

"That's a classic," Mabel said, nodding appreciatively. "So, what's the plan? We hunt down our family like it's a crime drama?"

"Maybe we start by confronting Mom," Claire suggested, her resolve hardening. "We ask her directly about what she wrote. I think we deserve that much. We can't keep dancing around it."

The thought sent a chill down my spine. "What if she refuses to talk? What if she pushes us away again?"

Mabel stepped in, her voice firm and supportive. "Then we push back. Gently, of course. But you're right, Claire. We need to approach this as a united front. If she's kept this secret all these years, there's a reason. We have to understand it."

As the conversation deepened, I found myself sliding into a reverie, thinking about the life I had known—an existence painted with love and warmth, yet marked by the ink of hidden truths. My childhood had been a soft embrace, a steady rhythm of family traditions that now felt like mere echoes, shadows of a past that might not have been as pristine as I'd imagined.

"What's the worst that can happen?" Claire asked, a hint of defiance in her voice. "She yells? She cries? Maybe she locks us out? It's already hard to picture her hiding things from us. But it can't be worse than carrying this secret around."

Mabel interjected, "And what if there's a whole other side to your family? What if they're wonderful? Maybe they'll be even more interesting than a cat stealing a wedding ring."

"Or maybe they'll be just as weird," I replied, thinking of the quirky relatives that peppered my childhood memories. "I mean, it's a family trait at this point."

Mabel smiled, but there was an undercurrent of concern in her eyes. "Whatever happens, we're in this together. You know that, right?"

I nodded, feeling the weight of her words settle in my chest. It was a promise wrapped in warmth, and I clung to it as tightly as I could. The truth was, I didn't want to face this revelation alone, and I knew deep down that I couldn't.

As night enveloped us, the soft glow of the lamp turned our living room into a sanctuary, a bubble of safety amidst the impending storm. Claire, who had been biting her lip, finally broke the silence. "Let's do it tomorrow. We'll talk to Mom before it gets too late. We'll find a way to make her listen."

The urgency in her voice sent a jolt through me. "What if she doesn't want to? What if she's been waiting for us to pry? Or worse, what if she tells us it's none of our business?"

"Then we take it from there," Claire insisted, her determination unwavering. "But we can't keep dancing around this. We need to know."

I took a deep breath, steeling myself against the whirlwind of emotions swirling within me. It was time to peel back the layers, to face whatever truth lay hidden in the shadows of our past.

As we made plans for the morning, I couldn't shake the feeling that this was more than just a confrontation; it was a reckoning. Our family story, so carefully woven over the years, was about to be unraveled, thread by fragile thread. And I had to hope that whatever we uncovered would still lead us back to the love that had always anchored us.

When the evening finally wound down, and the last of the tea had cooled, I found myself stealing glances at Mabel, who had settled beside me on the couch. Her presence felt like a lighthouse in a raging storm, guiding me toward clarity. "You know," I said softly, "no matter what happens tomorrow, I'm grateful for you. I wouldn't want anyone else by my side for this."

She turned to me, her expression serious yet softened by affection. "You're stuck with me, love. Always. Besides, what's family without a little chaos?"

And with that, I smiled, holding on to her words like a lifeline as we faced an uncertain future together.

The morning sun broke through the blinds, casting sharp, slanting rays across the living room, illuminating the remnants of last night's emotional whirlwind. I blinked against the brightness, the memories of Claire's revelation crashing over me like a cold wave, each detail surfacing with a clarity that felt both daunting and inevitable. The house was too quiet, the soft rustle of leaves outside providing a stark contrast to the chaos brewing within me.

Mabel had stayed over, her presence a comforting weight beside me, though sleep had evaded both of us. She stirred, rubbing the remnants of sleep from her eyes. "What time is it?" she murmured, voice thick with remnants of dreams that hung just beyond reach.

"Too early for existential crises," I replied, attempting a smile that didn't quite reach my eyes.

"Speak for yourself," she chuckled, the sound drawing a little warmth back into the room. "I had a dream that we were on a game show, and the prize was—get this—a lifetime supply of artisanal cheese. How's that for motivation?"

"Sounds delicious," I said, but my thoughts were already swirling, back to the confrontation ahead. "How do you feel about confronting my mother today?"

Mabel propped herself up on her elbows, her gaze steady. "Nervous. But it's about time we got some answers. Remember, we're not just digging up dirt; we're looking for the truth. There's a big difference."

I nodded, knowing that today would not just be about seeking answers but also about wrestling with the uncomfortable notion that I might not know my family at all. A pang of fear twisted in my gut, as I wondered what it would mean for my relationship with Claire and Mabel if the truths we unearthed threatened to fracture the bonds that had always held us together.

After a hasty breakfast that consisted of toast smeared with too much butter and a few cups of coffee strong enough to put hair on my chest, we made our way to Claire's house. The drive was punctuated by a silence thick with unspoken worries, the kind that crawled under your skin, leaving a chill in their wake.

As we parked outside Claire's, my heart raced, a drumbeat that drowned out the chirping of birds and the rustling of leaves. "Okay, deep breaths," Mabel whispered, squeezing my hand as we stepped out of the car. "You've got this."

Inside, the house was quiet, the air heavy with the scent of freshly brewed coffee. Claire was already there, pacing the small kitchen with the nervous energy of a coiled spring. "You're here! I thought I'd have to start without you," she said, her voice a mix of relief and anxiety.

"Let's not start without the main character," I replied, trying to inject some levity into the situation. "After all, she's the one with all the secrets."

Claire shot me a look, her eyebrows raised in mock exasperation. "Can we just focus on the task at hand? Mom's going to be home soon."

The mention of our mother felt like a match struck against dry kindling, igniting my simmering nerves. "Right. The task. Which I'm still trying to wrap my head around," I said, my voice quaking slightly. "What if she shuts down? What if she throws us out?"

"Then we dig our heels in and refuse to budge," Mabel said, her tone light but fierce. "We're not kids anymore. We can handle a little confrontation."

As if on cue, the front door creaked open, and the familiar sound of my mother's footsteps echoed down the hallway. My heart thudded louder, each beat echoing the questions I wanted to ask, the truths I hoped to uncover.

"Hello?" Mom called, her voice cheerful, oblivious to the storm brewing just behind the surface. "I brought donuts! You'll never believe the new bakery that opened down the street."

"Of course, she brings donuts," Claire muttered under her breath, her eyes darting toward the kitchen where our mother was headed.

"Keep it light," I urged, trying to summon some courage. "Let's just ease into it."

Mom entered, a bright smile lighting up her face. "Good morning, darlings! You're all here so early. What a lovely surprise!" She set the box of donuts on the table, her hands moving swiftly as she arranged them like a bouquet of pastries.

The sweet, sugary aroma filled the air, but it felt suffocating rather than inviting. "Thanks, Mom," I managed, trying to force a smile as I met her gaze.

"Before we dive into the sugar coma, we need to talk," Claire said, her tone serious as she stepped forward.

My mother's smile faltered for a fraction of a second, a flicker of concern crossing her face. "Talk? About what?"

"About your past," I interjected, feeling a wave of defiance swell within me. "About the things you've kept hidden from us."

The atmosphere shifted, an almost tangible weight settling over the room. My mother's expression hardened, and I could see the tension coiling in her shoulders. "What are you talking about?" she asked, her voice tightening.

"Mom, we found your journal," Claire said, her voice steady. "We know there are things you've kept from us—things about Dad, your family. We deserve to know the truth."

My mother's gaze flickered between us, her eyes wide with disbelief and something else—fear? Guilt? "That journal was not meant for you," she said sharply. "You have no right to invade my privacy like this."

"Privacy?" I couldn't keep the anger from spilling over. "You've built a wall around us, and it's not just your privacy we're talking about. It's our lives!"

Mabel stepped forward, her voice calm yet firm. "We're not here to attack you, but we need answers. You can't keep shutting us out. This is about us—your daughters, your family."

Silence fell heavy in the room, thick as fog, and for a moment, I thought my mother might bolt. But instead, she inhaled sharply, her hands trembling slightly as she gripped the table. "You think you're ready for the truth?"

The challenge in her voice sent a shiver down my spine. "We are. We need to know," I pressed, my heart racing as the moment stretched like a taut wire about to snap.

"I can't just tell you everything. You have to understand, some truths are meant to protect."

"Protect or imprison?" Claire shot back, her voice fierce. "We're tired of being protected from our own lives."

Just then, the doorbell rang, slicing through the tension like a knife. We all paused, exchanging wary glances. "Who could that be?" my mother asked, her brows knitting together in confusion.

"I have no idea," I said, my pulse quickening. "Maybe it's the ghost of our family secrets coming to haunt us."

But as my mother moved to answer the door, I felt a sudden surge of dread. What if the truth was more than we bargained for? What if the answers we sought were the very foundation of our family's destruction?

The door creaked open, and a figure stepped inside, casting a long shadow that filled the entryway. The blood drained from my face as I recognized the silhouette.

"Surprise!" the figure exclaimed, a smile spreading across his face that was eerily familiar, yet jarring in its suddenness. "I'm back, and it's time for us to talk."

The breath caught in my throat, the reality of the moment slamming into me like a freight train. The past, with all its secrets and shadows, had just walked through the door.

Chapter 10: Fractured Reflections

The kitchen, with its timeworn oak table and mismatched chairs, felt both familiar and foreign, like a favorite book with pages missing. Sunlight streamed through the window, casting a golden glow that danced upon the faded linoleum, illuminating dust motes that swirled like lost thoughts in the stillness. It should have been a warm, inviting space, the heart of our childhood home, yet today, it was heavy with unspoken words and repressed emotions, the air thickening as I braced myself to face my sister.

Adelaide sat across from me, her fingers fidgeting with a loose thread on her worn sweater. I tried to find solace in the way she always tucked her hair behind her ear when nervous, a gesture from our shared past that used to bring me comfort. But now, the way she avoided my gaze sent a chill down my spine, igniting a flicker of something dangerous in my chest—was it fear or betrayal?

"So," I began, the word sticking to my tongue like the remnants of last night's dinner, cold and unappetizing. I had rehearsed this moment in my mind countless times, imagining a confrontation that might bring us closer. But with each heartbeat, I felt myself drifting further from that goal. "What is it you wanted to tell me?"

Her eyes finally met mine, and for a fleeting moment, I caught a glimpse of the sister who used to laugh with me over shared secrets, the girl who would sneak out to catch fireflies in the dusky summer air. But that glimmer quickly extinguished, replaced by something I could only describe as resignation. "I think... I think it's time you knew the truth about Mom and Dad."

The words hit me like a sudden downpour, each drop cold and unforgiving. My heart raced, confusion and anger clawing at the edges of my sanity. "What truth?" I managed, though I could barely keep the tremor from my voice. I leaned in, desperate for clarity, but her face remained inscrutable.

Adelaide drew a deep breath, her gaze fixed on a spot just past my shoulder. "They... they weren't who you thought they were."

With each revelation, I felt a layer of my past begin to peel away, like paint flaking from an old wall, revealing the ghostly hues beneath. "What do you mean? They were our parents, Addie. They loved us." I struggled to mask the quaver in my tone, pulling at the threads of my memory, hoping to weave a semblance of familiarity around me.

"No," she said, her voice firm but soft, as if she were cradling a fragile bird in her hands. "That's just it. Their love... it wasn't as simple as that. There were things they hid from us, things that changed everything."

Her words hung in the air like a bitter aftertaste. I pressed my palms against the table, feeling the grainy surface beneath my fingers. "You're not making sense. What are you talking about?"

Adelaide's fingers stilled, and she finally looked at me, her expression shifting from uncertainty to something more profound—fear. "I found out that they weren't really our biological parents. They adopted us after... after something happened. Something terrible."

Each word felt like a stone dropped into a still pond, rippling across the surface of my understanding, shattering it into a million tiny pieces. "What do you mean, terrible? What happened?" The question burst forth before I could stop it, and I realized I was holding my breath, waiting for her to spill the secrets like marbles rolling across the floor.

"There was an accident, a car crash," she said, her voice a whisper now, as if she feared the very walls might listen. "Mom and Dad were in it. They survived, but..." Her gaze fell again, and I felt the edges of my world begin to fray. "They were in the process of adopting us when it happened. We were only a few months old. They loved us, yes, but it was never that simple."

I inhaled sharply, the room spinning ever so slightly. This new reality felt foreign, unsettling, a puzzle missing crucial pieces. "Why didn't you tell me sooner?" I managed to choke out, a wave of betrayal rising within me. "How could you keep this from me?"

"I thought you'd be happier not knowing," she said, her voice thick with emotion. "You had your life, your dreams. I didn't want to burden you with the truth."

"Burden?!" I snapped, the heat of my anger spilling over. "Do you know what a burden is? It's being lied to, living a lie! You think I'd be better off in the dark?"

Mabel's presence felt like a cool breeze on a hot day as she stepped into the kitchen, her gentle energy infusing the tense atmosphere. She cast a quick glance between us, her eyes searching for the right words. "What's going on?" she asked softly, concern lacing her tone.

"Just a family discussion," I said, forcing a smile that felt more like a grimace. I didn't want Mabel to see the cracks forming in my carefully built world.

"Family discussions can get heated," she said, settling beside me. "But remember, sometimes the truth, however difficult, can bring you closer." Her words resonated, washing over me like a balm, soothing the raw edges of my anger.

Adelaide shifted in her seat, and the air between us felt charged with the weight of unsaid apologies and unresolved emotions. "I just didn't want to ruin everything," she whispered, her voice barely above a murmur. "But I realize now that keeping secrets is its own kind of ruin."

As I looked at her, the stranger who wore my sister's face, I saw something shift behind her eyes. It was the flicker of understanding, the kind that sparked when two people stood on the brink of revelation. I felt the tension wane slightly, the storm clouds beginning to disperse, making way for clarity. The journey ahead would be daunting, fraught with unknowns, but perhaps, just perhaps, we could face it together.

The warmth of Mabel's presence grounded me, though the lingering shock of Adelaide's revelation left me teetering on the edge of chaos. I took a moment, letting her words settle like dust in the sunlight. I needed to center myself, to find a foothold in this shifting terrain where everything I believed was being called into question. "So, let me get this straight," I said, trying to infuse my tone with a lightness I didn't feel. "We were adopted? And our entire childhood was a well-scripted performance? A sitcom without the laugh track?"

Adelaide's lips twitched, and I caught a glimpse of the sister I knew beneath the veneer of her revelation. "Not a performance," she replied, her voice steadier now. "More like a documentary with some serious editing. They loved us, but they had to navigate their own pasts too."

A part of me wanted to laugh at the absurdity, to dismiss it as yet another one of Adelaide's wild theories, but I couldn't shake the feeling that the truth was slithering beneath the surface, too slippery to grasp. Mabel leaned in, her dark curls brushing against my arm. "You know, my family had its fair share of secrets too," she said, her voice a gentle balm. "It's like we're all just trying to figure out the right way to live in a world that sometimes feels like it's hiding the good stuff behind closed doors."

I appreciated Mabel's attempt to bridge the emotional chasm that had opened up between my sister and me, but the irony of her words gnawed at me. What good were those revelations when they served only to deepen the rift? "So what now?" I asked, my voice a little sharper than intended. "Do we dive into the family archives? Is there a dusty box somewhere labeled 'Secret Origins' that we can unravel together?"

Adelaide sighed, and for the first time, the weariness in her eyes struck me. "It's not that simple, trust me. We can't just sift through old papers and expect to understand everything. Our parents carried their own burdens, and I think they hoped we'd never have to carry them too."

"Or they hoped we'd just be ignorant enough to be happy," I snapped before I could stop myself, the bitterness spilling out like a broken faucet.

"Look," Adelaide said, frustration edging her voice. "I get it. You're angry, and you have every right to be. But the truth is, they were trying to protect us. They were afraid of what we'd uncover."

"Protect us from what, exactly? The truth? News flash: It's too late for that!" I shot back, my heart pounding with the urgency of the conversation. The once-familiar kitchen walls felt like they were closing in on me, the air thick with tension and unspoken fears.

Just then, the sound of a glass clinking against the table interrupted our charged atmosphere. Mabel had poured herself a glass of water, the droplets trickling down the sides like time slipping away. "What if you both take a breath?" she suggested, her eyes flitting between us. "This is a lot. Maybe talking about it isn't the best way to process it all right now."

"Great idea, Mabel," I replied, sarcasm slipping through the cracks in my facade. "What I really need is a glass of water to help me swallow this bitter pill."

"Okay, no one's making you drink it," Mabel countered, her playful smile breaking through the tension. "But maybe you can think of it as just water. The truth is still hard to digest, but it doesn't have to drown you."

Adelaide nodded slowly, absorbing Mabel's words. "We should take a step back," she said, her voice softer now, tinged with regret. "I didn't mean to drop this bombshell on you without a plan. I just thought... maybe we could start to rebuild."

"Rebuild?" I echoed, incredulity coloring my voice. "You mean like Legos? We can just snap everything back together? Because right now, I feel like I'm standing in a pile of broken bricks."

"Rebuilding doesn't mean you have to ignore the wreckage," she insisted. "It's about figuring out how to make something new from what's left."

As the storm of emotions within me settled into a low rumble, I caught sight of the photos lining the walls of the kitchen. They captured moments of us as children—grinning on summer days, arms slung over each other's shoulders, all the sweet and tender memories we had forged together. Those memories were now tangled in the truth of who we were, and I could feel a strange compulsion to reach out and reclaim them.

"Maybe," I began cautiously, "we could start with a story. Tell me what you know. Not just the facts, but what you felt, what it was like growing up with this weight hanging over us. Maybe that will give us a better foundation."

Adelaide's brow furrowed, surprise flickering across her face. "You really want to know?"

"Of course I do," I said, trying to sound more confident than I felt. "But only if you're ready to share. I'm tired of feeling like I'm navigating this labyrinth of our past alone."

With a reluctant nod, she leaned back, her shoulders easing slightly. "Okay. But this isn't going to be easy."

"Wouldn't want it any other way," I replied, crossing my arms with a half-smirk that masked the tremor of anxiety buzzing just beneath my skin.

Adelaide's eyes softened as she began, her voice weaving a tapestry of our childhood. "Remember when we'd sneak into the attic, looking for treasures? We'd always find those boxes filled with old clothes and dusty books. There was a time when I thought those were the most exciting things ever."

"Yeah, and I also remember how terrified I was of that old trunk you thought was haunted," I interjected, a small chuckle escaping my lips despite the tension still thick in the air.

She smiled, the memory drawing her in. "Right? I convinced you that it held the spirits of old relatives, didn't I? I thought I'd get you to stop asking so many questions."

"Those were the days when ignorance truly was bliss."

"I wish we could go back to that," she said softly. "But we can't. We have to face what's real now. There's so much I never understood—like why they were so protective. I thought they were just being parents, but now... it feels like they were guarding secrets."

The gravity of her words hung between us, a reminder of the uncharted territory we were venturing into. With every layer she peeled back, I felt the delicate fabric of our shared history unravel just a bit more, revealing truths we would need to confront together. As Mabel listened, her presence a steady anchor in the turbulent sea of revelations, I felt the first stirrings of hope. Perhaps this fractured reflection of our past could illuminate a path forward, one paved with honesty and healing.

"Tell me more," I urged, leaning forward, my heart a wild drumbeat in my chest. "I can't wrap my head around this whole idea of us being... adopted."

Adelaide's gaze flickered momentarily to the old photo on the wall of us dressed in our Halloween costumes—me as a princess with a lopsided tiara, and her as a pirate with a plastic sword held high. Those were innocent days, unmarred by the reality of a hidden past. "It's not just that we were adopted," she said, her voice steady but low, as if the very air might betray us. "It's what came before. There were reasons they chose to adopt us, reasons they never shared. I think it's time we explored that, together."

The implication hung between us, and I felt a mix of dread and curiosity. What was so sinister in their past that they thought it best to shield us from the truth? "You're talking about our parents like they're characters in a drama," I said, trying to keep my voice light even as a chill crept down my spine. "What do you think was going on in their lives that led them to adopt two little girls? Did they think we were some kind of charity project?"

"I don't think it was that simple," she replied, her eyes narrowing as she processed my flippant remark. "They were happy when they got us, and I know they loved us deeply. But maybe they were trying to escape something—a past they didn't want us to inherit."

"What could possibly be worse than lying about our origins? Is there a family of angry wolves waiting to come claim us?" I scoffed, but the playful tone didn't quite mask my rising anxiety.

"Maybe," she said, a hint of a smile ghosting her lips before vanishing. "But it's more likely something much worse. You remember how they avoided talking about family history? How they brushed off questions about grandparents or even where they met?"

"Yeah, but I thought that was just their quirk. Everyone has their skeletons," I replied, my voice steadier now, even as unease gnawed at the corners of my mind. "What's the big deal? We could just Google it."

"Some things don't fit neatly into a search bar," Adelaide countered, her tone shifting to something serious. "We need to uncover the stories that aren't written down. I stumbled upon some old letters and documents in the attic. They hinted at something much darker, something that could have torn our family apart."

Mabel, who had been quietly observing, chimed in. "This is a lot for anyone to handle. Have you both thought about how you want to approach this? Diving into the past might be painful."

"Painful or not, it feels like we need to do this," I said, my voice firmer now. "I don't want to keep pretending that everything is fine when clearly, it's not. If I have to break my own heart to find out the truth, then so be it."

Adelaide nodded, a flicker of gratitude in her eyes, and I felt a slight warmth bloom in my chest. "Okay. Let's start by revisiting those old letters. We can't let our parents' decisions shape our understanding of who we are. We need to carve our own path."

"Great, we'll be like detectives," I declared, trying to inject a bit of levity into the atmosphere. "Finding the truth one dusty letter at a time. A modern-day Nancy Drew and her ever-so-hesitant sidekick."

"I'd rather be your Watson than your Drew," Mabel replied with a grin, her playful tone a reminder that amidst the upheaval, we still had moments of connection that brought light into the chaos.

The atmosphere shifted as we began to draw a map of our family history, our own minds like chalkboards being wiped clean and re-written with questions. What would we discover? What truths lay buried beneath the surface of our family's façade?

"Let's check the attic tomorrow," Adelaide said, her voice laced with determination. "If we're going to dive into this, we might as well do it right."

"Agreed. The sooner we start, the sooner we can get to the bottom of this," I replied, feeling the weight of purpose settle around us like a warm blanket.

That night, sleep eluded me. I tossed and turned, my mind spiraling through fragments of memories and shadows of fears, until finally, dawn broke with a whisper of light spilling through my window. I found myself standing in the kitchen, a hot cup of coffee warming my hands, staring out at the world still wrapped in the soft embrace of morning mist.

As I sipped my coffee, I caught sight of Mabel, who had emerged from her room, rubbing sleep from her eyes. "You're up early. Coffee in the morning is becoming your thing, huh?"

"It's an acquired taste," I said, forcing a lightness I didn't quite feel. "Besides, I thought I'd brace myself for the emotional rollercoaster that awaits us today."

She leaned against the counter, her brows knitting together. "You sure about this? Digging into the past can sometimes open wounds you didn't even know were there."

"I don't think I can live in the dark anymore," I replied, my voice resolute. "Not when I have a sister across the table willing to face it with me. It feels right to uncover the truth, even if it hurts."

Just as Mabel nodded, agreeing with a soft smile, a loud crash erupted from the attic. We both jumped, adrenaline shooting through me like a lightning bolt. "Did you hear that?" I asked, my heart racing.

Mabel straightened, eyes wide. "What was that?"

"I don't know, but it sounded like something fell. Maybe the ghosts of family secrets are already trying to sabotage our plan," I joked, though my voice wavered slightly, betraying my nervousness.

"Should we check it out?" she asked, taking a step toward the stairs.

"Why not? Let's embrace the chaos," I said, setting my coffee cup down with a thud, adrenaline replacing the warmth of the drink.

As we climbed the creaky stairs, my mind swirled with possibilities, each creak of the floorboards echoing the tension building inside me. What if we stumbled upon something crucial, something that could shift our understanding? Or worse, what if it was a remnant of the past—a painful reminder that shattered our fragile resolve?

We reached the attic door, the dim light filtering through a dusty window revealing a world of boxes and cobwebs, the air thick with the scent of old wood and forgotten memories. Just as I reached for the doorknob, the door swung open, and I stumbled backward.

Standing in the doorway, framed by shadows, was a figure I recognized all too well—an unexpected visitor from our past. My breath caught in my throat, the weight of unspoken history crashing over me like a tidal wave.

"Hello, girls," they said, their voice a haunting echo of my childhood.

Chapter 11: Healing Old Wounds

The door clicked softly behind me, a finality echoing in the quiet room that had, until moments ago, been a sanctuary of solitude. The air was heavy with the scent of lavender and the faint traces of last night's rain, both comforting and suffocating in their familiarity. I leaned against the door, my heart pounding like a trapped bird, desperate to escape the tangled emotions that swirled inside me. Mabel, however, was a persistent force, her gentle prodding a warm light cutting through the fog of my thoughts.

"Come on," she said, her voice a melodic whisper that coaxed me back from the edge. "You can't just shut me out. Not after all that."

The walls I had fortified over years of hurt threatened to crack, but something about her presence made me hesitate. It wasn't just her unwavering support; it was the way she looked at me, as if she saw through the façade I had so carefully constructed. The last thing I wanted was to share the raw truths that lingered beneath my skin, but in her gaze, I felt an invitation—one that whispered of understanding, of a sanctuary where my truths would be met with compassion rather than judgment.

I sank onto the edge of my bed, a safe harbor in the storm of my emotions. Mabel settled beside me, our shoulders brushing, an electrifying reminder of how close we had become. "What are you so afraid of?" she asked, her voice low and soothing, like the rustle of leaves in a gentle breeze.

I stared at the worn carpet, my mind racing back to the years I spent grappling with unfulfilled expectations and the suffocating grip of disappointment. "It's not about fear," I finally admitted, my voice barely above a whisper. "It's about... everything. My childhood was a minefield of expectations, and every misstep was like setting off an explosion."

Mabel turned to me, her eyes wide and shimmering with a deep understanding that made my heart flutter uneasily. "Tell me. I want to hear it," she urged, and her words spilled over me like a warm embrace, drawing me into a space where vulnerability felt safe.

I took a breath, the memories swirling like autumn leaves caught in a whirlwind. "I grew up in a house where success was the only currency," I began, my voice steadying as I found my rhythm. "My parents had a plan for me—high grades, prestigious college, an impressive career. Anything less was a failure in their eyes. They had this image of perfection that I never quite fit into."

I paused, watching the way Mabel nodded, her expression reflecting an empathy that encouraged me to continue. "Every time I stumbled, it felt like the ground fell away beneath me. My parents didn't yell; they didn't have to. Their silence spoke volumes. It was like they had this invisible scale, measuring my worth against their dreams, and I was always coming up short."

Mabel leaned closer, her shoulder warm against mine. "That sounds... so hard. No wonder you built those walls," she murmured, her tone a blend of admiration and sympathy.

"Yeah, and those walls became my fortress. I didn't let anyone in, not friends, not even myself. I stuffed everything down so deep that I forgot what it felt like to be honest, to just be me without the weight of everyone's expectations." I could feel the tears pricking at the corners of my eyes, and I blinked them away, unwilling to surrender to the flood.

"But now?" she prompted gently, and I could see the concern etched in her features.

"Now," I sighed, looking out the window where the sun had dipped low, painting the sky in hues of orange and purple, "I'm at a crossroads. I don't want to be that person anymore. I'm tired of pretending, but it's hard to break free from the chains of my past. I've carried those scars for so long; it feels impossible to let them go."

"You're not alone in this," Mabel said softly, her hand brushing against mine, a simple gesture that sparked something deep within. "It's okay to share that burden. It's okay to heal. Sometimes, the first step is simply letting someone else see the real you."

Her words hung in the air, a lifeline thrown into turbulent waters, and I found myself drawn closer, a moth to a flame. "What if I can't? What if I'm just... broken?" I felt the vulnerability creeping in, threatening to unravel me.

"Broken things can be beautiful," Mabel replied, her voice steady and confident. "They tell stories of resilience, of strength. Besides, who wants to be perfectly whole? That's boring."

A laugh escaped me, light and genuine, cutting through the tension like a breath of fresh air. "You have a way with words, you know?"

"Years of practice," she quipped, a teasing glint in her eye that reminded me of how easily we had slipped into banter. "But seriously, I'm here for you. Whatever it takes, we'll get through this together."

In that moment, something shifted. The connection between us felt palpable, an electric charge that crackled in the air. Mabel's warmth enveloped me, and I could feel the edges of my heart soften, the fortress I had built beginning to crumble under the weight of her compassion.

"Thank you," I whispered, the sincerity flooding my voice. "For everything. You have no idea how much this means to me."

As our eyes locked, I could see it—the flicker of something deeper, a bond that went beyond friendship, an unspoken understanding that wove us together. The past still lingered like a shadow, but in this moment, with Mabel by my side, it felt lighter, less daunting. Perhaps this was the beginning of a new chapter, one where I could embrace my truth and allow myself to be seen, scars and all.

The moment hung between us, a fragile bubble of vulnerability suspended in the air. Mabel's presence, like a warm hearth on a winter's night, made it all too easy to forget the world outside—the unyielding pressure of expectations, the weight of a past that clung to me like shadows. Instead, I found solace in the bright curiosity sparkling in her eyes, urging me to go deeper.

"Have you ever felt like you were meant for something more?" I blurted, surprising myself with the question. It had lingered in my mind for so long, a ghost whispering through the dark corners of my thoughts. "Like you're walking a path that doesn't feel right, but you're too afraid to veer off?"

Mabel tilted her head, a thoughtful frown crossing her features. "All the time. I used to think I was destined to be a corporate superstar, until I realized my talent lay more in concocting the perfect coffee blend than balancing spreadsheets. Now, I'm just a barista who moonlights as a motivational speaker for my houseplants." She grinned, the corner of her mouth lifting, and I couldn't help but chuckle.

"Motivational speaker for houseplants?" I echoed, raising an eyebrow. "That sounds oddly specific."

"Oh, you wouldn't believe the kind of encouragement those little green guys need," she retorted, her laughter bubbling over like the froth on her cappuccino. "Honestly, I think they might be my toughest audience yet. But in all seriousness, I get it. We all have these paths laid out for us, like a giant treasure map, but sometimes the 'X' marking the spot doesn't feel like home."

Her words sank into me, stirring something deep within, as I recalled my own treasure map—full of detours, misdirections, and landmarks that turned out to be mere illusions. "You know, for a while, I thought success meant being everything my parents wanted me to be," I confessed, a hint of bitterness creeping into my tone. "But in trying to please them, I lost sight of what I wanted."

"Don't we all?" Mabel replied, her voice soft yet fierce. "But you're not them. You don't have to follow that map. You can create your own."

Her conviction tugged at me, a lifeline thrown into turbulent waters. "What if I don't know how?" I whispered, the admission feeling like a confession of a sin I'd carried for years.

"Then let's figure it out together," she said, her tone unwavering. "It doesn't have to be perfect. It just has to be yours. Besides, I'm pretty good at making bad decisions, so I can help steer you away from my epic fails."

Her playful attitude made the weight of my confession seem lighter, and I felt a smile creeping onto my face. "Bad decisions, huh? Care to share some?"

"Oh, where do I start?" Mabel laughed, leaning back against the headboard. "There was that time I decided to try and impress a date with my cooking skills and nearly set my apartment on fire. Or the time I bought a karaoke machine because I thought it would be fun for a 'ladies' night in'—turns out, I'm better at belting show tunes in the shower than in front of an audience."

I could see it now—the picture of her fumbling through a smoky kitchen or crooning off-key while her friends laughed. "I can't believe you thought karaoke was a good idea," I said, grinning. "Didn't you think it might scare them off?"

"Oh, it did," she replied, her eyes sparkling with mischief. "But it also broke the ice, and who doesn't love a good laugh? It's all part of the journey, right? Like a rollercoaster you didn't ask to get on but ended up loving."

The lightness in her words made me think about my own journey—one of missed turns and wrong exits, but also moments of laughter and joy hidden among the pain. "I guess that's true. Life's unpredictable, isn't it?"

"Exactly!" Mabel leaned forward, her excitement infectious. "We just have to learn to roll with it, like a good wave at the beach. Sometimes you wipe out, but you always get back up. And sometimes, the wipeouts make for the best stories."

"I've definitely got a few wipeouts in my own story," I said, my heart swelling with the truth in her words. "But maybe it's time I start writing new chapters instead of dwelling on the old ones."

"Now you're talking," Mabel said, her enthusiasm wrapping around me like a comforting shawl. "Let's find a way to rewrite your story. What do you want to be? Who do you want to become?"

"I want to be someone who isn't afraid to speak up," I found myself saying. "Someone who embraces her own story, scars and all, without fear of judgment."

"And what's stopping you?" she asked, her brow arching as if challenging me to find an answer.

"Old habits die hard," I admitted, feeling the truth in my chest. "I've spent so long hiding from myself that breaking free feels... overwhelming."

"Sure, it's overwhelming," she acknowledged, her tone gentle yet firm. "But you're not alone in this. You have me, and I'm a certified distraction if I ever saw one. Plus, there's plenty of coffee and terrible karaoke waiting to be had."

The thought made me laugh again, and as we sat there, the afternoon sun spilling golden light through the window, I began to feel a glimmer of hope. Mabel's presence transformed the daunting task of healing into an adventure, each shared moment an opportunity for connection and growth.

As the sunlight danced in the room, I realized that the walls I had built around myself were not impenetrable. With each word exchanged, I felt them crumbling, not with a crash, but gently, like autumn leaves surrendering to the wind. I could take this leap—this terrifying, beautiful leap into the unknown. With Mabel beside me, perhaps I wouldn't just survive the ride; maybe I would finally learn to enjoy it.

With the warmth of Mabel's laughter still lingering in the air, I felt a shift inside me, as if the gears of a long-stalled engine were finally catching. I didn't just want to heal; I wanted to thrive, and for the first time, it felt like a possibility rather than a pipe dream. Mabel's easygoing charm wrapped around me, making the prospect of revealing more of myself less daunting. I could almost hear the faint hum of potential swirling around us, like the sweet scent of fresh coffee blending with the crisp autumn air.

"What's the first step, then?" I asked, feigning casualness as my heart fluttered with a blend of hope and anxiety. "Do we start by finding a new career path, or should I take a crash course in karaoke?"

"Definitely karaoke," Mabel shot back, her eyes sparkling with mischief. "You need to be ready to dazzle your audience. Plus, it's scientifically proven to release endorphins and reduce stress. Who doesn't want to sing their way into happiness?"

"Right, because nothing screams 'I'm totally together' like belting out power ballads in a dive bar," I replied, rolling my eyes, but I couldn't suppress my smile. The idea of stepping outside my comfort zone suddenly seemed less terrifying and more exhilarating.

"Exactly!" she exclaimed, her enthusiasm infectious. "Imagine it: you on stage, a glittery mic in hand, captivating the crowd with your rendition of 'I Will Survive.' Just think of the post-performance glow. The world won't know what hit it!"

I let out a laugh, picturing the scene in my mind. "Maybe I should hire you as my hype woman."

"Absolutely, as long as there are snacks involved," she said, her tone serious. "What's the point of conquering fears without some celebratory chips and salsa?"

"Sounds like a fair trade," I agreed, our shared laughter creating an intimacy that felt like a secret pact. "But really, I think I need to confront my fears head-on, not just in karaoke bars but in every aspect of my life. It's like I've been hiding in plain sight."

"Hiding in plain sight sounds like the title of a bestseller," she mused, leaning back and crossing her arms, a thoughtful look on her face. "And if you need help with that, you know I'm all in. Let's turn that hiding into thriving."

"Okay, then. Let's do it," I said, feeling a surge of determination. "But if we're going to face my past, we need to tackle the big stuff first—the parental expectations, the disappointments. It's time to confront my ghosts."

"Bring them on," Mabel said, her smile unwavering. "Ghosts, ghouls, or even that neighbor's yappy dog that won't shut up—nothing can scare me away now."

As we plotted our way through an imaginary list of all the things I wanted to confront, the air crackled with anticipation. For the first time in ages, I felt as though the heavy veil of my past was beginning to lift, and the colors of life were sharpening into focus. But just as the warmth of connection began to settle into something deeper, I noticed a change in Mabel's expression—a flicker of uncertainty shadowing her bright demeanor.

"Hey," I said, catching her gaze. "What's going on?"

She hesitated, biting her lip. "It's nothing," she said too quickly, and that familiar sense of concern prickled at the back of my mind.

"Mabel," I pressed gently, "I can tell when something's up. You know I'm here for you too, right?"

Her eyes met mine, a storm of emotions swirling within them. "It's just... I've never been the person anyone leans on for big, heavy stuff. I'm usually the one who deflects, you know? I didn't want to bring any of my baggage into this."

"Everyone has baggage. It's called being human," I said, trying to keep my voice light, but my heart raced. "If we're going to do this, we need to be honest with each other. No more hiding."

She let out a breath, a mixture of relief and anxiety washing over her. "Okay, you're right. But promise me, once I share this, you won't treat me any differently."

"I promise. No judgments, just truth," I said, holding her gaze.

With a deep breath, Mabel began to unravel her own story, and my heart ached as she revealed pieces of her past—fragments of broken relationships and friendships that had left scars on her heart. "It's not that I haven't tried to open up," she admitted, her voice trembling slightly. "It's just easier to be the funny one, the carefree one. I've spent so long pretending I'm okay that I don't know how to be anything else."

"That's not fair to you," I replied, my chest tightening at the realization that we were both navigating the same treacherous waters. "You don't have to carry that weight alone. We can help each other."

"Yeah, but it's not just about me," she said, a flicker of hesitation passing through her eyes. "There are things I haven't shared—things that could change everything."

"What do you mean?" I asked, suddenly intrigued, the air between us thickening with tension.

She hesitated, biting her lip again, and in that brief silence, I could feel the magnitude of her words hanging in the balance, teetering on the edge of revelation. Just as she opened her mouth to speak, a loud knock shattered the moment, echoing through the room and causing us both to jump.

"Ugh, what now?" Mabel groaned, clearly frustrated by the interruption.

"Who is it?" I called out, instinctively leaning forward, eager to know what had pulled us away from this moment of truth.

"It's me," came a muffled voice from the other side of the door—deep and familiar, sending a jolt of unexpected tension through my veins.

I exchanged a glance with Mabel, uncertainty flickering in her expression, and in that instant, I realized our conversation had been drifting toward something monumental. I felt the weight of unspoken words resting heavily on my chest, while Mabel's face reflected a blend of dread and resignation.

"Are you going to let me in, or do I have to start reciting Shakespeare?" the voice continued, laced with sarcasm, but there was an undercurrent of concern that sent my heart racing.

Mabel's eyes widened, the moment shattered, and I could sense a shift—a sudden urgency hanging in the air, heavy with unexpressed fears. "We have to get this out," I said, my voice resolute, but doubt tugged at the edges of my mind.

Mabel nodded, but the tension between us was palpable. "Fine, let's put a pin in this," she said, her tone barely masking the frustration bubbling beneath the surface. "Just... be ready for anything."

I glanced back at the door, anxiety curling in my stomach as I took a deep breath, the weight of the moment pressing down on us both. Whatever waited behind that door was about to shift the dynamics of everything we had begun to build, and in that heartbeat, I could feel the fragile threads of our newfound connection quivering on the brink of revelation.

Chapter 12: The Quiet Before the Storm

Autumn's breath hung in the air like the promise of a secret. The vibrant hues of orange and gold dripped from the trees, the leaves swirling in a whimsical dance as if choreographed by nature itself. The sun was a soft, golden orb, casting long shadows that stretched across the town square, where preparations for the annual Harvest Festival unfurled like an elaborate tapestry. The chatter of townsfolk mingled with the rustle of hay bales and the sweet scent of freshly baked apple pies wafting from the bakery down the street.

Mabel, my sister and my truest champion, flitted around like a firefly caught in the glow of summer's last light, her excitement infectious. "What if I set up a booth where people can write their own short stories? We could call it 'The Tales of Maplewood,'" she exclaimed, her eyes sparkling with possibilities. Her curly hair bounced with each enthusiastic gesture, catching the light and casting little rainbows in the air. She was vibrant, an explosion of joy in a world that often felt like it faded into muted tones.

"Do you really think people will want to share their stories?" I asked, my voice barely louder than a whisper, as if fearing the very question would extinguish her zeal. I tugged at the hem of my sweater, suddenly aware of the fabric's rough texture against my skin. It was comforting in a way, grounding, yet it couldn't smother the rising tide of anxiety that churned in my chest.

"Of course! Everyone has a story," Mabel replied, her brow furrowed in that endearing way when she was deep in thought. "And this festival is the perfect chance for them to express themselves! Just imagine the stories we could collect!"

Her enthusiasm was like a balm, and for a fleeting moment, I almost believed in the beauty of her vision. But beneath her bright exterior, my own darkness loomed like a heavy storm cloud, its thunder rumbling deep within. I could feel the weight of our parents' expectations pressing down on me like the heat of the sun—unrelenting and suffocating. Mabel's joy clashed with the fear festering inside me, a war that raged silently, rendering me a spectator to my own turmoil.

"Maybe we should just keep it simple," I suggested, trying to steer her toward less ambitious shores. "What if we just have a few paper and pens? That way, people can jot down their thoughts, and we won't need to worry about crowds."

"Are you kidding?" Mabel shot back, hands on her hips, eyes narrowing in mock seriousness. "You're not getting out of this that easily. You're going to help me decorate the booth with fairy lights, and we'll need a catchy sign. Plus, I'm going to need you there to encourage people! You know how shy they can be."

"Shy? I'm pretty sure I'm the shy one here." I glanced down, half-expecting my insecurities to manifest in the gathering shadows of the square.

"Exactly! That's why you'll be perfect," she countered, nudging me playfully. "Think about it. You're going to face your fears. And I'll be right there with you."

Her unwavering belief in my potential was like a warm blanket, but the underlying anxiety curled up in the corner, watching like a hawk. It wasn't that I didn't want to support Mabel; it was the gnawing realization that she was asking me to reveal the very part of myself I had carefully tucked away. My writing had always been a sanctuary—a hidden garden of emotions I tended to quietly, away from prying eyes. The thought of putting it on display felt akin to baring my soul in a crowded room, every word an invitation for judgment.

"Okay, fine. I'll help with the booth," I relented, forcing a smile that felt more like a grimace. "But you have to promise me we'll keep it low-key. No crowds."

"Deal!" she beamed, the very definition of unyielding optimism. "We'll make it intimate—just like our writing sessions! I'll bring the cupcakes, and you can read some of your poems aloud. It'll be magical!"

"Poems?" I squeaked, feeling my insides twist. "You know I can't do that!"

"Why not? You're brilliant! You've been writing poetry since we were kids."

"Brilliance is a stretch," I muttered, biting my lip to suppress the rising panic. The thought of standing in front of people, my heart racing, palms sweaty, words tumbling from my mouth like clumsy toddlers learning to walk, made me want to bolt.

"Everyone gets nervous," she coaxed, her tone softening. "But it's about sharing. About connecting. And if anyone judges you, they'll have to answer to me."

I chuckled, my heart fluttering with warmth at her fierce loyalty. "What if I just... write something new? Something that speaks to all of this?"

"That's the spirit!" Mabel clapped her hands, her laughter ringing like the chime of a bell. "We'll get you a lovely little notebook, and you can write down everything you're afraid of. You can even decorate it with flowers! It'll be a special project for the festival."

"Flowers?" I echoed, caught off guard. "What is this, a kindergarten art class?"

"Hey, flowers make everything better," she said, grinning impishly. "Besides, if you're going to spill your secrets, you might as well do it with a little flair."

As we bickered back and forth, a spark ignited within me—a small flicker of hope amidst the encroaching shadows. Perhaps, just perhaps, sharing my fears could lead to something unexpected. Maybe I wouldn't just be unearthing my vulnerability; I might also discover strength in the act of creation, a sense of community woven into the fabric of our town.

But just as the warmth began to spread, the whisper of my sister's earlier revelation crept back into my thoughts, dragging my heart into familiar trepidation. What was I hiding from? And what did it mean for me to step into the light when the dark secrets loomed so close?

The days dwindled like the last rays of sun before twilight, each one bleeding into the next with a familiarity that both comforted and unnerved me. The town, wrapped in a blanket of autumn splendor, thrummed with life, as if the very earth was celebrating the end of a season. Mabel's enthusiasm was the heartbeat of the preparations, her laughter ringing out like music, infectious and bright. Yet, while she twirled around in a flurry of ideas, I found myself standing on the sidelines, tethered by my own anxiety.

Everywhere I looked, signs of the Harvest Festival took shape. Colorful banners fluttered in the crisp breeze, and local vendors set up stalls overflowing with produce—pumpkins, apples, and those strange little gourds that looked more like decorative props than food. Mabel had commandeered a corner of our small town library for our booth, her vision sprawling before us like a wild garden. She had even invited friends to join us, convinced that their creativity would bring a unique flair to the booth.

"Don't you think it'll be fun to have a little 'Story Slam' at the booth?" she proposed one morning over breakfast, her cereal bowl nearly empty. "We can invite people to share their tales right there! It'll be like a live version of our favorite podcast, but with more drama and less editing!"

My fork paused mid-air, contemplating the horror of impromptu storytelling. "You want me to participate in this... Story

Slam? Like a gladiator of narratives?" I replied, attempting to inject humor into my growing apprehension.

"Exactly! Just imagine," she said, her eyes sparkling with mischief. "You could deliver a heartfelt poem about your deepest fears, and I'll be right there cheering you on like a loyal sidekick. We'll have the crowd eating out of our hands!"

"Or they'll flee in terror, screaming about how I've exposed their deepest insecurities," I countered, an exaggerated shiver running down my spine. "Nothing screams 'Harvest Festival' like an emotional breakdown."

Mabel laughed, her joyous sound bubbling like a brook in spring. "You're being dramatic. This is a celebration! We're here to connect with people, share stories, and yes, maybe even spill our fears on a stage. But think of it this way—if we're brave enough to be vulnerable, we might inspire others to do the same."

In theory, that sounded wonderful. In practice, I was less convinced. The idea of baring my soul, however cathartic it could potentially be, felt like preparing for a dive into icy waters. Each time I considered it, a wave of nausea threatened to pull me under. Yet there was something about Mabel's relentless spirit that tugged at my heart. Perhaps it was time to trade my fear for courage, to let the storm within me break free rather than allowing it to rage unnoticed.

The week wore on, each day filled with last-minute details and the frenetic energy of festival preparations. Mabel recruited our friends for last-minute crafts, all with an easy charm that made every task seem like a game rather than work. We cut paper leaves for decorations, each snip of the scissors punctuated by laughter and light-hearted banter. I helped Mabel fashion a garland from twine and bits of colored paper, where our visitors could clip their stories for others to read—a visual tapestry of shared experiences.

On the eve of the festival, our booth stood like a beacon in the town square, colorful and inviting. Fairy lights twinkled overhead, casting a warm glow that wrapped around us like a cozy shawl. Mabel beamed, her cheeks flushed with excitement as she stepped back to admire our work. "Look at this! We've created a little haven of creativity right here in Maplewood!"

"It does look good," I admitted, pride creeping into my voice despite the anxiety still simmering beneath the surface. "I can't believe we actually pulled it off."

"Now, all we need is the perfect plan to lure people in," she said, rubbing her hands together. "You know, like a magician with a bag of tricks. What do you think about a sign that reads, 'Share Your Story, Gain a Cookie!'?"

"Are we bribing them now? Because I'm not sure I can uphold any literary standards if there are cookies involved." I couldn't help but grin at her enthusiasm. "Though it's a solid marketing strategy."

"Oh, come on! Who doesn't love cookies?" she shot back, her eyes dancing with mischief. "Plus, I'll bake them myself! Everyone will feel obligated to write something just to get one of my famous chocolate chip cookies."

"Famous? Since when are your cookies famous?" I asked, half-teasing, half-serious.

"Since I made them last year at the festival, and even Mrs. Henderson asked for my secret recipe," she replied, a hint of pride creeping into her tone. "That's practically celebrity status in Maplewood!"

As night fell, I found myself standing in front of the booth, heart racing, anticipation building. The square began to fill with people, laughter echoing in the night air. The vibrant sounds of the festival danced around us like fireflies, igniting a sense of magic that made my pulse quicken. Yet, just beneath that excitement lurked a shadow of uncertainty, the nagging fear of judgment and exposure clawing at my insides.

"Ready?" Mabel asked, her voice full of encouragement as she handed me a small notebook—my "secret weapon," as she called it. "This is where you'll write your poem. You can start small, jot down your thoughts, and then we'll build up to something grand!"

"Small, like a post-it note?" I replied, chuckling nervously.

"More like a heartfelt haiku," she grinned, nudging me playfully. "Now, let's get this party started! I see someone from school coming. Go be social!"

"Ah, socializing—the sport I never trained for," I muttered under my breath, but my feet moved of their own accord, propelled by Mabel's unwavering faith. I joined the throng of festival-goers, the energy vibrant and electric.

As I mingled, a sense of unease lingered in my chest, a reminder of the quiet storm brewing within me. But every laugh shared and story exchanged chipped away at that wall, replacing it with a fragile sense of belonging. I watched Mabel glide through the crowd, her infectious laughter drawing people in like moths to a flame. Each moment spent at the booth slowly started to peel back layers of my apprehension.

Suddenly, a familiar face appeared—Sarah, a friend from high school I hadn't seen in years. Her wide smile and bright eyes felt like a lifeline amidst the sea of strangers. "Hey! I didn't know you'd be here!" she exclaimed, her voice bubbling with excitement.

"I wasn't sure either," I admitted, the warmth of her presence washing over me. "Mabel dragged me into this booth idea, and here I am, still not quite sure what I'm doing."

Sarah chuckled, leaning in conspiratorially. "Honestly, it looks amazing. I'd be intimidated if I were you. What's the plan? Are you reading something?"

I felt my throat tighten, words caught in a vise of apprehension. "Maybe? It's all still a bit surreal."

"Surreal is good. It means you're stepping out of your comfort zone!" She nudged me playfully. "Besides, I'll be right here if you need a cheerleader."

Just as I prepared to respond, a gust of wind swept through the square, rustling the leaves and lifting the corner of our booth's sign. Mabel dashed over, laughter escaping her lips like a tune on the breeze. "Did you see that? The universe is telling us we're destined for greatness!"

"Or that we need to anchor our booth better," I countered, but her optimism was infectious.

"Either way, it's a sign we're ready for this!" she said, clapping her hands together.

The vibrant colors of the festival swirled around us, the warm lights twinkling like stars against the velvety night. With each passing moment, my anxiety began to fade, and I felt the gentle pull of camaraderie wrapping around me like a soft blanket. It wasn't just a booth, or a festival; it was an opportunity to weave my story into the fabric of our town, to embrace the storm inside rather than hide from it. And perhaps, just perhaps, I was ready to take that leap—into the unknown, into the light, and into my own truth.

The festival reached a crescendo as night deepened, and the flickering lights began to mingle with the stars, casting a spell over the square. Laughter bubbled around us, weaving through the crowd like a lively melody. Mabel, in her element, beckoned to passersby with an infectious energy that ignited even my fading spirit. "Come! Share your story and earn a cookie!" she called, her voice ringing clear above the din.

It was a small miracle how she managed to rally interest so effortlessly. I watched as families stopped to inspect our booth, curiosity dancing in their eyes. A little girl, clutching her mother's hand, leaned in closer, captivated by the colorful leaves that adorned our display. My heart fluttered, a strange mix of pride and fear swelling inside me. For every joyful cheer Mabel inspired, my own anxiety hissed a reminder of the uncertainty that lingered.

"You look like a deer caught in headlights," Sarah said, sidling up beside me, her gaze tracking my shifting expression. "This isn't a horror movie, you know."

"It certainly feels like one," I shot back, trying to laugh off the knot tightening in my chest. "I'm pretty sure the last time I felt this way was during the school spelling bee. I almost fainted."

"Right, but you survived that, didn't you?" Sarah nudged me gently. "This is different. It's just sharing your heart. Not a spelling bee. Think of it more as a heart slam."

"Ah, yes. The old heart slam. Sounds delightful," I quipped, my voice dripping with sarcasm.

"Listen, how about I read first? You can see how easy it is to spill your guts in front of a crowd," she suggested, a sly smile creeping onto her lips.

As she stepped up to the makeshift podium we'd created, the crowd began to gather, curiosity ignited by the girl who promised cookies for stories. Sarah cleared her throat, her expression a perfect blend of excitement and nervousness. The crowd quieted, anticipation crackling in the air like electricity.

"I don't have a fancy story," she started, her voice steady. "But here goes nothing." She paused, glancing at me, then began to recount a humorous tale from our high school days, how we had accidentally locked ourselves in the school's supply closet for an entire lunch period. Her animated retelling, complete with exaggerated gestures, had the audience laughing within moments. I found myself smiling, a warmth spreading through me, a reminder of the joy that could be found in vulnerability.

As her story concluded to wild applause, a sense of relief washed over me. It was like watching a dam break, releasing a flood of joy into the room. Mabel bounced on her toes, her eyes shining with pride. "See? You can do that! And think of all the good cookies we can make!"

The festival pulsed with life, and I felt the weight of my fears begin to lift, inch by inch. Perhaps I could join them, share my own words without the fear of judgment. The thought was intoxicating, and for a moment, I thought maybe I could.

"Okay, I'll go next!" I blurted out, the words escaping before I could fully grasp what I was saying. Mabel's eyes widened with excitement, and Sarah shot me a thumbs-up, her grin impossibly bright.

As I stepped to the front, I could feel the crowd's gaze like a gentle tide against my skin. My heart thudded against my ribs, a wild drum echoing in my ears. I looked out at the sea of faces, some familiar, some new, and felt the intensity of their attention wash over me. In that moment, the world around me began to blur, and all I could hear was the steady rhythm of my heart.

"Um, hi, everyone," I began, the words tumbling out like loose marbles. "So, I'm... uh... here to share a poem." I inhaled deeply, forcing my racing thoughts to coalesce into something coherent. "This one is about fears—like my fear of standing in front of you right now."

Laughter rippled through the crowd, and I found my footing amidst their warm response. "But also, about what happens when you let those fears speak, and how scary it can be to share your truth."

With each word, my nerves eased slightly, and I found the flow of my thoughts anchoring me, guiding me through the words I had penned in the solitude of my room. The poem unfurled, a delicate thread of vulnerability laced with humor, the kind that made people lean in closer as if they were discovering a secret. The rhythmic cadence of my voice began to weave a tapestry of connection, each line drawing the audience deeper into my world.

"Sometimes it's hard to show the things we hide, / To expose the frayed edges of our insides. / But in this little town, we all belong, / Together we'll sing our awkward song."

The crowd murmured in appreciation, and I caught sight of Mabel, her smile radiating pride like a lighthouse guiding a ship home. Encouragement buzzed in the air like the soft glow of the fairy lights overhead. It felt exhilarating to bare my soul, to pull back the curtain on my vulnerabilities while standing among people I cared for.

As I finished, a rush of applause erupted, drowning me in warmth. It was as if the town had wrapped its arms around me, squeezing tight in a way that made my heart swell. I stepped back from the podium, my cheeks flushed, a giddy mix of relief and exhilaration coursing through me.

"See? That wasn't so bad!" Mabel exclaimed, rushing to my side. "You were brilliant! Now we just need to keep this momentum going!"

Just as I was about to respond, an unexpected commotion broke out near the edge of the crowd. A group of strangers had appeared, their voices rising above the merriment, a sharp discord in the otherwise harmonious atmosphere. I turned to see a tall figure with an unmistakable demeanor, his posture rigid, face set in a scowl that could freeze a wildfire.

"Can you believe they're letting this nonsense happen in our town?" he bellowed, gesturing emphatically toward our booth. "What is this, some sort of joke?"

The crowd stilled, eyes darting between him and the festival, the laughter and joy draining like air from a balloon. My heart sank, a shadow creeping back over the bright night as I exchanged worried glances with Mabel and Sarah.

"Who does he think he is?" Sarah whispered, her expression a mix of shock and anger.

"I don't know, but this isn't good," I replied, feeling the tension rise, a storm brewing just beyond the surface.

Mabel stepped forward, her spirit still ablaze. "This is a celebration of our community! We're here to share stories, not to tear each other down."

The man sneered, eyes narrowing as he dismissed her with a wave of his hand. "Community? Ha! You're ruining what this town stands for. No one wants to hear your nonsense."

Anger flared within me, a fire igniting against the chill of his words. "We're creating something beautiful here! Sharing our voices matters!" I found myself stepping alongside Mabel, confronting the negativity head-on.

As the crowd began to murmur, I could feel the collective heartbeat of the town shifting, unity swelling amidst the rising tide of tension. But before I could grasp the direction this confrontation would take, a loud crash reverberated through the square—a toppled display table, books and papers scattering like fallen leaves.

In that moment, time slowed, and the night sky darkened with the weight of unspoken fears and unresolved conflicts. The sense of community was at a precipice, teetering on the brink of chaos. The storm wasn't just within me anymore; it had swept into the heart of our celebration, threatening to drown out the voices that had fought so hard to be heard.

And in that moment, as the tension thickened, I understood: the night was just beginning, and the real story was about to unfold.

Chapter 13: A Festival of Fear

The Harvest Festival bursts into life like a well-timed punchline, each element a flourish of color and sound, weaving through the air like a vibrant tapestry. Mabel's booth stands at the heart of it all, festooned with bright ribbons and twinkling fairy lights, the kind that seem to dance in tandem with the laughter of children darting past, sticky fingers clutching caramel apples that glisten in the waning sunlight. The scent of pumpkin spice wafts through the crowd, rich and inviting, stirring memories of childhoods spent huddled in cozy corners, far removed from the chaos that now thrums just outside.

Mabel, ever the enchantress, stands at the helm of her little kingdom, drawing in the curious and the lost with the flick of her wrist and the lilt of her voice. Her hair, a riot of curls that bounce with every enthusiastic gesture, catches the golden light, haloing her like some whimsical fairy godmother. She turns to me, her eyes sparkling with that familiar mischief, the kind that suggests she might just persuade a stone statue to join in the festivities.

"Come on, sis! You can't just hide behind me all night," she teases, leaning in closer, her voice a conspiratorial whisper amidst the cacophony. "They want to hear your story, too."

I offer a tight smile, feeling the edges of my resolve fray as I force myself to glance at the gathering crowd. They buzz like bees, swarming around Mabel's infectious enthusiasm, faces alight with wonder. My heart races, a frantic drumbeat echoing the unease knotting my stomach. The idea of sharing my own journey feels like standing at the edge of a cliff, the ground crumbling beneath my feet, the fall more exhilarating than terrifying yet riddled with the fear of what awaits below.

"Not today," I murmur, my voice almost lost in the laughter swirling around us. "I'm not ready." The words taste bitter, each syllable a reminder of the walls I've built.

But Mabel, ever the optimist, merely shakes her head, a playful grin stretching across her face. "You're stronger than you think, and your story deserves to be told. Plus, I'm pretty sure the crowd's dying to hear about the time you accidentally dressed as a scarecrow for Halloween!"

I roll my eyes, the familiar warmth of embarrassment flooding my cheeks. "That wasn't my fault! It was a mix-up at the thrift store. I ended up winning the contest, didn't I?"

"Only because everyone felt sorry for you!" Mabel cackles, a sound that makes heads turn and smiles broaden. "Just think of how fun it would be to share your version of it all. You're not just the scarecrow; you're the girl who turned a costume mishap into a victory lap."

As she continues to weave her magic, her laughter blending into the festival's symphony, I feel the weight of my own story settle heavily on my shoulders. The sensation is almost suffocating, like a thick fog closing in around me. I can feel Mabel's eyes on me, the unspoken challenge hanging between us like a delicate thread, ready to snap.

"Okay, maybe just a little," I finally relent, the words slipping out before I can fully consider their implications. A thrill of fear and excitement courses through me, a fraying rope taut with possibility. "But only if you help me!"

Mabel's grin widens, her eyes shining with glee. "That's the spirit! Just wait until they hear how you made that field of corn your personal catwalk. You'll have them rolling with laughter in no time."

I chuckle softly, imagining my clumsy attempts at posing amidst the tall stalks, the corn leaves scraping my skin, and the inevitable falls that left me laughing and covered in dirt. I pull the memory close, letting the warmth of laughter light a flicker of courage in my heart.

As the sun dips lower, painting the sky with hues of orange and pink, the air fills with the sound of laughter and music, the atmosphere charged with a palpable energy. The festival transforms, shadows creeping in to join the revelry, turning the vibrant fair into something more magical, almost otherworldly. I watch as families gather, children darting between legs, eyes wide with wonder, absorbing the spectacle unfolding before them. The night wraps itself around us like a cozy blanket, tucking us in, whispering secrets of the season.

With a deep breath, I step closer to the booth, my heart racing in sync with the pulse of the festival. The crowd buzzes with anticipation, and as Mabel gestures for me to join her, I take a tentative step forward.

"Alright, everyone!" she calls, her voice rising above the din. "Gather 'round! My sister has a story to tell!"

A ripple of excitement spreads through the crowd as I feel a rush of heat creep up my neck. I can't back out now. The air crackles with energy, the festival's glow illuminating faces eager to listen.

"Um, hi," I stammer, my voice wavering as I clasp my hands together, feeling the weight of their gaze. "So, there was this one time at a Halloween party..."

And just like that, the dam bursts, my voice rising and falling with the laughter and gasps that follow, as I find myself swept into the flow of my own narrative, buoyed by the collective breath of the crowd. Each word I share becomes a stepping stone, leading me further away from fear and closer to the joy that lives in sharing our stories.

The crowd swells, laughter bubbling around me like the sweet cider simmering at a nearby stall, mingling with the spicy notes of cinnamon that waft through the air. Mabel is in her element, spinning tales that draw gasps and giggles from her audience. With each flick of her wrist, she paints vivid images that dance in the minds of those gathered, their faces illuminated by the glow of hanging lanterns. I can't help but admire her gift, the way she effortlessly captures the hearts of everyone around her.

"Isn't she brilliant?" a voice pipes up, belonging to a young woman leaning against a nearby hay bale, a caramel apple poised dangerously close to her face. Her eyes shimmer with admiration, mirroring what I feel yet can't articulate. "I could listen to her all night!"

"Right?" I reply, a hint of pride slipping into my tone. "She's like a bard of the harvest, spinning tales that even the pumpkins must envy." My attempt at humor earns me a chuckle from the woman, and I feel a spark of encouragement flicker to life within me. Maybe this isn't just a stage for Mabel; perhaps it can be a platform for me as well.

Mabel catches my eye again, her gaze steady and encouraging, and for a moment, I almost forget the fear clawing at my insides. "Don't just stand there, sister. Come join me!" she beckons, her voice laced with that familiar teasing edge. I can feel the warmth of the crowd, an almost tangible wave of support washing over me.

Taking a deep breath, I step into the spotlight. "So, about that time I turned a Halloween party into a scarecrow fashion show…" I start, my voice trembling slightly at first, then gathering momentum as I lean into the absurdity of it all. I recount the chaotic evening, the laughter bubbling up in the telling, and as I describe my makeshift costume—a tattered plaid shirt with hay poking out at odd angles—the audience erupts in laughter, their delight becoming a balm for my nerves.

"Did you really think a pair of rubber boots would make you look fashionable?" Mabel interjects, her laughter infectious. "You ended up looking more like a trendy farmer than a scarecrow!"

I smirk, leaning into the banter. "I was going for chic rustic! Clearly, the vision was lost on most." The laughter grows, and for the first time, I feel the weight of my sister's encouragement lift my spirits. Sharing my story becomes a dance, the rhythm of our dialogue flowing effortlessly as I lean into the connection forming with the crowd.

Yet, beneath the laughter, an undercurrent of tension hums, as if the festival itself holds its breath in anticipation. The joyous atmosphere is tinged with a strange thrill, and I can't shake the feeling that something is waiting just beneath the surface. A glance at Mabel reveals a slight furrow in her brow, her laughter more forced as the night wears on. I wonder if she feels it too—an inexplicable pull that seems to whisper promises and threats in equal measure.

As I conclude my story, the applause washes over me like a warm tide, and I revel in the moment, the sweet taste of acceptance lifting my spirits higher than I thought possible. Mabel squeezes my hand, her eyes sparkling with pride. "See? You were amazing! Who knew scarecrows could steal the spotlight?"

"Right? Move over, Mabel. I might just take over your booth," I quip, nudging her playfully. But beneath the jest, a flicker of doubt creeps in, reminding me that sharing my story was only the first step.

The festival continues to unfold around us, music swelling in the background, mingling with the joyful shouts of children playing games. I spot a couple dancing under the stars, their movements weaving a narrative of their own, and I feel an ache of longing stir within me. The kind of longing that whispers of missed moments and lost connections, stirring memories I'd rather keep buried.

"Hey, I'll be right back," I tell Mabel, my voice barely above the din. She nods, her focus already on the next eager crowd forming at our booth. I slip away, drawn by the music and laughter spilling from a nearby bonfire.

The glow of the flames casts flickering shadows that dance like specters around the edges of my mind. I find a spot at the edge of the gathering, where the light bathes everything in a golden hue. People are sharing ghost stories, their voices rising and falling with the crackling of the fire. Each tale carries a weight of mystery, a haunting beauty that draws me in, tethering me to this moment.

As the storyteller shares an eerie account of the legend of Old Man Simmons, who wandered the woods and never returned, I can't help but feel the hairs on the back of my neck stand on end. It's a perfect blend of suspense and nostalgia, a reminder of the fears that have shaped us all. But beneath the thrill of the story, I sense an energy—a palpable tension that seems to dance in the air.

Suddenly, the storyteller pauses, glancing over my shoulder. "And they say, if you listen closely, you can hear the whispers of those who were lost..." His voice trails off, leaving the crowd in rapt silence. I turn to see what has captured his attention, and my heart stutters as I spot a figure lurking at the fringes of the firelight, half-hidden in shadow.

My pulse quickens, a mix of intrigue and apprehension swirling within me. The figure seems to shimmer at the edges, as if caught between this world and another, and a sense of foreboding washes over the crowd. The warmth of the festival feels distant now, the laughter fading as the tension builds like an impending storm.

"What is that?" a voice whispers from beside me, barely audible over the crackling flames. I can feel the collective breath of the crowd, the shift from joy to unease. The figure takes a step forward, revealing a hooded cloak that sways with a ghostly grace, and the air grows colder, wrapping around us like a chilling embrace.

Mabel's laughter rings in my ears, a distant echo of warmth amidst the gathering storm, and I realize that the night has shifted, and we're no longer just participants in a festival; we are now part of something larger, something that stirs the edges of our fear and beckons us to confront it. The joy that once bubbled through me now collides with a growing uncertainty, and I find myself standing on the precipice of a new story, one that promises to test everything I thought I knew about fear, courage, and the bonds that hold us together.

The figure in the shadows steps closer, illuminated briefly by the flickering bonfire, revealing a face that seems both familiar and foreign. My heart races, a wild drumbeat echoing in my chest as recognition dances at the edges of my consciousness. It's as if I've stumbled upon an old photograph, the edges worn and frayed, the memory barely holding together. The crowd stirs, a ripple of nervous energy cascading through them, and I can feel the air thicken with an electric charge.

"Who are you?" someone finally calls out, breaking the heavy silence that had enveloped us. The figure straightens, the hood slipping back just enough to reveal a shock of tousled hair that glints like silver under the firelight. The moment stretches, fraught with tension, and I feel every breath held tight in collective anticipation.

"I am a traveler," the figure replies, their voice smooth yet haunting, carrying a cadence that sends shivers down my spine. "A keeper of stories and secrets. But tonight, I come with a warning."

The atmosphere shifts again, laughter from earlier evaporating into the chill of the night, replaced by a curiosity mixed with apprehension. "A warning? What kind of warning?" I find myself asking, my voice firm despite the fluttering in my stomach.

"There are things that lie beneath the surface of this festival," the traveler continues, glancing at the swirling leaves dancing in the night air. "Things that thrive on the fears you harbor, the fears you try to ignore. Tonight, they awaken."

A murmur of unease spreads through the crowd, and I feel my heart thump harder, a palpable echo of the words just spoken. My mind races, a chaotic whirlwind of thoughts crashing together.

Could this be just a clever ruse, a staged performance meant to heighten the festival's allure? Or is there a grain of truth in the traveler's ominous proclamation?

Mabel's voice cuts through the tension like a warm knife through butter, a playful edge masked beneath concern. "I mean, I've heard of some pretty weird things happening at festivals, but this is a whole new level of dramatic, don't you think?" Her attempt at levity draws a few nervous chuckles, but it does little to quell the unease coiling in my gut.

The traveler, unperturbed, locks eyes with me, their gaze penetrating as if peeling back the layers I've carefully constructed. "You carry the weight of your own fear, don't you?" They lean closer, their voice dropping to a conspiratorial whisper. "What are you afraid of, really?"

I swallow hard, caught off guard by their insight. The words swirl around me, tightening like a noose. It feels as though they can see right through the facade I've so painstakingly crafted, the doubts and insecurities I've buried deep. I've spent so long avoiding the truth, and now, standing here under the scrutiny of both the crowd and this mysterious figure, I feel exposed.

But before I can answer, a gust of wind sweeps through, knocking over a stack of hay bales nearby, sending a shiver through the crowd. Gasps rise into the night, the fire sputters, casting shadows that flicker like anxious spirits. The traveler smirks, a knowing glint in their eye. "Fear is not just a feeling; it's a force, and it can take on a life of its own."

The darkness seems to press in closer, the joyous atmosphere of the festival giving way to something more sinister. The laughter now feels distant, like a fading echo, replaced by the heavy silence that blankets us. I turn to Mabel, seeking the comfort of her presence, but she stands frozen, eyes wide, caught between fascination and dread.

"Mabel?" I say, my voice trembling. "Are you okay?"

She nods slowly, though the color has drained from her face. "I just... I feel like we should leave. Now."

The urgency in her tone snaps me back into the moment. I glance back at the traveler, who watches us with an almost predatory interest. "It's too late to leave," they say, their voice a low murmur, laced with an eerie calm. "You're already part of the story."

My heart pounds in my chest as I feel the collective gaze of the crowd shift, all eyes on us now. Whispers swirl like the autumn leaves, curling around my thoughts, drowning out reason. "What do you mean we're part of the story?" I demand, though the tremor in my voice betrays my fear.

"Fear is a powerful storyteller," the traveler replies, stepping back as the shadows deepen around us. "And it feeds on your doubt, your insecurities. It draws in the lost and the wandering, and soon, the festival will be a canvas for its tales."

Before I can process the weight of their words, the bonfire flickers violently, sending sparks cascading into the night sky, each one bursting like a firework, the brilliant glow illuminating faces twisted in confusion. The ground beneath us rumbles slightly, a low growl that reverberates through the very air, igniting a spark of panic in the crowd.

"Did you feel that?" someone shouts, their voice cracking with fear. "What's happening?"

"I don't know," I reply, turning to Mabel, who looks at me with a mixture of determination and terror. "We need to find a way out of here."

But just as we begin to move, a shadow looms larger, towering over us like a dark specter. The traveler stands resolute, their voice steady yet laced with urgency. "To confront your fear, you must first understand it. There's power in embracing the unknown."

"Unknown?" I repeat, my voice barely above a whisper. "You mean like whatever is lurking in those shadows?"

"Yes, but more importantly, what's lurking in your mind." They gesture towards the festival, where the laughter has turned to murmurs of uncertainty. "Face it now, or be consumed by it later."

A chill races down my spine as the reality of their words sinks in. The shadows around us pulse, shifting as if alive, and I can feel the very ground beneath my feet trembling in anticipation.

"Stay together!" Mabel shouts, gripping my hand tightly as we instinctively move closer to each other. The crowd begins to scatter, panic sparking like dry tinder. The warmth of the festival feels like a distant memory as dread creeps in like an unwelcome guest, wrapping itself around us.

"Embrace your fear, or it will consume you," the traveler warns, their voice echoing like a haunting melody. I can feel the weight of their gaze, the insistence that I confront what I've tried so desperately to avoid.

I take a deep breath, the air heavy with uncertainty. "What if we don't want to be part of this story?"

But the traveler only smiles, a knowing glimmer in their eye as the night seems to draw closer, wrapping around us like a cloak. "Oh, but you already are. The night has just begun."

As the festival devolves into chaos, I grasp Mabel's hand tighter, the warmth of her skin a lifeline in the dark. The shadows writhe, and the ground shakes beneath us, drawing us toward an unknown fate that looms just beyond the flickering flames. In that moment, with fear coursing through my veins, I realize we stand at a crossroads where choices and consequences entwine, and the thrill of uncertainty pulls me forward, into the darkness.

Chapter 14: Bursting the Bubble

The room hums with an electric tension, the air thick with a mingling of nervous energy and the scent of stale coffee from the cups lining the tables. Mabel stands beside me, her presence a steady anchor against the tide of emotions swirling inside me. I can feel her unwavering belief in me like a warm blanket, urging me to step into the spotlight. My heart races, and as I glance at the audience, a ragtag collection of faces reflecting every shade of curiosity, I know there's no turning back. In that moment, spontaneity overrides hesitation, and with a deep breath, I take a step forward.

"Here goes nothing," I murmur under my breath, but the words feel like a battle cry instead of a whisper. The chatter fades as I begin to speak, my voice breaking the silence like glass shattering underfoot. I don't care about being perfect or polished; this is my story, and I'm done hiding it.

"I never thought I'd be here," I start, feeling the weight of every word. "If you had told me a year ago that I would be standing in front of all of you, sharing my deepest fears and failures, I would have laughed in your face. Hard." A few chuckles ripple through the crowd, the ice beginning to thaw. I pause, letting the laughter linger like a promise of camaraderie. "But here I am, living proof that life can throw you curveballs you never see coming."

As I delve deeper into my past, the words come tumbling out, raw and unfiltered. I recount my turbulent relationship with my sister, the one person who should have been my biggest supporter but instead became the catalyst for my deepest insecurities. My voice shakes as I describe the moment she moved away, leaving behind a void so vast I couldn't even begin to fill it. "We had our differences," I say, my heart aching at the memory. "But I always thought we'd figure it out. That she'd be my forever partner in crime."

I glance around, taking in the sea of faces. The audience leans in, rapt with attention, and I see tears glistening in the eyes of those who've been through their own struggles. It's in this shared vulnerability that I realize I'm not alone. My story, once steeped in shame, now serves as a bridge connecting me to each of them.

"Honestly, I used to think I was the odd one out," I continue, finding my rhythm. "The quirky sister who never quite fit into the mold. But then I realized, fitting in is overrated. It's far more interesting to stand out, to embrace every bizarre quirk that makes us human." Laughter erupts, and I bask in it, feeling the warmth of their understanding wrap around me.

The air shifts as I dive into the darker corners of my journey—the moments of despair when I felt lost, as though I were wading through a murky swamp with no solid ground in sight. "There were days when getting out of bed felt like climbing Everest. I lost touch with who I was, drowning in a sea of 'shoulds' and 'coulds.'" My voice softens, tinged with the weight of honesty. "But in that darkness, I found something unexpected. A flicker of resilience I didn't know I had. And that flicker... it grew into a flame."

The audience is with me now, nodding in solidarity, their own experiences echoing in the space between my words. I see the moments of recognition—the smiles, the tears, the deep, knowing glances. It's as if I've peeled back a layer of armor, exposing the raw, beating heart beneath.

"Then there's Mabel," I say, a smile creeping onto my lips at the thought of her. "She waltzed into my life with her boundless energy and a penchant for terrible puns. Seriously, I think she could single-handedly revive the dad joke industry." Laughter erupts again, and I can see Mabel beaming in the corner, her eyes twinkling with mischief.

"But beyond the jokes, she's been my lifeline. She showed me that vulnerability isn't a weakness; it's a superpower. It takes courage to stand in your truth, to bare your soul, and it's something we should celebrate, not shy away from." I catch Mabel's eye, a silent exchange of gratitude passing between us.

As I approach the end of my story, I feel the tension in the room shift, morphing into something lighter, something hopeful. "So here I am, a work in progress," I say, my voice steady and strong. "And I'm okay with that. I'm learning to embrace the chaos and dance in the rain, one quirky step at a time."

The applause that follows is thunderous, a wave of warmth washing over me. I stand there, breathless and exposed, but instead of fear, I feel an undeniable surge of strength. The crowd's response is a balm to my soul, igniting something within me—a glimmer of hope that maybe, just maybe, I can rediscover happiness in the midst of life's beautiful messiness.

As the clapping dies down, I scan the room and see smiles, nods, and even a few people dabbing at their eyes. In that moment, I realize I'm not just telling my story; I'm inviting everyone to join me in the messy, wonderful dance of life. I take a deep breath, allowing the laughter and warmth to cradle me, knowing I've stepped out of my comfort zone and into something far more meaningful—a connection forged in vulnerability, a celebration of resilience.

As the applause reverberates through the room, I feel a strange mix of exhilaration and disbelief. Mabel's enthusiastic clapping rings out above the rest, her hands moving with the fervor of a marching band conductor. I can't help but smile at her infectious energy; it's the kind of encouragement that makes you feel invincible, even if just for a moment. I stand tall, soaking in the warmth radiating from the audience, their faces glowing with newfound understanding.

Yet, amidst this beautiful moment, a small voice in my head whispers doubts that bubble beneath the surface. Was I too much? Too raw? I shake my head, pushing those thoughts aside like fallen leaves in a brisk wind. The truth is, I've spent far too long being the keeper of my own secrets, and I'm finally beginning to see the light. Mabel nudges me playfully, breaking through my spiraling thoughts. "See? You were amazing! I told you those words of yours would make them weep."

"Or maybe they were just laughing at my terrible jokes," I reply, feigning a dramatic sigh. "The only thing that might keep me from becoming a professional comedian."

"Oh, don't sell yourself short. The world needs more humor, especially when it's coming from a bright, shiny mess like you." She winks, and I can't help but laugh. Mabel has this way of making every insecurity feel like a minor inconvenience, easily brushed aside with a well-timed joke.

I step down from the makeshift stage, my legs tingling with the residual adrenaline, and the chatter begins to fill the air once more. The crowd disperses, but a few stragglers linger, approaching me with smiles and gentle words. Each connection is a small thread weaving a tapestry of shared experiences. I'm reminded that vulnerability isn't merely a personal act; it's a communal experience, a dance of hearts and minds.

A woman with soft brown eyes and a comforting demeanor approaches first. "Thank you for sharing your story. I could relate to so much of what you said about family. My sister and I are like oil and water." She chuckles, and I see the warmth behind her laughter. "We love each other fiercely, but sometimes it feels like we're in separate orbits."

"I completely understand," I reply, my heart swelling with empathy. "Sometimes it's as if we're speaking different languages, even when we're in the same room."

Her nod of understanding feels like a gentle affirmation, and I find myself enveloped in an unexpected camaraderie. The conversation flows easily, shifting from shared struggles to laughter over our most ridiculous family gatherings. It's liberating to connect in such an authentic way, and I realize how refreshing it feels to peel back the layers of pretense that often shroud our lives.

Mabel bounces over, grabbing my arm and pulling me away from the small group. "Let's get out of here for a bit," she says, her eyes dancing with mischief. "I have a surprise."

"A surprise? What kind of surprise?" I can't help but feel a rush of curiosity mixed with trepidation. Mabel's surprises tend to be wildly unpredictable, and half the time I end up with a story I'm not sure I'm ready to tell.

"You'll see!" she insists, leading me through the crowd, weaving past familiar faces and unfamiliar strangers alike. We slip out into the crisp evening air, the moon a glowing crescent hanging low in the sky. The chill is invigorating, sharpening my senses and making me feel alive.

Mabel pulls me down a narrow alley, illuminated by soft, flickering lights. The aroma of something sweet wafts through the air, and my stomach grumbles in agreement. "What are we doing, Mabel?"

"Trust me," she says, a twinkle in her eye. "You'll love this."

Moments later, we arrive at a tiny dessert shop tucked between two larger buildings, its sign hanging askew but exuding a charm that makes my heart flutter. The place is decorated with twinkling fairy lights, and the display case is filled with an assortment of decadent pastries. My mouth waters at the sight.

"What is this place?" I ask, my voice barely above a whisper.

"It's my little secret. I come here to indulge when I need to celebrate life, or when I'm feeling particularly melancholy. Tonight, we're celebrating you," she says with a grin, her enthusiasm infectious.

We step inside, the bell above the door jingling softly, and I'm immediately enveloped by the warm, sugary scent that wraps around me like a cozy blanket. "Okay, I'll have whatever you're having," I declare, feeling lighter than I have in ages.

"Good choice!" Mabel exclaims, pointing to a whimsical-looking dessert that resembles a miniature mountain range topped with whipped cream and drizzled with chocolate. "That's the 'Sierra Surprise.' It's rumored to be a mood booster."

"Sounds like something I need," I chuckle, but deep down, I realize that the real mood booster is Mabel's unwavering support and the warmth of the connections I made tonight.

As we settle at a small table, our desserts in front of us, Mabel leans in, her expression turning serious. "You know, tonight was a big step for you, right?"

"Yeah, I guess so." I push a spoonful of the decadent dessert into my mouth, and it's like a burst of happiness explodes on my taste buds.

"It was more than that. You opened up in a way that can change everything," she continues, her eyes serious but filled with warmth. "You're not just a quirky mess. You're a force of nature, and I want you to own that."

"Easy for you to say. You're not the one spilling your guts on a stage." I poke at my dessert, suddenly feeling the weight of her words settle heavily on my shoulders.

"Yes, but you did it. You took the leap, and now the net is there. You're going to soar," Mabel insists, leaning back in her chair with an air of confidence that makes me want to believe her.

We clink our forks together like we're toasting to something monumental, and as I savor another bite of the 'Sierra Surprise,' I can't help but feel a shift within myself. In that moment, amidst the sweet chaos of life, I understand that the true adventure is just beginning.

Sinking my fork into the remaining mountains of the 'Sierra Surprise,' I feel an overwhelming sense of gratitude wash over me. The sweet, velvety cream drips down the sides, pooling on the plate like happy little puddles. Mabel watches me with an amused smile, her eyes sparkling with mischief. "You look like you've just discovered the meaning of life," she teases, leaning back in her chair as if she's about to deliver the most profound of wisdoms.

"Maybe I have! It's sugar," I reply, savoring another bite. "It really is the secret to everything." The laughter between us flows easily, creating an invisible thread binding our friendship even tighter. I glance around the dessert shop, taking in the vibrant murals painted on the walls—bright swirls of color that dance around the rustic, wooden beams overhead. Each detail breathes life into the small space, and I feel a flicker of hope that maybe, just maybe, I'm beginning to embrace the chaos of my own life, too.

As we continue to indulge in our sweet treats, the conversation shifts from light banter to deeper reflections. Mabel shares her own stories of triumph and defeat, revealing her struggles with self-doubt and the fear that lurked in the shadows, waiting to pounce when she least expected it. "You'd think I was the one without a care in the world, always the life of the party," she says, shaking her head. "But inside, I was a tangled mess of insecurities."

"Really?" I ask, raising an eyebrow. "I find that hard to believe. You seem so... well, put together."

"Ah, the magic of good mascara and well-timed jokes," she quips, flashing me a grin that is equal parts playful and genuine. "But seriously, everyone has their battles. Yours just happens to be a little louder than mine."

Our laughter mingles with the comforting buzz of the shop, a symphony of voices and clinking silverware. Each chuckle feels like a step towards forging an unshakeable bond, and I realize how much I've come to rely on Mabel's unwavering support. It's like discovering a wellspring of encouragement that I never knew existed, bubbling up to the surface when I needed it most.

As the clock ticks closer to closing time, the shop begins to empty, and the staff starts cleaning up, dimming the lights slightly. I glance at Mabel, who seems lost in thought. "What's on your mind?" I ask, my curiosity piqued.

"Oh, you know, the usual," she replies, twirling her fork absentmindedly. "Just contemplating the mysteries of the universe, like why I always end up dating guys who are allergic to commitment."

I chuckle, recognizing the truth in her words. "It's a conspiracy, I swear. They must have a secret club or something."

"But hey," she adds, suddenly serious, "what about you? What's next for you after tonight? You really opened up in front of everyone. What are you going to do with that newfound courage?"

The question hangs in the air like the lingering aroma of pastries, and I can feel the weight of her inquiry pressing down on me. What was next? The thought of venturing into uncharted territory sends a thrill coursing through my veins. "I think I want to keep sharing my story. I want to help others feel less alone, maybe start a blog or something," I confess, surprised at the confidence in my own voice.

Mabel's eyes light up. "That's brilliant! You should totally do it. There are so many people out there looking for a connection, a lifeline, and you could be that for them."

As we finish our desserts, a sense of possibility envelops me, warming me from the inside out. Maybe this is the start of something new, a chapter yet to be written. My mind races with ideas and visions of what could be, and for the first time in a long while, I feel hopeful.

We step outside, and the cool night air is invigorating, wrapping around us like a gentle hug. Mabel turns to me, her expression softening. "You know, you've come so far. I'm really proud of you."

"Thanks, Mabel. I couldn't have done it without you. You've been my cheerleader through all this."

"Just doing my job," she replies with a wink, but her eyes shimmer with sincerity.

As we stroll down the sidewalk, the city around us twinkling with life, a sudden noise disrupts the serenity. A cacophony of shouting erupts from a nearby alley, the sound jagged and alarming. Mabel freezes, her eyes widening. "Did you hear that?"

Before I can answer, a figure bursts from the shadows of the alley, stumbling into view. He's disheveled, his clothes torn, and his face is a canvas of fear and desperation. "Help! Please!" he gasps, his breath ragged as he stumbles toward us, panic etched in every line of his face.

"What happened?" Mabel steps forward instinctively, her protective instincts kicking in.

"They're after me! I—I can't go back!" He looks over his shoulder, his eyes darting wildly.

"Mabel, maybe we should call the police?" I suggest, my heart racing with both fear and intrigue.

"No! No police!" he cries, his voice tinged with urgency. "They'll find me if you call them. Please, I just need a place to hide for a moment."

The weight of his plea hangs heavily between us, and I can feel my pulse quickening, the adrenaline surging through my veins. Mabel and I exchange a glance, an unspoken understanding passing between us. This night, filled with laughter and hope, has suddenly taken a dark turn.

"Okay," Mabel says, her voice steady despite the chaos around us. "We'll help you. Just tell us what we need to do."

Before I can comprehend the gravity of the situation, I feel the world around me tilt as the alley looms ominously behind him. The air thickens, charged with an unsettling tension, and the night suddenly feels darker than before. What have we stepped into? I can't shake the feeling that our lives are about to change in ways I could never have anticipated.

Chapter 15: Whispered Confessions

The night air is thick with the scent of popcorn and the faint waft of cotton candy, mixing in a way that feels almost magical under the soft glow of fairy lights strung between trees. The laughter of festival-goers drifts like music, vibrant and alive, yet here we are, ensconced in our own little universe. I can hear Mabel's breath catch slightly as I recount my spontaneous moment on stage, the crowd's cheers still ringing in my ears, a euphoric echo that dances around us like fireflies in the dusk.

"It was incredible," I say, the memory igniting my senses. "I never thought I'd have the guts to do it, you know? One minute I was standing there, clutching my drink like a lifeline, and the next, I was up there singing like I belonged."

Mabel laughs, a sound that feels like the sweetest melody I've ever known. Her eyes glimmer in the low light, a shade of warmth that rivals the lanterns hanging overhead. "I wish I could have seen it. I'm sure the crowd went wild," she teases, nudging my shoulder with her own. The light touch sends a pleasant jolt through me, grounding me in the moment.

"Oh, they did!" I lean in, sharing the thrilling details, the way my heart raced like a runaway train, each beat echoing in time with the melody. "But the real rush was when I spotted you in the front row, your face lit up like you'd just won the lottery. It made me feel invincible."

"Invincible, huh?" she replies, raising an eyebrow in that playful way she always does when she's teasing. "So, does that mean I'm the secret to your superpowers?"

"Maybe. But be careful, Mabel. I might just make you my sidekick," I say, grinning as I take a sip from my cup, trying to hide the way my pulse quickens at the thought of us becoming something more than just friends.

As I talk, the world around us fades into a haze of color and sound, the laughter of others growing distant, as if we've carved out a niche in the chaos. The warm evening wraps around us like a blanket, shielding us from the outside world and allowing this moment to linger, to deepen.

I notice how the shadows play across her face, accentuating the curve of her smile, the way her hair catches the light just so, framing her features like a halo. It's intoxicating, the way she looks at me, as if I'm more than just a person; I'm a puzzle she's eager to solve.

"Let's talk about you, then," I say, shifting the spotlight back to her, wanting to know what fires burn beneath her calm exterior. "You've been a quiet force of nature tonight, and I want to know your secret."

She takes a moment, her gaze drifting to the stars, which twinkle like little pinpricks of magic against the deep indigo sky. "There's nothing secretive about me," she replies, her voice soft but layered with a hint of mischief. "I just prefer to let the fireworks happen around me."

"Ah, a classic wallflower! But you're more than that. You have a whole constellation of talent up your sleeves," I say, genuinely curious. The way she lights up when she talks about her passions—a small art project, her secret baking endeavors, or her occasional forays into photography—makes me want to know every detail.

"Maybe," she muses, a playful lilt in her voice. "But I guess I'm just waiting for my moment. Like you had yours tonight."

I nod, the weight of her words settling in, mingling with the thrill of my performance. "You deserve that moment, Mabel. It's out there, just waiting for you to claim it."

The atmosphere shifts, a tension hanging in the air, thickening with unspoken words. My heart pounds as I lean in, the distance between us shrinking like the space on a crowded dance floor. There's an electricity crackling in the air, and before I fully register the impulse, I find myself brushing my lips against hers, tentative at first, tasting sweetness and a hint of uncertainty.

It feels surreal, like I'm kissing the stars themselves. The world around us blurs, fading into a gentle hum, and I lose myself in the warmth of her presence. As the kiss deepens, igniting a fire within me that had been smoldering for too long, I let go of the panic that often clings to me. This is what I've wanted, what I've yearned for, and it feels breathtakingly right.

But just as everything aligns, that familiar rush of fear swells in my chest, a sudden tide pulling me back from the precipice of something new. I pull away, a wave of anxiety crashing over me as I struggle to breathe. "Mabel, I—"

"What's wrong?" Her brow furrows slightly, concern etching lines across her forehead. I can see the way she searches my eyes, trying to decipher the mix of emotions swirling within.

"I didn't mean to— I just got caught up in the moment," I stammer, words tumbling out before I can catch them. The joy of the festival, the connection between us, all of it feels fragile, like a soap bubble that might burst with the slightest prick.

"You kissed me," she states simply, her voice steady. "That seems pretty intentional."

"I know. But everything is changing so fast, and I—" I struggle to articulate the fear creeping in, the worry that I'm stepping into a territory where I might lose everything if I misstep.

Mabel tilts her head slightly, her expression softening. "What are you afraid of?" she asks, and it's not just a question; it's an invitation to be vulnerable, to peel back the layers of my guarded heart.

"Of this," I say, gesturing vaguely between us, the sky stretching above like a canvas yet to be painted. "Of us. I've always been... cautious, you know? What if I ruin everything?"

She moves closer, her eyes sparkling like the stars we sit beneath. "Maybe it's worth the risk. Maybe you won't."

For a heartbeat, silence reigns, filled only by the soft sounds of the festival drifting from afar, echoing the uncertainty that now hangs between us.

The silence stretches, charged with an unspoken energy, and I can feel the warmth radiating from Mabel as if it could chase away the chill of uncertainty creeping in. "You know," she says slowly, her voice a tender brush against the stillness, "if you're waiting for the perfect moment to happen, you might be waiting forever."

Her words hang in the air like a challenge, teasing at the edges of my carefully constructed defenses. "Is that what this is? A perfect moment?" I ask, the wryness in my voice barely disguising my trepidation. "Because I've never been good at being perfect."

"Good thing we're not aiming for perfection then," she replies, her smile softening the blow of my insecurities. "We're aiming for real, and that's far more interesting."

There's something in her tone, a spark that draws me in and propels me forward. The festival sounds blur into a distant symphony, but here, under the vast sky, it's just us, cocooned in our own little world. My heart races, not just from the kiss we shared but from the intoxicating thrill of possibility. What if I could allow myself to embrace this uncertainty? What if I could leap into whatever this is with both feet?

But then the inevitable voice of doubt crashes through my thoughts, a dissonant note in this otherwise harmonious night. "And if it doesn't work out?" I whisper, the fear spilling from my lips like a confession. "What if I screw things up and ruin everything we have?"

"Everything we have?" Mabel's eyebrows dance upwards, a flicker of mischief illuminating her expression. "You make it sound like we've built an empire together."

"Isn't it? We've built this—whatever this is," I gesture broadly, my arm sweeping over the expanse of the festival, the lights twinkling like our shared laughter. "You've been my anchor, and now I'm afraid to set sail."

Her laughter spills out, bright and unfiltered. "You're dramatic. But I like it," she says, the teasing glint in her eyes making it impossible for me to hold on to my anxious thoughts. "Look, no one said it would be easy. But isn't it worth a little chaos for something real?"

The challenge in her voice rekindles my earlier exhilaration, igniting a flicker of courage deep within. "Maybe you're right. Chaos does have a certain charm to it," I admit, a hesitant smile breaking through my initial panic. "I just don't want to mess things up for you."

"Oh, honey," she replies, the warmth of her voice wrapping around me like a soft blanket. "The only thing you could mess up is this perfect moment we're sharing. So, stop thinking so much and just... be."

"Be?" I echo, the word lingering in the air, heavy with meaning. It sounds so simple, yet it feels monumental, an invitation to relinquish control and lean into the unknown. I take a deep breath, filling my lungs with the sweet, crisp air of the night, allowing the tension to slowly unwind within me. "All right then, let's just be."

Before I can overthink it, I reach for her hand, intertwining our fingers. Her skin is warm against mine, a grounding sensation that sends delightful shivers through me. I study her face, the way the light dances in her eyes, and for a moment, I feel the swirling chaos of the world around us fade into a quiet hum.

"You know," Mabel begins, her gaze shifting to the horizon, "sometimes I think the universe conspires to bring people together in the most unexpected ways. Like a cosmic matchmaking service."

"Ah, so you believe in fate? A starry-eyed romantic, are we?" I tease, nudging her shoulder gently.

"Maybe," she concedes, her eyes sparkling like the stars overhead. "Or maybe I just like to imagine that there's a little magic in the air. Like tonight. We could've easily missed each other at the festival, but here we are, under the stars, talking about life and dreams."

"That's a good point," I say, pausing to savor the sweetness of the moment. "And we've got a good view of the cosmos too. There's something comforting about being so small in the grand scheme of things, isn't there?"

"Very comforting," she replies, the softness in her voice intertwining with the gentle breeze. "Like a reminder that no matter how heavy things feel, there's a whole universe out there, vast and open."

I look up at the star-studded sky, and for the first time, I feel a sense of belonging, as if each star is a possibility waiting to be explored. The weight of my worries begins to lift, and I find myself chuckling softly at my earlier fears. "Maybe I could use some of that cosmic magic in my life," I admit.

Mabel turns to face me, her expression shifting to something more serious, yet gentle. "You already have it, you know. Just look at how far you've come tonight."

"True," I say, recalling the rush of emotions from the stage. "It's just the aftermath that has me a little dizzy. It's overwhelming to think about what's next."

"Then take it one step at a time," she advises, her thumb tracing small circles on my palm, grounding me. "We'll figure it out together. You've got me on your side. You're not alone in this."

Her words wrap around me like a warm embrace, easing the lingering tension in my chest. "You really mean that?" I ask, the vulnerability in my voice surprising even me.

"Absolutely," she affirms, her gaze steady and sincere. "And you can't scare me off that easily. Just know that whatever happens, I'll be here."

The promise in her voice sends ripples of warmth through me, and I can't help but lean in closer, feeling the magnetic pull between us. "Well, then," I say, a spark of mischief igniting in my tone, "I guess I'd better make sure I'm worth the risk, huh?"

Mabel smirks, her eyes gleaming with that playful challenge I've come to adore. "Oh, I have no doubt you're worth it. Just remember to keep the drama to a minimum."

"Drama? Me? Never," I retort, my voice dripping with feigned innocence. "But I might have a few surprises up my sleeve."

"Surprises?" she repeats, her brow arched in mock skepticism. "Now I'm intrigued. What kind of surprises are we talking about?"

I lean back slightly, a smirk playing on my lips. "The kind that may or may not involve spontaneous dance parties in the middle of the street."

"Oh, well, now I'm definitely in!" Mabel exclaims, laughter spilling from her lips like music. "Let's make some memories worth remembering."

And just like that, the tension shifts, morphing into something lighter, infused with hope and laughter. It feels like a delicate balance, a dance between what is and what could be, and for the first time, I'm ready to step into the unknown, hand in hand with the girl who makes chaos feel like home.

The moment lingers between us, heavy with uncharted possibilities, and I'm still reeling from the warmth of her lips against mine. Mabel's breath quickens slightly, her eyes wide as if she's trying to decode the whirlwind of emotions swirling between us. "So, this is where we're at now?" she asks, her tone playful yet probing, a hint of challenge lacing her words.

"Maybe," I reply, my heart racing. "Unless I've completely misread the moment."

"Oh, don't worry," she says, laughter bubbling beneath her breath. "You've definitely read it correctly. But I didn't think we were getting into a relationship analysis quite yet."

"Who needs a relationship analysis when we have this?" I gesture to the festival still buzzing with life around us, the sounds of laughter and distant music like a heartbeat. "It's like we've got our own little universe right here."

"I like that," she replies, her gaze drifting back to the stars, their shimmer reminding me of the spark ignited between us. "A universe just for us. But remember, every universe has its quirks. For instance, I tend to be a bit of a troublemaker."

"Troublemaker?" I feign shock, pressing a hand to my chest. "What kind of trouble could you possibly cause?"

"Let's just say I have a knack for making things interesting," she says, her smile mischievous. "And I might drag you along for the ride."

"I'm not sure I'm ready for the kind of trouble you bring," I joke, feigning wariness, but the fluttering in my stomach suggests I'm ready for anything as long as it includes her.

"Ready or not, I think you're already on board," she counters, her gaze penetrating, daring me to commit. "Besides, we're in this cosmic dance together now. Might as well see where it takes us."

"Is that how you see it? A dance?" I ask, a grin creeping onto my face.

"It's the perfect analogy," she replies, her eyes twinkling with enthusiasm. "Two people moving in sync, even if they occasionally step on each other's toes."

I chuckle, the tension from moments before fading like mist in the sunlight. "Well, I can promise I'm not the best dancer. But if we're going to trip over each other, at least we'll do it with style."

She leans in closer, her shoulder brushing against mine. "Style is key," she whispers, a conspiratorial glint in her eyes. "And we can always make it more interesting with a little adventure."

"Adventure?" I echo, intrigued. "Like what? What's on your agenda?"

"Let's sneak into the photo booth and take some ridiculous pictures. I want to see you in a pirate hat and an inflatable parrot."

"A pirate hat?" I laugh, the absurdity making me grin. "Okay, now you're just pushing it. But I'm in if it means spending more time with you."

"Deal!" she exclaims, her excitement contagious as she grabs my hand and pulls me up from our cozy spot. I'm still buzzing from the kiss, and now the promise of a night filled with laughter makes my heart race again—this time for all the right reasons.

Navigating through the scattered clusters of people, we weave our way past colorful booths and food stands still buzzing with activity. Each stall seems alive with energy, from the tempting aroma of grilled meats to the sweet scent of funnel cakes, and we laugh as we dodge festival-goers and stray balloons.

When we finally reach the photo booth, it's tucked away in a quieter corner, a hidden gem amidst the festival chaos. The small, red-striped tent beckons us closer, the cheerful banner announcing it in bright, playful colors. I can't help but feel a sense of giddy anticipation as we step inside.

"Okay, let's see what we've got!" she declares, surveying the array of props hanging from the walls—feather boas, oversized glasses, and a multitude of hats. "I call dibs on the pirate hat!"

"Fine, but I want the boa. It's my turn to bring some flair to this shindig," I counter, my playful competitiveness rising to the surface.

We both start rummaging through the props, our laughter filling the small space like a joyful symphony. As I put on the fluffy pink boa, Mabel can't help but double over in laughter. "You look ridiculous!" she exclaims, wiping tears from her eyes.

"Ridiculous is my middle name," I retort, striking a pose with the boa dramatically draped over my shoulders. "Now, where's my pirate hat?"

"Right here!" she announces, placing the hat on my head with a flourish, and I can't help but burst into laughter at how absurdly wonderful this moment feels.

"Now, are you ready for some epic pirate photos?" I ask, my voice slipping into a dramatic accent that makes her giggle uncontrollably.

"I can't believe I'm doing this," she says, shaking her head in mock disbelief but clearly reveling in the spontaneity.

"Believe it! And now, let's capture our very own adventure!"

With the camera timer set, we pose in ridiculous stances, a mix of exaggerated expressions and playful antics that leave us both breathless with laughter. The flash goes off repeatedly, capturing our joy in snapshots—moments suspended in time, chaotic yet beautiful.

"Okay, we're definitely going to frame these," I declare, wiping a tear of laughter from my eye as we finally finish our impromptu photo shoot. "They're worth their weight in gold."

Just as we settle back into the booth, the lights dim momentarily, and the muffled sounds of the festival fade into a hushed whisper. "What's happening?" I wonder aloud, glancing at Mabel, who looks equally perplexed.

"Maybe it's just part of the festival? A special surprise?" she suggests, but there's a hint of unease in her voice that I can't ignore.

Suddenly, the lights flash back on, brighter than before, and the crowd erupts into a cheer, drawing our attention. "Let's see what's going on!" Mabel urges, tugging me toward the exit of the booth.

We step outside to find a large group of festival-goers gathered around the main stage, their voices rising in excitement. A figure steps into the spotlight, and I squint, trying to make out who it is.

As the crowd settles, the announcer's voice booms, "Ladies and gentlemen, we have a special guest tonight!"

"What guest?" I ask, curiosity piquing.

Mabel squeezes my hand, her grip tightening as the figure steps forward, and I feel my stomach drop at the sight.

"It can't be—" I start, but before I can finish my thought, the crowd roars in recognition, and my heart races for an entirely different reason.

"Mabel, do you see who that is?"

She stares in shock, her eyes wide as realization dawns. "Oh my God, it's him!"

A chill runs down my spine as I take in the figure on stage. It's someone I never thought would cross my path again—a shadow from my past that I thought I'd left behind, and now he's here, staring out into the crowd with a smile that sends shivers through me.

And suddenly, our magical night feels perilously uncertain, a precarious tightrope stretched over a canyon of memories I thought I had safely tucked away. Mabel's hand slips from mine as I step back, the world swirling around us, and I can't shake the feeling that this night is only just beginning.

Chapter 16: Unraveling Threads

The air is thick with the scent of stale beer and the faint echo of laughter lingering long after the last patron has stumbled out. I wipe down the bar with a cloth that has seen better days, the texture coarse against my fingertips, as if it's trying to remind me of all the moments that have slipped through my grasp. I've been working at The Rusty Nail for years now, my sanctuary amid the chaos of my life, but tonight, the familiar rhythm feels different. It feels strained, like a taut string waiting to snap.

Mabel had left an imprint on my world, bright and vibrant, yet now she feels like a ghost haunting the very space we once filled with laughter. I can't shake the image of her hurt expression from my mind, flickering across the mirror like an unwanted reflection. Her eyes, usually sparkling with mischief, had dulled, dimmed by something I had yet to articulate. I set the rag down, my mind racing with thoughts I'm desperate to untangle.

"Hey, you okay?" Sam, my colleague, asks, leaning against the bar, his brow furrowed in concern. Sam's always had an uncanny ability to read people, a gift that sometimes feels intrusive but is mostly a blessing. He's like the big brother I never asked for but desperately need.

"Yeah, just a long shift. You know how it is," I reply, plastering on a smile that I can only hope looks genuine. The truth is, I'm anything but fine. "Mabel and I... we're not on the best terms right now."

"Right." Sam's tone is laced with skepticism. "You're not on the best terms with the girl you kissed? Shocking." He rolls his eyes, smirking slightly, and I can't help but laugh. Sam's ability to make light of my disastrous romantic life is a skill worthy of applause.

"Thanks for the support, Sam," I retort, shaking my head as I grab a bottle of whiskey, pouring myself a generous splash. "I just...

I don't know how to fix this. It feels like the universe is throwing everything at me, and I'm fumbling with it all."

"Maybe you should stop waiting for the universe to give you a sign and just talk to her. Sounds like a plan, right?" His casual demeanor belies the weight of his words. "Communication, or whatever the experts call it."

I raise an eyebrow, half-impressed, half-annoyed. "Since when did you become the relationship guru?"

He shrugs, a crooked smile on his face. "I've been watching you two dance around each other for weeks. It's like a rom-com without the happy ending."

"More like a tragicomedy," I mutter, swirling the whiskey in my glass. "One wrong word and poof, I lose her for good."

Sam pushes off the bar, his face suddenly serious. "Look, you care about her. She cares about you. Just lay it all out there. You might be surprised."

I nod, contemplating his advice as I finish my drink. With every passing moment, the tension between Mabel and me stretches like a fraying rope, and I know I have to act before it snaps completely. The night wears on, and I find myself distracted, replaying memories of Mabel—the sound of her laughter, the way her hair catches the light, her quick wit that keeps me on my toes.

Finally, as the clock inches toward closing time, I shove my cleaning rag into the nearby bucket and decide I can't delay any longer. My heart thrums in my chest as I step outside, the cool evening air hitting me like a splash of cold water. The streets are quiet, the kind of stillness that feels both comforting and ominous, and I head toward her apartment, each step feeling heavier than the last.

As I approach her door, I hesitate, my hand hovering over the knocker. What if she doesn't want to see me? What if I've already messed things up beyond repair? My thoughts race as I stand there, a living statue of indecision, but just then, I hear her voice float through the thin walls, tinged with something that sounds like laughter.

I knock lightly, the sound echoing in the silence that follows. Moments stretch, and I can feel the air shift, electric and charged. The door creaks open, revealing Mabel, a vision of confusion and surprise. She stands there, her hair tousled, wearing an oversized sweatshirt that swallows her whole and somehow makes her look even more irresistible.

"Um, hey," she stammers, brushing a stray strand of hair behind her ear, an instinctual move that pulls at my heartstrings.

"Hey," I manage, suddenly feeling small and inadequate under her gaze. "Can we talk?"

Her expression shifts, vulnerability flickering across her face, but she steps aside, gesturing for me to enter. I cross the threshold, heart pounding, as the familiar scent of lavender and vanilla envelops me. The living room is cozy, adorned with mismatched furniture and a stack of books piled haphazardly on the coffee table. It's her sanctuary, a space that speaks volumes about who she is.

"Would you like some tea or something?" Mabel asks, breaking the silence as she moves toward the kitchen, her back turned to me.

"No, I just… I need to say something." I can feel the weight of the moment pressing down on us, suffocating and electric.

She turns slowly, her expression shifting from surprise to a guarded sort of hope. "Okay."

Taking a deep breath, I plunge into the words that have been building inside me, a dam finally breaking. "I've been thinking about that kiss, about everything. And I don't want to pretend like it didn't happen or like I don't care. I do care, Mabel. A lot."

The silence that follows is heavy, a moment stretching into eternity, and I can see the turmoil in her eyes. It's both exhilarating and terrifying, the uncertainty palpable as we stand on the precipice of something monumental. "But I'm scared, too," I admit, vulnerability creeping into my voice. "Scared of ruining what we have. Scared that maybe... maybe you don't feel the same."

Mabel takes a step closer, her gaze searching mine. "You're right. I've been scared too. But I also know that we can't just ignore what's happening between us."

I nod, the truth settling like a warm blanket around us. Her words spark a flicker of hope, igniting something I thought was fading. It's a mess, this tangled web we've woven, but it's our mess, and I suddenly don't want to untangle it alone.

The distance between us closes, the air charged with the promise of honesty.

The air between us is charged with a tension I can almost taste, a blend of hope and fear swirling in the cozy space of her living room. Mabel stands close enough that I can see the slight rise and fall of her chest, her breath mingling with mine. Every passing second feels like a deliberate tick on the clock, a countdown to something monumental.

"Look, this is all very dramatic, and I didn't mean to make it weird," I say, trying to inject some levity into the moment, my attempt at humor landing like a stone. "But it's also terrifying, and you know how much I hate spiders and feelings."

Mabel's lips twitch, barely suppressing a grin, and the tension begins to loosen, if only just. "You know, I think you're more afraid of feelings than you are of actual spiders. I don't know how you survived that time we found that tarantula in the garden."

"Let's not dwell on that. I'm still not sure what it was doing there, minding its own business like it owned the place." I lean against her wall, trying to appear nonchalant, but the nervous energy radiating from me is palpable. "Anyway, I'm sorry for how I've handled everything since... you know, that moment."

She crosses her arms, the gesture both defensive and inviting, like she's shielding herself while also saying she's ready to engage. "It's just that we've always had this… dynamic, you know? We've danced around the idea of us for a while now, and it was so easy until it wasn't."

"Exactly! I'm good at dancing—two-step, cha-cha, awkward shuffles when no one's looking—but this? This is like trying to tango while standing on a trampoline. I keep bouncing around without knowing what the hell I'm doing." My heart races, and I can't believe I'm confessing my ineptitude in the realm of romance.

Mabel laughs, the sound bubbling up like sparkling water, cutting through the tension like a knife through butter. "A trampoline? That's quite the image. I must admit, it's not one I expected."

We share a moment, the air shifting as a smile breaks across her face, illuminating her features in a way that feels both familiar and breathtakingly new. "So, we're both clumsy dancers, then?"

"More like two left feet attempting to salsa at a wedding," I reply, my nerves beginning to settle. "But maybe we can figure it out together? I mean, it might involve a few missteps along the way."

"Missteps can be entertaining," she counters, tilting her head slightly. "What's the worst that could happen? We end up with a spectacularly awkward dance routine that becomes a viral sensation?"

"Perfect! I can already envision the headlines: 'Local Barista and Mystery Woman Stumble Their Way Into Love—and a Viral Dance.'"

The moment stretches, the laughter weaving a fragile bond between us. It feels like the first ray of sunlight breaking through a cloudy sky, and suddenly, everything seems possible. "I want to take the risk, Mabel. I really do," I say, feeling the words spill out, earnest and raw.

Her gaze softens, and I can almost see the cogs turning in her mind as she weighs her options, the air thickening with the weight of her contemplation. "Okay," she finally breathes, her voice barely above a whisper. "Let's take that risk, but I need you to promise me something."

"Anything." My heart races, caught between excitement and trepidation.

"Promise me that if this gets messy—and it probably will—you'll be honest. No dodging, no running away. Just... us."

I nod, the gravity of her request settling over me like a warm blanket. "I promise. I'm not going anywhere."

"Good," she replies, her smile returning, brighter than before. "Because I'm not either."

Before I know it, she closes the distance, and her fingers brush against mine, a soft electric shock that sends my heart into overdrive. "So, what now?" she asks, her voice teasing, eyes dancing with mischief.

"Now, I think we should have a dance party," I declare, a sudden burst of inspiration guiding my next words. "Like, a real one. No skills required, just two people trying to keep their balance."

Mabel arches an eyebrow, feigning skepticism. "A dance party? In here?"

"Why not? The living room has great acoustics," I reply, gesturing around the cozy space. "Plus, I'm not against making a fool of myself. It's basically my superpower."

"I'm not sure 'dance party' is what I had in mind," she muses, a playful glint in her eye. "But I'm intrigued."

"Let's put on some music, and I'll show you my best moves."

"Alright, Mr. Superpower, you're on," she says, and I can hear the challenge in her voice.

I reach for my phone, scrolling through my playlist, finally settling on a track that feels right—something upbeat and infectious that beckons the spirit of celebration. The moment the first notes spill into the air, I can't help but sway to the rhythm, my enthusiasm spilling over like a fizzy soda left too long without a cap.

Mabel watches for a moment, laughter bubbling in her chest, before she joins me, her movements light and carefree. She spins, her hair fanning out like a halo, and I can't help but mimic her, arms flailing in a mix of enthusiasm and sheer delight.

"Is this your signature move? The flail?" she teases, hands on her hips, her laughter infectious.

"Absolutely! It's all the rage!" I spin her into a dramatic twirl, and as she lands back in my arms, the world around us fades.

As the song progresses, we dance wildly, our laughter echoing through the room, drowning out any remnants of the doubts that once loomed heavy in the air. Each twirl, each unexpected spin pulls us closer, weaving threads of connection that feel both fragile and unbreakable. The walls seem to close in around us, but instead of feeling claustrophobic, I feel a warmth that envelops us, a sense of intimacy that makes my heart race.

Just as I'm lost in the moment, a sharp knock on the door breaks through our laughter, the sudden intrusion pulling us back into reality. I freeze, wide-eyed and breathless, exchanging a glance with Mabel that mirrors my surprise. "Who could that be?" she whispers, peering toward the door as if the answer is written on the wood itself.

"Maybe it's the dance police," I joke, attempting to lighten the mood as I inch toward the door, curiosity bubbling within me. "Or a pizza delivery—I did mention my love for carbs."

Mabel rolls her eyes, but there's an unmistakable hint of nervous excitement dancing in her expression. "I don't think they'd send a pizza delivery to investigate an impromptu dance party."

"Guess we'll find out." I pull the door open, revealing a figure that sends my heart plummeting into my stomach. Standing there, disheveled but undeniably striking, is an old friend, Jenna, with an expression that oscillates between confusion and curiosity.

"Hey," she says, glancing between me and Mabel, her brow knitting together. "Am I interrupting something?"

The air shifts again, but this time, it feels heavy with unspoken questions and unresolved tension. I glance back at Mabel, whose expression mirrors my own uncertainty, and just like that, the warmth of our newfound connection feels a little less secure, a little more precarious, and I wonder if this uninvited visitor might unravel the fragile threads we've just begun to weave.

The moment hangs thick in the air, heavy with unsaid words as Jenna's presence looms between us like an unexpected storm cloud, darkening the vibrant sunshine we had just begun to share. She stands in the doorway, hands shoved deep into the pockets of her worn-out jeans, looking like she just stepped off a different planet. My mind races, trying to read her expression, searching for a clue in her stormy gray eyes that might hint at her intentions.

"Mabel, is this a bad time?" Jenna's tone is casual, but her gaze darts between Mabel and me, and I can almost hear the unspoken questions swirling in the space around us.

"Not at all," Mabel replies, her voice steady, yet I can sense a tremor beneath the surface. "We were just having a little impromptu dance party." She glances back at me, and the moment feels suspended, our laughter and carefree moments now tangled in the fabric of this uninvited reality.

"Dance party, huh?" Jenna raises an eyebrow, a teasing smirk playing on her lips. "Looks more like a hot mess from where I'm standing."

I try to shake off the sudden awkwardness, feeling like a deer caught in headlights, unsure whether to laugh or cringe. "You should have seen my moves—definitely worthy of a viral video," I quip, gesturing wildly, trying to lighten the mood. "It was all flailing and questionable rhythm."

"Sounds about right," Jenna replies, but her eyes narrow as she studies us closely. "But seriously, is everything okay? You both look like you've just been caught in a very personal moment."

I can feel the heat rising to my cheeks, a flush of embarrassment mixed with the vulnerability of being exposed in front of someone who used to know all my secrets. "We were just discussing... well, life and stuff." I'm not even sure what I'm trying to cover up, but I can feel Mabel's eyes on me, silently encouraging me to navigate this delicate terrain.

"Life and stuff, huh? Sounds intense," Jenna replies, crossing her arms and leaning against the doorframe with a confidence that makes me feel like I'm being put on display.

"More like life and feelings," Mabel jumps in, her voice steady despite the slight tension crackling in the air. "We were figuring things out."

"Ah," Jenna says, the hint of a smile playing at the corner of her lips. "Figuring things out in the middle of a dance party. Classic." Her gaze lingers on Mabel for a moment longer than necessary, and I wonder if there's history I'm unaware of, something unspoken hanging in the air between them.

"Do you want to come in, Jenna?" Mabel asks, breaking the silence that feels increasingly uncomfortable. The invitation is tentative, and I can almost hear the gears turning in her head, weighing the risk of inviting Jenna into our chaotic mix.

Jenna glances back at me, a flicker of mischief in her eyes. "If I come in, I expect to see some real moves, not just this flailing you've been selling."

I can't help but laugh, a nervous sound that echoes in the small space. "Alright, if you insist. But you'll have to join in."

"Please," Jenna scoffs, stepping into the apartment. "I could teach both of you a thing or two."

With Jenna now in the room, the dynamic shifts again, the air charged with a different kind of energy. I want to be annoyed by her sudden intrusion, to feel the tension ease back into a comfortable silence, but as Jenna begins to sway to the music, it's hard not to be drawn in by her contagious enthusiasm.

"Let's see what you've got, flail master!" she calls out, challenging me with a playful grin.

I take a deep breath, channeling every ounce of my playful spirit, and start to move with a little more conviction, shaking off the remnants of my earlier discomfort. Mabel watches, her eyes dancing with amusement, and as I execute a surprisingly decent spin, I catch her laughter in my peripheral vision.

"Okay, okay! Maybe I was wrong about the whole flailing thing," Jenna admits, jumping in with a few exaggerated hip movements. The three of us quickly fall into a rhythm, and the laughter returns, vibrant and infectious, drowning out the earlier awkwardness.

Just as I begin to feel like I can breathe again, I catch a glimpse of Mabel's expression—her laughter softening into something else, something more vulnerable. The moment feels fleeting, a delicate pause in the chaos of our impromptu dance party, and I wonder if she's still processing the weight of our earlier conversation.

"Do you two ever think about how life can just throw curveballs?" Jenna asks suddenly, her voice cutting through the laughter as she pulls away from the makeshift dance floor. "Like, one minute you're enjoying a perfect moment, and the next you're facing some unexpected truth?"

Mabel's eyes widen slightly, a subtle shift as if Jenna's words have pierced through the bubble we've created. "All the time," Mabel replies, her voice quieter now, the lightheartedness draining away.

"Sometimes it feels like a constant game of dodgeball, and I'm just trying not to get hit."

"Exactly! Or like you're standing at the edge of a cliff, and you have to decide whether to leap or turn back," Jenna adds, her eyes darting between us. "But let's be honest, if you don't take the leap, you might miss out on something incredible."

The atmosphere shifts again, becoming heavier, as Jenna's words hang in the air like a tangible force. It feels as though she's speaking directly to me and Mabel, addressing the unacknowledged feelings that linger just beneath the surface. My heart races, the earlier warmth replaced by a rush of uncertainty as I meet Mabel's gaze, and the unspoken connection between us flares back to life.

"Sometimes, leaping is the only way to find out what's waiting for you on the other side," I whisper, my voice barely above the music, the weight of my confession hanging between us like a thread ready to snap.

"Or it could mean crashing and burning," Mabel replies, a hint of challenge in her tone.

I feel the challenge bounce back and forth between us, a palpable push and pull. "Maybe crashing and burning is just part of the process. Maybe it's how you find out what you're made of."

Jenna leans back, watching us like a spectator at a tennis match, her expression amused yet insightful, as if she understands the gravity of this conversation. "Or maybe it's how you discover what really matters to you."

The music fades into the background, our laughter simmering down to a gentle hum as we stand there, the moment stretching into something profound. "So, what do you really want?" Jenna's question is direct, cutting through the layers of laughter and flirtation, and I feel Mabel's gaze on me, searching for an answer that's been swirling around us all night.

"I want..." I begin, my heart pounding, the truth teetering on the tip of my tongue. "I want to stop running from what's right in front of me."

Suddenly, the doorbell rings again, slicing through the fragile moment we've created. The sound is startling, pulling me back to the reality of the world outside. "Oh, great. More interruptions," I mutter, my heart sinking as I turn toward the door.

"Maybe it's the universe telling you to face whatever's next," Jenna quips, trying to lighten the mood again, but I can't shake the feeling of impending chaos.

Mabel and Jenna exchange a glance, and I can see the uncertainty in Mabel's eyes reflected in my own. "Do you want to get that?" Mabel asks, her voice hesitant, as if the simple act of answering the door carries a weight far beyond its physicality.

"Yeah, I'll check," I say, my voice steadier than I feel as I move toward the door. With each step, my heart races faster, my mind swirling with possibilities and fears. I reach for the doorknob, the cool metal grounding me as I take a breath, preparing for whatever awaits on the other side.

But as I pull the door open, the sight before me sends shockwaves of confusion and disbelief racing through my veins. Standing there, cloaked in shadows with a wild expression that seems to oscillate between anger and desperation, is someone I never expected to see again—a figure from my past, with a history intertwined with my present. The weight of unresolved feelings crashes over me like a tidal wave, and I realize that this unexpected reunion could unravel everything I've been trying to hold together.

Chapter 17: Heartfelt Confrontations

The river murmured softly as I led Mabel to my sanctuary, a hidden nook where the world felt like it had paused just for us. Sunlight danced on the surface of the water, casting flickering patterns like playful spirits darting across the current. I had discovered this spot during one of my many exploratory walks, the kind where I lost myself in thought, and it had quickly become my refuge. Here, the scent of damp earth mingled with the sweet, floral notes of wildflowers that sprouted defiantly from the banks, creating a harmony that echoed my longing for solace and connection.

Mabel stepped lightly beside me, her laughter trailing like a warm breeze as she remarked on the vibrant greenery. "You always find the best places to hide," she teased, her voice lilting through the air. It struck me then how her presence could turn any moment into a sweet melody. She wore a flowing sundress that caught the breeze, the fabric swirling around her like petals caught in a gentle gust. I tried to focus on the moment, but the gravity of what I was about to share weighed heavily in my chest.

As we settled on the worn blanket I had laid out, I could feel the texture of the fabric against my skin, a familiar comfort amidst my rising anxiety. The soft sound of the water lapping against the stones seemed to coax my thoughts into order, urging me to speak the words I had rehearsed countless times in my mind. But now that the moment was upon us, it felt as though the words had retreated into the shadows, leaving me standing in the stark light of my fears.

"Mabel," I began, the name rolling off my tongue like an invocation. "I wanted to bring you here because there's something I need to tell you." My heart raced as I met her gaze, those deep, knowing eyes that seemed to see into the very fabric of my being. She nodded, encouraging me, her expression a blend of curiosity and concern.

I took a deep breath, the cool air filling my lungs as I prepared to unearth the tangled roots of my past. "This relationship—everything about it has been... overwhelming," I confessed, my voice barely above a whisper. "I'm scared. I haven't let myself feel this way in a long time, and it terrifies me." The confession spilled from my lips, raw and unpolished.

Mabel's brow furrowed slightly, her lips parting as if to respond, but I pressed on, needing to spill the truth before it choked me. "I'm not sure I can keep up with the pace of everything," I continued, the words tumbling over one another in their haste to escape. "You're wonderful, and I don't want to push you away, but my past... it makes trusting so hard."

The moment hung in the air, thick with vulnerability. The sunlight shifted, casting long shadows that seemed to stretch across the ground, mimicking the shadows of my insecurities. I could see the flicker of emotion in her eyes—a mixture of empathy and understanding. As I finished speaking, the silence was palpable, a fragile thread connecting us in this moment of honesty.

Her hand reached out, warm and gentle, as she took mine in hers. "You're not alone in feeling this way," she said softly, her thumb brushing across my knuckles, sending a rush of comfort through me. "I've struggled too, you know. I've spent so long believing that I didn't deserve love, that maybe it was just a fleeting shadow that would never catch me."

There was a shared understanding in her voice, a vulnerability that mirrored my own. "It's like standing on the edge of a cliff, isn't it?" she mused, her gaze drifting to the flowing water, a pensive look crossing her features. "You want to leap, but the fear of falling holds you back."

"Yes!" I exclaimed, the word escaping me like a breath I had been holding for too long. "Exactly that. I want to dive in, but I don't know how to swim in these feelings without drowning."

Her laughter, soft and melodic, broke through the weight of the moment. "Then let's learn to swim together," she proposed, her eyes sparkling with mischief. "We'll figure it out. I promise I won't let you drown."

I laughed, the sound echoing off the riverbanks, buoyed by her lightness. "You make it sound so easy," I replied, a teasing lilt in my tone. "What's next, synchronized swimming?"

"Why not?" she countered, her expression shifting from playful to serious. "Life is too short to tread water. We'll have to make a splash."

And just like that, the heaviness in my chest began to lift. I realized that this shared moment of vulnerability had not only opened the door to my fears but had also invited her in, allowing us both to peel back the layers we had wrapped around ourselves like protective armor.

Mabel squeezed my hand, her warmth grounding me, reminding me of the vibrant world around us. The trees whispered secrets to one another, and the river sang its ageless song, all while we sat on the precipice of our own truths. It was a turning point, an unveiling that felt like the first rays of dawn breaking through a long night. As the sun dipped lower in the sky, painting the horizon with hues of gold and rose, I understood that this was just the beginning of our journey—together, unearthing the tangled threads of our pasts to weave a new tapestry of trust and love.

The afternoon sun, now casting its golden glow through the branches, seemed to wrap us in a cocoon of warmth. It felt surreal, as if time itself had slowed to let us savor this moment of honesty. Mabel's fingers entwined with mine, her touch a reminder that vulnerability doesn't have to be a solo venture. As she spoke, the sincerity in her voice unfurled like the petals of a blossom—delicate yet strong.

"I spent years convinced I was unlovable," she confessed, her voice steady despite the tremor beneath it. "Like a ghost haunting my own life, watching everyone else find their joy while I stood on the sidelines." There was a glimmer of vulnerability in her eyes that mirrored my own, a fleeting shadow of the hurt that had once occupied too much space in our lives.

"Ghosts can be tricky," I replied, trying to lighten the mood, "especially when they start throwing their own haunting parties." She chuckled softly, the sound warming my heart. It was in these small exchanges that I found comfort—humor and pain woven together like an intricate tapestry, each thread telling a story of its own.

"I think I'm just tired of running," she said, her gaze drifting back to the water. "Tired of being the girl who is always waiting for the other shoe to drop." I felt the weight of her words settle between us, heavy with unspoken fears. The river whispered as it flowed, echoing our hidden thoughts, reminding us that we were both moving forward, whether we liked it or not.

"Mabel, if there's one thing I've learned, it's that life is a series of leaps of faith," I said, the truth of my own journey shining through the uncertainty. "We leap, and sometimes we fall, but every time we do, we get back up. You're not a ghost—you're the life of the party." I squeezed her hand, hoping to ignite a spark of belief in her.

She looked at me then, a mix of surprise and admiration flickering across her features. "That's an optimistic view. Are you sure you're not just trying to be the cheerleader for the team that never makes it past the first round?"

"Maybe I'm just a hopeless romantic at heart," I shot back, a smirk playing on my lips. "Or maybe I've just seen too many movies where the underdog ends up winning the big game."

"Now I'm picturing us in matching outfits, rallying the crowd," she laughed, her eyes sparkling with mischief. "But seriously, what if I'm not cut out for the spotlight? What if I just... fade into the background again?"

"Then we'll make it a duet," I countered, my voice light and teasing. "You and I will paint the world with our mismatched colors. Together, we can create a masterpiece. Besides, fading into the background sounds so much less fun than blazing a trail."

Her laughter rang out, bright and free, scattering my fears like leaves in the wind. In that moment, I felt a shift in the air, as if we were no longer standing on the precipice of our fears but rather at the cusp of something extraordinary. The sunlight dipped lower, igniting the river with a fire-like glow, and I realized that I wanted to keep this warmth alive, to nurture it and let it grow.

"What do you say we make a pact?" I proposed, feeling bold. "A promise that we'll face whatever comes together. No ghosts, no fading—just two people committed to exploring every messy, beautiful part of this life."

"Deal," Mabel said, her voice filled with a newfound determination. "But only if you promise to stop with the horror movie metaphors."

"Fine, fine," I laughed, holding my hands up in mock surrender. "No more ghosts or eerie shadows. Just sunshine and rainbows from now on."

As we settled into a comfortable silence, the river's murmurs wrapping around us like a gentle embrace, I felt an undeniable shift within me. Mabel's honesty had opened a door, and as I peered through it, I realized there was a world of possibilities waiting for us—one that could be filled with laughter, connection, and love.

But life, as it often does, threw a curveball when I noticed a shadow lurking at the edge of our peaceful haven. My heart skipped a beat as I turned to see a figure emerging from the thicket—a familiar face framed by disheveled hair and a coat that seemed two sizes too big. It was Jenny, my estranged sister, her eyes wide with a mixture of desperation and anger.

"Surprise, surprise," she said, her voice laced with sarcasm as she stepped closer, the leaves crunching underfoot. "Nice to see you've found a little slice of paradise while the rest of us are left to pick up the pieces."

Mabel's grip tightened around my hand, a silent support grounding me as I braced for the confrontation that was inevitable. "What are you doing here, Jenny?" I managed, my heart racing as the warmth of our moment felt abruptly chilled by her presence.

"Oh, just wandering through the woods, looking for my favorite sibling," she replied, a biting edge to her words. "You know, the one who abandoned me when things got tough."

"Mabel's here with me," I said, trying to assert my own space against the tide of anger rising between us. "This is our time. You don't get to barge in and ruin it."

Jenny crossed her arms, a defiant stance that felt all too familiar. "You think I wanted to interrupt your little love fest? Please. I'm here because I need your help, and you're the last person I'd ever want to rely on."

I felt Mabel's eyes on me, a silent question lingering in the air. I knew this confrontation could unravel the delicate threads we had just woven together. But as I looked into my sister's eyes, I saw the flicker of a vulnerability that echoed my own—a yearning for connection that we both desperately needed, even if we were too stubborn to admit it.

"I don't know if I can help you," I replied, my voice steady, though my heart raced. "But I'm willing to listen. If you're ready to talk."

Jenny's defenses dropped for a moment, and I caught a glimpse of the sister I had once known—the girl who laughed too loudly and who believed in magic, who always seemed to have my back when the world grew too dark.

"Fine," she said, her voice softer now, "but you'd better brace yourself. This isn't the fairy tale you're hoping for."

"Who said anything about fairy tales?" I shot back, determination coursing through me. "This is just another chapter in our story—let's make it a good one."

And as the sun dipped lower in the sky, painting the river with its fiery hues, I knew we were standing at the edge of a new beginning, ready to dive into the unknown depths of our tangled lives.

The tension in the air was palpable, but the warmth from our earlier conversation wrapped around me like a comforting shawl, bolstering my resolve as I faced Jenny. Her presence was an unexpected storm, disrupting the fragile calm Mabel and I had created. The shadows seemed to deepen around us, and I could feel Mabel's hand, warm and steady, providing an anchor amidst the swirling emotions.

"Help?" I echoed, raising an eyebrow at Jenny, who stood there with an expression that was a mix of defiance and something softer, more vulnerable. "You know, you could've sent a text. It's less dramatic."

"Because texting you about my life falling apart would've been so much easier," she snapped back, rolling her eyes. "Besides, this is your fault. You're the one who decided to ghost me. Now you're suddenly the expert on relationships?"

"I'm not ghosting you. I'm trying to figure my life out too." My voice trembled slightly, a reminder of the past I thought I had buried. "And I'm trying to move forward, not backwards."

"Newsflash: You don't just get to decide that when it's convenient for you," she shot back, her eyes flashing. "I'm not the one who ditched family for some fairytale romance."

My heart thudded painfully against my ribs. "This isn't about Mabel," I insisted, though I could feel the weight of the accusation lingering between us. "It's about us. About what we lost and what we need to face together."

"And what do you think we need to face? The fact that you've been living in your little bubble while the rest of us are still picking up the pieces?" Her voice cracked, and for a moment, I glimpsed the hurt that lay beneath her bravado.

"Mabel and I are trying to build something real," I said, my frustration boiling over. "But that doesn't mean I want to forget where I came from. It doesn't mean I don't care."

"What do you want from me?" Jenny challenged, her tone shifting to a mix of anger and desperation. "You want me to apologize for needing you? For thinking that family means something?"

"Family does mean something," I replied, my voice softer now. "But it's not just about blood. It's about support, about showing up for one another. And that's something we've both fallen short on."

Mabel remained silent beside me, but I could feel her support radiating like warmth on a chilly day. With her presence, I felt the courage to stand firm, to bridge the gap between the past and present.

"I'm here now," I continued, forcing my voice to steady. "But you have to meet me halfway. Let's talk about what's really going on."

A flicker of hesitation crossed Jenny's face, and for a brief moment, I thought I saw the wall she'd built start to crack. "Fine. But don't act like it's that easy," she muttered, crossing her arms defensively. "I didn't come here for a family reunion."

"What did you come here for?" Mabel interjected, her voice calm but firm.

"Maybe I wanted to figure out why I feel so lost without you two," Jenny admitted, the words spilling out as if they had been bottled up for too long. "You both moved on, and I'm still stuck in the same place. I thought coming here might help me find my way."

The honesty of her confession caught me off guard, like a sudden gust of wind that lifted the tension from the air. "Then let's help each other," I suggested, feeling a flicker of hope ignite in my chest. "But we can't do that if we keep pointing fingers."

She looked between us, her expression softening. "Maybe I've been a bit harsh," she conceded reluctantly, her stubbornness evident but cracking. "It's just...hard to see you two so happy when I'm still drowning."

Mabel stepped forward slightly, her eyes earnest. "We want you to be happy too, Jenny. We're all in this together. But we can't help if you keep pushing us away."

There was a beat of silence as Jenny considered our words, the shadows of her past clinging to her like an unwelcome cloak. "I don't know how to stop feeling like a failure," she admitted finally, the bravado fading from her voice.

"Then let's work on it," I said, my heart aching for the sister I had known, the one who had once shared my laughter and dreams. "We can take small steps. I'm here for you, and I'll always be. Just don't shut us out again."

A flicker of vulnerability crossed her face, and I thought maybe—just maybe—we were making progress. But then the wind shifted, and the serenity of our riverside sanctuary suddenly felt fragile, like the threads of our conversation were unraveling too quickly.

Before Jenny could respond, a distant sound broke the air, sharp and jarring—a shout, followed by a commotion that cut through our moment like a knife. My heart raced as I turned toward the sound, a gut instinct urging me to stand.

"What was that?" Mabel asked, her voice taut with concern, her hand instinctively tightening around mine.

"I have no idea," I replied, my mind racing. It was a sound too frantic to ignore, too urgent to dismiss as mere background noise. A moment later, the underbrush rustled violently, and out of the thicket burst a figure—a man, his shirt torn and eyes wide with fear.

"Help!" he gasped, stumbling toward us. "They're coming! We need to get out of here!"

The sense of urgency in his voice sent chills down my spine. I glanced at Mabel, and then back to Jenny, confusion and alarm flashing in our shared gaze.

"Who's coming?" I managed, my throat dry as the weight of the moment crashed down upon us.

"The people from the camp!" he exclaimed, glancing over his shoulder as if expecting shadows to leap from the trees. "They're looking for me—looking for all of us! We have to run!"

My pulse quickened, a rush of adrenaline igniting the air. In the span of a heartbeat, the serenity of the river transformed into a backdrop for chaos, and the threads of our fragile reunion began to fray.

"Wait! What are you talking about?" Jenny shouted, her voice tinged with panic.

But he didn't answer; instead, he grabbed my arm, his grip like iron. "There's no time! If we don't leave now, we're all in danger!"

I looked at Mabel, her face mirroring my own disbelief, uncertainty swirling in her eyes. My heart raced as I weighed my choices, the world around us teetering on the edge of something dark and uncertain.

"Let's go," I said, the decision coiling in my gut, a tightrope of instinct urging me forward. "We can figure it out on the way."

As we turned to flee, the river flowed behind us, its gentle current now a haunting echo of what we had just shared. And as the trees closed in around us, a sense of foreboding gripped my heart, whispering that this was only the beginning of a much darker chapter unfolding.

Chapter 18: The Weight of Decisions

The sun cast a golden hue over Silver Springs, its rays filtering through the towering oaks and dappling the cobblestone streets with patches of light that danced like spirits come to life. Mabel and I strolled side by side, our fingers just brushing against each other's, a gentle electricity crackling in the air. The scent of fresh pastries wafted from the café down the street, mingling with the earthy aroma of the nearby flower market. Each step felt like a small rebellion against the world outside our little bubble, where laughter came easily and worries lingered just out of reach.

"This town really knows how to do charm," Mabel mused, her eyes glimmering as she paused to admire a cluster of daisies, their bright yellow centers resembling tiny suns. "It's like stepping into a postcard. Who wouldn't want to live here?"

"People with a fear of quaintness, I suppose," I replied, unable to suppress a grin. "Or anyone allergic to sunshine and joy."

She laughed, the sound bubbling up like a brook over smooth stones. "So, you're saying you're all in on the sunshine and joy, then?"

"Absolutely. It's the perfect antidote to... well, life." The shadow of my sister's recent return hovered at the edge of my mind like a thundercloud, but I pushed it away. Mabel had a way of making the world seem lighter, brighter, and I was determined to embrace this moment.

We wandered through the vibrant shops that lined Main Street, their doors flung open to invite passersby in like old friends. I marveled at the eclectic assortment of wares—handmade pottery, vintage clothing, and rows of books that promised new adventures. My heart fluttered at the thought of losing myself in their pages, yet I was equally captivated by the warmth of the company beside me.

Mabel caught me gazing at a quaint bookstore with a sign that read "Last Chapter," and her brows arched playfully. "You want to go in, don't you?"

"It's like a siren song," I confessed. "But I don't want to drag you into a literary rabbit hole when we could be exploring. Besides, the last thing I need is to become a hermit among the stacks."

She tilted her head, a sly smile playing on her lips. "You do realize hermits have their own charm, right? Just think—no one to interrupt your thoughts. No obligations to smile politely while pretending to care about someone's recipe for kale chips."

I laughed, picturing myself ensconced in dusty shelves, escaping the chaos of my family drama. But the thought of being alone in that way suddenly felt heavy. "True, but I'd rather take my chances with a few interruptions than miss moments like this with you."

Her smile widened, illuminating her face like the sun breaking through clouds. "Well, let's promise not to become hermits. A little adventure and a little reading—balance, right?"

As we continued our journey, Mabel's presence enveloped me in a cocoon of warmth and laughter, making the burdens of my heart seem lighter, almost negligible. But as the sun dipped lower in the sky, painting the world in shades of orange and purple, I felt the familiar weight settle back into my chest. My sister's reemergence was like an unexpected storm front, dark and looming, threatening to disrupt the tranquility we'd found.

Later that evening, nestled in the corner of our favorite café, I sipped my latte, the foam art swirling into a delicate heart shape. Mabel perched across from me, her fingers tracing the rim of her cup absentmindedly.

"What's on your mind?" she asked, the easy cadence of her voice laced with genuine concern.

I hesitated, torn between the urge to confide and the instinct to protect the fragile peace we'd created. "It's just... my sister is back. She wants to talk, to rebuild things. And it's like, I've finally started to breathe again, and now..."

"Now she's asking for a piece of that air?" Mabel finished, her expression turning serious. "It's complicated, isn't it?"

"More than I'd like to admit. I thought I could leave it all behind, just focus on what makes me happy for once. And now she's showing up, wanting forgiveness like it's as easy as breathing."

The tension in the air thickened as I spoke, each word punctuated by the weight of my emotions. Mabel's gaze remained steady, encouraging me to unravel my thoughts.

"Forgiveness isn't easy," she replied softly. "It takes time. You can't rush what needs to heal. You deserve to put yourself first for a change. But it's also okay to want a relationship with her."

"Right. It's just... what if by trying to mend things, I end up losing what I have with you?"

Her lips pursed as she considered my words, the silence stretching between us like a taut wire. "You won't lose me, not unless you push me away. Just remember that your happiness matters too. Whatever decision you make, I'll be here. But it's okay to take your time."

I nodded, grateful for her understanding yet wrestling with the turmoil inside me. In that moment, the café felt like a refuge, the soft chatter of patrons a soothing backdrop to my inner chaos. Yet, I could feel the storm of my sister's request brewing on the horizon, its implications heavy and real.

Mabel reached across the table, her hand covering mine, grounding me amidst the swirling thoughts. "We'll figure it out together, whatever 'it' is."

The sincerity in her eyes kindled a flicker of hope in my heart. But as I held her gaze, I felt the specter of my sister looming larger, the weight of decisions pressing down like the humidity before a summer storm. It was a reminder that even in moments of serenity, the world had a way of reminding us of the storm clouds yet to come.

Mornings in Silver Springs had an exquisite way of unfolding, like a well-loved book whose pages are crisp but familiar. I watched as sunlight streamed through my bedroom window, casting playful shadows on the walls, and I couldn't help but smile at the memory of Mabel's laughter from the night before. We had spent hours sprawled across the worn sofa in her living room, dissecting our favorite books and engaging in friendly debates over plot twists and character motivations, our voices weaving a tapestry of shared ideas that wrapped around us like a cozy blanket.

Yet, even as I lay there relishing the quiet, my phone buzzed insistently on the bedside table, dragging me back to reality. The name on the screen sent a chill down my spine: Ava. My sister, with her history of well-intentioned chaos. I let it ring twice before silencing it, the weight of her request still looming large. Mabel had promised me that I could take my time, but the pressure felt like an elastic band pulled taut, threatening to snap at any moment.

After a lazy breakfast, complete with buttered toast and strawberry jam—Mabel's secret weapon against a sour mood—I found myself unable to focus on anything but the unanswered call. Maybe I should just call her back and get it over with. The thought of facing her after so long felt like stepping into a chilly lake. Awkward and shocking, but maybe, just maybe, invigorating once I was fully submerged.

"Are you planning to stare at that phone all day?" Mabel leaned against the kitchen counter, her dark curls bouncing as she poured herself another cup of coffee. The warmth from the mug seeped into her palms, and her brow furrowed in that adorable way that made me want to kiss her right there. "I'm starting to think it's a new art installation: 'The Phone of Regret.'"

I chuckled, shaking my head. "I think it's more like a ticking time bomb. My sister is... complicated."

"Complicated? I think you mean 'an absolute whirlwind of chaos wrapped in a pretty package.'" Mabel's voice was teasing, but I could see the concern lurking in her eyes. "What's the worst that could happen?"

I had to laugh at that; it was a solid question. "Well, she could ask for a family reunion, and I could have a panic attack."

"True, but you could also just tell her you're not ready for that yet. Just because she's knocking on your door doesn't mean you have to answer it immediately. You're not a doorbell; you don't exist to be rung."

"Someone's been reading her self-help books," I shot back, enjoying the way her lips curved into a smile.

"Guilty as charged. It's my new obsession. But really, just think of it like this: You're the one holding the keys here, not her. If you don't want to open the door, then don't."

"Philosophy 101 with Mabel. I like it." I could feel the tension slowly loosening its grip, if only a little. I took a deep breath, attempting to breathe in the possibility of taking control.

After a moment, I made my decision. "Fine. I'll call her. But only if you promise to be on the other end of the line for moral support."

"Deal."

I reached for my phone, the moment stretching like taffy as I dialed Ava's number. Each ring felt like an eternity, and just when I thought she might not pick up, she answered, her voice bright yet tinged with a nervous energy. "Hey! It's been a while!"

"Ava," I managed, my heart racing. "You called?"

"Yeah! I wanted to talk. Can we meet up?" The enthusiasm in her voice was layered with an undercurrent of sincerity, almost foreign to me after the distance we'd kept.

I glanced at Mabel, who raised her eyebrows in encouragement. "Um, sure. When were you thinking?"

"How about today? I know this little coffee place you'll love."

The tension returned, wrapping around my chest like a vice. "Today? I mean, okay. I guess that works."

"Great! I'll text you the address."

After we hung up, I looked over at Mabel, who was trying not to look too smug. "See? That wasn't so hard, was it?"

"Not yet," I replied, "but give it time. She has a knack for turning simple meetings into soap operas."

"Then let's make this a fun soap opera. If she starts with the dramatics, just hit her with your best one-liners. I mean, it's either that or tears, right?"

"Good point," I said, a grin creeping onto my face. "And if all else fails, I can always just say, 'I'm really sorry, but I can't hear you over how much fun I'm having with my new girlfriend.'"

Mabel laughed, and her laughter was a bright beacon as I prepared to face the storm. The café was just a few blocks away, and with every step, I felt a mix of apprehension and excitement bubbling up. I needed to keep my heart open, no matter how scared I was.

When I arrived, the aroma of freshly brewed coffee embraced me, and the cozy atmosphere felt like a warm hug. Ava was already seated at a table near the window, her fingers nervously tapping against the table as she scanned the crowd. She looked a bit different—older, maybe—but the familiar glint of mischief still sparkled in her eyes.

"Hey!" I greeted, forcing a smile that felt slightly more authentic than I expected.

"Thanks for coming!" She stood and hugged me tightly, her arms wrapping around me in a way that felt both familiar and strange. As I pulled back, I studied her face. "You look good. It's... nice to see you."

"You too," she replied, a hint of vulnerability in her voice. "I missed you."

The words struck me like a rogue wave, unexpected and powerful. "I missed you too, I guess. It's been a long time."

We settled into our seats, the chatter of the café swirling around us, a comforting backdrop to our impending conversation. I was acutely aware of Mabel's earlier words echoing in my mind, but as we exchanged small talk, the atmosphere lightened. Maybe this wouldn't be as difficult as I feared.

"I wanted to apologize for everything that happened," Ava began, her voice dropping to a softer tone. "I know I messed up, and I've been doing a lot of thinking."

I nodded, my heart caught between the past and present. "I appreciate that. It just felt like... like you weren't really there when I needed you."

Her expression softened, and for a moment, I saw the sister I had loved through the tangled web of disappointment. "I get it. I was selfish, and I'm sorry. I just want to make it right, if you'll let me."

Her words hung in the air, weighted with both sincerity and a flicker of hope. But just as I felt the tiniest spark of optimism, the door swung open with a dramatic flourish, allowing a gust of wind to swirl into the café. My heart dropped as I recognized the figure stepping inside—an all-too-familiar face that sent a shiver down my spine.

The café's door swung open with a creak that sliced through the air, and my breath caught in my throat. Ava had been one thing, a familiar presence I was still trying to navigate, but the newcomer—Megan—was a tempest, the kind that could wreak havoc with little more than a glance. Her entrance felt like the moment in a movie when the music shifts from a sweet melody to a discordant note, signaling that trouble is about to unfold. She spotted me immediately, her expression morphing from surprise to what I could only describe as mischief.

"Megan," I whispered, my heart racing. This was the last thing I needed. Just when I thought I was ready to have a calm conversation with my sister, Megan appeared like a siren in a sea of chaos, ready to drag me under.

"Fancy meeting you here, sis," she chirped, sliding into the booth beside Ava as though she belonged. "I hope I'm not interrupting anything important." Her smirk was sharp, a knife's edge, and I could feel the tension in the air shift, thickening around us like fog.

"Oh, just a little family reunion," Ava said, trying to maintain a veneer of composure, but I could hear the strain in her voice. "You know, no big deal."

Megan's laughter rang out, bright and mocking. "Family reunion? Is that what we're calling it now? Looks more like a therapy session gone wrong." She leaned back in her seat, clearly reveling in the discomfort she was causing.

I glanced at Mabel, who sat across from me, her brows furrowed as she took in the unfolding drama. I could see the instinct in her eyes—she wanted to help, to shield me from this onslaught. But I couldn't expect her to step in. This was my fight, after all, tangled up in a family web that was as familiar as it was suffocating.

"Why are you here, Megan?" I asked, trying to keep my voice steady, though it felt like my heart was pounding in my ears. "I thought you were too busy chasing your latest obsession."

"Oh, I took a break," she replied with a flippant wave of her hand, like she was brushing away a pesky fly. "And besides, I heard through the grapevine that you were having a little sisterly bonding moment. I couldn't resist dropping by to see how the other half lives."

"Why don't you go back to whatever hole you crawled out of?" I snapped, irritation bubbling to the surface. I glanced at Mabel, who was watching me with an expression that danced between concern and admiration. I was glad she was there, but I could feel the riptide pulling me away from her, dragging me back to familiar patterns of confrontation.

Megan raised an eyebrow, her smile unfaltering. "Aw, come on! Can't we all just play nice? I'm here to spread a little sunshine."

"Sunshine, or a thunderstorm?" Mabel interjected, her tone cool but playful, and I couldn't help but admire her for it. "You're stepping into a fragile situation. You might want to tread lightly."

"Oh, I like her," Megan said, her eyes narrowing with a calculating gleam. "Feisty! Just like you, sis. But you know what they say about feistiness. It's only cute until it isn't."

"Enough." I raised my voice, feeling a surge of anger mixed with desperation. I didn't want this meeting to devolve into chaos. I wanted answers, understanding, something that felt solid beneath my feet. "We're not doing this here. Not now."

Megan shrugged, unperturbed. "Suit yourself. I'm just here for the entertainment. And it looks like I hit the jackpot."

Ava shifted in her seat, clearly flustered. "Megan, we're trying to have a conversation about forgiveness. This isn't about you."

"Forgiveness? How quaint!" Megan exclaimed, leaning in closer, her voice dripping with sarcasm. "Why not just hang a banner? 'Welcome back to the family! Please disregard the emotional wreckage.'"

I felt a deep ache in my chest, a knot of frustration and sadness that threatened to spill over. This was supposed to be a moment of healing, a chance to mend the fractures that had split our family apart. And yet here was Megan, a walking embodiment of the chaos I was trying to escape.

"Megan, please just leave," I said, my voice wavering slightly. "This is between Ava and me."

But she only laughed, the sound echoing around us. "Oh, honey, you're too naive if you think this is just between you two. Family drama is like a game of chess. You can't just ignore the pawns."

"Family drama?" I echoed incredulously. "Is that what you call this? Because to me, it feels more like a circus."

"I'd pay to see that," Mabel chimed in, a hint of laughter breaking through her tense demeanor. "But I'm pretty sure the ringmaster just walked in."

Megan feigned a gasp, clutching her chest. "Oh, darling, you wound me! You really think I'm the villain here?"

"Honestly? Yes!" I shot back, the words spilling from my lips before I could rein them in.

Her grin faltered for a moment, and I could see the mask slip. "Well, good luck with your little heart-to-heart, then. But let's be real—you can't just sweep things under the rug and pretend everything's fine."

Mabel's hand slipped into mine beneath the table, her warmth a soothing balm against the gathering storm. I felt a rush of gratitude for her steadiness, a reminder that I didn't have to face this alone. "You're right, Megan. We can't just pretend. But that doesn't mean you get to barge in and dictate how we deal with our issues."

Megan's expression shifted to something darker, her smile tightening. "Oh, sweet sister. You really think you're in control here? You're standing on the edge of a cliff, and you're about to jump without a parachute."

Ava shifted uncomfortably, her eyes darting between us, caught in the crossfire. "Can we just try to talk like adults? This isn't helping anyone."

"Adults?" Megan scoffed. "Look around. You're surrounded by a bunch of children playing at family. How could this ever be helpful?"

"Maybe it starts with honesty," I said, my voice firmer now, feeling a flicker of determination surge within me. "Ava wants to talk. I want to talk. If you can't respect that, then—"

"Then what?" Megan's voice dripped with condescension. "You'll throw me out of the family? Good luck with that."

Before I could respond, the door swung open again, a gust of wind carrying in the unmistakable scent of rain. In walked a figure I had not expected—my mother, her face pale, as though she had just seen a ghost. "Girls..." she began, her voice trembling, but the words fell flat as she took in the scene before her.

"Megan," I said, my heart sinking as I realized my mother's arrival would only add fuel to the fire. The tension in the café thickened, like the heavy clouds gathering outside, ready to burst. "What now?"

Megan's smirk widened as she turned toward our mother. "Well, well, look who decided to join the party. Mom, we were just talking about family—our favorite subject."

And just like that, the air shifted, the storm poised to break, with everything hanging in the balance, as if the very fate of our family was about to be decided in that crowded café.

Chapter 19: Rebuilding Bridges

The café was alive with the aroma of freshly brewed coffee and the soft murmur of conversations swirling around me, each voice a thread weaving a tapestry of warmth and familiarity. The Broken Compass had always been my sanctuary, a cozy nook tucked away from the frenetic pace of life outside. Today, however, the usual comfort of the place felt different, charged with an electricity that left me both anxious and excited. I sat at my favorite corner table, the one with the mismatched chairs that creaked under pressure, clutching a latte that had long since cooled, while my heart raced like a rabbit cornered by an unexpected predator.

Mabel appeared in the doorway, her silhouette framed by the golden light filtering through the glass. I almost didn't recognize her. Gone was the sister who once defined my childhood, the one who filled our house with laughter and mischief. Instead, standing before me was a woman who seemed to carry the weight of her choices like a heavy cloak draped over her shoulders. Her hair, once a vibrant chestnut, was now dulled, and her eyes—those mischievous, twinkling eyes—held a hint of something deeper, something shadowed. She hesitated for a moment, scanning the café as if trying to find her bearings in a place she had once known so well.

"Hey," she finally said, her voice breaking the spell of silence that had cocooned us. The warmth that accompanied the word was familiar, yet it felt so foreign in the air between us. I nodded, a small gesture that felt monumental, the weight of our history hanging like a shroud around us.

"Thanks for meeting me," she continued, sliding into the seat across from me. The table was small, just a few inches separating us, but it felt like an entire ocean of unresolved emotions lay in that space. "I know it's been a while."

"A while," I echoed, my tone laced with unspoken words. It was an understatement, really. The years had stretched between us, filled with distance and misunderstandings that morphed into barriers too daunting to dismantle.

"I've missed you," Mabel said, and the sincerity in her voice made my heart flutter uneasily. It was a truth wrapped in a sorrow that danced just beneath the surface of her words. I could see her fighting against the tide of regret, her hands fidgeting with the edge of the table as if grasping for stability.

"I miss you too," I admitted, the admission tasting both sweet and bitter. It was a small truth, but in that moment, it felt like a lifeline thrown into turbulent waters.

Her gaze dropped to the latte in front of her, and I watched as she took a deep breath, collecting herself before she plunged into the depths of what had led us to this precarious moment. "I know I hurt you," she said finally, her voice almost a whisper, vulnerable and raw. "And I'm so sorry for that. I was selfish, caught up in my own world, and I didn't see how my actions affected you."

The truth hung in the air, tangible and heavy, a palpable reminder of the scars left in the wake of our shared past. I remembered the nights spent in tears, the long silences stretched across our home like a chasm, and the joy that had once filled our lives becoming an echo of laughter that no longer resonated.

"I felt like I was losing you," I confessed, my own voice trembling slightly. "And it hurt. It still hurts."

Mabel's eyes glistened, reflecting an understanding that transcended words. "I didn't realize how much I took for granted until it was gone. I thought I could navigate my life without really considering how it impacted you. I'm trying to change, to be better."

Her words were a balm and a burden, stirring a tumult of emotions within me. Part of me wanted to hurl my frustrations at her, to unleash years of pent-up anger and disappointment, but another part—a softer, gentler part—yearned for the connection we once shared.

We sat in silence for a moment, the café around us bustling with life while we hovered in our own little universe, caught between what had been and what might still be. The clinking of cups, the laughter of strangers, and the soft strains of a guitar playing in the background faded into a comforting hum as I navigated the complexities of my feelings.

"Maybe we can start over," I suggested, my voice steadier than I felt. "Not like nothing happened, but... like we're rebuilding something. A bridge, perhaps?"

Mabel's face lit up with a tentative hope, a spark igniting in her eyes that reminded me of the sister I once knew. "I'd like that," she said, her smile tentative yet genuine, as if she was afraid to break the fragile moment we had created.

Our conversation unfolded, rich with shared memories, laughter, and the tentative exploration of forgiveness. Each story we exchanged was a thread, weaving us closer together, patching up the frayed edges of our bond. The past was not erased; instead, it became a tapestry of lessons learned, scars borne, and the hard-won wisdom that only time could offer.

As we sipped our lattes, the warmth seeped through the ceramic mugs into our palms, an invitation to stay grounded amid the emotional whirlwind swirling around us. The café, once just a backdrop to my solitary musings, transformed into a vibrant canvas painted with the colors of rekindled connection. I could see a flicker of the sister I once adored, her laughter a balm to my heart, a promise of potential reconciliation.

But deep down, uncertainty lurked like a shadow, reminding me that the journey ahead would be fraught with challenges. Forgiveness was not an easy path, and the road to rebuilding bridges was often riddled with obstacles. Yet, in that moment, as I looked into Mabel's eyes, I felt a cautious optimism bloom within me—a fragile flower fighting to break through the cracks of our shared past.

A few days later, as I walked through the bustling streets of our little town, the autumn air crackled with a crispness that made everything feel alive. Leaves swirled like confetti around my feet, each one a small celebration of change. I was on my way to meet Mabel again, the first time since that bittersweet reunion at The Broken Compass. The sun draped everything in golden light, but my heart felt heavy with uncertainty.

The café had become a symbol of our tentative steps toward rebuilding, but today, I was both excited and apprehensive. I pushed open the door and was greeted by the comforting blend of coffee and baked goods. Mabel was already there, a pumpkin spice latte cradled in her hands. I couldn't help but notice the way she absentmindedly traced the rim of her cup, a nervous habit that had never changed.

"Hey, look who finally made it!" she exclaimed, her voice a mix of teasing and genuine warmth. "I was starting to think you'd found a better offer. Did someone promise you free muffins?"

I chuckled, sliding into the chair across from her. "As tempting as that sounds, nothing beats our little coffee chats. Though I will say, it's a close second." I glanced around, noticing a few regulars tucked into their corners, but my focus remained on her.

The banter felt familiar, yet it was underscored by a gravity that neither of us could ignore. "So, how's life treating you?" I asked, hoping to keep the conversation light while gauging her mood.

"Better, I think," she replied, a glimmer of hope flickering in her eyes. "I've started volunteering at the animal shelter. You know, working with those furballs has a way of putting things in perspective."

I raised an eyebrow, intrigued. "Is that code for 'I've adopted three cats and a dog'?"

"Not yet! I'm holding strong. Although, I may or may not be fostering a particularly needy tabby named Mr. Whiskers," she grinned, and for a moment, the atmosphere around us softened, the tension easing as laughter bubbled to the surface.

"Mr. Whiskers? Are you trying to win the title of 'crazy cat lady' before you're thirty?"

"Maybe! I mean, have you seen the way he looks at me? It's like I'm the only person in his universe. I can't resist his charm." Her enthusiasm was infectious, and I felt a warmth spreading through my chest. It was moments like these that reminded me of the bond we once shared, the lightness we had both seemingly lost.

"Do you think we could resurrect that charm between us?" I asked, the question hanging in the air like a balloon ready to pop.

Mabel's expression shifted, her smile faltering slightly. "I hope so. I really do. But I know I've got a lot to prove, and it won't be easy."

"Nothing worthwhile ever is," I agreed. "But I'm willing to try, if you are."

"Absolutely. It's like riding a bike, right? Just a little rusty and in need of some grease."

I chuckled, shaking my head at the analogy. "I'm not sure I like the idea of us being bikes—though I suppose it beats being stuck in a ditch."

"Touché. Let's aim for a smooth ride then," she said, and the hint of mischief returned to her eyes.

We talked about everything—her newfound love for animals, my latest obsession with mystery novels, and the absurdities of our teenage years. Laughter flowed freely, spilling over into the moments of silence, each shared story acting as a thread in the fabric of our renewed relationship. It felt like a fragile bridge, but one worth building.

As we finished our drinks, Mabel's expression turned serious again. "I know it's still early, but I'd like to do something special for you. Something to show I'm committed to making this work."

I looked at her curiously. "What do you have in mind? A giant banner that reads 'Sisterly Forgiveness?' Because I'm not sure that'll go over well with the neighbors."

"Maybe not," she laughed, but her gaze grew earnest. "I was thinking we could do a weekend getaway. Just us. Some place where we can relax, talk, and maybe even get lost a little. No distractions, just us reconnecting."

The idea tugged at my heart. "You mean like a sister retreat? I'm not sure I can handle the level of bonding that might entail. You know how emotional I get."

"That's the point!" Mabel exclaimed, her eyes shining with enthusiasm. "We can be goofy, cry over old photos, and maybe even have a dance party in the middle of the woods. Just think about it: no interruptions, no outside noise. Just us."

The vision she painted was tempting, a tantalizing escape that felt like a breath of fresh air after a long winter. But lurking beneath the excitement was a whisper of caution. "What if we don't like what we find?"

Mabel leaned in closer, her voice softening. "What if we do? This is our chance to find out. We can face the past and see what still binds us."

A flicker of hope ignited within me, battling against my hesitation. "Okay. I'll consider it. But no promises on the dance party."

"Deal! But be warned—I'm bringing my best playlist."

As we stood to leave, I felt a renewed sense of purpose. The journey ahead wasn't going to be easy, but perhaps we could navigate it together, one step at a time. With each conversation, each shared moment, I sensed the possibility of healing, and the prospect of a rekindled sisterhood began to feel like more than just a distant dream.

Walking out of The Broken Compass, I felt lighter, the weight of our past still present but less suffocating. Mabel had extended her hand, and I was ready to reach back, not knowing where the road would lead but hopeful that, together, we could rebuild not just the bridges but the very essence of our sisterhood.

The following weekend, as we loaded our bags into Mabel's car, a nervous excitement fizzled in the air, crackling like static. The sunlight filtered through the trees, casting playful shadows on the pavement, and I couldn't help but feel a sense of adventure bubbling up inside me. The prospect of a weekend away, just the two of us, held the promise of both healing and chaos. My sister had planned a little escape to a cozy cabin nestled in the woods, far from the reminders of our complicated past. I wasn't sure what to expect, but the idea of getting lost in nature sounded like just what we needed.

"Remember to grab the snacks!" Mabel called out, her voice a perfect blend of enthusiasm and urgency. I turned to find her wrestling with a gigantic bag of chips that seemed far too large for our short trip. "What if we encounter a bear? We'll need sustenance!"

"Or a raccoon," I countered, raising an eyebrow. "But sure, let's stock up on junk food like we're about to embark on a month-long expedition."

She laughed, a sound that felt refreshing against the backdrop of our recent past. "It's all about survival, sister! Besides, junk food is part of the bonding experience."

As we hit the road, the familiar rhythm of our banter began to ease the tension that had hovered over us for weeks. The scenery transformed from the bustling town to the serene countryside, lush greens giving way to golden hues as the sun dipped lower in the sky. Mabel sang along to the radio, her voice surprisingly on pitch, and

I found myself joining in despite my reluctance. We belted out pop anthems from our youth, our laughter echoing off the car windows, blending seamlessly into the melody.

"Okay, but can we agree to never speak of this moment again?" I joked, faking a serious expression as I turned to her. "I have a reputation to uphold."

"Your secret is safe with me, but only if you promise to dance like nobody's watching tonight," she shot back, her eyes sparkling with mischief.

"Deal. But no TikTok-worthy moves, please. I'm saving those for a true crisis."

The cabin came into view just as twilight settled in, the wooden structure hugging the forest as if it belonged there. A faint smell of pine enveloped us as we stepped out of the car. Mabel tossed her bags over her shoulder, already moving toward the door, and I felt a twinge of nerves mingling with my excitement.

Inside, the cabin was warm and inviting, decorated with rustic charm and hints of a life once lived. The fireplace beckoned, its mantle lined with weathered photographs of families gathered for laughter and meals. "We should definitely recreate one of these," I suggested, running my fingers over the edges of a picture frame.

Mabel grinned. "With our artistic skills? I can see it now—abstract, impressionist take on a sisters' gathering. It'll be an exhibition in every gallery."

As night descended, we settled on the couch, a patchwork of cushions and blankets offering cozy warmth. The crackling fire danced in front of us, flickering shadows that seemed to narrate stories of their own. We sipped on mugs of hot cocoa, the rich chocolate contrasting with the cool air that wafted through the open window.

"Okay, let's get serious for a moment," I said, glancing at her over the rim of my cup. "This weekend is about us. No more skirting around the issues. What do you really want?"

Mabel took a deep breath, her gaze thoughtful as she stirred her drink. "I want to fix what's broken between us. I know I hurt you, and I don't expect you to forget that, but I want to try to make it right."

I nodded, my heart pounding. "And how do you plan on doing that? Trust isn't just handed out like candy."

"By being here. By showing up, not just physically but emotionally. I'm not perfect, and I can't erase the past, but I can promise to be different moving forward."

The sincerity in her voice wrapped around me like a warm blanket, but doubts still lurked at the edges of my mind. "But can you? Can we?"

Before she could respond, a sudden noise shattered the moment. A loud thump echoed from outside, followed by a rustle of leaves. Mabel and I exchanged bewildered glances.

"Did you hear that?" she asked, her eyes wide with curiosity and a hint of fear.

"Yeah. Maybe it's just the wind?" I suggested, but even I could hear the uncertainty in my voice.

"Or it could be a bear looking for its midnight snack," she replied, a nervous laugh escaping her lips.

"Let's hope Mr. Whiskers isn't out there scouting for food," I joked, though I felt the tension creeping back in.

Mabel pushed the curtain aside to peer out the window, her silhouette framed by the warm glow of the firelight. "It's probably nothing," she said, but her voice trembled slightly.

I joined her at the window, peering into the darkness that cloaked the forest. The trees stood tall and imposing, shadows flickering as the wind swayed them like dancers. For a moment, everything felt still, as if the world was holding its breath.

Just then, another noise echoed—a distinct crack, like a twig snapping underfoot. We both jumped back, our eyes wide. "Okay, definitely not just the wind," I whispered.

"What if it's someone out there?" Mabel asked, her voice barely above a whisper.

"Then I hope they're friendly," I replied, trying to maintain my composure. "Let's just pretend we're not home, right?"

But as we stood there, the hairs on my arms began to prickle, a sensation of being watched washing over me. I caught a glimpse of movement near the edge of the trees—something darker than the night around it, shifting with purpose.

"Mabel…"

Before I could finish, she had already stepped toward the door. "I need to see what that was," she declared, a spark of bravery igniting her features.

"Mabel, wait! We should—"

But it was too late. She flung open the door, the sound echoing through the stillness. "Hello?" she called, her voice ringing with defiance, yet I could hear the tremor beneath it.

And that's when I saw it—a figure emerging from the shadows, cloaked in darkness, standing just beyond the reach of the cabin light. A moment stretched, taut as a bowstring, as the world around us seemed to spiral into chaos, the promise of what this night held flickering just out of reach, leaving us at the brink of uncertainty.

Chapter 20: The Balancing Act

The café buzzes with a familiar energy, the clinking of mugs and the soft hum of conversation weaving a cozy tapestry around us. The air is thick with the rich aroma of freshly brewed coffee, mingling with the sweet scent of pastries on the display counter. I watch as Mabel stirs her cup, her brow furrowed in thought, casting fleeting glances my way as if to gauge my emotional temperature. The sunlight streaming through the window casts a warm glow over her curly hair, making it look almost ethereal, like a halo trying to convince me that everything is alright. But the truth is, it feels anything but.

I take a sip of my latte, its warmth a brief comfort against the gnawing anxiety coiled within me. The creamy foam swirls on top, almost taunting me with the illusion of calm. Mabel's hands dance over the table as she speaks, her animated gestures punctuating her words, but I'm only half-listening, trapped in my thoughts. My sister's return has been nothing short of a storm, her voice echoing in my mind, an uninvited whisper urging me to choose sides.

"I mean, seriously, if we don't get the muffins before they sell out, I might just go into a full-on pastry meltdown," Mabel says, snapping me out of my reverie. Her teasing tone manages to elicit a smile, if only briefly.

"I'll take my chances," I reply, my attempt at lightheartedness falling flat. "I'm not sure what I'd do if I had to deal with a muffin crisis."

Mabel's laughter dances through the café, and it's the kind of sound that draws smiles from strangers. "You'd probably write a heartfelt letter to the bakery. 'Dear Muffin Makers, I regret to inform you that my emotional state hinges on your baked goods…'"

The absurdity of it tugs at my lips, and for a moment, I imagine Mabel's scenario—me, penning a desperate plea for blueberry muffins, each word dripping with melodrama. "Okay, that's not entirely inaccurate," I concede, trying to shake off the clouds looming overhead.

But as the laughter fades, the shadows creep back in. I glance around the café, noticing the couples entwined in whispered conversations, the friends leaning in close, sharing secrets like precious treasures. I can't help but feel like an intruder in my own life, watching from a distance as others revel in uncomplicated connections. It's disheartening, the way my mind oscillates between gratitude for Mabel's presence and guilt over my sister's growing influence.

"I can't believe she just waltzed back in," Mabel says, her tone suddenly serious, an undercurrent of tension threading through her words. "After everything that happened, it feels like she's trying to claim a part of you she lost."

I nod, biting my lip as I contemplate my response. "It's... complicated. She's trying to make amends, but it's like trying to fit a square peg into a round hole." I take a deep breath, forcing the words out. "There's a part of me that wants to forgive, to embrace the sister I used to know, but another part is terrified of what that might mean."

Mabel reaches across the table, her hand warm and reassuring against mine. "You're not obligated to take her back just because she's showing up again. Your feelings matter, too. Don't forget that."

Her words are a lifeline, a reminder that amidst the chaos, my emotional truth holds weight. Yet the guilt swells again, an unwelcome companion whispering that my sister deserves a chance. I can feel the two sides of myself waging war, each demanding my allegiance.

"I just wish it didn't feel like a betrayal," I admit, the admission tasting bitter on my tongue. "I'm trying to balance everything, but it's like walking a tightrope. One misstep, and I could fall."

"Life is messy," Mabel says, a spark of mischief lighting her eyes. "But hey, if you do fall, at least you'll have some good stories to tell. Maybe even a dramatic muffin rescue mission."

Her attempt to lighten the mood is welcome, and I chuckle, but the laughter fades too quickly. "What if the story ends with me losing both of you?" The thought hangs heavy in the air, a specter lurking just beyond the edges of our conversation.

"You won't lose me," Mabel assures, her voice steady. "But you've got to set boundaries. If she pushes you into a corner, you need to stand up for yourself. You've been through enough already."

"Boundaries," I echo, the word tasting foreign on my tongue. I've spent so long avoiding conflict, tiptoeing around fragile emotions, that the idea of drawing lines feels daunting. "What if she gets angry? What if I hurt her feelings?"

Mabel rolls her eyes playfully. "You're not responsible for her feelings. If she can't handle you needing space, that's on her. You can't pour from an empty cup, right?"

The truth of her words seeps in, and I lean back, letting her wisdom settle around me like a comforting blanket. I want to believe I can hold my ground without collapsing under the weight of obligation. "Maybe you're right," I say softly, testing the idea.

"Of course I'm right," she replies, a cheeky grin spreading across her face. "Now, let's get those muffins before I have a meltdown of my own."

As we stand to order, I feel a flicker of hope igniting within me. Perhaps I can navigate this balancing act without losing myself entirely. Maybe, just maybe, I can carve out a space where I can honor my past with my sister while cherishing the friendship that keeps me grounded.

The bell above the café door jingles as we step outside, releasing us into the crisp afternoon air that dances playfully around us. Autumn is creeping in, painting the world with splashes of gold and crimson, the leaves swirling like confetti at a party I wasn't quite invited to. Mabel tilts her head back, inhaling deeply, her smile bright as if the sun itself has taken residence in her cheeks. "This weather is basically begging us to have a pumpkin spice adventure," she declares, and I can't help but laugh. The lightness of her spirit is infectious, a much-needed balm for my troubled thoughts.

"Ah, yes, the sacred autumn ritual of caffeinated gourd beverages," I reply, rolling my eyes with mock seriousness. "We must pay our respects to the season before winter descends like a grumpy old troll."

"Exactly! Plus, it's a chance to wear sweaters that have been sitting in the closet, judging me for months." Mabel gestures dramatically, as if the sweaters themselves are part of some grand conspiracy against her social life.

I shake my head, letting the absurdity pull me back into the moment, but beneath the humor, the weight of my reality still tugs at the corners of my mind. Mabel and I stroll down the street, the vibrant energy of the city wrapping around us. Each step feels heavier than the last, my thoughts spiraling into the mess that is my sister and the reemerging ties that bind us. The trees lining the sidewalk rustle, their leaves whispering secrets I'm not yet ready to hear.

"Why don't we check out that new market around the corner?" Mabel suggests, her voice slicing through my reverie. "I heard they have the best caramel apples in the city, and I am absolutely determined to have one without making a fool of myself."

"Ah, a noble quest," I say, leaning into her enthusiasm, the thought of sticky sweetness momentarily distracting me. "You'll just have to remember not to bite into it like an overzealous toddler."

"Please, like you have room to talk. You once nearly declared war on a slice of chocolate cake," she retorts, her laughter bubbling up like the most effervescent of sodas.

We reach the market, a riot of colors and sounds that envelops us. Vendors shout their wares, the scent of cinnamon and roasted nuts mingling in the air, wrapping around us like a soft embrace. Mabel drags me through the throng of shoppers, her excitement palpable as she gestures toward a stand overflowing with glistening caramel apples, each one coated in a glossy sheen that promises both danger and delight.

"Look at those!" Mabel exclaims, her eyes wide with wonder as if she's just spotted a treasure chest overflowing with riches. "It's a caramel apple wonderland! I need one—preferably two. One for the aesthetic and one for… emotional support."

I chuckle at her exaggerated urgency. "Then I'd better get in line before you spontaneously combust from caramel-induced enthusiasm."

As we wait, I can't shake the feeling that something is brewing beneath the surface, an undercurrent of tension I can't quite identify. Mabel chats animatedly about flavors and toppings, her voice rising and falling like the waves of the ocean, but I find myself glancing around, half-listening. The laughter and chatter of the crowd become a dull roar, and my mind drifts back to my sister, her return a relentless specter looming at the edges of my thoughts.

"Hey, are you with me?" Mabel's voice cuts through my reverie, pulling me back to the present. "You look like you just watched a horror movie trailer on repeat."

"Sorry, I was just… thinking," I admit, forcing a smile. "About my sister, and how she's like an unexpected plot twist in a really bad rom-com."

"Plot twist? More like a rogue character who forgot their lines but is still stealing the show," Mabel quips, her laughter ringing out like a bell. "What's her angle, anyway? You don't need that kind of drama in your life."

"Exactly! I thought we had closed that chapter, but now it's like she's come back for the sequel, and I didn't even want the original," I grumble, my frustration bubbling over like a pot of boiling water. "Every time I try to focus on what's in front of me—what I've built with you—she pops back up like a bad penny."

Mabel tilts her head, a thoughtful look crossing her face. "Maybe it's time to flip the script. You have the power to decide how much of her story you let into your life. Set the boundaries we talked about earlier. You're the main character here; don't let her overshadow you."

"I know, I know," I reply, rubbing my temples as if I can massage away the tension. "But what if she takes it personally? What if I lose her again?"

"Then maybe she wasn't meant to be in your story in the first place," Mabel says, her gaze steady. "It's hard, but you can't be everyone's hero without losing yourself in the process."

The vendor finally hands us our caramel apples, their glossy surfaces glistening under the sun, and I can't help but admire the way Mabel lights up, her troubles momentarily forgotten as she clutches the sweet treat like a trophy. "To new beginnings, and the occasional sticky situation!" she declares, raising her apple as if proposing a toast.

"To new beginnings," I echo, raising mine, the tension in my chest easing just a fraction.

But as we bite into our apples, the rich caramel giving way to the crispness of the fruit, I can't shake the feeling that the weight of my choices is just beginning to settle in. Each bite is both sweet and heavy, the juxtaposition of flavors echoing the complexities of my life. There's a sweetness in Mabel's laughter and the warmth of our friendship, yet the bitter notes of unresolved issues linger like an unwelcome guest, refusing to leave.

"Hey, what do you think about trying that pumpkin spice place next?" Mabel asks, her eyes sparkling with excitement.

"Sure," I reply, though my thoughts are still caught in the web of my sister's reemergence. As we wander deeper into the market, I realize that no matter how sweet the caramel is, I must confront the messy truths swirling around me. Each step forward is a chance to reclaim my narrative, to draw the lines I so desperately need. And maybe, just maybe, I can find a way to balance the love for my sister with the fierce loyalty I owe to myself.

The pumpkin spice café is a treasure chest of autumnal delights, its walls adorned with cozy string lights that twinkle like stars against the backdrop of rich burgundy and soft beige. Mabel and I step inside, the air infused with the warm scent of baked goods and spiced lattes. As I take a deep breath, I feel a brief sense of comfort settle around me, like a well-worn sweater.

"I swear, if I don't leave this place with a muffin and a pumpkin spice latte, it might just ruin my entire week," Mabel proclaims, her eyes lighting up as they scan the menu board, as if it's a map to buried treasure.

"Not to mention your emotional well-being," I quip, nudging her playfully. "It's practically a public service to indulge in seasonal flavors."

"Exactly! We're practically saving the world, one pastry at a time," she replies, her voice gleeful as she bounces on her heels, making me laugh.

As we wait in line, the barista, a tattooed whirlwind of energy, takes our orders with a charming smile. Mabel leans in closer, her excitement palpable. "You know, I read somewhere that pumpkin spice is actually a magical elixir. They say it has healing properties. You know, for the soul."

"Right, because nothing says 'I'm feeling great' like a belly full of sugar and spice," I reply, rolling my eyes dramatically. But a part of me savors the lightness of this moment, the simple joy of being here with her, away from the spiraling chaos of my family life.

With our drinks and a selection of muffins balanced precariously in hand, we settle at a small table by the window, the golden light spilling over us like syrup. I take a sip of my latte, the warmth spreading through me, momentarily distracting me from the storm brewing in my heart.

"So, tell me," Mabel begins, leaning forward, her elbows resting on the table, "how do you feel about your sister? Really?"

I pause, the question settling heavy between us like a boulder. "I wish I could say I'm excited, but... it's complicated." The words tumble out, tinged with a mixture of frustration and uncertainty. "I want to give her a chance, but every time I think about her, I feel this knot in my stomach. It's like trying to find a signal in a thunderstorm."

Mabel nods, her expression serious, yet understanding. "You're allowed to have mixed feelings, you know. It's not like she's just going to magically turn into the sister you remember."

"Exactly!" I exclaim, grateful for her validation. "I keep trying to remind myself that she's not the same person I grew up with. That girl is long gone, replaced by... whatever this is." I gesture vaguely, a wave of exasperation washing over me. "She wants to play the role of the devoted sister now, but I can't shake the feeling that it's all an act."

Mabel takes a bite of her muffin, her eyes sparkling with mischief. "So, you think she's auditioning for a part in your life?"

"More like she's reading from a script she didn't bother to memorize." I take a sip of my latte, feeling the heat burn my throat. "And here I am, just sitting in the audience, trying to figure out if I want to clap or throw tomatoes."

"Sounds like a classic case of mixed signals," Mabel muses, the corners of her lips curling into a smirk. "You could always send her to acting school. Might help her learn how to improvise."

"Maybe I should just hand her a mirror," I shoot back, a grin creeping across my face. "Here, take a good look at yourself, and tell me if this is who you really want to be."

The laughter fades, and a moment of silence envelops us. I feel the tension creeping back in, a reminder of the delicate balance I'm trying to maintain. Mabel's eyes soften, and she leans back in her chair, clearly sensing the shift. "You know I'm here for you, right? Whatever happens with your sister, I've got your back."

"Thank you," I reply, my voice barely a whisper. "It means more than you know."

Our conversation drifts back to lighter topics, the warmth of friendship momentarily chasing away the shadows. We share stories about our pasts, goofy memories that bubble to the surface like the froth on my latte. But even as we laugh, the knot in my stomach remains, a stubborn reminder of the unresolved conflict lurking in my life.

As the afternoon sun begins its descent, casting long shadows across the café, my phone buzzes on the table. The sudden vibration sends a jolt through me, and I pick it up, my heart racing as I glance at the screen. It's a message from my sister.

Can we talk?

I freeze, the laughter fading as the weight of her request settles like a stone in my chest. Mabel notices my change in demeanor, her eyes narrowing with concern. "What's up?"

"It's my sister. She wants to talk," I reply, my voice strained as I try to gauge my own feelings.

"What do you want to do?" Mabel asks, her tone steady, urging me to confront the decision I've been avoiding.

I take a deep breath, the air thick with uncertainty. "I don't know. Part of me wants to ignore her, to pretend like everything is fine. But... maybe we do need to have a conversation."

"Then have it," Mabel encourages, her expression fierce. "Just make sure you're standing your ground. You're not her emotional punching bag anymore."

"I know," I say, but the doubt creeps back in. "What if she pushes me too far? What if this only makes things worse?"

Mabel leans forward, her eyes piercing mine. "You're stronger than you think. You've come this far; don't let fear dictate your choices. Talk to her on your terms."

With a shaky hand, I type a response, my heart pounding like a drum in my chest.

What do you want to talk about?

I hit send, and a chill rushes through me, the kind of chill that settles deep in the bones. As we wait, the atmosphere shifts, the café bustling around us, oblivious to the turmoil brewing at our table. The seconds stretch into an eternity, my breath shallow as I try to read Mabel's expression.

Then my phone buzzes again, and I open the message, my heart sinking at the words that flash across the screen.

We need to meet. I have something important to tell you.

"Shit," I mutter, the air thickening with tension as I process the weight of her request. "This can't be good."

"What did she say?" Mabel asks, concern etched on her face.

"She wants to meet," I reply, dread pooling in my stomach like lead. "And I have a feeling it's not just to catch up over coffee."

"Are you going to?"

"I don't know," I whisper, feeling the walls closing in around me. "But I can't ignore this. Not now."

As I look out the window, the sun dips below the horizon, the world outside cloaked in darkness. My heart races as I realize I'm standing at a precipice, teetering on the edge of a decision that could change everything.

Suddenly, my phone buzzes again, and I pick it up, my breath catching in my throat.

It's about Mom.

My mind races, the implications unfurling like a dark cloud looming overhead, and as I meet Mabel's concerned gaze, I know that the balancing act I've been trying so hard to maintain is about to come crashing down.

Chapter 21: An Unexpected Visitor

The atmosphere in The Broken Compass buzzed with life as I wiped down the bar, the scent of roasted coffee beans mingling with the warm, sugary aroma of freshly baked pastries. I loved the rhythm of this place, the way laughter erupted like champagne bubbles, filling the air with a comforting buzz that made me forget, even for a moment, my worries. The polished wood of the bar gleamed under the soft, amber glow of the hanging pendant lights, casting a cozy warmth across the mismatched furniture and eclectic decor that adorned the walls. Each piece told a story—a battered antique mirror, a framed photograph of the town from decades past, a collection of vintage liquor bottles that stood as silent witnesses to countless toasts and heartbreaks.

Just as I was about to pour myself a much-deserved cup of coffee, the bell above the door chimed, and I turned to greet the next customer, my smile fading into a tight-lipped line. There he was: Jake. My ex-boyfriend. The man who had been the bright star in my teenage dreams, now a constellation of contradictions. His hair was tousled in a way that suggested he'd spent the last few years wrestling with life itself, a rugged charm clinging to him like the remnants of a summer storm. He was dressed in a leather jacket, the fabric worn and cracked, and jeans that hung just right on his lean frame. That smirk, the one that had once sent my heart racing, now pulled at the edges of my resolve.

"Hey, can I get a whiskey neat?" he said, his voice smooth, but it felt like a jagged stone lodged in my throat. I nodded, the muscles in my jaw tightening as I reached for the bottle. Mabel, my steadfast companion behind the counter, caught my eye from across the room, her brow furrowed in concern. She knew better than to intervene but was silently urging me to take a deep breath. "How've you been?"

Jake asked, leaning against the bar, casual, as if we were just picking up where we left off after all those years apart.

"Busy," I replied, the word escaping my lips sharper than I intended. It was true. The Broken Compass had become my sanctuary, my lifeline to a community that needed me. I poured the whiskey with precision, watching the golden liquid swirl in the glass, wishing it could drown my swirling thoughts. I slid the drink toward him, feeling the tension between us thicken like syrup.

"I've heard this place has a killer vibe," he said, lifting the glass to his lips. "I remember when it was just a dive bar with questionable karaoke nights."

"Yeah, well, some things change," I said, attempting a playful tone, though the weight of our history loomed like a fog. "Others... don't."

"Touché." He chuckled, a sound that was both familiar and foreign, tugging at the frayed edges of my heart. "So, how's life treating you?"

I leaned against the bar, forcing a nonchalant air as I attempted to keep my emotions at bay. "I've been managing. You know how it is." I gestured toward a group of patrons laughing at a nearby table, their carefree joy a stark contrast to the heaviness that had settled between us. "Life goes on, right?"

He studied me for a moment, those deep, expressive eyes searching my face as if trying to decipher a puzzle he'd once been able to solve effortlessly. "You're looking good, Emma," he said, and the sincerity in his voice caught me off guard.

"Thanks. And you... you look different. Good different." I meant it, but I couldn't help feeling a little pang of jealousy. "Rugged."

"Guess I've been roughing it a bit," he said, flashing that disarming smile, which reminded me of the summer nights spent talking under starlit skies, where our dreams felt boundless. I shifted, uncomfortably aware of how easily our chemistry rekindled.

Just as I was about to navigate the treacherous waters of our past, the door swung open again, and a gust of wind swept through the bar, bringing with it an unexpected chill. A tall figure stepped inside, and I felt a wave of recognition wash over me. It was Sarah, my friend and self-appointed life coach, her usual vibrancy dimmed by the sharp lines of anxiety etched across her face. She spotted me, her eyes widening in alarm as she approached.

"Emma! I—" she began, but her words faltered when she caught sight of Jake.

"Oh, great," I muttered under my breath. The two people in my life I'd been avoiding were now colliding in the same moment. "What's up?"

"Just came to check on you. You seem... tense," she said, glancing at Jake with a mixture of curiosity and apprehension.

"Is that what you call it?" I replied, attempting to inject a lightness into my voice that was rapidly slipping away. "I thought it was my natural charm."

Sarah shot me a knowing look. "I'll just grab a drink and hang out over there." She gestured vaguely toward a corner table, but her hesitation spoke volumes. I could feel the weight of her concern, her instincts screaming at her to intervene.

"Good idea," Jake said, his voice tinged with a hint of annoyance, though it wasn't aimed at Sarah. I caught a flicker of protectiveness in his gaze as he watched her walk away. "You're doing a great job running this place, Emma. It looks amazing."

"Thanks," I replied, feeling an unexpected swell of pride at his compliment. "It's been a lot of work, but worth it."

"Glad to hear that. I mean it." His sincerity wrapped around me like a warm blanket, threatening to thaw the cold walls I'd built around my heart. I found myself wondering why it felt so easy to fall back into this rhythm with him, despite the past lurking like a shadow just out of reach.

As the evening unfolded, the atmosphere thickened with unsaid words and unacknowledged feelings. The tension crackled in the air, both electric and disconcerting. I watched him from behind the bar, my mind racing. What did he want? What did I want? And why did everything seem to spiral into chaos the moment he walked through that door?

The minutes stretched like taffy as I served drinks and attempted to ignore the weight of Jake's presence at the bar. My mind felt like a crowded room, full of echoes and half-formed thoughts clamoring for attention. Mabel, ever the perceptive friend, busied herself with a pile of napkins but shot me furtive glances, a silent plea for me to keep it together. Her dark curls bounced as she sidled closer, pretending to rearrange the cocktail garnishes, her bright eyes flickering between Jake and me.

"Another whiskey, Jake?" I asked, forcing a smile that felt more like a grimace.

He shook his head, his expression softening. "No, I'm good. Just catching up with old friends."

"Old friends," I echoed, the phrase tasting bitter on my tongue.

He raised an eyebrow, a playful challenge sparking in his gaze. "And we're not old friends, Emma? You know what they say about old flames."

"Yeah, they tend to burn down the house," I shot back, the words escaping before I could reel them in.

A laugh escaped him, genuine and rich, and I felt a tiny crack in my carefully constructed walls. "Touché. But maybe we could at least put the flames in a controlled environment, like a cozy campfire? Roast some marshmallows?"

"Sure, and while we're at it, let's pitch a tent and sing campfire songs." I didn't mean to be snarky, but sarcasm was my shield. The truth was, the idea of rekindling anything with Jake was terrifying.

"You know, I used to love those campfire songs," he replied, leaning in closer, his voice low and conspiratorial. "I think I still remember the words to 'Kumbaya.'"

"Oh, how nostalgic." I rolled my eyes, but my lips betrayed me, curling into a reluctant smile. "That really takes me back."

"See? There's a soft spot in there." He nodded knowingly, his gaze unwavering. "You've always been the one who wears her heart on her sleeve, Emma."

"Yeah, well, I also learned how to tuck it away when necessary." I poured another drink, my hands trembling slightly as I concentrated on the task. "Let's not pretend this is a heartwarming reunion."

The atmosphere around us thickened, charged with unspoken truths. I could feel the eyes of the patrons darting between us, their curiosity a palpable entity. Mabel busied herself washing glasses, her attention clearly divided.

"Fair enough," Jake conceded, the playfulness in his tone fading. "But can we at least acknowledge that we're here now? In this moment?"

I paused, the weight of his words hanging in the air like a delicate thread. "What do you want from me, Jake?"

He leaned back against the bar, his expression shifting to something more serious, more contemplative. "Honestly? I just wanted to see how you were doing. It's been a while, and I felt like... I owed you that much."

Owed me? The word lingered, prickling at the edges of my defenses. "Owed me?" I echoed, trying to wrap my head around the implication. "You think just showing up after all this time is enough?"

He took a breath, clearly weighing his response. "No, I don't. But I'd like to start somewhere. Maybe even make up for... everything."

The truth was, I'd spent years putting the pieces of my heart back together after our breakup, and here he was, a dark specter from the past, trying to stir the pot of emotions I had simmering just beneath the surface. "Jake, you have no idea what I've been through since then."

"I want to know," he said earnestly, leaning forward, his elbows resting on the bar as he met my gaze. "Just give me a chance."

The warmth of his sincerity was disarming, wrapping around me like a soft blanket, but it only made me want to retreat further. The last thing I needed was to open old wounds. I glanced over at Mabel, who looked like she was about to intervene, her expression a mix of concern and encouragement.

"Emma, do you want to talk about it?" she asked gently, her voice cutting through the charged atmosphere.

"No, I—" I began, but Jake cut in.

"I do," he insisted, a sense of urgency creeping into his tone. "I want to hear your side. I want to understand."

The sincerity in his eyes made my stomach flip. This wasn't the boy I remembered; he had transformed into someone who seemed genuinely invested in my story, and it was unnerving.

"Alright," I said, my voice barely above a whisper. "If you want to know... I've been rebuilding my life. I bought this place, turned it into something worthwhile. I've poured my heart and soul into it."

"Emma, I—"

"Let me finish," I interrupted, my emotions flaring. "It's not easy watching everything you built alone. I was so focused on proving to myself that I could make it without you, without anyone, that I didn't realize how lonely it felt."

Jake's eyes softened, and I could see the flicker of regret there. "I had no idea."

"Of course you didn't," I snapped, my anger flaring up like a sudden wildfire. "You disappeared, remember? You left without a word. No texts, no calls, nothing. You made your choice."

He winced, a shadow passing over his features. "I know. I was young and stupid, thinking I could handle everything on my own. But I'm here now. Can't we at least try to talk?"

Before I could respond, the door swung open again, and in walked a boisterous group of friends, the kind who seemed to emit energy like a thousand-watt bulb. Laughter erupted, filling the space and momentarily shattering the tension that had enveloped us.

"Emma!" one of them called, her voice cutting through my tangled thoughts. "Let's order some shots!"

I turned to the newcomers, grateful for the distraction. "Sure! What can I get you?"

Jake leaned back, an amused smile playing on his lips. "Looks like you've got a party to attend to. Maybe we'll just pick this up later?"

"Maybe," I replied, my heart a chaotic mix of hope and trepidation. As I turned to the bar, the bittersweet taste of unresolved feelings hung heavy in the air, leaving me wondering if I'd ever truly be able to move on.

The laughter of the newcomers enveloped The Broken Compass like a warm embrace, momentarily lifting the weight of the past off my shoulders. I turned to the group, their faces bright with excitement, and for a heartbeat, the bar transformed into a playground of nostalgia, where old friends reunited and stories spilled like the drinks I poured.

"Emma, we need shots! It's a celebration!" a tall woman with fiery red hair exclaimed, her arms flailing as if conducting a symphony of jubilation.

"Of what, exactly?" I asked, smirking, trying to catch my breath amidst the flurry of enthusiasm.

"Of surviving another week! And you know, that's a feat worth celebrating!" she said with mock seriousness, causing a ripple of laughter among her friends.

"Alright, alright," I relented, reaching for the tequila. "But I expect you to keep it together. We can't have a repeat of last month's karaoke night."

Her laughter rang out again, rich and infectious. "Fair point! I promise to keep my performance strictly to the shower from now on."

As I prepared the shots, I couldn't shake the sensation of Jake's gaze on me, his presence an unwelcome ghost looming in the corner of my mind. I glanced back at him, half-expecting to find him rolling his eyes at the antics of my patrons. Instead, he was smiling, a genuine smile that caused an unexpected flutter in my chest. It was strange to see him so relaxed, so far removed from the tense, fraught moments we had just shared.

"Here's to surviving another week!" I raised my voice, lifting the shot glasses toward the group. They all joined in, cheers echoing through the bar as the clinking of glass punctuated the air. I felt the energy shift, the lightness of the moment pulling me away from the weight of the conversation I'd just had with Jake.

"Emma, you've outdone yourself! This place is thriving!" Jake called over the din, his tone teasing yet sincere, a twinge of admiration lacing his words.

"Glad you approve," I replied, trying to maintain a light-hearted façade. "It's not easy managing the chaos, but I think I'm getting the hang of it."

He nodded, his eyes flickering with something I couldn't quite place—nostalgia, regret, or perhaps a glimmer of pride? Whatever it was, it sent a ripple of warmth through me, and I quickly turned back to the lively group, pouring more shots, ready to lose myself in the buzz of camaraderie.

As the night unfolded, the energy in the bar intensified, fueled by laughter and the joyous clamor of friends reconnecting. I joined the revelry, serving drinks, sharing stories, and trying to ignore the magnetic pull of Jake's gaze. With every passing minute, my internal battle raged on—could I truly put the past behind me, or was I merely stoking the fires of old wounds?

"Another round, Emma!" one of the friends called, her cheeks flushed from a mix of alcohol and merriment. I complied, pouring shots as the clinking glass became a melody of celebration.

"Just keep an eye on it, alright? I can't be responsible for any more late-night karaoke disasters," I said with a laugh, tossing the woman a playful wink.

"Only if you promise to join us next time," she shot back, the challenge in her voice playful yet pointed.

"Oh, you don't want that," I replied, shaking my head with a laugh. "My singing voice is reserved for my dog."

As I wiped down the bar, I felt Jake's presence draw closer, and the noise around us faded into a dull hum. "You should have sung with them," he said, his voice low and teasing. "I'm sure your dog would have appreciated it."

I turned to face him, a smirk tugging at my lips. "Only if I want to scare away all the customers."

His laughter filled the space, rich and melodic, reminding me of simpler times, of sun-soaked afternoons and late-night drives with music blasting. "You've always had a way with words, Emma. Just like back then."

"Is that a compliment or a dig?" I shot back, raising an eyebrow.

"Definitely a compliment," he said, leaning against the bar, his expression earnest. "You have this incredible gift for making people feel at home. It's no wonder this place has become such a success."

I felt a warmth creep into my cheeks. "Thanks. It's nice to hear that from you, of all people."

His gaze turned contemplative, as if he were peering into the depths of our shared past. "You've done well for yourself, haven't you?"

"Thanks for noticing," I replied, my tone slightly defensive. "But it hasn't been easy, especially after everything."

"Emma, I—"

The door swung open yet again, this time revealing a dark figure silhouetted against the neon glow of the streetlights. The buzz of conversation dwindled to a hush as the figure stepped inside, the atmosphere shifting abruptly. It was Ray, a local journalist who had been digging into the underbelly of our town's latest scandal—the kind that threatened to expose secrets buried deeper than my past with Jake.

"Emma! We need to talk!" Ray's voice sliced through the tension, his tone urgent, his eyes wide with a mixture of excitement and concern.

I exchanged a glance with Jake, confusion swirling between us. "What's going on, Ray?"

"It's about the old mill site," he said, rushing toward me, his breath coming in quick bursts. "There's something happening there, something big, and I think you might be in danger."

Danger? My heart skipped a beat, and I felt the color drain from my face. The mill had been abandoned for years, a relic of the town's industrial past, but recent whispers had hinted at shady dealings involving land developers and possibly even illegal activities.

"Danger? How?" I asked, my pulse racing.

"It's complicated, but I need your help. There are people involved who won't hesitate to keep their secrets buried," Ray said, glancing around the bar as if expecting someone to jump out from the shadows.

Jake straightened, the playful demeanor vanishing, replaced by a sharp focus. "What do you mean, Emma might be in danger?"

"Not here," Ray said quickly, his voice low, glancing nervously at the patrons now whispering among themselves. "Let's talk outside."

A shiver of unease ran down my spine, and I felt the weight of Jake's gaze bore into me as I hesitated. The tension crackled in the air, an invisible thread tugging me toward a choice I hadn't anticipated. "Wait, Ray. What are you talking about?"

But before Ray could respond, the door swung open again, and in walked a couple of rough-looking men, their expressions unreadable. The bar felt smaller, the walls closing in, and I suddenly wished for the comfort of my past, the simplicity of laughter and drinks, before the shadow of danger loomed over us.

"Emma, we need to leave," Jake said, his voice steady but laced with urgency.

I looked back at Ray, who nodded, his eyes wide with fear. "Please, trust me."

But before I could respond, the men approached, their intentions unclear, and just like that, the world I had carefully crafted began to unravel around me, leaving me teetering on the edge of an unexpected abyss.

Chapter 22: The Ghosts of the Past

A late afternoon sun dipped low in the sky, spilling golden hues across the café's patio, where the rich aroma of roasted coffee intertwined with the crisp scent of autumn leaves. I absently twirled the last sip of my caramel macchiato in its glass, the sweet warmth echoing the bittersweet memories that danced through my mind like leaves caught in a gust of wind. There, sitting across from me, was Jake—an old chapter of my life I thought I'd carefully tucked away. His laughter, infectious and vibrant, cut through the air, but the sound felt like a double-edged sword, slicing through my resolve.

"Remember that time we thought we could hike the cliffs at Windy Point?" he asked, a mischievous glint in his eyes that once made my heart flutter. His dark hair caught the light, framing his face with an allure I had long ago tried to forget. "You insisted we could make it to the top before sunset, and we ended up stuck in that weird little cave while the sun dipped below the horizon."

I couldn't help but smile, the memory as clear as the bright blue sky of that day. I remembered the way the cool breeze felt against my sun-kissed skin, how it had wrapped around us like a comforting blanket. But then there was the aftermath—the argument that had spiraled into months of resentment and silent treatments. "Yeah, and we nearly got lost. You were convinced your way was better," I teased, raising an eyebrow. I tried to keep my tone light, but the weight of his presence bore down on me, and I could sense Mabel's watchful eyes burning into my side.

Mabel, ever the perceptive friend, had picked up on the tension brewing between us. She sat next to me, her fingers nervously fidgeting with the edge of her notebook, a smattering of colorful pens scattered haphazardly across the table like fallen leaves. "You should ask him about the hike where he got stuck in a tree," she interjected, trying to lighten the mood. "I swear he spent more time trying to climb it than actually hiking."

"Hey, that tree was my Everest!" Jake shot back with mock indignation, and for a brief moment, we were transported back to those carefree days, the world a simpler place where heartbreak was just a distant whisper. Yet, as my gaze flickered to Mabel, I felt the weight of uncertainty settle between us like a thick fog. She was the one who had been there through the fallout, picking up the pieces when my heart shattered like glass.

"Speaking of the past," Jake continued, his tone shifting to something softer, almost wistful. "What if we relived some of those old memories? Just for old times' sake. There's a new bistro downtown I think you'd love." His eyes locked onto mine, and I felt a familiar tug at my heart, a seductive pull towards the comfort of nostalgia.

But what was nostalgia if not a gilded cage? I could almost hear the echoes of our past, the whispers of betrayal and disappointment mingling with laughter. The shadows of our shared history loomed over the table, ghostly reminders of promises unkept. "I don't know, Jake. It's been a while," I said, my voice faltering.

Mabel's hand found mine beneath the table, her warmth grounding me. "You know, sometimes it's good to revisit old haunts. Just...be careful," she murmured, concern lacing her words like a gentle caress. Her eyes darted between us, a mix of curiosity and protectiveness swirling in their depths.

"I promise I'm not here to stir things up. I just thought it might be nice," Jake insisted, leaning in a fraction closer, his sincerity almost tangible. "Things ended... badly, I know. But it doesn't have to be like that now."

I searched his gaze, searching for the boy I had once loved, but all I found was a stranger who wore his old face. The conflict inside me deepened, a whirlwind of emotions threatening to pull me apart. The idea of spending time with him felt like stepping onto a tightrope strung between two worlds—one where I could get lost in the warm embrace of old memories, and the other where I had fought so hard to build something new and steady.

"Remember the way you used to tease me about my cooking?" I shifted the conversation, attempting to deflect while keeping the nostalgia alive. "I still can't believe I thought I could make a soufflé."

His laughter was a soft echo of the past. "You set off the smoke alarm twice that night. I think the fire department was on speed dial." His smile was genuine, but it stung, reminding me of the sweetness that had long since turned to bitterness.

"Okay, fine," I said, my voice stronger than I felt. "You can take me to that bistro, but I'm bringing Mabel. No arguing. If we're revisiting the past, I need a safety net."

Mabel's eyes lit up, relief flooding her features. "See, I told you! It'll be fun!"

Jake nodded, a triumphant grin spreading across his face. "It's a date then. Just like old times."

As the sun dipped lower, casting long shadows across the café, I couldn't shake the feeling that I was stepping into a well-rehearsed play, the lines perfectly memorized but the script still unpredictable. The laughter and shared memories danced in the air around us, but the specter of what had come before lingered, waiting to pounce. What if the ghosts of our past were more than just echoes? What if they had teeth?

The night air was cool and crisp as we strolled through the streets, Mabel's laughter blending with the sounds of the bustling city. The bistro Jake had chosen was tucked away in a narrow alley, its string lights twinkling like stars against the deepening indigo sky. Each step felt laden with both trepidation and exhilaration, a tightrope walk between memories that seemed to dance just out of reach. I could sense the weight of anticipation—Mabel's eyes sparkled with curiosity, while Jake's demeanor radiated a confident charm that was both familiar and foreign.

As we reached the entrance, the warmth of the bistro enveloped us like a soft blanket, the rich scent of garlic and rosemary wafting from the kitchen, mingling with the faint notes of jazz that floated through the air. The ambiance was intimate, with candlelit tables arranged closely together, their flickering flames casting playful shadows on the walls. Jake guided us to a cozy corner table, his easy demeanor easing the knot of anxiety that had settled in my stomach.

"I hope the food is good; I've heard mixed reviews," he remarked, his eyes dancing with mischief as he settled into his seat across from me. "But I'm confident you'll manage to get a soufflé out of me at some point tonight."

Mabel snorted, almost choking on her water. "Oh, we have to hear the story of the great soufflé disaster! Did it involve more smoke than egg whites?"

I rolled my eyes playfully, shooting Jake a conspiratorial smile. "You have no idea. I've since perfected my skills—at least enough to avoid calling 911."

"Maybe you should give me a cooking lesson sometime," he teased, leaning forward, elbows on the table. "I might need it for the next time I attempt a gourmet meal."

Mabel leaned back, her expression a mixture of amusement and caution. "Just don't try any crazy recipes, or I might have to rescue you again."

The conversation flowed easily, each shared laugh stitching together the frayed edges of our past. The more I spoke with Jake, the more I found myself entranced by the charm that had initially drawn me to him. The nostalgia wrapped around me like a cozy scarf, blurring the harsh lines of our history. I momentarily forgot the ache of betrayal, the stinging memories that had once felt like a suffocating weight.

But every now and then, a shadow flickered across my thoughts—a ghost I couldn't quite shake off. Jake caught me staring off into space, and his brow furrowed, genuine concern flickering in his eyes. "Hey, you okay? You seem a million miles away."

"Just thinking," I replied, forcing a smile. "About how quickly things can change."

"Yeah, I get that." He paused, his tone shifting to something softer. "You know, I didn't mean to hurt you back then. I was an idiot."

I bit my lip, weighing the sincerity of his words. "You didn't just hurt me, Jake. You shattered everything I believed about us."

The air between us thickened, and for a moment, it felt as if the room had faded away, leaving just the two of us suspended in a fragile bubble. Mabel cleared her throat, the noise echoing like a gentle nudge back to reality. "So, what's next on the agenda after this delightful meal? Another trip down memory lane?"

Jake chuckled, his laughter breaking the tension like a stone tossed into still water. "How about a walk by the river? I hear it's beautiful at night, especially with the city lights reflecting off the water."

"Sounds lovely," Mabel said, her enthusiasm genuine. "As long as you promise not to get us lost again, Jake."

With the playful banter returning, we finished our meal amid laughter and stories, Jake's charm wrapping around us like the warmth of a snug blanket on a cold night. I found myself leaning into the moment, the familiar thrill of his presence igniting old sparks I had thought extinguished.

But the longer I spent with him, the more the nagging thought persisted: Was I reopening a door best left shut? The evening air felt electric as we stepped outside, the chill swirling around us, mingling with the warmth of the bistro.

As we walked toward the river, the sound of water lapping against the shore harmonized with the distant hum of city life. The path was illuminated by a string of lights hanging overhead, casting a soft glow on our faces. Mabel walked slightly ahead, her phone buzzing in her pocket as she pointed out landmarks and amusing anecdotes, effortlessly breaking the silence with her infectious energy.

"Look at that!" she exclaimed, gesturing toward a group of swans gliding gracefully across the water. "They're so serene, like little floaty dream boats."

I chuckled, watching the swans bobbing along as if choreographed to the music of the night. "And they look so dignified until you realize they're just waiting for someone to throw them bread."

Jake leaned closer, lowering his voice to a conspiratorial whisper. "I heard they actually prefer crackers. You know, for the crunch."

I burst out laughing, shaking my head at his unexpected wit. "Crackers, really? Is that in the swan handbook?"

"I could write it," he replied, his grin infectious. "Swan Snacks 101."

Mabel sighed dramatically. "If only the world knew the wisdom of Jake. You'd be a bestseller!"

The laughter trailed off as we reached the riverbank, the water reflecting the moonlight like a silver blanket. A cool breeze danced across my skin, and for a moment, I closed my eyes, allowing myself to absorb the beauty of the scene. But even as I marveled at the moment, the tension simmered beneath the surface, a reminder that this was not just a picturesque evening—it was a crossroads.

Jake stepped closer, his expression shifting from playful to earnest. "You know, I've missed this—us. The way we could just... be. No pretenses."

The sincerity in his voice struck a chord within me, a longing I hadn't fully acknowledged until that moment. "I've missed it too, but it's complicated. What we had was... special, but it was also broken."

His eyes searched mine, and I felt the familiar pang of emotions battling for dominance. "Maybe it doesn't have to be broken anymore. People change, you know?"

"Change can be good," I replied, feeling the weight of uncertainty hanging heavy in the air. "But it can also mask old habits."

The moment stretched, charged with possibilities and the weight of the past. Mabel, sensing the shift, stepped back, giving us space while still keeping an eye on the river. As the tension thickened, I wondered if we were standing at the edge of a new beginning or a return to old patterns, the swans gliding by, utterly unaware of the turmoil brewing between us. The night was pregnant with unspoken words, and the path ahead seemed as murky as the water beneath our feet.

The water sparkled under the moonlight, casting rippling reflections that danced like fleeting memories across the surface. Jake stood beside me, the tension between us a taut line, ready to snap at the slightest provocation. Mabel, ever the mediator, leaned against a nearby railing, her eyes darting between us, as if she were a referee in an unannounced match. I wished I could read her thoughts, to understand whether she was rooting for Jake or for the part of me that had spent years healing from his ghost.

"Change, huh?" I finally broke the silence, my voice steady despite the fluttering in my chest. "People can change, but can they truly erase the past?"

Jake's gaze bore into mine, earnest and intense. "I think they can learn from it. I know I've had to." His words hung in the air like a promise and a challenge, both comforting and unnerving.

Mabel, sensing the weight of our exchange, interjected with her signature flair. "Well, learning is all well and good, but let's not pretend this is a soap opera where we can just sweep everything under the rug. What are you really saying, Jake?"

He chuckled, the tension easing slightly. "You always did have a way of cutting through the nonsense, Mabel. I'm saying I want another chance—maybe not the same kind, but something new, something better."

My heart raced. The air felt thick with the potential of a new beginning, but the shadows of our past loomed like storm clouds on the horizon. "What if I'm not ready for a 'something new'? What if I still have too many ghosts lurking around?"

"Then let's chase them away together," Jake offered, his sincerity resonating with an unexpected warmth. "We don't have to rush into anything. Just... let's figure it out as we go. One step at a time."

I bit my lip, contemplating the invitation. It felt reckless, like stepping onto a bridge that swayed in the wind, uncertain but tantalizing. Mabel shifted her weight, her expression a mix of support and worry. "You know you don't have to do this just because he asked, right?"

"I know," I replied, turning my attention back to the shimmering water. "But the idea of exploring this... whatever it is, is enticing. Like a mystery novel I want to unravel."

"Then go for it," Mabel urged. "Just remember that some stories come with plot twists."

"Plot twists?" Jake quirked an eyebrow, a smirk tugging at his lips. "Are we writing a novel here? I thought we were just trying to navigate some awkward emotions."

I laughed, the sound breaking the tension further. "Oh, trust me, if we were writing a novel, this would be a bestseller—full of drama, suspense, and a smattering of unrequited love."

"Perfect, we can market it as a self-help guide on what not to do in relationships," he quipped, the ease of our banter gradually rebuilding the fragile bridge between us.

"Or a guide to surviving bad soufflés," I shot back, my heart lifting at the playful exchange. Perhaps we weren't entirely lost. Perhaps there was still a thread of connection woven through our shared history.

As we wandered along the riverbank, the air filled with the sound of rustling leaves and distant laughter from late-night revelers, I felt a flicker of hope ignite in my chest. Maybe I could explore the possibilities of friendship—something simpler, yet grounded in the weight of our past.

But just as I was starting to feel at ease, the atmosphere shifted. A commotion erupted further down the path, drawing our attention. A group of people were gathered, their voices rising in alarm. Mabel's curiosity piqued, and she tugged my arm, urging me forward.

"What's happening?" she asked, her eyes wide with intrigue and concern.

"I don't know," I replied, a knot forming in my stomach. We approached the crowd, the faces around us reflecting a mixture of confusion and concern. I could feel Jake's presence at my back, a comforting force as we pushed through the throng to see what was going on.

Then I saw it—a couple of figures silhouetted against the backdrop of the river, one of them crumpled on the ground. My heart raced. "Is that—"

Before I could finish my thought, a shout broke through the murmurs of the crowd. "Call an ambulance! Someone get help!"

The reality of the situation struck me like a jolt of cold water. The excitement of the evening faded, replaced by a sinking dread. I strained to see through the gaps in the crowd, my stomach twisting into knots. The figures became clearer, and my breath caught in my throat as I recognized one of them—a familiar face that sent a chill racing down my spine.

"Is that... No way..." I whispered, but the words felt like shards of ice lodged in my throat.

"What? Who is it?" Mabel pressed, her voice urgent.

"Jake!" I shouted, panic seeping into my voice. "It's Jake!"

"What?" Mabel turned, her eyes wide with disbelief. "That's impossible!"

But it wasn't. My heart raced as I squeezed through the crowd, my mind racing with memories, fears, and the haunting realization that whatever was unfolding before us could change everything. I reached the front, the scene before me sharp and unyielding, and my breath caught once more as I faced the truth.

Jake was on the ground, and the world around me blurred into a cacophony of shouts, sirens, and the unmistakable sense that time was slipping away. I felt the earth shift beneath me, a fracture in the night that threatened to swallow everything whole.

Chapter 23: A Choice to Make

The café hums with energy, the rich aroma of freshly brewed coffee mingling with the sweet scent of pastries, creating an intoxicating atmosphere that buzzes with life. I push the door open, and the bell chimes cheerfully above me, a welcoming note in a symphony of clinking cups and laughter. Sunlight pours through the large windows, illuminating the faces of patrons engrossed in their conversations. Yet, despite the warmth around me, an icy chill wraps around my heart as I spot Jake at a secluded table in the back, his familiar smile stirring memories both sweet and bitter.

Sitting across from him feels like stepping onto a stage where I must perform a delicate dance between past and present. He looks the same—dark hair tousled just so, those deep blue eyes sparkling with mischief as they always did. I can't help but remember how those very eyes once filled with promises that turned into shadows, haunting me long after our paths diverged. Yet here we are, two characters pulled back together by the plot of life, each of us with our own script, but sharing a scene that could change everything.

"Hey," he says, his voice warm and inviting, as though no time has passed between us. "You look good."

I nod, unable to find words that feel genuine. The old charm slips over me like a well-worn sweater, cozy yet suffocating. "Thanks. You too," I manage, forcing a smile that feels more like a mask than a reflection of my true feelings. As we settle into our conversation, I take a sip of my coffee, the bitterness grounding me, reminding me of the truth that simmered beneath the surface of our past.

"So, how's life treating you?" Jake leans in, genuine interest etched across his features. His casual demeanor belies the weight of the conversation I know is looming, a ticking clock counting down to the inevitable moment when I'll have to confront the demons of our shared history.

"It's... complicated," I reply, the words tumbling out as if uninvited. "I've been focusing on Mabel, you know? She's at a crucial point in her life, and I want to make sure she's okay." The name hangs in the air like a lifeline thrown into turbulent waters, a reminder of everything I've fought for since that tumultuous chapter closed.

"Mabel?" He raises an eyebrow, curiosity piqued. "How's she doing?"

A fond smile tugs at my lips as I think of her bright spirit, her laughter echoing in my mind like a favorite melody. "She's amazing, actually. She's taking her first steps toward independence. It's terrifying but exhilarating for both of us." I can see the flicker of surprise in his eyes, as if my life has shifted into a dimension he never quite anticipated.

"That's great to hear," he says, the sincerity in his voice cutting through the tension like a knife through butter. "I always knew she had it in her. You're a good influence on her."

I take a deep breath, gathering my thoughts like pieces of a shattered mirror. "You know, Jake, that's part of why we're here today. I've been thinking a lot about everything—the way things ended between us, the trust that was broken. It's not something I can just brush aside." The words tumble from my lips, sharp and clear, carrying the weight of memories that cling to me like shadows.

His expression shifts, the carefree charm replaced by a flicker of vulnerability. "I know I messed up," he admits, his voice low. "I was young and stupid, and I hurt you. I've regretted it every day since." The genuine remorse in his eyes is almost enough to soften the jagged edges of my heart. Almost.

"It was more than just a mistake, Jake. You shattered my trust. I can't just forget that." My voice trembles slightly, but I push on, determined to make him understand the depth of my pain. "I've worked so hard to rebuild my life, to be there for Mabel, and to create something worth fighting for."

"I get it," he says, his tone earnest, almost pleading. "And I'm not asking you to forget. I just... I want a chance to make things right. To show you I've changed."

I shake my head, conflicted. For a moment, the air is thick with unspoken words, the weight of our history pressing down on us like a heavy fog. Just as I start to imagine a world where forgiveness is possible, Mabel's face flashes in my mind, her laughter, her determination. She represents everything I've come to cherish—the future I'm fighting for.

As I glance out the window, the bustling life outside continues, oblivious to the turmoil inside. I take another sip of coffee, letting its warmth seep into my bones, grounding me. "I need time, Jake. Time to think about what you've said and what it means for my life now."

His nod is almost imperceptible, but there's understanding in his gaze. "I can respect that," he replies, though a hint of disappointment lingers in his voice. "I just hope it won't be too late."

The words settle between us, heavy with implications. As I rise to leave, the world outside the café feels brighter, more vibrant, yet my heart is burdened with a decision that could alter the course of my life. I step into the sunlight, feeling its warmth against my skin, and for a brief moment, the chaos inside me quiets. But I know it won't last.

With every step I take, I can feel the weight of my choices pressing down, the crossroads I stand upon growing more pronounced. It's not just my relationship with Jake that hangs in the balance; it's the future I've built with Mabel, the life we're crafting together, one lesson at a time. The choice is mine to make, and as I walk away from the café, I feel the lingering shadows of my past brush against me, a reminder that some ghosts refuse to stay buried.

The sun beats down on my back as I stroll through the park, the vibrant colors of autumn swirling around me like a painter's palette. Leaves, painted in shades of crimson and gold, crunch beneath my feet, each step a reminder of the beauty that can exist even amid turmoil. Mabel is somewhere out there, likely in the midst of her own vibrant chaos, and the thought brings a warmth to my chest. We've become each other's safe spaces, a bond woven from late-night talks and shared dreams, but now that connection feels like it's being tested by the very person I thought I had closed the door on.

I find a bench and plop down, the wood warm from the sun. The serenity around me contrasts sharply with the storm of emotions whirling in my mind. I take a deep breath, inhaling the crisp air mixed with the faint aroma of caramel from a nearby vendor. As I glance at the laughter of children chasing each other in the distance, I can't help but think about Mabel's laughter, her joy brightening even the gloomiest days. She's my priority, the anchor in my world of uncertainty.

"Hey, Earth to Luna," a voice interrupts my reverie, pulling me from my thoughts. I look up to see Mabel, her hair a wild mess of curls bouncing around her face, a canvas of energy in motion. She holds two cups of steaming hot chocolate, topped with clouds of whipped cream, the kind that could make anyone's heart melt. "I come bearing treats!"

"Is that a bribe to share your latest gossip?" I tease, accepting one of the cups and relishing the warmth spreading through my hands.

"Maybe," she replies, plopping down next to me with an exaggerated huff. "But first, I need to tell you about the latest drama in the cafeteria. You won't believe who tried to take my seat today!"

I laugh, feeling the tension of earlier dissolve like sugar in the warm drink. Mabel has this incredible ability to draw me back into the present, making the chaos of the past fade into the background. "Let me guess. It was the same kid who thought he could outsmart you in math class?"

She rolls her eyes, a practiced maneuver that feels like second nature to her. "Of course! Can you believe he thought he could outwit me over geometry? I mean, please! I could solve for x in my sleep."

Her enthusiasm is infectious, and for a moment, I lose myself in her world, a place where numbers and cafeteria politics reign supreme. But the weight of my earlier encounter lurks at the edges of my mind, a dark cloud I can't shake.

"Speaking of school," I say, hesitant but needing to gauge where her thoughts lie. "How are you feeling about your upcoming exams?"

Her face shifts, a flicker of vulnerability crossing her features. "Honestly? I'm nervous. I want to do well, but sometimes it feels like everyone else has it all figured out. I'm just... me."

"Me is pretty amazing," I reassure her, taking a sip of my hot chocolate. "You've worked hard. Just remember, it's not about being perfect. It's about doing your best."

She nods, her gaze distant for a moment as if she's contemplating my words. "Yeah, but it's hard not to compare myself to everyone else."

I want to tell her how easy it is to lose sight of oneself amid comparisons, how I'm struggling with the same thing in my own way. But I swallow the words, knowing that this moment is about lifting her up, not dragging myself down. "What about your study group? I thought you liked working with them."

"Ugh, don't get me started on them," she groans dramatically. "It's like trying to herd cats. Half of them spend more time talking about TikTok trends than actually studying. I swear, sometimes I'm tempted to pull a 'teacher' move and start assigning detentions."

The laughter bubbles up uncontrollably, the kind that feels cathartic, breaking through the weight of my own thoughts. "Just don't start handing out extra credit for creative dance moves, okay?"

"Noted," she grins, her eyes twinkling with mischief. "Though I might consider it if they can't keep it together before the big test.

Maybe I'll make it a part of my study guide—'How to Ace Your Exam While Dancing.'"

As our conversation drifts toward more trivial matters, I can't shake the underlying tension of my earlier meeting with Jake. Part of me wishes I could confide in Mabel about him, about the ghosts of our past that threaten to re-enter our lives. But the thought of her reaction—her disappointment, her worry—stops me cold. I don't want to burden her with the weight of my choices, the complexities that have suddenly unraveled in a single afternoon.

"Luna?" Mabel's voice cuts through my thoughts, the concern in her gaze pulling me back. "You okay? You seem a little... distant."

"Yeah, just... thinking," I say, hoping my smile doesn't falter. "You know how it is. Sometimes my mind runs off on its own little adventures."

"Well, if it's anything like my study group, you might want to rein it back in." She nudges me with her shoulder, her playful tone easing the lingering weight in my heart.

"Touché," I reply, my voice lighter now. "But seriously, I'm just trying to figure some stuff out. You know how life can be a bit of a rollercoaster."

"Tell me about it. But remember, you don't have to ride it alone. I'm here."

Her words hang in the air like a promise, a tether to the world we've created together. In that moment, I realize how fiercely I want to protect this relationship, this slice of happiness carved out from the chaos.

As we finish our drinks, the sun begins to dip lower in the sky, casting golden rays that filter through the trees. The world is alive with the sounds of laughter and the rustle of leaves, a backdrop to the internal struggle simmering beneath my surface. I want to be honest with Mabel, to share the parts of my life that feel heavy. But fear grips me—fear of shattering the bond we've built, of unraveling the fabric of our everyday joy.

Suddenly, a commotion nearby catches my attention. A group of children races by, their laughter ringing out like music, and one of them tumbles, landing with a thud. Instantly, Mabel leaps to her feet, her instincts kicking in. "Oh no! Are you okay?" she calls, rushing toward the small boy, her concern evident.

As she kneels beside him, a wave of pride washes over me. This is Mabel in her element—compassionate, brave, and fiercely protective. Watching her, I'm reminded of the choices I face, the path ahead, and the uncharted territory of vulnerability. As she helps the boy to his feet, brushing off dirt and assuring him it's all part of the game, I realize that no matter how tumultuous my past may be, my present is filled with moments like this—small, significant, and worth fighting for.

And suddenly, I know that the choice I need to make isn't just about forgiveness or letting go. It's about choosing to embrace the beauty of now, the joy of shared experiences, and the love that binds us together in this vibrant tapestry we're weaving. The shadows may linger, but for every ghost, there's a ray of light—and I'm determined to follow it.

The afternoon sun hangs low in the sky as Mabel and I stroll through the park, her energy infectious as she recounts her latest triumph in a math competition. The world around us seems to fade away, leaving only the rhythmic crunch of leaves underfoot and her animated voice, which dances through the air with an enthusiasm that could light up the gloomiest of days.

"Did I tell you that I used my dance moves as a mnemonic device to remember the quadratic formula?" she exclaims, her eyes sparkling with mischief. "I mean, who doesn't want to break out in an interpretive dance during a test?"

"You know, I could see that becoming a viral sensation," I chuckle, nudging her playfully. "Mabel's Math Moves: Where Algebra Meets the Cha-Cha!"

"Exactly!" She spins on her heel, throwing her arms wide, as if she's already performing for an audience. "And you could be my manager! Just think of the hashtags."

"I'll add that to my growing list of side hustles," I tease, the warmth of her laughter enveloping me like a cozy blanket. But just as I'm swept away in our banter, the nagging thought of Jake creeps back into my mind, a reminder that my heart still carries unspoken words.

As we pass a playground, the sound of children's laughter cuts through my reverie. Mabel's gaze drifts to a group of kids playing tag, and I can see the longing in her eyes. "I miss that. Just running around without a care in the world."

"Ah, the golden days of youthful freedom. It's like riding a bike—until someone knocks you off," I reply, the truth of those words weighing heavily on me.

She raises an eyebrow. "You think someone's gonna knock you off your bike? What are you, five?"

"Hey, you never know! Life is unpredictable." I glance sideways at her, gauging how much of my own unpredictability I should reveal. "Just like life has a way of throwing unexpected people back into your path."

Mabel's expression shifts, a flicker of concern shadowing her playful demeanor. "You're not talking about Jake, are you?"

My stomach twists at the mention of his name, and I can't help but feel as if the ground is shifting beneath me. "Well, I did run into him," I admit, keeping my tone light, though the words feel heavy on my tongue.

"Luna, you know I'm always here if you want to talk about it." Her offer hangs in the air, genuine and open, but the weight of my secret keeps me from fully stepping into that light.

"Yeah, I know," I reply, trying to smile despite the turmoil brewing inside me. "I just don't want to drag you into my drama. You've got enough on your plate with school."

"But I care! And you can't pretend it's not weighing on you. If you don't talk about it, it'll just fester like last week's leftovers."

A laugh escapes me, but it's tinged with anxiety. "Okay, fair point. But right now, let's focus on conquering the world, one math dance at a time."

Mabel rolls her eyes, a familiar gesture of feigned exasperation that makes my heart swell. We continue walking, the park sprawling around us in a kaleidoscope of colors, but the shadows of my encounter with Jake loom large in my thoughts, the unresolved tension pulling at my heartstrings.

As the sun begins to set, painting the sky in hues of pink and orange, Mabel and I make our way back toward my apartment. The city hums with life, the bustling streets filled with the sounds of honking horns and distant chatter. Mabel's phone buzzes, breaking the comfortable silence. She pulls it out, glancing at the screen. "Ugh, it's my group chat. They're still arguing about whether pineapple belongs on pizza."

"People have strong opinions on fruit toppings, I'll give them that," I say, shaking my head. "I still don't understand how anyone can enjoy warm pineapple."

"Right? It's like chewing on a fuzzy basketball," she quips, laughing again. But as she types a quick response, her expression shifts, and a sense of unease washes over me.

"Mabel, can I ask you something?" I venture, the words barely escaping my lips.

"Of course! Hit me."

I take a deep breath, steeling myself against the vulnerability I feel. "If someone from your past suddenly wanted to reconnect, how would you feel?"

She tilts her head, her brow furrowing in thought. "That depends. Did they hurt me? If they did, then I'd probably want to shove them off a cliff."

"Noted," I say, trying to keep the tone light, even as my heart races. "What if it was someone you thought you'd forgiven?"

Her eyes narrow slightly as she processes my question. "Honestly? It would depend on whether they're really sorry or just trying to make themselves feel better."

I nod, feeling the weight of her words. "That's fair. It's just... complicated."

"Life usually is. But if they were truly sorry and you could see that they've changed, then maybe it's worth considering."

"I guess," I reply, though uncertainty lingers in my chest. Just then, my phone buzzes in my pocket, startling me. I pull it out to see a message from Jake, and my stomach drops.

"Everything okay?" Mabel asks, noticing my sudden shift in demeanor.

"Uh, yeah. Just a message," I say, trying to sound casual, but my heart is racing. The text reads: Can we talk? I need to explain something important.

"Is it about Jake?" Mabel presses, her eyes sharp with curiosity.

"Just a... casual chat," I say, but the weight of his words hangs heavy.

"Luna, you've been avoiding the topic all day. Just say the word and I'm ready to call in the cavalry."

I give her a half-smile, knowing that her intentions are pure, but the fear of dragging her into the storm brewing in my heart keeps my lips sealed. "I'll handle it. I promise."

As we approach my apartment, I stop short, a decision looming like a shadow before me. "I think I need a minute."

"Okay. Just don't overthink it. You'll be fine," she reassures me, squeezing my arm before heading inside.

Standing at the threshold, I feel as if I'm at the edge of a cliff, staring down into the unknown. The phone buzzes in my hand again, and I can't help but glance at the screen. This time, the message is different: I didn't mean to hurt you, and I have something to tell you that could change everything.

The tension crackles in the air, and my heart pounds in my chest, anticipation mingling with dread. I stare at the screen, the weight of his words sinking in. What could possibly be so important that it demands my attention now?

Just as I'm about to reply, a figure steps out of the shadows behind me, a voice that sends chills down my spine. "Are you really going to talk to him?"

I turn slowly, my heart racing, only to find someone from my past standing there, a ghost I thought I'd buried long ago.

Chapter 24: Love in the Open

The sun dipped lower, casting its golden hues across Silver Springs as I walked alongside Mabel, the air infused with the scent of blooming wildflowers and the distant hint of barbecues from backyard gatherings. Our steps were light, the gravel crunching beneath our feet, almost like a soundtrack to our shared anticipation. I glanced at her, the way her hair danced in the breeze, golden strands catching the light and framing her face, reminding me of the sun itself. In those moments, with laughter bubbling between us, everything felt possible.

The iconic overlook loomed ahead, a beloved spot where the townsfolk often gathered to marvel at nature's artistry. As we reached the edge, I paused, breathless at the vista before us. The valley spread like an artist's palette, vibrant and alive, the fading sunlight dappling the fields in shades of amber and emerald. I felt a sense of awe wash over me, mingling with the excitement that coursed through my veins. It was as if the world held its breath, waiting for our next move.

"Wow," Mabel breathed, her eyes wide, reflecting the brilliance of the horizon. "Isn't it amazing?"

"It really is," I replied, settling beside her on the worn wooden bench. "It's hard to believe we live in a place this beautiful."

As the sun began its descent, I took a deep breath, steeling myself for what I had to share. I turned to Mabel, the warmth of her presence grounding me. "So, I had that meeting with Jake today."

Her expression shifted, curiosity dancing in her hazel eyes. "The Jake? The one you've been trying to avoid like a rash?"

I chuckled nervously, the tension in my chest easing slightly. "Yeah, that Jake. You know, the one I've been dodging since the day I realized my heart had its own plan."

Her brow furrowed in genuine concern. "And? How did it go?"

The words spilled out like an open faucet, my heart racing as I detailed the meeting, how Jake had approached me with that familiar cocky grin, the same one that had once sent shivers of confusion through me. "He was charming, of course, like always," I said, unable to hide the roll of my eyes. "He tried to convince me that we could just pick up where we left off, but—"

"But?" Mabel prodded, her fingers brushing against mine, a gentle anchor amidst my swirling thoughts.

"But it's different now. I'm different. I'm not that girl who got swept up in his whirlwind anymore." I looked into her eyes, searching for understanding. "I care about you, Mabel. You're the one who makes me feel... whole."

The vulnerability in my confession hung in the air between us, heavy and precious. Mabel's gaze softened, her lips curving into a smile that lit up her entire face. "You know, I never thought I'd see the day when you'd finally stand up to him. I'm proud of you."

The warmth of her compliment wrapped around me like a comforting embrace. "It wasn't easy. He knows how to play his cards right. But I've come to realize that love isn't about being swept away; it's about being grounded in what really matters."

"Wise words from a woman who has battled her own romantic tornadoes." Mabel's teasing tone brought a laugh bubbling up from my throat, easing the tension further. "So, what now? Are you going to throw Jake a curveball, or are you just going to ghost him again?"

"Maybe a little of both," I said, my playful smirk matching hers. "I mean, how many second chances does one guy need? He should be happy I'm not sending him a fruit basket and a note that says 'thanks for the memories, but no thanks.'"

Mabel laughed, a musical sound that echoed against the backdrop of chirping crickets. The heaviness of my earlier thoughts began to fade. "You really are the queen of rejection letters," she teased, nudging my shoulder. "I could write a whole handbook on how to tell someone you're not interested without being a total jerk."

"Let's start a publishing company. We can call it 'No Thanks Publishing.' We'll make millions!" My tone was laced with sarcasm, but the idea lingered in the air between us, whimsical and light.

As the sky deepened into twilight, stars began to pepper the heavens, flickering like diamonds on velvet. The moment felt sacred, wrapped in a cocoon of understanding and shared history. "You know, I've always believed that love isn't just about finding the right person; it's about becoming the right person, too," I said, my voice softening as I gazed into the valley below. "I feel like I'm still figuring that part out."

Mabel turned to me, her eyes searching mine. "You've already taken the first step. You've recognized what you want, and it's not Jake. That's huge."

"Is it wrong to want both freedom and connection?" I asked, the weight of my choices pressing down on me. "Sometimes I think I'm a walking contradiction."

"Contradictions make life interesting," Mabel replied, her tone playful but firm. "Besides, who wants to be predictable? Life is about balance, like a good recipe. A pinch of this, a dash of that, and voilà! You've got yourself something delicious."

I smiled, captivated by her perspective. The tension that had coiled tightly in my stomach began to unfurl. "You really should consider a side career as a life coach," I said, my voice teasing. "Or maybe even a professional philosopher."

"Or perhaps just your personal cheerleader?" she winked, nudging me again. "Because I'm here for it all. Every glorious moment of your unpredictability."

The warmth of her words enveloped me, wrapping me in a sense of belonging I hadn't realized I craved. "You really are incredible, you know that?" I said, leaning closer, the distance between us dissolving.

Her laughter was soft and melodic, wrapping around us like a protective cocoon. In that moment, I knew I had chosen the right path. I leaned in, capturing her lips with mine, the kiss electric and warm, a vibrant thread stitching us together against the canvas of the world.

The kiss lingered, electric and sweet, igniting a spark that resonated deep within me. Mabel pulled back slightly, her cheeks flushed and her smile blooming like the wildflowers that framed our view. The warmth of the sunset cast a golden glow around us, making the moment feel almost surreal, like a scene from a romantic movie. Yet, as the silence enveloped us, a ripple of uncertainty danced at the edges of my mind.

"So…," Mabel began, her tone playful, as she tucked a loose strand of hair behind her ear, "is this the part where you declare your undying love and we run off to live in a tiny house with a bunch of rescue dogs?"

I laughed, the sound breaking the tension that had gathered in the air. "As tempting as that sounds, I think I need to take it one step at a time. Maybe we can start with coffee first?"

"Coffee?" she teased, arching an eyebrow. "What are we, a couple of college kids going on a first date? Please, I expect at least dinner and a candlelit atmosphere next time."

"Fine, dinner it is," I replied, my heart racing at the thought of our next step together. "I'll even throw in dessert—perhaps a slice of that ridiculous chocolate cake from the diner?"

Her eyes sparkled with mischief. "You know the way to my heart is through my stomach. Just be warned: I have high standards."

The playful banter felt like a safety net, catching me as I navigated the sudden depth of my feelings. It was in these moments, amidst laughter and light teasing, that I could let down my guard and truly embrace what was unfolding between us.

As the sun dipped below the horizon, painting the sky in twilight hues, I turned my gaze back to the valley, the shadows creeping over the landscape like a slow tide. "You ever think about what the future holds?" I asked, my voice low, almost lost to the rustle of leaves in the gentle breeze.

Mabel considered this, her expression thoughtful as she leaned back against the bench, her eyes searching the darkening sky. "Sometimes," she admitted, her voice tinged with a hint of wistfulness. "But mostly, I try to live in the moment. The future has a way of surprising you, and I prefer to let it unfold organically."

Her words resonated deeply within me. It was a philosophy I admired yet struggled to embody. I had spent so much time planning, overthinking every potential outcome that I'd lost sight of the beauty in spontaneity. "Organic, huh? So, you're saying I should just throw caution to the wind and see where this crazy ride takes us?"

"Exactly! Life is a wild ride," she laughed, nudging me playfully. "You don't want to be the person who sits on the sidelines, afraid to join in the fun. Plus, where's the excitement in that?"

Her laughter was infectious, a melody that brightened the dusk. I found myself leaning closer, drawn to the warmth of her presence, wanting to bask in her adventurous spirit. "Okay, Ms. Spontaneity, let's take your advice. I'll embrace the chaos and see what happens."

"Good! Just remember, chaos often leads to the most memorable moments," she winked, her confidence making my heart race in a delightful, unexpected way.

Just then, a faint rustling interrupted our playful exchange, drawing our attention. A group of teenagers had wandered onto the overlook, laughter bubbling over as they snapped selfies against the backdrop of the fading light. Their energy was infectious, a reminder of the simplicity of youth, and I couldn't help but smile at their unrestrained joy.

Mabel rolled her eyes playfully. "Ah, the vibrant sound of adolescence. Isn't it delightful?"

"Delightful, indeed," I replied, a soft chuckle escaping my lips. "You know, at their age, I was definitely not as cool as they think they are."

"Oh, I can't wait to hear the 'back in my day' stories," she teased, nudging me again, her laughter intertwining with the fading sounds of the teens.

But as the group became more boisterous, I felt a knot tightening in my stomach. I tried to push it aside, reminding myself that I had chosen this moment. "You know what? This is nice," I said, attempting to mask the growing unease within me. "We should come here more often, even with the noise."

"Definitely," Mabel replied, her tone bright. "We can make it a tradition. A weekly ritual of watching the sun set and listening to teenage drama. What could be better?"

"Sign me up!" I said with a mock enthusiasm that made her laugh again. The knot in my stomach slowly began to loosen, yet my mind couldn't help but drift back to Jake and the unresolved feelings that lingered there.

As we sat together, watching the vibrant pinks and blues bleed into one another, I knew that I had to confront those feelings sooner rather than later. The truth was, despite the strides I'd made, there was still a lingering sense of obligation to Jake, an echo of a past that refused to stay buried.

"Hey," Mabel's voice cut through my thoughts, gentle and probing. "What's going on in that beautiful head of yours?"

I hesitated, caught between wanting to confide in her and fearing that it would shatter the blissful moment we shared. "It's just... I need to resolve things with Jake," I admitted finally, the weight of the words heavy on my tongue.

Mabel turned fully towards me, her expression shifting to one of understanding. "What do you mean?"

"I feel like I owe him something, you know? He was a big part of my life, even if it was a turbulent part." I sighed, frustration simmering just beneath the surface. "It's hard to shake that feeling, even after everything."

She nodded slowly, her eyes full of empathy. "You can acknowledge your past without letting it dictate your future. It's okay to care about what he feels, but don't lose yourself trying to appease him."

"Easier said than done," I replied, running a hand through my hair, the reality of her words settling into my consciousness.

"Perhaps, but that's where I come in," she grinned, the light returning to her eyes. "I'll be your cheerleader, helping you navigate this chaotic emotional landscape. We'll face it together."

"Together," I echoed, the word wrapping around me like a promise.

As the stars began to twinkle above us, I felt a sense of clarity take root. It was in this moment, with Mabel beside me, that I realized I had already begun to choose my own path. The beauty of the night spread out before us, vast and full of possibilities, just waiting for us to dive in.

The kiss lingered, a gentle exclamation mark punctuating the vulnerability that had settled between us. As I pulled back, Mabel's eyes sparkled, reflecting the soft glow of the evening stars. I felt an exhilarating sense of freedom mixed with an unsettling weight of responsibility. While our connection flourished in this moment, Jake loomed in the corners of my mind like a ghost haunting an old, forgotten house.

"Let's make a pact," Mabel said suddenly, breaking the silence with an energy that felt almost electric. "No more secrets between us. If something's bothering you, you spill it. No matter how uncomfortable."

I chuckled, a mix of admiration and disbelief swirling in my chest. "You're really putting me on the spot, huh?"

"Just trying to be a good partner," she said, leaning back against the wooden bench, her eyes narrowing playfully. "And besides, I'm not afraid of a little discomfort. I mean, have you seen the state of my kitchen when I'm attempting a new recipe? That's discomfort."

"Fair point," I admitted, smiling at the mental image of her flour-covered counter and chaotic culinary experiments. "But what if I don't know how to articulate what's bothering me?"

"Then we'll figure it out together," she replied confidently. "Like a detective duo unraveling a mystery. I'll bring the snacks; you bring the angst."

Her playful demeanor was a welcome distraction, but the truth sat heavy on my tongue. "Okay, but just to be clear, Jake isn't some ancient history for me. It's complicated, and I don't want to burden you with it."

"Does it ever get less complicated?" she asked, tilting her head as her fingers played with the hem of her sweater. "I mean, my love life is a soap opera at best."

I laughed, but the tension in my gut tightened again. "I think your soap opera is more like a romantic comedy. It's light and funny. Mine is... well, it's more of a suspense thriller, riddled with cliffhangers."

"Then we'll be the perfect duo. You bring the thrill, and I'll bring the laughs. It's the best of both worlds." She nudged me again, her eyes glinting with mischief. "But seriously, if you need to talk about Jake, I'm all ears."

The weight of her offer hung in the air, and I realized that I wanted to tell her, needed to, but the words seemed tangled in my throat. Just as I was about to muster the courage, the shrill ring of my phone sliced through the tranquil night, the sound shocking me back to reality.

Mabel glanced at me, her brow raised. "Is it Jake?"

"Probably," I replied, feeling a surge of annoyance mixed with apprehension. "He's persistent, I'll give him that."

"Then answer it! Let's see what kind of drama he brings to the table," she said, her voice a mix of encouragement and challenge.

With a reluctant sigh, I fished my phone from my pocket. The screen lit up with Jake's name, the bright letters almost mocking in their familiarity. "Here goes nothing," I muttered, swiping to answer.

"Hey, you." Jake's voice was smooth, almost too smooth, like honey dripping from a spoon. "I hope I'm not interrupting anything too important."

I shot Mabel a glance, her expression a mix of amusement and curiosity, and I forced a smile. "Just enjoying the sunset. What's up?"

"I wanted to talk," he said, the seriousness in his tone setting off alarm bells in my head. "Can we meet? I think we need to sort this out face-to-face."

The casual mention of meeting sent a jolt of anxiety coursing through me. "Meet? You mean like in person?"

"Yeah, I know it's been a while, but I really think we can work this out. There are things we need to clarify," he urged, his voice firm yet surprisingly soft.

I felt the knot in my stomach tighten again, and I could feel Mabel's gaze boring into me, a silent support that made the moment both easier and more difficult. "When were you thinking?" I asked, trying to keep my tone steady.

"Tonight. I know it's short notice, but I'm in town, and I really think we should do this. Let's not drag it out any longer."

"Tonight?" I echoed, my heart racing. The idea of facing Jake again sent shivers of both dread and anticipation down my spine. "I'll need to think about it."

"Don't think too hard. Just let me know where and when," he replied, a hint of impatience creeping into his voice. "I'll be waiting."

As he hung up, a thick silence settled between us, and I turned to Mabel, who looked as if she'd just witnessed a train wreck. "So, that happened," I said, trying to inject some humor into the tension that crackled between us.

Mabel crossed her arms, her expression serious. "Are you really considering meeting him tonight? After everything?"

"I don't know. Part of me feels like I owe it to him to at least hear him out. But the other part of me knows that it might just open a can of worms I'm not ready to deal with."

Her gaze held mine, steady and unwavering. "You don't have to do anything you're not comfortable with. It's your life, not his."

"Right," I replied, wrestling with the inner turmoil. "But I also don't want to leave any loose ends. I don't want to regret not confronting this."

"Then maybe you should go," she said, her voice softer now, like a gentle breeze that calms a storm. "But promise me one thing: if it gets too intense, you'll walk away. You're not obligated to make yourself uncomfortable just because he wants to talk."

"Promise," I said, feeling the weight of her words settle into my resolve.

Mabel stood, brushing the dirt from her jeans, her expression shifting from concern to determination. "Then let's get you ready for this. If you're going to face Jake, you need a game plan."

I stood, my pulse quickening with the prospect of the evening ahead. "Game plan, huh? What do you suggest?"

She took a step closer, her eyes glinting with mischief. "Channel your inner superhero. You'll go in there, and you'll show him that you're not the same person he once knew. You're stronger, more resilient, and you won't let him waltz back into your life without a fight."

"Inner superhero, I can do," I said, a hint of excitement bubbling beneath my anxiety. "But what if I falter?"

"Then I'll be your sidekick," she declared, a grin spreading across her face. "You've got this. Just remember that you're not alone."

With her words echoing in my mind, I took a deep breath, steeling myself for what lay ahead. The night stretched out before me, a tangled web of uncertainty and possibility. I turned to Mabel, a smile breaking through the tension. "Let's do this together."

But just as we turned to leave, a shadow passed over the path ahead, and I felt a chill sweep through the air, like the whisper of a storm. I squinted into the darkness, my heart thumping wildly. "Did you see that?"

Mabel's eyes widened as she peered into the gloom. "See what?"

Before I could answer, a figure emerged from the shadows—familiar, yet startling. Jake stood there, his face etched with urgency and something unrecognizable, a mixture of hope and desperation. "There you are," he said, his voice laced with tension. "We need to talk. Now."

In that instant, the world around us faded, and I felt the weight of a decision that could change everything, hanging in the balance.

Chapter 25: Tides of Change

Mabel's laughter rang out like wind chimes in a gentle breeze, lifting my spirits as we stood in the kitchen, flour dust swirling around us. She flourished her hands, coated in a fine white powder, as she crafted yet another batch of her legendary biscuits. The scent of melting butter and sugar danced in the air, weaving a tapestry of warmth and nostalgia that wrapped around us like a favorite blanket. Mabel had a knack for filling a room with light, and as she worked her magic, I couldn't help but smile, letting the sweetness of the moment distract me from the storm brewing inside my heart.

"Okay, but can we agree that I'm better at eating them than baking?" I teased, watching as she expertly folded the dough, her movements graceful and practiced. It was a little ritual we'd shared ever since I moved to the coastal town, and though I often took on the role of sous-chef, it was no secret that my culinary skills began and ended with opening a box of takeout.

"Only if you promise to try not to eat all of them before they hit the cooling rack," she shot back, winking at me. "You know what they say about too many cooks in the kitchen. I'm just here to keep you from burning the place down."

The light banter felt like a balm, and I immersed myself in it, laughing and teasing back, but in the back of my mind, Jake's face loomed like a distant thundercloud, darkening the sunny kitchen. It was maddening how easily he slipped back into my thoughts, a ghost haunting my every waking moment. Mabel, with her uncanny intuition, caught my eye and paused, her hands resting on the countertop. The levity of the moment dissipated, leaving behind a palpable tension.

"You're thinking about him again, aren't you?" Her voice was gentle but direct, piercing through my defenses with the accuracy of an arrow. I opened my mouth to deny it, but the look on her face told me she saw right through my half-hearted facade.

"Maybe," I finally admitted, watching a bead of flour tumble from her fingertips to the countertop. It landed softly, almost lost amidst the chaos of our cooking session, much like my own feelings, scattered and untethered. "It's just... he was a big part of my life. And now he's back, and I don't know how to feel about it."

"Jake's back," Mabel echoed, her brow furrowed slightly. "But that doesn't mean you have to slip back into old habits or let him pull you into that past. You're not the same person you were when he left. You're stronger."

Her words hung in the air, like the scent of baking cookies, sweet yet suffocating. I admired her conviction, the way she believed in me without question. But even as I nodded, a part of me wrestled with doubt. Jake wasn't just a name or a memory; he was laughter on lazy summer days, soft kisses under the stars, a warmth that seeped into my bones. But he was also heartbreak, shattered trust, and the weight of unspoken words. How could I reconcile the two?

As if sensing my struggle, Mabel changed the subject, urging me to knead the dough. I found myself pouring my energy into the task, fingers working the mixture with determination, as if I could mold my feelings into something more manageable. The rhythmic squishing of the dough mirrored the internal battle I faced, each push and fold a release of pent-up emotions.

"Let's think about this practically," Mabel suggested, breaking the silence as she measured out sugar. "What do you want, really?"

The question hung between us, suspended in the warm air. Did I even know? A part of me yearned for the familiarity of Jake's embrace, the way he made me laugh until my sides ached. But another part of me, one that had grown during his absence, whispered that I deserved more than the ghosts of our past. I wanted a love that felt like a lighthouse in the fog—steady, unwavering, guiding me through the turbulent waters of uncertainty.

"Honestly, I'm terrified," I confessed, the truth spilling out before I could censor it. "What if I get swept up in the tide of what we had and lose sight of what I want now? I don't want to hurt Mabel in the process."

Mabel put down her measuring cup and stepped closer, a look of earnestness in her eyes. "You can't control how someone else feels. If Jake really cares about you, he'll understand your boundaries. But you need to set them first. It's your heart, after all."

Her words felt like a compass, guiding me toward the truth I had buried beneath layers of uncertainty. I took a deep breath, inhaling the sweetness of the moment, grounding myself in the reality that I could honor my past with Jake while still choosing to embrace my present with Mabel.

In that moment of clarity, I made a decision. I would talk to Jake. I would figure out where we stood, where I stood. If I wanted to move forward, I had to confront the shadows he cast. But before I could voice my resolution, the sharp ring of my phone sliced through the air, jarring me from my thoughts.

I glanced at the screen, my heart leaping into my throat. Jake's name glowed back at me like a beacon in the night, and for a heartbeat, I hesitated, fingers hovering above the screen. Mabel's encouraging nod urged me on, and with a mixture of excitement and dread, I swiped to answer.

"Hello?" My voice trembled, a fragile note in the symphony of emotions swirling within me.

"Hey," Jake's voice flowed through the line, warm and familiar, sending a shiver down my spine. "Can we talk?"

The world narrowed to the soft clatter of Mabel's flour-covered hands as I stood frozen, caught between the past and an uncertain future.

The words hung in the air like the scent of fresh bread, both comforting and unnerving. I could hear the waves of the nearby shore crashing rhythmically against the rocks, a natural metronome to the uncertainty swirling in my mind. Jake's voice had stirred something deep within me, and as I clutched my phone tighter, I felt the warmth of familiarity mixed with a storm of emotions I thought I had tucked away neatly.

"Mabel is here," I said, my voice a curious blend of assertiveness and apprehension. "What do you want to talk about?"

There was a pause on the other end, the kind that stretched out like a rubber band, full of unspoken words and unmade choices. I could picture him—probably leaning against the door frame of his apartment, hands shoved deep into his pockets, the familiar tousle of his hair framing those penetrating blue eyes.

"I need to explain," he finally said, his tone serious, almost grave. "I owe you that much."

The weight of those words pressed down on me, and I could almost hear Mabel in the background, rolling out more dough, blissfully unaware of the emotional earthquake about to unfold. I glanced over at her, where she hummed to herself, and a pang of guilt twisted in my gut. Was I ready to dive back into this?

"Okay," I replied, my heart thumping against my ribs. "Where are you?"

"Can I come over?" His request was quiet, almost tentative, but it ignited a flicker of something I couldn't quite define—fear, excitement, hope. "I promise, I'll explain everything. I need you to understand."

"Fine. But only if you bring coffee," I said, attempting to mask my rising anxiety with humor. "Otherwise, I might forget to listen."

A low chuckle escaped him, and I found myself smiling despite the gravity of the situation. "I'll bring the good stuff. Just... don't go too easy on me, alright?"

The line went dead, and I was left standing in the warm kitchen with Mabel, the delicious aroma of her biscuits fading into the background as the reality of the moment settled over me like a heavy blanket.

"Are you okay?" she asked, her brow creased with concern as she wiped her hands on a towel and walked over to me.

"I think so," I said, forcing a smile that didn't quite reach my eyes. "Jake wants to talk. Like, face-to-face talk."

"Ah, the plot thickens," she replied, her eyes sparkling with a mixture of mischief and empathy. "Do you think you're ready for that?"

"I have to be," I said, my voice barely above a whisper. "I can't keep letting him linger like a shadow over my life. It's not fair to either of us."

Mabel nodded, her understanding palpable. "Just remember, whatever happens, you've got me. You don't have to carry this weight alone."

As I prepared for Jake's arrival, I found myself moving like a marionette with tangled strings, my thoughts darting back to the time when our lives intertwined so effortlessly. The laughter, the whispered secrets shared under a blanket of stars, all the moments that felt suspended in time. I shook my head, trying to clear the fog of nostalgia that threatened to cloud my judgment.

When Jake arrived, I was caught off guard by how the world outside faded, leaving only the two of us in the room. He stood on my doorstep, an imposing figure wrapped in a denim jacket, with a paper coffee cup in one hand and an air of uncertainty that mirrored my own.

"Hey," he said, his voice low, laced with vulnerability as he took in the sight of me.

"Hey," I replied, stepping aside to let him in. The door closed behind us with a soft click, sealing the moment and everything that came with it.

We stood in the kitchen, the tension thick enough to slice through. I gestured toward the counter, where Mabel's baking chaos reigned supreme. "Want some biscuits? Mabel's baking."

Jake's eyes flickered with a hint of a smile, but it was quickly overshadowed by a shadow of concern. "No, thanks. I don't think I could eat anything right now. I just... I want to talk."

"Then talk," I urged, my voice steadier than I felt. "I'm listening."

He took a deep breath, as if summoning courage from the depths of his being. "When I left, it was never about you. It was about me, my headspace. I thought I was doing the right thing. I didn't want to drag you down with my baggage."

"Your baggage?" I scoffed, crossing my arms. "It sounds like you thought you could just walk away and it would all magically disappear. You didn't even give me a chance to help you."

"I didn't think I deserved help," he shot back, his voice laced with frustration. "I thought it was better for both of us if I disappeared."

Silence wrapped around us like a shroud, and I could feel the weight of unexpressed emotions hanging heavily in the air.

"Do you think it worked?" I challenged, leaning closer, my heart racing as the truth poured out. "Because all it did was leave me with memories and questions that have been eating at me since you left."

Jake's expression softened, regret flashing in his eyes. "I know I messed up, and I'm not asking for forgiveness. I just want you to know I'm back now, and I'm here for you—if you'll have me."

A million thoughts raced through my mind, and the chaos of emotions threatened to topple me over. "Jake, it's not that simple. I've moved on in ways you don't understand. There's someone else in my life now."

His expression darkened, a mixture of surprise and hurt flickering across his features. "You mean Mabel?"

"No!" I almost shouted, before taking a calming breath. "I mean, yes, but that's not what I meant. She's a friend, and an amazing one at that. But I've found myself, Jake. I don't know what you think this will look like, but it can't be the way it was. I won't be that person again."

He stepped closer, vulnerability etched across his face. "Then let's find out what we can be. I'm not asking you to forgive me overnight, but I want the chance to show you I can be better. We can figure this out together."

His words hung in the air, pregnant with possibilities and uncertainties, and the weight of our shared history pressed down on my chest. I knew that what lay ahead was not going to be easy. There was a chasm between us, one built of heartbreak and regret, but maybe—just maybe—there was a way to bridge it.

The storm of emotions raged within me, but amidst the chaos, a small ember of hope flickered to life. Perhaps this was our moment to redefine everything we once had, to carve out a new space that didn't erase the past but rather embraced it as a part of our journey.

The silence in the kitchen grew thick, filled with unsaid words and fragile hopes as Jake's gaze bore into mine. I could feel the air crackling between us, an electric tension that sparked with each passing moment. He took a small step closer, his expression shifting from determination to something softer, almost vulnerable.

"I just want to be honest with you," he said, his voice low. "I never stopped thinking about you. Not for a second. I know I messed up, but I can't let you slip away again without trying."

I felt my heart stutter, caught in a crossfire of emotions I hadn't anticipated. "But what does that mean, Jake? What do you think can happen between us now?"

He ran a hand through his hair, a gesture I recognized all too well. "I don't know. Maybe we start as friends, see where it goes? I've changed, I promise. I'm not the same person I was when I left."

His honesty pulled at my heartstrings, but doubts loomed larger. The space we once occupied together had been invaded by time and circumstance, and rebuilding it felt like trying to reassemble a shattered vase.

"Starting as friends sounds... manageable," I admitted, my voice barely above a whisper. "But I can't go back to the way things were. It's not fair to either of us."

"I'm not asking you to," he replied earnestly. "I'm just asking for a chance. Let's figure this out, one step at a time."

The way he looked at me, with those deep, searching eyes, was enough to make my heart race. Yet, I could hear Mabel in the back of my mind, reminding me that I had to protect what I'd built in her absence.

"Okay," I finally said, steeling myself. "But there's something you need to know first."

He tilted his head, curiosity sparking in his gaze. "What is it?"

"I've started something new with Mabel. It's been... different. Special."

His expression shifted, the light in his eyes dimming momentarily. "Are you saying you're dating her?"

"No! Not dating. But we've built a bond that means a lot to me."

"Got it," he said, his tone stiffening. "So, what happens if this... whatever this is, between us, doesn't work out? I can't be the reason you lose her too."

I crossed my arms, frustration bubbling to the surface. "You're not going to lose her if this doesn't work out. Mabel is my friend, and she deserves the truth. She wouldn't want me to put my life on hold because of the past."

Jake seemed to wrestle with my words, the internal conflict etched across his face. "So we just go back to being strangers, then? Is that really what you want?"

I opened my mouth to respond, but the doorbell rang, slicing through the tension like a hot knife through butter. I glanced at Jake, whose expression shifted from concern to confusion, and then back again.

"Is that...?" he began, but I didn't wait to finish. I made my way to the door, my heart thrumming in my chest.

When I swung it open, I was met with a whirlwind of energy that was Mabel, her arms laden with grocery bags and a smile that lit up her face. "Surprise! I thought we could whip up something special tonight," she said, her enthusiasm as infectious as ever.

I felt a rush of relief wash over me, but it quickly dissipated when I caught sight of Jake behind me. Mabel's eyes widened, flicking from me to him in a way that suggested she sensed the gravity of the moment.

"Hey! You must be Jake," she said, her tone bright, masking any tension that loomed in the air. "I've heard so much about you."

Jake stepped forward, a hesitant smile spreading across his face as he extended his hand. "Nice to finally meet you, Mabel. I've heard about you too—mostly good things."

Her laugh rang out, light and airy. "Well, I hope they were all good! I'm always happy to hear I've made a positive impression."

As she juggled the bags and began unpacking them onto the counter, I felt like I was witnessing a precarious balancing act. Mabel had a unique gift for diffusing tension with her energy, yet I couldn't shake the unease brewing beneath the surface.

"Are you staying for dinner, Jake?" she asked, tossing a sideways glance at me. I felt the weight of her question, the subtle implication that she had picked up on our earlier conversation.

I opened my mouth to respond, but Jake beat me to it. "I don't want to intrude. I was just here to talk."

"Nonsense! The more, the merrier!" Mabel declared, her hands moving briskly as she sliced vegetables and set the stove to simmer. "We can make a feast! I'm thinking pasta with a creamy garlic sauce, garlic bread, and a fresh salad."

"Sounds great," Jake replied, glancing at me, his expression a mixture of resignation and acceptance. It was evident he was unsure about this new dynamic but willing to embrace it for now.

I took a breath, allowing the aroma of Mabel's cooking to fill the kitchen, hoping the flavors would mask the complexities swirling in my heart. As we settled into the rhythm of preparing dinner, laughter erupted, the three of us weaving between jokes and lighthearted banter, the weight of the earlier conversation slowly fading.

But with each shared smile and playful jab, I felt the tension between Jake and me stretch like a taut string, ready to snap at the slightest provocation. The dance of friendship was a delicate one, and with every passing minute, I couldn't shake the feeling that the ground beneath us was shifting.

When dinner was finally served, we gathered around the small kitchen table, the warm glow of candlelight illuminating our faces. Mabel poured us each a glass of red wine, the rich color swirling like velvet.

"To new beginnings," she toasted, her smile genuine and bright. I clinked my glass against hers and Jake's, feeling the warmth of the moment blend with the chill of the lingering uncertainty in my heart.

The meal unfolded beautifully, punctuated by Mabel's laughter and Jake's occasional witty remarks, but my mind was elsewhere, caught in a labyrinth of thoughts. Every glance I exchanged with Jake felt loaded, each shared joke an echo of a life we once had together.

I was trapped between the comfort of nostalgia and the thrill of something new.

As dessert approached—chocolate lava cake, a recipe Mabel swore could melt anyone's heart—I felt my phone buzz on the table, an unwelcome interruption. I reached for it, hoping for a distraction, but my breath hitched in my throat when I saw the name flashing across the screen.

It was an unknown number, but something in my gut told me it was important. "Sorry, I need to take this," I muttered, excusing myself from the table.

Stepping into the living room, I answered the call, my heart racing with each ring. "Hello?"

"Is this [Your Name]?" A voice crackled on the other end, urgent and unfamiliar. "I have news about Jake."

My stomach dropped, a chill rushing through me as I glanced back at the kitchen, where Mabel and Jake shared a laugh, blissfully unaware of the storm that was about to break.

"What news?" I asked, my voice steady, though my heart pounded in my chest.

"Meet me at the pier. I can't discuss it over the phone." The line went dead before I could respond, leaving me standing in the living room with my pulse racing and questions swirling in my mind.

Turning back to the kitchen, I found Jake's gaze already on me, a flicker of concern shadowing his features. I could feel the air thickening around us, the weight of secrets pressing down like the encroaching tide.

"What was that about?" he asked, and I could see the glimmer of worry in his eyes.

"I—" I hesitated, my mind racing. I had to make a choice, and in that moment, I felt the world shift beneath my feet.

"I'll be back," I said, summoning every ounce of courage. "I just need to check something."

As I rushed for the door, the sound of my heartbeat thundered in my ears, drowning out the laughter behind me. Whatever news awaited me at the pier could change everything, and as the door clicked shut behind me, I realized I was stepping into a storm that might just unravel everything I had fought so hard to hold together.

Chapter 26: The Bonds We Forge

The engine purred like a contented cat, a sound I'd come to cherish over the years, the rhythmic thrum of my small, beloved hatchback reassuring me as we hit the open road. I had always preferred the spontaneity of driving without a destination, the thrill of uncertainty mingling with the promise of adventure. But today, the pull of the coast was undeniable, a siren call echoing through my mind as I glanced sideways at Mabel. Her eyes sparkled with excitement, a radiant contrast to the gray morning sky, and I could see the anticipation dancing on her lips, which were painted a bold shade of coral.

"Are we really doing this?" she asked, her laughter bubbling up like the surf we were heading towards, infectious and genuine. It was a sound that filled the car, wrapping around me like a warm blanket.

"Why not?" I grinned, my heart lightening at her enthusiasm. "The coast is just a few hours away. Fresh air, saltwater, and all the seafood we can eat. Plus, I need a break from the city's chaos, don't you?"

She nodded vigorously, and the sunlight caught the edges of her wild curls, illuminating her like a halo. "If I had known you were this spontaneous, I would have invited myself on all your past adventures."

"Trust me, they were mostly filled with anxiety and overpriced coffee."

Mabel chuckled, leaning back against the worn leather seat. The scenery outside began to change as we navigated through quaint towns and sprawling fields, each mile drawing us closer to the sea. I couldn't help but notice how the mundane aspects of our journey—stoplights, roadside diners, and clusters of trees—seemed more vibrant, as if they were painted anew just for us.

"Did you ever think you'd be on a road trip like this?" she mused, watching the world whiz by, her fingers tapping a rhythm on her knee.

"Honestly? No. I was convinced I'd be tied to my desk forever, drowning in spreadsheets and the hum of fluorescent lights." I shook my head, letting the wind ruffle my hair. "But here I am, freeing myself from all that. Who knows? Maybe we'll discover something amazing."

"Like what? A hidden beach with glittering sands and friendly dolphins?"

"Exactly! Or perhaps a tiny café that serves the best key lime pie this side of Florida." I leaned into her enthusiasm, imagining the possibilities stretching out before us like the winding roads ahead.

We entered a stretch where the land opened up, revealing rolling hills that cascaded down into the vast, blue ocean. The air shifted, carrying with it the unmistakable scent of salt and adventure. The excitement buzzing between us felt like electricity, palpable and exhilarating. I could see her breath catch as the waves crashed against the rocks, their rhythm a hypnotic soundtrack to our journey.

"Look!" Mabel pointed, her face lighting up as we pulled into a scenic overlook. "Can we stop here?"

I couldn't say no. The view was breathtaking—a panoramic masterpiece of jagged cliffs and foamy waves. As we stepped out of the car, the salty breeze tousled our hair, sending the scent of the sea swirling around us. I closed my eyes, letting the sounds wash over me: the roar of the ocean, the distant calls of seagulls, and Mabel's laughter as she took in the sight.

"This is stunning," she breathed, her voice almost lost in the wind. "I can't believe we've never done this before."

"Life has a funny way of keeping us busy," I replied, but I couldn't help but wonder if it was something more—an unwillingness to step outside my comfort zone. "But maybe that's about to change."

We stood side by side, the sun dipping lower in the sky, painting everything in hues of gold and orange. I felt a wave of gratitude wash over me. Here was this incredible woman, a friend who had brought warmth and laughter into my life, sharing this moment with me.

"Okay, what's next?" she asked, bouncing on her heels, her energy contagious.

"Let's hit the shops and find something unique to remember this trip by," I suggested, and she nodded, her eyes shining with mischief.

As we wandered through the charming coastal town, each shop we entered was like stepping into a different world—each filled with handmade treasures, local art, and the lingering scent of fresh baked goods. We laughed over a selection of quirky souvenirs, debated the merits of whimsical sea-themed decor, and finally settled on matching bracelets—simple leather bands that promised to remind us of this day, a small token of our blossoming friendship.

"Perfect," Mabel grinned, holding up the bands. "Whenever I wear this, I'll remember our spontaneous escape from reality."

"And I'll remember that you're not just my friend; you're my partner in crime," I replied, slipping mine on.

But as we strolled along the bustling boardwalk, a gentle tug in my chest reminded me of the life I was momentarily escaping. The shadows of the past loomed just beyond the vibrant joy of the day. I couldn't shake the feeling that I was still tethered to something heavy, a weight I couldn't yet articulate.

"Hey," Mabel's voice broke through my reverie. "You okay?"

"Yeah, just... thinking."

"About what?"

"About how grateful I am for this," I admitted, searching for the right words. "But also how much I need it. It's easy to get lost in the grind."

Mabel studied me, her gaze piercing but gentle. "I get it. Life can feel like a loop sometimes. But that's why we need these moments—to remind us of who we are beyond the daily grind."

Her insight settled over me, a warm embrace in a cool breeze. Maybe she was right; perhaps it was time to finally sever the ties that bound me to my past. The bonds we forge don't always have to carry the weight of our history. Sometimes, they can lift us, letting us soar into the unknown. And as I looked at Mabel, radiant and alive, I knew this adventure was just the beginning.

We ambled through the bustling streets of the coastal town, Mabel leading the way like a navigator charting an undiscovered territory. Her laughter mingled with the distant cries of seagulls and the rhythmic crash of the waves, creating a melody that made my heart race with anticipation. We passed small cafes with vibrant awnings, their doors wide open, inviting the salty breeze to weave its way through the chatter of patrons and the clinking of glasses.

Mabel paused in front of a store adorned with colorful wind chimes that danced in the breeze, their melodic tinkling echoing in the air. "Can we go in? I need to find something utterly impractical to decorate my apartment," she declared, her eyes gleaming with mischief.

"Only if you promise to get something that's completely absurd," I replied, grinning as I followed her inside.

The shop was a cornucopia of eccentricities—every shelf teetered under the weight of trinkets that begged for attention. Giant, inflatable flamingos lounged next to handcrafted pottery, while quirky prints of animals dressed as famous historical figures hung on the walls. Mabel's enthusiasm was infectious as she wandered, fingers trailing along the colorful array of goods.

"Look at this!" she exclaimed, holding up a small, ceramic octopus with an absurdly happy face. "This little guy could cheer anyone up."

I burst out laughing. "Only you would find joy in a ceramic cephalopod. But I admit, it's oddly charming."

She placed it back on the shelf, her brows furrowing slightly as she searched for something else. "I want something that captures this day—something that reminds me of our adventure. Something with character."

As I rifled through a basket of postcards depicting sun-soaked beaches and whimsical illustrations, I stumbled upon a card featuring a majestic lighthouse against a stormy sky. The words "Find your light" were emblazoned across the front in elegant script. I turned it over and found that it was blank inside, just waiting for a message.

"Hey, how about this?" I called to Mabel, holding up the card. "It's beautiful, and I think it encapsulates the journey we're on."

She took it from my hands, studying it with a thoughtful expression. "It's perfect. It reminds me that even on the darkest days, there's always a light to guide us."

We made our purchases, and as we stepped back into the sunlight, I could feel the warmth of the day wrapping around us like a soft embrace. "Let's grab something to eat before heading to the beach," Mabel suggested, her stomach rumbling audibly.

"Seafood?" I asked, a grin spreading across my face.

"Absolutely!" she replied, her enthusiasm a delightful contrast to my hesitation. I had always found myself drawn to the sea's bounty, but my past experiences with seafood had been... questionable.

We wandered into a small seaside shack that smelled of fried fish and melted butter. It was the kind of place where the decor consisted of mismatched chairs and string lights strung haphazardly overhead, creating an inviting, bohemian vibe. We ordered a variety of dishes—grilled shrimp tacos, clam chowder in bread bowls, and a plate of garlic butter mussels.

As we sat at a rickety wooden table, the waves crashed in the distance, their steady rhythm echoing the laughter and chatter around us. Mabel dug into her food with abandon, her eyes widening as she savored each bite. "This is incredible!" she exclaimed, her mouth half-full.

I watched her, feeling a warm swell of happiness. "You're enjoying that a little too much. Are you sure you didn't miss your calling as a food critic?"

"Only if the job description includes being dramatic and using food metaphors," she shot back, her eyes sparkling. "I would be phenomenal at it. 'This taco dances on the taste buds like a ballerina in a sea of flavor.'"

"Bravo! I can already see you on television, critiquing dishes while wearing a beret and holding a tiny fork."

"Now you're just trying to make me laugh," she grinned. "And it's working. Seriously though, this is the best decision we've made all year."

A comfortable silence enveloped us as we finished our meals, punctuated only by the sound of waves and the occasional call of a seagull. With our stomachs full and laughter still bubbling between us, we made our way toward the beach. The sun hung low in the sky, casting a warm golden hue across the sand, inviting us into its embrace.

Mabel kicked off her sandals and raced ahead, leaving a trail of laughter in her wake. I followed her lead, letting my shoes drop to the side as I plunged my feet into the cool, wet sand. It felt like stepping into a new world—soft, inviting, and free from the constraints of everyday life.

The tide rolled in, retreating in a soft, foamy kiss that washed over our feet, leaving behind delicate shells and the promise of secrets from the sea. Mabel squealed, jumping back as a wave nipped at her ankles. "Careful! The ocean's trying to get you!"

"Noted," I chuckled, splashing water in her direction. She squealed again, her laughter ringing out like a bell.

As the sun began to dip below the horizon, casting a tapestry of oranges and purples across the sky, we settled onto a blanket we had hastily grabbed from the car. The world around us faded as we chatted, our conversation flowing easily from silly anecdotes to dreams we hadn't dared to share with anyone else.

"Do you ever think about what you really want?" Mabel asked, her voice dropping to a more contemplative tone. "Like, if you could have anything, what would it be?"

I stared out at the ocean, watching the waves dance under the fading light. "I suppose I want to feel free—unburdened by the past. I want to explore, to create memories like this one. But sometimes, I feel like there's a shadow looming behind me, holding me back."

"Shadow?" she asked, her gaze steady and sincere.

I hesitated, but there was something in her expression that urged me to share. "It's just... a mix of choices and circumstances, I guess. Times when I didn't choose myself or let others dictate my path. It's like I'm still sorting through it all."

Mabel nodded slowly, as if processing my words. "You know, shadows only exist when there's light. Maybe it's time to step into the light and see what you can create."

Her insight settled in me, igniting a flicker of hope. Maybe this road trip, this newfound friendship, could be the catalyst I needed to finally break free from the shadows of my past. The sun dipped lower, casting a brilliant orange glow across the water, as if urging me to embrace the unknown.

In that moment, with the ocean's symphony surrounding us and Mabel's unwavering gaze guiding me, I felt the weight begin to lift. Perhaps the bonds we forge aren't just connections to others; they can also be the threads that weave us into our own narrative—a narrative filled with possibility, laughter, and the promise of brighter days ahead.

With the sun dipping low on the horizon, painting the sky in strokes of orange and lavender, our laughter cascaded through the car as we sped along the coastal highway. The scent of salt and adventure wrapped around us, a sweet reminder of the freedom that lay just beyond the open windows. Mabel leaned back in her seat, her hair dancing in the wind like wild waves, a perfect mirror to the ocean that shimmered beside us.

"Why does the ocean always look like it's ready to swallow the sun?" she mused, her voice laced with a playful seriousness that made me chuckle. "Like, it's got a hungry crush on our star."

"Maybe it just wants to drown in its light," I shot back, grinning at her. "A classic case of unrequited love, if you ask me." Mabel rolled her eyes dramatically, but the corners of her mouth betrayed her amusement.

We turned into a small beach town, where the storefronts looked like they'd been painted by someone who loved bright colors a little too much. Each shop was a delightful cacophony of candy stripes and pastel hues, bursting with trinkets and treasures that seemed to whisper secrets of the sea. As we parked the car and stepped out, the salty breeze wrapped around us like a welcoming embrace, mingling with the scent of fried calamari from a nearby food stand.

Mabel's eyes sparkled with curiosity. "Let's get something to eat first. I need fuel for my inner explorer!"

"Fuel? You mean you just want to chow down on calamari and ice cream?" I teased, nudging her shoulder playfully as we walked toward the food stall.

"Details, details," she replied, waving a dismissive hand, her laughter spilling into the air like champagne bubbles.

As we savored our food—squid rings that were crispy and golden and ice cream that dripped down our hands—we strolled along the beach, the waves lapping at our feet like playful puppies. Mabel recounted her childhood adventures, painting vivid pictures of lazy summer days and daring escapades. With each story, I felt the weight of my past lighten a little more, replaced by the buoyancy of our shared joy.

"Mabel, you're like a walking adventure book," I said, nudging her with my elbow. "I might just need to take notes."

"And you, my friend, are the editor," she quipped, flicking a drop of melting ice cream at me with a mischievous grin. "Here to polish my stories until they shine!"

The sun began its slow descent, casting golden hues across the beach, and we found a secluded spot to settle in. The sand was warm beneath us, and the rhythmic sound of the ocean created a serene backdrop to our growing connection. We watched as the sky transformed, vibrant colors bleeding into one another, a canvas of fleeting beauty.

"I used to think love was all about grand gestures and passionate kisses," I confessed, breaking the comfortable silence that enveloped us. "But now? I think it's about moments like this—silly conversations, shared laughter, and the peace of just being together."

Mabel turned to me, her expression thoughtful. "You know, it's the little things that build the strongest bonds. It's like friendship is the foundation, and love is just the icing on the cake. Except it's not just icing—it's the whole party."

"Now you're just making me hungry again," I teased, nudging her shoulder once more. "But seriously, you've got a point. It's those ordinary moments that weave the extraordinary into our lives."

As night fell, we walked along the shore, our footprints washing away with each wave, like whispered secrets between us and the universe. The stars began to twinkle overhead, revealing constellations that seemed to reflect our conversations—chaotic yet beautiful.

Just as we paused to admire the view, a distant shout cut through the night, sharp and urgent. My heart raced as I turned to Mabel. "Did you hear that?"

Before she could respond, a figure stumbled out of the shadows, drenched and wild-eyed. "Help! Please!" The words tumbled out in a rush, thick with desperation.

Mabel and I exchanged a look, the laughter of earlier evaporating into the salty air. "What happened?" I called out, taking a cautious step forward.

"They... they're out there! In the water!" the stranger gasped, pointing toward the dark expanse beyond the shore. "Two of my friends... they were swimming and got caught in a rip current!"

Without hesitation, Mabel took a step forward, her face resolute. "We have to help them!"

"Wait!" I called after her, panic gripping me. "It's too dangerous! We need to call for help first!"

But she was already sprinting toward the water, her determination propelling her forward. I hesitated, torn between fear and the urge to follow. The ocean glimmered ominously under the starlight, waves crashing with a ferocity that whispered of danger. I could feel the weight of my indecision anchoring me in place, yet the sight of Mabel plunging into the surf ignited a flame of courage within me.

"Don't you dare go in there alone!" I shouted, breaking into a run, heart pounding as I plunged into the cold water. The shock jolted me, but I forced my body to move, pushing through the waves toward where Mabel had disappeared.

As I swam deeper, the world above faded, and the dark water enveloped me. Adrenaline surged through my veins, propelling me forward. I called out for Mabel, but the roar of the ocean swallowed my words. Panic clawed at my insides as I scanned the churning waves, searching for a glimpse of her.

Then, suddenly, I caught sight of her—her figure struggling against the current, arms flailing as she fought to reach two shadowy forms just beyond her grasp.

"Mabel!" I shouted, desperation lacing my voice as I swam harder, each stroke feeling like a battle against an unseen foe. Just as I reached her side, I realized we were not alone. Two more figures emerged from the depths, gasping for air, their faces painted with fear.

The realization hit me like a wave crashing against the rocks: we were in over our heads, and the night was far from over.

Chapter 27: Cracks in the Foundation

The air was thick with the scent of freshly mowed grass, a faint sweetness mingling with the earthy undertones of the soil that still clung to the soles of my shoes. I stepped onto the porch, a creaking old thing with splinters that caught the light in the soft, golden hues of dusk. It was our little sanctuary, where laughter had danced through the air just days before, but now the silence settled heavily around us, a weight that threatened to pull us both under. Mabel sat there, her silhouette framed against the fading sky, the light casting gentle shadows that softened her features. She was a portrait of stillness, and in that moment, I felt the distance that had crept between us like an uninvited guest.

"Hey," I said softly, hesitant to disrupt the fragile peace, as if the wrong word might shatter the moment altogether. She looked up, her blue eyes reflecting the fading light, and offered a small, almost imperceptible smile. The kind of smile that didn't quite reach her eyes, as if they were holding on to something darker.

"Hey," she replied, her voice barely above a whisper.

I settled into the chair beside her, the wood cool against my skin, a stark contrast to the warmth of the day that had lingered long into the evening. "You've been quiet since we got back," I ventured, not wanting to sound accusatory but rather concerned. It felt like walking on the edge of a cliff, the ground shifting beneath me with every word.

Mabel sighed, a sound that seemed to carry the weight of the world. "It's nothing," she said, but I could hear the tremor in her tone. There was an unease lurking just beneath the surface, and I was beginning to realize how well I had ignored it.

"Really?" I pressed gently, hoping to coax her thoughts into the open. "Because it feels like you're a million miles away."

She shifted in her seat, the chair groaning under her movement, and I felt the urge to reach for her hand, to anchor her here with me. But I hesitated, unsure if the gesture would be welcome.

"It's just... I don't know," she started, her gaze drifting to the horizon where the sun had dipped low, leaving behind a palette of purples and pinks that looked almost like a bruise. "After everything we experienced on that trip, I thought we'd come back different, maybe more connected. But I feel... I don't know, adrift."

Her vulnerability struck me like a sudden gust of wind, swirling around us, stirring up the leaves that had begun to scatter across the porch. My heart ached with the realization that I had been so wrapped up in my own whirlwind of emotions that I had inadvertently neglected her. "Mabel, you know you're everything to me, right? That trip didn't change that," I said, my voice earnest, hoping to bridge the gap that had widened between us.

"Didn't it?" she shot back, a flash of defensiveness igniting her words. "It seems like you're still haunted by Jake and what he did. You can't seem to shake it off. And I'm here, standing on the sidelines, wondering if I'm enough to pull you back."

Her words hung in the air, thick and charged. The truth of them struck deep, a painful reminder of the lingering shadows I had allowed to cast over our relationship. "You are enough," I said firmly, my gaze locking onto hers. "You've always been enough."

"Do you really believe that?" she asked, her voice cracking just slightly, the vulnerability laid bare before me like an open book.

"I do," I said, the sincerity behind my words wrapping around us like a warm embrace. "I've been so caught up in my own stuff that I've failed to see how my struggles have affected you. I'm sorry for that, Mabel. You deserve to be reminded of how important you are to me, every day."

As she looked at me, I could see the turmoil shifting within her, the conflict of emotions wrestling for dominance. "Sometimes,

I just feel like I'm not living up to what the world expects of me," she admitted, her voice barely above a whisper. "Like I'm failing at everything—my job, my friendships, even this," she gestured between us, "our relationship."

"Expectations are overrated," I replied, leaning closer, wanting her to feel the earnestness behind my words. "They're like ghosts—always lurking, whispering that we're not enough, when the truth is we get to define what enough means for us."

Her brows furrowed slightly, and for a moment, I could see her wrestling with the weight of her thoughts. "You make it sound so easy," she said, a wry smile teasing at her lips. "But when you're standing in front of the mirror, questioning every choice you've made, it's not so simple."

"No," I agreed, "but it's a process. A messy, complicated process that we all navigate. You're not alone in this, Mabel. We can figure it out together."

The words hung in the air between us, fragile yet hopeful, like a thread of light cutting through the shadows. I reached for her hand this time, intertwining my fingers with hers, and I felt the tension begin to ease, if only slightly.

"I don't want to feel like I'm losing you," she said, her voice trembling with sincerity. "I need to know you're here with me, really here, and not just lost in your own head."

"I promise," I said, squeezing her hand gently, grounding us both in the reality of the moment. "I'm here, right now. And I'm going to make sure you know how much you mean to me every single day. No more ghosts, okay?"

Her laughter broke through the heaviness, a melodic sound that filled the space with warmth. "No more ghosts. Just us, and maybe a glass of wine?"

"Definitely a glass of wine," I replied, grinning. "It's a date."

As the evening deepened around us, I felt the warmth of connection blossom anew, a reminder that even amidst the chaos, there was still space for growth, for understanding, and for love. And in that moment, with the stars beginning to twinkle overhead, I felt a flicker of hope ignite between us, a promise that no matter how turbulent the waters, we would navigate them together, hand in hand.

The next morning, the sun streamed through the kitchen window, casting a warm glow over the table where Mabel had laid out a spread of breakfast. The aroma of coffee mingled with the sweetness of fresh pastries, and for a fleeting moment, the chaos of the previous evening faded into the background. I stood at the counter, trying to decide whether to grab a croissant or the blueberry muffin, when Mabel walked in, her hair tousled and eyes still heavy with sleep.

"Look at you, all bright-eyed and bushy-tailed," I teased, flashing her a grin that I hoped conveyed a sense of normalcy. "Did you get enough beauty sleep last night?"

She smirked, stirring her coffee with a delicate touch. "If by 'beauty sleep' you mean tossing and turning while rehashing my life choices, then yes, I'm positively radiant."

"Ah, well, at least you can blame your mood on lack of sleep," I quipped, grabbing the muffin. "I, on the other hand, am just a natural disaster waiting to happen."

"Never thought I'd say this, but you're right," she replied, her playful banter breaking through the lingering tension. "I'm glad you're embracing your inner chaos."

We both chuckled, and the air began to feel a bit lighter. As we settled into our breakfast, I noticed the way she took her time with each bite, as if savoring not just the food but the moments between us. It was a small gesture, but one that spoke volumes about her desire to reconnect.

"What do you think about going for a walk after this?" I suggested, hoping the fresh air might clear the remnants of last night's heaviness. "Maybe we can check out that new café downtown? I hear they have great lattes."

"Café and a walk? Now you're talking my language," she said, her enthusiasm bubbling just below the surface. "But let's make a pact: no deep discussions. Just coffee and pastries, and maybe I can convince you to try that ridiculous avocado toast everyone's raving about."

"Deal," I said, raising my coffee cup in mock solemnity. "No existential crises until after breakfast."

Once we had finished eating, we slipped into our shoes, and I felt a rush of anticipation as we stepped outside. The air was crisp, the kind of freshness that invigorated your lungs and made everything seem just a little bit brighter. The neighborhood was waking up, with families tending to gardens and dogs tugging eagerly at their leashes. Mabel and I walked side by side, the comfortable silence wrapped around us like a soft blanket.

As we approached the café, the quaint little building stood adorned with colorful flower boxes, each petal a burst of cheerfulness against the pale blue facade. Mabel glanced at the chalkboard sign that swayed gently in the breeze, advertising their seasonal specialties, and her face lit up with genuine excitement. "Look! They have pumpkin spice everything. It's officially fall, and I'm here for it."

"Pumpkin spice? We just left summer behind! I thought we agreed to enjoy our sun-soaked moments while they last," I teased, nudging her playfully.

"Maybe I'm just ready for sweater weather and cozy blankets," she retorted, eyes sparkling. "Besides, I'm not the one who has a muffin in hand."

As we entered the café, the aroma of roasted coffee beans wrapped around us like a warm embrace. The atmosphere buzzed with the lively chatter of patrons and the rhythmic clinking of cups. We ordered our drinks and snagged a table by the window, the perfect spot for people-watching and observing the world in motion.

Settling in, Mabel glanced outside, a contemplative look crossing her face. "You know," she said slowly, "it's funny how life feels both fast and slow at the same time. One minute, we're on an adventure, and the next, we're back to ordinary routines."

"Ordinary can be good, though," I countered, leaning back in my chair. "It's where we find stability, the quiet moments that help us recharge."

"True," she conceded, her gaze lingering on the passersby. "But I think sometimes we need a little chaos to remind us what we're made of. Like the time we went skydiving—"

"—And you nearly lost your lunch mid-air? Yeah, I remember," I interrupted with a chuckle. "That was a lesson in trust, for sure."

"It was," she agreed, her expression softening. "But it was also a reminder that life isn't always about feeling safe. Sometimes, it's about taking a leap, even when you're terrified."

"I think I preferred it when you were just talking about pumpkin spice," I joked, raising an eyebrow.

"Alright, alright. Back to pastries and lattes," she laughed, the tension from earlier melting away with each passing moment.

We exchanged playful stories, weaving through memories both fond and silly, and I felt the distance between us shrink. Yet, beneath the surface, I sensed the underlying currents of unspoken fears still lurking. Mabel's earlier admission haunted me, the echo of her insecurities threading through our laughter like an unseen thread.

As we finished our drinks and prepared to leave, Mabel's phone buzzed, cutting through our moment. She glanced at the screen, her expression shifting subtly. "It's Jake," she said, her tone dropping an octave. "He wants to meet up."

A tight knot formed in my stomach, a mix of surprise and dread. "Jake? Today?"

"Apparently," she replied, her fingers hesitating over the screen. "He says it's important."

"Important how?" I asked, my heart racing. The chaos of my past was crashing back into our present like a rogue wave threatening to pull us under.

"I don't know," she admitted, glancing back at me, her eyes searching mine. "He just wants to talk."

"Talk? That's rich coming from him," I said, a spark of indignation flaring in my chest. "What could he possibly want? To apologize? To stir up more trouble?"

Mabel hesitated, clearly weighing her options. "I can ignore it if you think it's best. But maybe... maybe I should hear him out? Just to put this behind us for good?"

"Behind us?" I echoed, disbelief creeping into my voice. "This isn't just about you and him anymore, Mabel. It's about us. Are you sure you want to open that door?"

"I don't know!" she snapped, her frustration bubbling to the surface. "I just don't want to be haunted by his ghost anymore."

"Then let's close that door together," I suggested, leaning forward, my heart pounding in my chest. "No more ghosts. Just you and me."

Her eyes flickered, uncertainty dancing in their depths. The tension crackled between us, charged with the weight of decisions unmade and futures uncharted. It felt like the precipice of a cliff, and I couldn't help but wonder whether we would soar or plunge.

Mabel's gaze drifted toward the window, her fingers absentmindedly tracing the rim of her coffee cup as if it were a magic orb revealing her fate. "It's not just about Jake," she finally said, her voice soft yet steady, pulling me back from the anxious thoughts spiraling in my mind. "I thought I could handle this whole situation, but every time he reaches out, it's like he throws me into a tailspin."

The café buzzed with life around us, but at that moment, we were cocooned in our bubble of concern, the outside world fading into a blur. I leaned closer, wanting to bridge that gap of uncertainty. "You know I'm here, right? Whatever he wants to say, you don't have to face it alone. I mean, you can just tell him to take a hike."

Her lips quirked into a half-smile, a flicker of light breaking through the clouds. "If only it were that easy. I mean, part of me wants to be the person who just walks away from the drama. But I also want closure. I don't want to feel like I'm holding onto something that's not there anymore."

"And what about us?" I asked, feeling the weight of those words. "What if meeting with him opens old wounds?"

Mabel took a deep breath, her expression shifting as if she were standing on the edge of a precipice, peering into an abyss. "What if it helps us heal? Maybe I need to confront this, to make sure I'm not bringing that past into our future."

"Your past is your past, Mabel. But we're building something together now," I pressed, my heart racing. "Don't let him take that away from us."

"I know," she replied, her voice barely above a whisper, the flicker of resolve mingling with uncertainty. "I'll think about it. But I can't keep running away from him forever."

We lingered in that moment, each lost in the tangled web of our thoughts. The noise of the café faded away, leaving only the heartbeat of the world around us. Just as I was about to suggest a detour to the park, my phone buzzed violently against the table, shattering the fragile atmosphere we'd cultivated.

I glanced down at the screen, and my stomach sank. It was a text from Jake.

"Talk soon?" I read aloud, unable to suppress the incredulous tone that colored my voice. "What does that even mean?"

Mabel's eyes widened, her expression shifting from contemplation to alarm. "What does he want?"

"Beats me," I said, my fingers trembling as I considered my options. "Part of me wants to respond with a resounding 'no' and block him for good, but another part of me is wondering if this is a baiting tactic."

"I mean, he's a master of manipulation," she agreed, a shadow crossing her features. "But he's also your past, not mine. Just be careful, okay?"

"I'm always careful," I shot back, perhaps more defensively than I intended. "Well, mostly careful. You know what I mean."

She sighed, the tension in her shoulders easing slightly as she shifted her focus back to the window. "Maybe we should go home. I need to think about this, and I don't want to drag you into my emotional baggage any more than I already have."

I nodded, the disappointment swirling in my chest, mixing with a fierce protectiveness. I didn't want to leave her in that uncertain place, but I also recognized the gravity of the decisions that lay ahead. "Alright, but we're tackling this together, no matter what you decide."

As we made our way back, the day continued to unfold in a blur of mundane moments—the crunch of gravel beneath our feet, the laughter of children playing in nearby yards, the slight chill that hinted at autumn's impending arrival. But each step felt heavier than the last, weighted down by the anticipation of a confrontation that loomed like a storm cloud on the horizon.

Once we were home, I busied myself with small chores, trying to distract myself from the tension that seemed to linger in the air. I washed dishes, wiped counters, and even organized the spice cabinet, but every mundane task only served to highlight the unresolved tension simmering between us. Mabel remained quiet, lost in her thoughts, and I couldn't help but feel like a spectator in my own life.

As the sun dipped below the horizon, casting a warm golden glow through the window, Mabel finally broke the silence. "I think I want to meet him," she said, her voice steady but laced with a vulnerability that made my heart ache. "Just to see what he has to say. But I need you to promise me something."

"Anything," I replied, my pulse quickening with dread and determination. "Just name it."

"Promise me you won't let it affect us," she said, her gaze locking onto mine. "No matter what happens, you'll remind me of what we have. I don't want to lose that."

"I promise," I said firmly, though I could feel the uncertainty gnawing at my insides. "Just remember, you're in control of this. You don't owe him anything."

She nodded, a determined glint in her eyes, and I couldn't help but admire her bravery, even as a part of me wrestled with fear for her heart.

The following day, Mabel arranged to meet Jake at a local diner, a place known for its greasy burgers and questionable coffee. The moment felt like a scene from a movie, where the stakes were high, and everything hinged on a single conversation. I spent the morning pacing our small living room, waiting for the clock to tick down to the appointed hour.

"Stop worrying," Mabel said, her voice cutting through my anxious thoughts. She'd changed into a casual outfit that suited her perfectly—a cozy sweater and jeans that hugged her in all the right places. "I'll be fine."

"You're just meeting the guy who put you through emotional hell," I said, unable to hide my apprehension. "I'm not sure 'fine' is in the cards."

"I've got this," she assured me, though I could see the tension behind her smile. "And if anything goes wrong, I'll text you."

As she headed out the door, I felt a rush of mixed emotions—pride, fear, anticipation—and the tight knot in my stomach only grew tighter. She glanced back one last time, her expression a blend of hope and apprehension, and then she was gone, leaving me with the deafening silence of our empty home.

I tried to distract myself, diving into work, scrolling through my emails, but nothing could shake the looming worry that hung like a fog over me. Minutes turned into hours, and just when I thought I could finally settle into my own thoughts, my phone buzzed again, jolting me from my reverie.

A message from Mabel.

"Everything's fine. I'll text you later."

Relief washed over me, but it was short-lived. I couldn't shake the feeling that things were not as simple as she claimed. A knot of unease twisted in my stomach, a reminder that the ghosts of our pasts weren't so easily exorcised.

Time dragged on, and my mind raced with a million possibilities. Had she gotten the closure she needed? Was Jake putting on a show, using his charm to weave his way back into her life? I paced the floor, glancing at the clock every few minutes, each tick a reminder of the weight of anticipation pressing down on me.

Just as I was about to lose myself in another spiral of anxiety, my phone buzzed once more. This time, it was a call from Mabel. I answered immediately, my heart pounding in my chest.

"Mabel? Are you okay?" I asked, my voice taut with concern.

"Uh, yeah. But can you meet me?" Her tone was shaky, and I felt a chill run down my spine.

"Of course. Where?"

"Back at the diner. Please hurry."

The line went dead, and I felt the world around me tilt as a rush of panic surged through me. I grabbed my keys and dashed out the door, my heart pounding with a mixture of dread and determination. As I sped through town, the familiar streets blurred past me, a whirlwind of colors and shapes that barely registered in my frantic mind.

Pulling into the diner's parking lot, I spotted her car, the old blue sedan parked haphazardly as if she'd jumped out in a hurry. I rushed inside, the familiar bell jingling above the door, and my eyes scanned the room, landing on her seated at a booth in the far corner.

But it wasn't just Mabel sitting there. Jake was across from her, leaning forward with an intensity that made my skin crawl. Mabel's eyes darted to me as I approached, and the moment our gazes met, a flash of fear and uncertainty crossed her face.

"Hey," I said, forcing a casualness into my tone that I didn't feel. "What's going on?"

"Just having a conversation," Mabel replied, though her voice lacked its usual confidence.

Jake looked up, a smirk playing on his lips, and for a moment, everything fell silent. The tension crackled in the air like static electricity, and I could feel the ground shifting beneath us.

"Glad you could join us," Jake said, his voice dripping with false sweetness.

My heart raced as I caught Mabel's eye, searching for reassurance, but all I saw was uncertainty mingling with fear. It felt like standing at the edge of a cliff, the winds howling around us, and I was left to wonder just how far we were willing to fall.

Chapter 28: Strengthening Our Foundation

The scent of lilacs wafted through the air, a gentle reminder of spring's flirtation with summer, as I stood in the dim light of The Broken Compass, a world transformed from its usual spirited chaos into something intimate and warm. Fairy lights twinkled overhead, casting a soft glow that danced across the rustic wooden walls, highlighting the eclectic decor that was always a conversation starter but tonight served a new purpose. Each delicate strand of light felt like a tiny star captured in a glass bottle, ready to grant a wish or two for the evening.

I had spent the day preparing, carefully arranging her favorite flowers—blush peonies mingling with delicate white daisies—into mismatched vases I had scavenged from the back of the bar. They held stories of laughter and late-night confessions, now a backdrop to the evening I hoped would mend the fractures that had begun to form between us. My heart raced with a blend of hope and anxiety as I placed a handwritten note on the small table, the ink barely dry and full of words I could barely bring myself to say out loud. "You are extraordinary," it read, a simple truth that I wanted her to carry in her heart like a secret charm.

As I waited for Mabel, I couldn't help but reflect on our journey. She had stepped into my life like a wild breeze, shaking loose the cobwebs of routine and filling my days with laughter and spontaneity. Our adventures had woven a tapestry rich in colors—flashes of deep red from our spontaneous road trip to the mountains, the bright yellow of lazy afternoons at the park, where we had sprawled out on a blanket, munching on sandwiches while debating the merits of pineapple on pizza. But as with any beautifully crafted piece, there were threads that began to unravel, moments of tension where the laughter faded, and silence crept in like an unwelcome guest.

The jingle of the bell above the door announced her arrival, and my breath hitched in my throat. Mabel stepped in, her usual vibrant aura dimmed slightly by the shadows that clung to her, an uncharacteristic hesitance in her stride. The moment she took in the transformed space, her eyes widened in disbelief, a mix of confusion and wonder flashing across her face. "What in the world...?" she breathed, glancing around, and I could see the walls she had built, strong yet fragile, begin to crack just a little.

"Surprise," I said, forcing a grin that felt more like a plea than a celebration. "I thought we could use a night just for us."

Her smile blossomed like the flowers around us, tentative at first but brightening as she took a step further into the room. "This is... incredible. You did all this?" She moved closer, brushing her fingers against the delicate petals, and I couldn't help but feel the warmth of affection creeping back in. It was the little things, those effortless moments, that reminded me why I had fallen for her in the first place.

"I did. And for the record, it wasn't easy. I had to bribe a few of the regulars to keep their distance for the night." I gestured dramatically toward the bar where we usually served drinks, as if it were the most dangerous of missions. "You'd be surprised how many people are willing to barter their secrets for a free drink."

A soft laugh escaped her, and in that instant, the tension began to melt away like ice under a summer sun. "You're impossible," she said, shaking her head, but the corner of her mouth curled up, and I felt the familiar flutter of hope.

We settled into a cozy corner, where the light overhead shimmered like a soft halo. As we shared stories from our past, the air filled with a warm familiarity that felt like home. We laughed over our shared misadventures—like the time we tried to cook a gourmet dinner and ended up ordering pizza while the smoke alarm blared like a siren. "I still maintain that the burnt lasagna was a culinary masterpiece," I declared, and she rolled her eyes playfully, the shadows of doubt beginning to dissipate.

"Masterpiece or not, I think we should stick to takeout for our next 'gourmet' endeavor," she teased, and for a moment, it felt as though we were back to our carefree selves, before the weight of unspoken words and frustrations had begun to settle between us.

But as the evening progressed, the conversation turned more serious. I could see the glimmer of vulnerability in her eyes as she opened up about her fears—about our future, about the dreams we had shared but seemed to drift further apart with each passing day. The laughter faded, replaced by a gravity that hung in the air like a thick fog.

"Mabel, I know things have been rocky," I started, reaching across the table to take her hand. The warmth of her skin against mine sparked a flicker of courage. "But you're the heart of this place, of my life. I want us to be stronger together. You inspire me every day."

She searched my gaze, and for a moment, it felt as though the world outside had fallen away, leaving just the two of us in this pocket of intimacy. "I've just been so scared, you know? Scared that we're moving in different directions."

"Then let's change direction together," I urged, squeezing her hand, hoping my resolve would ground her. "Let's make sure we're on the same path."

The flickering lights reflected in her eyes, illuminating the path ahead, even if it remained a little foggy. We found ourselves wrapped in each other's arms, the barriers that had kept us apart dissolving like the last remnants of winter, our hearts beating in a rhythm that felt achingly familiar. But as I held her close, the warmth of her body against mine, I couldn't shake the nagging feeling that while we had fortified our connection for now, unseen challenges still loomed ahead, waiting patiently for their moment to strike.

In the quiet aftermath of our embrace, a soft hum of contentment enveloped us, but it was not long before the first hints of uncertainty crept back into the space between us. Mabel nestled her head against my shoulder, her breath warm and steady, yet I could feel the tension lingering just beneath the surface. It was a tension that had settled like dust in the corners of our lives, unnoticed until we began to clear away the clutter of everyday routines.

"So, what's next?" she asked, her voice a soft melody, laced with curiosity and something deeper. She looked up at me, those emerald eyes sparkling in the fairy lights, and I was reminded once more of how captivating she was. But beneath that spark, I sensed a question that needed answering. The weight of it pressed down on my chest, a question that both excited and terrified me.

"I don't know," I admitted, leaning back slightly to meet her gaze. "Maybe we should talk about the future more. I mean, really talk about it, not just throw around vague ideas like confetti." The slight frown that tugged at her lips told me I was right to be cautious.

"Are we talking about jobs, places, or...something else entirely?" she asked, a playful lilt to her tone, though the way she bit her lip suggested she was bracing for something heavier.

"Let's start with jobs." I chuckled, trying to lighten the mood, even as I felt the knot in my stomach tighten. "I mean, we can't just drop everything and become nomadic poets, no matter how romantic it sounds."

Her laugh rang out, a bright chime that filled the room, but the glimmer in her eyes soon dulled. "But isn't that what we talked about once? Just packing a bag and driving until we felt like stopping?"

I remembered that late-night conversation, illuminated by the glow of the moon, where dreams tumbled out like loose change. We had envisioned sunsets over distant horizons and laughter echoing through open fields, a world without responsibilities. Yet here we were, tangled in the reality of bills, responsibilities, and the growing divide that began with those little miscommunications that turned into mountains overnight.

"Maybe we can do that," I offered hesitantly, "but in a more sustainable way? Like, we can plan short trips, find new places that inspire us."

Her expression softened, but I saw the flicker of doubt cross her features. "Sustainable sounds safe. I thought we wanted to break free from that safe box."

"It's not about safety," I protested, my voice rising just a fraction too much, the air thickening with unspoken truths. "It's about building something together, something that lasts."

"Building? Like bricks and mortar? Or maybe just another pretty façade?" Her words dripped with sarcasm, and the sting of them left a bitter taste in my mouth. "What's the point of building if we're still stuck in the same place?"

It felt as if a door had swung wide open, and suddenly we were standing at the edge of a precipice, the ground beneath us shifting. "You're right," I conceded, pinching the bridge of my nose as I tried to collect my thoughts. "But change doesn't always have to mean everything falls apart. Maybe it's about finding a way to blend our dreams with reality."

Mabel regarded me for a long moment, her expression shifting from frustration to contemplation. "You know, I used to think we were on the same page. But lately, it feels like we're just rewriting our own stories, and I'm not sure our plots intersect anymore."

Her words felt like a slap, shocking me back into the present. I wanted to protest, to deny her doubts, but a part of me recognized the truth behind her confession. We had drifted, each caught in the whirlwind of our own aspirations, and I could sense her frustration was less about me and more about feeling adrift herself.

"Okay, let's stop skirting around it," I said, taking a deep breath. "What do you want, Mabel? What do you truly want?"

Her gaze fell, a fleeting shadow crossing her face. "I want to create something meaningful, not just a job that pays the bills. I want to explore art, to paint, to dive into the things that make my heart race, not just what's expected."

"And what's stopping you?" I pressed, my heart racing with a mix of urgency and fear. "You have that spark, and it's why I fell for you. Why can't we find a way to harness that?"

"It's easier said than done." She looked up, eyes fierce but filled with something softer, like hope peeking through a crack in a wall. "I just don't want to lose you in the process. It's like we're both on a tightrope, and I'm terrified of falling."

"I'm not going anywhere," I replied, my voice steadier than I felt. "We just need to figure out how to balance this together. If we're going to strengthen our foundation, we need to be honest, even if it's uncomfortable."

Silence fell, punctuated only by the soft hum of the fairy lights above. The weight of our conversation hung in the air, heavy yet strangely liberating. It was in this shared vulnerability that I began to sense a flicker of understanding.

"What if," I began cautiously, "we make a plan? Set aside time for both our dreams and our responsibilities? We can each pick one thing we want to pursue and see where that leads us."

Her expression shifted, curiosity dawning in her eyes. "Like an experiment?"

"Exactly! A passionate experiment." I grinned, feeling the tension begin to lift as the corners of her mouth curled upward. "We could hold each other accountable. Plus, think of the stories we could tell."

She considered my proposal, and I could almost see the gears turning in her mind. "Okay, I'm in. But we both need to be committed. No half-measures."

"Agreed," I said, feeling a sense of relief wash over me. "We'll chart our paths, but we'll do it together."

Just then, the chime of my phone interrupted our moment, breaking the spell. I glanced down to see a message from one of my old friends, but when I looked up, Mabel's expression had shifted again, an uncertainty flitting across her face.

"What is it?" I asked, noting the change in her demeanor.

"Nothing," she said too quickly, but the tension returned, thicker than before. I could sense it—an unspoken fear, a question left hanging in the air, begging for release. I leaned closer, determined to catch the truth.

"Mabel," I pressed gently, "whatever it is, we can talk about it. You don't have to carry it alone."

She hesitated, her gaze darting away before meeting mine again, vulnerability shining through the uncertainty. "It's just...what if all of this doesn't work out? What if we try to change, and it leads us further apart instead of closer?"

Her words echoed the very fears I harbored, yet it was in this moment of honesty that I felt the spark of connection reignite. "Then we'll figure it out together," I said, leaning in closer, our foreheads almost touching. "We won't let fear dictate our journey. It's about the adventure, right?"

As she nodded slowly, I could see the glimmer of hope returning to her eyes. Maybe we were not on the same page just yet, but we were finally writing in the same book, each stroke of the pen an affirmation that together we could face whatever the future held. In that moment, the world outside faded, leaving only us—the laughter, the dreams, and the promises still waiting to be fulfilled.

The air hummed with a blend of warmth and unresolved tension as Mabel and I sank deeper into our conversation. Our words flowed like a river, carving out new pathways through the rocky terrain of our relationship. I was acutely aware that we were standing on the brink of something significant, an unseen chasm that could either lead us to new heights or swallow us whole if we weren't careful.

"Okay, let's say we're committed to this plan," Mabel said, her eyes sparkling with renewed determination. "What's our first step?" She leaned forward, resting her chin on her hand, the corners of her mouth twitching with a hint of a smile that reminded me of the mischief we used to conjure up together.

"Let's create a vision board!" I declared, caught up in the enthusiasm of the moment. "We can cut out pictures from magazines, find quotes that resonate with us, and make it pretty. You know, the kind of project that screams 'We are taking control of our destiny!'"

Mabel arched an eyebrow, her expression teasingly skeptical. "I didn't realize I was in a craft class. Do we also need glitter and macaroni?"

"Only if we're feeling particularly avant-garde," I replied, grinning at the thought. "But seriously, I think it could help us clarify what we want. And if nothing else, it'll give us an excuse to spend an afternoon together doing something fun."

"Fun, huh?" She tilted her head, pretending to ponder. "I guess I can get behind that. But if you start gluing googly eyes on everything, we may have to have a serious talk about your creative choices."

"Hey, those googly eyes bring life to any project! Just wait until you see them in action." The laughter that followed felt like sunlight breaking through a cloudy sky, illuminating the shadows that had been lurking. It was a reminder that we had the power to reshape our narrative, to inject joy back into the story we were writing together.

As we tossed around ideas, my heart warmed at the thought of embarking on this journey. But just as I began to picture our vision board plastered with vibrant colors and wild dreams, the familiar chime of my phone interrupted the moment, this time with a sharp sense of urgency. A message from my old friend, Jake, flashed across the screen, and I felt a knot tighten in my stomach.

"Do you need to take that?" Mabel asked, her expression shifting to one of concern, the previous levity slipping away.

"Um, no, it can wait," I replied, forcing the words out, but the flicker of unease in my gut didn't dissipate. I had a feeling it wasn't just a casual catch-up. "It's just Jake."

"The one from college?"

"Yeah." I tried to sound nonchalant, but her piercing gaze told me I wasn't fooling anyone. "He's probably just checking in. You know how he is."

Mabel nodded, but the tension hung in the air like a heavy curtain, obscuring the warmth we'd just rekindled. "You seem off. Is everything okay with him?"

I hesitated, the truth threatening to spill over. Jake had always been the wild card in my life—charming, unpredictable, and sometimes a little reckless. He had a way of showing up just when I thought everything was settled, and tonight felt like one of those moments. "I mean, he's fine. Just... you know, life stuff."

She gave me a knowing look. "You can't keep everything bottled up, you know. Not after the whole 'let's be honest' moment we just had."

"I know," I said, frustration creeping in. "But some things are complicated. I just want this night to be about us."

Mabel sighed, a hint of exasperation dancing in her eyes. "You can't pretend everything's fine just because we're having a good moment. If there's something you need to deal with, you should deal with it. It's part of building a strong foundation, remember?"

I felt a rush of irritation bubble up. "And I thought we were supposed to be enjoying this time together, not dissecting my life choices!"

Mabel crossed her arms, her expression softening but still resolute. "Look, I care about you. I don't want you to feel like you have to hide things from me. If it's bothering you, let's talk about it. No walls, remember?"

"Fine!" I snapped, then took a deep breath to rein in my frustration. "Okay, let's just say Jake has a tendency to… stir the pot a bit."

"Stir the pot?" Mabel echoed, her brows knitting together. "What does that mean?"

"Let's just say he's been known to encourage impulsive decisions." I rubbed the back of my neck, feeling the weight of my words. "He's the friend who thinks a spontaneous trip to Vegas sounds like a great idea, and somehow I always end up in the middle of it."

Mabel's expression shifted, a mixture of concern and understanding. "And he's reaching out now because…"

"Because he wants to meet up," I admitted, the truth finally spilling out. "He's in town and wants to grab a drink."

"Are you going to?" The question hung in the air, thick and heavy, as though it could shift the very foundation we had just started to rebuild.

"I don't know," I replied, the conflict roiling inside me. "I mean, part of me wants to see him—he's fun, he's wild. But then there's the other part of me, the part that wants to stay grounded."

"Are you worried he'll pull you back into your old ways?"

"I'm not worried; I'm terrified," I admitted, my voice dropping. "Terrified I might slip, that all this we've just talked about could come crashing down."

Mabel's eyes softened, and she reached out to cup my face. "Then don't go. You know what you want, right? It's about the path you choose. You have the power to say no."

"Yeah, but saying no is so much harder when temptation is knocking on your door."

Just then, my phone buzzed again, and the sudden noise jolted me. Jake's message lit up the screen: "Let's meet up tonight. I'll be at The Broken Compass around 9. Can't wait to see you."

I glanced at Mabel, who had stiffened, her gaze fixated on my phone. "Wow," she said, her tone icy now. "That's... convenient."

"Convenient?" I asked, defensively. "He just wants to catch up. It doesn't mean anything."

"Doesn't it?" Mabel's eyes narrowed, and I could feel the distance growing between us once more, a chasm threatening to swallow our hard-won intimacy.

"Do you think I should go?" I asked, my voice suddenly raw.

Mabel let out a sigh, frustration etched across her features. "It's not about what I think. It's about what you want."

"Honestly? I don't know!" I threw my hands up in exasperation. "I just want to be here with you, but—"

"Then be here!" she exclaimed, her voice rising. "Make the choice that keeps us moving forward, not backward. It's your decision."

Her words hung in the air, and I could feel the weight of every unspoken moment pushing down on us. I glanced at my phone again, Jake's message glaring at me like a challenge.

Just then, the door swung open, and a burst of laughter flooded the room, cutting through the tension like a knife. A group of my old friends stepped in, bright and loud, a whirlwind of energy that instantly transformed the atmosphere.

"Mabel! You're here!" Jake shouted, his presence magnetic as he sauntered over, oblivious to the storm brewing just beneath the surface.

"Great," Mabel muttered under her breath, her expression shifting from curiosity to unease.

As Jake approached, the clock ticked ominously in the background, counting down the seconds until I would have to make a choice—a choice that could alter the course of everything we had worked for. Mabel's gaze was piercing, searching my face for the answer, the future we had begun to build suddenly teetering on the brink of uncertainty.

"Are we going to party, or what?" Jake asked, flashing that disarming grin of his that had always made him so irresistible.

I looked from Mabel to Jake, a sense of foreboding creeping in. I could feel the weight of their expectations pressing down on me, and in that moment, the path ahead split into two, each option pulling at me in opposite directions.

"Um..." I began, my voice faltering as I wrestled with my decision, the air thick with anticipation.

And then everything shifted—Mabel's eyes widened, and I caught a glimpse of something shifting in her expression. It was a look of determination mixed with a hint of desperation, as if she knew this moment could change everything.

"Are you coming?" Jake pressed, oblivious to the tension that crackled between us.

"Yeah, are you?" Mabel echoed, her voice sharp, slicing through the charged air like a razor's edge.

In that instant, I realized the gravity of the choice I faced—not just a choice between two friends, but between two paths of my life, and I could feel the chasm deepening, a swirling abyss waiting to swallow us whole.

Chapter 29: The Unexpected Twist

The Broken Compass had seen better days. It stood at the edge of the harbor, a weathered pub with chipped paint and a sagging roof that seemed to lean into the wind as if whispering secrets to the waves below. Inside, the scent of salt mingled with the smoky remnants of the day's fare—fried fish and spicy crab cakes mingled in the air like old friends catching up after a long separation. The dim light flickered overhead, casting shadows that danced on the walls, each flicker a reminder that life was full of movement, both forward and back.

I was nursing my third cup of coffee, its bitterness barely cutting through the sweet haze of nostalgia that wrapped around me like a well-loved blanket. Mabel, my anchor, was seated across from me, her fiery red hair a beacon of warmth and support. She tapped her fingers on the scarred table, her eyes darting toward the door as if she were a lighthouse keeper waiting for a ship that had long since lost its way.

"You know," she said, breaking the silence, "for a place called The Broken Compass, it certainly feels like you've found your true north."

I chuckled, though a part of me winced at the thought. Life had been an exhilarating roller coaster, filled with unexpected loops and sudden drops. I had thought I'd weathered the worst of it, convinced that my past was securely tucked away in the corners of my mind. But just as I took a sip of my coffee, the door swung open, and the cool breeze rushed in, carrying with it a familiar scent—Jake.

He strode in, his presence commanding the attention of every patron, as if he had choreographed his entrance for maximum impact. The chatter diminished, and I felt the temperature in the room drop a few degrees. There was a gravity to him, a magnetic pull that made my heart thud in my chest. He had changed since I last saw him, his hair tousled, and his cheeks slightly sunken as if he had been holding on to something heavy.

The moment he spotted me, the world shrank to just the two of us. I felt my breath hitch, an involuntary reaction to the memories flooding back—the laughter, the late-night confessions, the heartbreak. He approached me with an earnestness that sent shivers down my spine. The air crackled, charged with unspoken words, and I could feel the weight of everything we'd shared hanging between us like a delicate thread.

"Can we talk?" His voice was a low rumble, steady yet laced with uncertainty. It was a tone I had heard before, usually followed by something that would change everything.

Mabel's eyebrows shot up, a clear signal that she was both intrigued and wary. I glanced at her, seeking reassurance, but her eyes mirrored my own—curiosity tangled with apprehension. With a slight nod, I motioned for him to join us, the tension twisting around my chest like a vice.

"Do you want to sit?" I gestured to the empty chair, my voice steady despite the chaos brewing within me.

"Yeah." He lowered himself into the seat, and I could see the weight of his decision etched into the lines of his face. "I just... I needed to see you."

The words hung in the air, thick with meaning. I could taste the bitterness of missed opportunities and the sweetness of nostalgia swirling together, creating a cocktail that was hard to swallow. I opened my mouth to speak, but he cut me off, urgency in his eyes.

"I'm leaving town for good," he said, and the words crashed into me like a rogue wave, knocking the breath from my lungs. "I wanted to say goodbye. Properly."

I felt a million questions flood my mind—Why now? Why here? Did he really think a simple farewell would suffice? But instead, I found myself staring at him, seeking answers in his familiar gaze. "Leaving? Just like that?" I asked, incredulity leaking into my tone.

He nodded, the weight of his decision visibly pressing down on him. "I can't stay here. Not after everything that happened. I need a fresh start, somewhere I can breathe."

The honesty in his words pulled at something deep within me, a longing I thought had faded into the background of my life. I looked away, trying to gather my thoughts, to form a coherent response. Mabel shifted in her seat, her hand hovering near my own, an unspoken promise of support. I could feel her presence like an invisible shield, a reminder that I wasn't alone.

"Jake, I... I don't know what to say," I finally managed, the words heavy on my tongue. "We've been through so much. And now you're just... leaving?"

"It's complicated." He ran a hand through his hair, a gesture I had come to associate with his frustration. "I thought maybe we could talk about it, you know, find some closure before I go."

"Closure." The word tasted bitter. "Is that what you think we need?"

"I hope so," he said, his voice softer now, the bravado peeling away to reveal vulnerability underneath. "I can't carry this weight with me. Not anymore."

Mabel cleared her throat, breaking the tension that was spiraling dangerously close to overwhelming. "Maybe it's worth exploring," she suggested, her tone both gentle and firm. "After all, what's the harm in clearing the air?"

I shot her a grateful glance, her support wrapping around me like a warm embrace, and nodded slowly. "Alright, let's talk. But I'm not making any promises, Jake. This isn't just about you."

His eyes sparkled with a mix of hope and fear, a reflection of the man I once knew, standing before me on the brink of something new, and yet, still tethered to the past. We dove into conversation, the words flowing like a river that had been dammed for too long, but as the familiar cadence of our dialogue filled the air, I couldn't shake the feeling that this moment was just the beginning of something even more tumultuous.

The conversation flowed, each word steeped in a mix of nostalgia and tension that clung to the air like the salt from the sea outside. Jake's voice was a familiar melody, but it was one I hadn't heard in a long time, resonating with echoes of shared laughter and late-night confessions. His eyes darted between mine, searching for a sign, perhaps reassurance that I still cared, even as he prepared to walk out of my life for good.

"You know," he began, leaning in slightly, "when I decided to leave, it felt like pulling off a band-aid. Quick and clean. But now that I'm here…" His words trailed off, as if he were trying to navigate a treacherous sea of emotion.

"But now that you're here, what?" I prompted, my tone sharper than I intended. The air crackled between us, charged with unfulfilled promises and lingering glances.

Jake sighed, rubbing the back of his neck—a nervous habit I had always found endearing. "It feels like I'm about to step onto a plane without a destination. I thought I'd just slip away quietly, but being here with you, it feels monumental."

Mabel cleared her throat again, a gentle reminder of her presence, but her eyes glimmered with encouragement. "Sometimes the monumental things are the hardest to say goodbye to," she interjected, her voice low and steady. "Like all those half-finished stories we leave behind."

He nodded, as if Mabel's words held some hidden wisdom, then turned back to me, his gaze intense. "I don't want to just slip away, Lila. I want to leave with clarity, with understanding. Can we talk about us?"

Us. The word reverberated through my mind like the tolling of a bell, heavy and significant. The last time we spoke of "us," we were both still navigating our feelings with the grace of two drunken dancers. It had been messy and exhilarating, filled with unspoken promises that somehow got tangled in the reality of our choices.

"What is there to say?" I asked, my voice softer now, almost tentative. "We had our time, Jake. You left. I stayed."

He shifted in his seat, frustration flickering across his features. "I didn't leave because I wanted to. I left because I thought it was what you needed. What we both needed. I thought it would be easier."

"Easier for whom?" I shot back, the question bursting out before I could rein it in. "You took the easy way out, Jake. You made the choice for both of us."

The room fell silent, the ambient sounds of clinking glasses and muffled laughter fading into the background. I could see the storm brewing behind his eyes, a clash of regret and longing. Mabel glanced between us, her expression a mix of concern and intrigue, as if she were watching a riveting drama unfold.

"I know," he said, his voice almost a whisper. "I thought distance would make it all clear. But all it did was make me realize how much I missed you. Every day was a reminder of what I lost, and now..." He paused, inhaling deeply, as if summoning the courage to bare his soul. "Now I'm scared I'll leave and never find my way back."

My heart raced at the honesty of his admission, yet the weight of unresolved feelings hung heavily between us. "Jake, it's not just about you finding your way back. I've been building a life here. One that doesn't include you."

He leaned forward, urgency flickering in his eyes. "But what if it could? What if you and I could find a way to be a part of each other's lives again?"

The thought sent a rush of conflicting emotions surging through me. On one hand, there was the thrill of rekindled passion, the promise of laughter and warmth. On the other, the voice of reason warned of the pitfalls of opening old wounds. "And what happens when the shine wears off again?" I challenged, crossing my arms. "What happens when we fall back into old patterns?"

"That's the risk we take, isn't it?" His voice softened, a trace of vulnerability emerging as he leaned back in his chair, surrendering to the moment. "Life is about risks. And sometimes, the most beautiful things come from the messiest choices."

The gravity of his words settled over me like a blanket, warming yet suffocating. I glanced at Mabel, who was watching us intently, her eyes wide with anticipation, as if she were about to witness a momentous shift in the universe. I could almost hear her internal debate: to encourage or to protect.

I took a deep breath, weighing my options. "I don't know, Jake. I don't want to be your safety net. I've done that before, and it only leads to heartbreak."

"Then let's not do that," he said, his gaze unwavering. "Let's build something new. From the ground up. No safety nets, just honesty and a little risk."

His words hung in the air like a fragile promise, and for a moment, I felt the old thrill spark between us. It was intoxicating, this idea of diving back into the depths of our connection. But what lay beneath the surface? Could we truly navigate the waters of our past without capsizing?

Just then, the door swung open again, and the chill from the outside world rushed in. A figure stepped through, silhouetted against the waning light—a familiar face that made my heart skip a beat. It was Sam, the bartender from the pub, his usual easy smile faltering as he took in the scene before him.

"Uh, am I interrupting something?" he asked, glancing between Jake and me.

"No," I said quickly, perhaps too quickly, feeling a flush rise to my cheeks. "We were just... talking."

Jake shot me a look, an eyebrow raised in amusement, as if he could sense the sudden shift in atmosphere. Sam's presence was like a sudden downpour on a warm day, unexpected and jarring. But as the words settled between us, a thread of tension eased, and I felt the moment recalibrate.

"Right," Sam replied, rubbing the back of his neck. "Well, I just came to let you know that the fish special is running out. Thought you might want to grab some before it's all gone."

"Thanks, Sam," I said, grateful for the interruption, but part of me longed to dismiss him, to return to the intimate space Jake and I had carved out in the bustling pub. "I'll be right there."

With a nod, Sam retreated, leaving behind a lingering trace of awkwardness, but his timing had opened a new avenue of thought. I turned back to Jake, the air between us charged once more, yet the introduction of the unexpected twist had shifted the narrative in a way I couldn't ignore.

"Maybe we should take a moment," I suggested, my heart racing with the potential for both clarity and chaos. "Let's step outside for some air. It's getting a bit stuffy in here."

He nodded, understanding that the conversation needed a change of scenery. We both stood, leaving Mabel behind with her knowing smile, and stepped out into the evening chill. The world beyond the doors was a living tapestry of color and sound, the setting sun casting a golden hue across the water. It felt like a new beginning, or perhaps a final farewell, waiting just beyond the horizon.

The evening air outside The Broken Compass was crisp, laced with the salty tang of the sea and the faint hum of distant laughter spilling from the pub. It felt like stepping into another world—one where possibilities fluttered like moths drawn to a flame, lighting up the shadows of my doubts. I leaned against the weathered railing of the deck, trying to gather my thoughts as Jake stepped beside me, the tension between us palpable.

"So," he said, breaking the silence, "this is the place where you've been finding yourself?"

I shot him a sideways glance, unable to resist a smirk. "Something like that. It's more a place to drink bad coffee and contemplate life choices."

"Ah, the existential crisis corner." He chuckled, and the sound wrapped around me like a familiar embrace. "We should probably hang a sign."

"Right next to the 'Welcome to Emotional Turmoil' banner," I quipped, the humor lightening the mood, even if only momentarily.

We stood together, the gentle breeze tousling our hair, and for a fleeting moment, it felt like old times. The kind of easy camaraderie that had once formed the foundation of our relationship, yet now felt weighted with unspoken words and what-ifs. I could sense his gaze drifting toward the horizon, where the last vestiges of daylight melted into the ocean, creating a fiery canvas of oranges and purples.

"You know," he said after a beat, "I didn't just come back to say goodbye. I came back because I realized I can't just walk away from us without knowing if we've really closed the door."

His words sliced through the air, leaving a sudden chill in their wake. I turned to face him fully, the gravity of what he was saying settling into my bones. "What are you saying, Jake? You want to pick up where we left off?"

"I'm saying maybe we could start fresh. I know it's messy, but if we don't at least try, won't we always wonder?" His voice was earnest, his eyes searching mine, and for a second, I felt the pull of his proposal, like a tide drawing me closer.

"But fresh starts come with baggage," I replied, keeping my voice steady. "We can't just erase the past like it never happened. You walked away."

"Because I thought that was what you wanted!" His frustration bubbled to the surface, his hands clenching into fists at his sides. "I was trying to do the right thing!"

"Maybe you thought it was the right thing," I countered, heat creeping into my words, "but it was your choice, Jake. You didn't give me a say in it."

He exhaled sharply, a mix of anger and remorse flickering across his features. "I see that now. I really do. I thought distance would help me, but it only made me realize how much I care about you. How much I still want you in my life."

The honesty of his admission was like a jolt of electricity, causing my heart to race even faster. A part of me wanted to reach out, to take his hand and promise we could navigate this tangled mess together. But another part warned me that falling back into the same patterns would only lead to more heartache.

"Caring doesn't erase the hurt," I said, my voice softening. "What if we try to piece together what we had, only to find it's still broken?"

His gaze remained steady, and I could see the vulnerability shimmering beneath his bravado. "Then we can be brave enough to let it go. But if we don't try, we'll always be stuck in this limbo."

I looked out over the water, the waves crashing against the rocks below, mirroring the turmoil within me. Was it possible to step back into a relationship that had left me feeling so adrift? Could we really build something new without being haunted by our history?

"I need time," I finally said, my heart heavy with uncertainty. "I can't just jump back in and pretend everything is fine."

"I understand." He nodded, a mix of relief and resignation in his eyes. "But can we keep talking? Not just tonight but... moving forward?"

The question hung between us, heavy with implications. I could almost feel the weight of the uncharted territory stretching out before us, like a vast ocean with unseen depths. "I don't know, Jake," I admitted, feeling vulnerable. "I don't want to keep going in circles."

Before he could respond, a loud crash shattered the fragile moment, jolting me from my thoughts. I whipped around to see a group of rowdy tourists stumbling out of the pub, their laughter ringing through the air like a discordant symphony. One of them, a burly man in a baseball cap, lost his balance and nearly toppled over the railing, grasping for anything to steady himself.

"Hey! Watch it!" Jake shouted, instinctively stepping closer to me, his protective instincts kicking in.

The commotion quickly subsided, the group breaking into raucous laughter as the man regained his footing, oblivious to the tense energy still hanging in the air. I couldn't help but chuckle at the absurdity of the moment, the tension between Jake and me momentarily diffused by the unexpected distraction.

"See? Life's messy," I said, shaking my head. "Maybe we should embrace the chaos instead of trying to control it."

"Chaos can be fun," he agreed, a wry smile creeping onto his face. "But it can also drown you if you're not careful."

"Speaking of drowning..." I started, my heart still racing, when a sudden siren blared through the evening, cutting through the laughter. A police car sped by, its lights flashing like a disco ball in the night, drawing our attention away from each other once more.

"What's going on?" I asked, frowning. The energy had shifted again, a ripple of unease slicing through the atmosphere.

Jake squinted in the direction of the commotion. "I don't know, but it doesn't look good." He glanced back at me, concern etched across his features. "Do you want to check it out?"

Before I could answer, another figure emerged from the shadows, rushing toward us with urgency. It was Sam again, his usual smile replaced by a worried frown. "Lila! You need to come inside. Something's happened!"

My stomach dropped at the urgency in his voice. "What do you mean? What's going on?"

"Just come on!" he urged, grabbing my arm and pulling me back toward the pub. The sound of muffled voices filled the air, mingling with the sirens that echoed in the distance.

Jake followed closely behind, his presence a reassuring anchor as we navigated the throng of people spilling out of the bar. The sense of something being terribly wrong hung in the air, an electric charge that made my skin prickle.

"What happened?" I asked Sam again as we pushed through the crowd.

"There's been an accident," he said, his expression grave. "A boat capsized in the harbor. They're pulling people out, but they need help."

I felt my heart race, panic swirling in my chest. "Are there injuries?"

"Some serious ones. They called for backup." Sam looked back at me, his gaze pleading. "They might need more hands. Can you help?"

I exchanged a quick glance with Jake, who nodded, determination flaring in his eyes. "Let's do this," he said, and in that moment, I knew that whatever lay ahead—uncertainty, chaos, or perhaps even clarity—was something we would face together.

But just as we stepped into the chaotic crowd, a distant scream sliced through the air, followed by a commotion near the edge of the harbor. A crowd had gathered, their voices rising in alarm, and my heart dropped.

I sprinted toward the noise, adrenaline surging, not knowing what awaited us but acutely aware that this night had just shifted into uncharted territory. As we reached the edge of the crowd, I spotted a figure flailing in the water, desperately grasping at something unseen beneath the waves.

"Someone's out there!" I shouted, my voice barely cutting through the rising panic.

Jake's hand tightened around mine, and together we pushed forward, ready to face whatever chaos lay ahead. The night was no longer just a backdrop to our unresolved feelings; it was a storm of uncertainty that threatened to unravel everything we had just begun to piece together. And in that moment, as we stared into the dark abyss of the harbor, the only certainty was that our lives were about to change irrevocably.

Milton Keynes UK
Ingram Content Group UK Ltd.
UKHW020757231024
450026UK00001B/70